HAVEN ENDURING

THE LEGION OF PNEUMOS, BOOK II

H.B. RENEAU

VESALIAN PUBLISHING

Acknowledgments

This book would not have been possible without the love and encouragement of untold family and friends. This series has become near and dear to my heart, and I feel so lucky to have been able to bring this next chapter to the pages before you.

Special thanks go to my beta readers Mary R. Lanni, Perry Sheneman, Marjorie S., and others who shall go unnamed but not unappreciated! Your early feedback and suggestions were absolutely essential to the writing and editing process. Additional thanks go to my editor Lara Kennedy, whose insight and guidance helped turn this manuscript into the finished product before you. Thank you also to Natalia Junqueira for yet another gorgeous cover design. You did it again!

Finally, this book is dedicated to all those who wander in search of meaning and peace from the memories that haunt them. May you find the haven you seek.

"The whole value of solitude depends upon oneself; it may be a sanctuary or a prison, a haven of repose or a place of punishment, a heaven or a hell, as we ourselves make it."
—John Lubbock

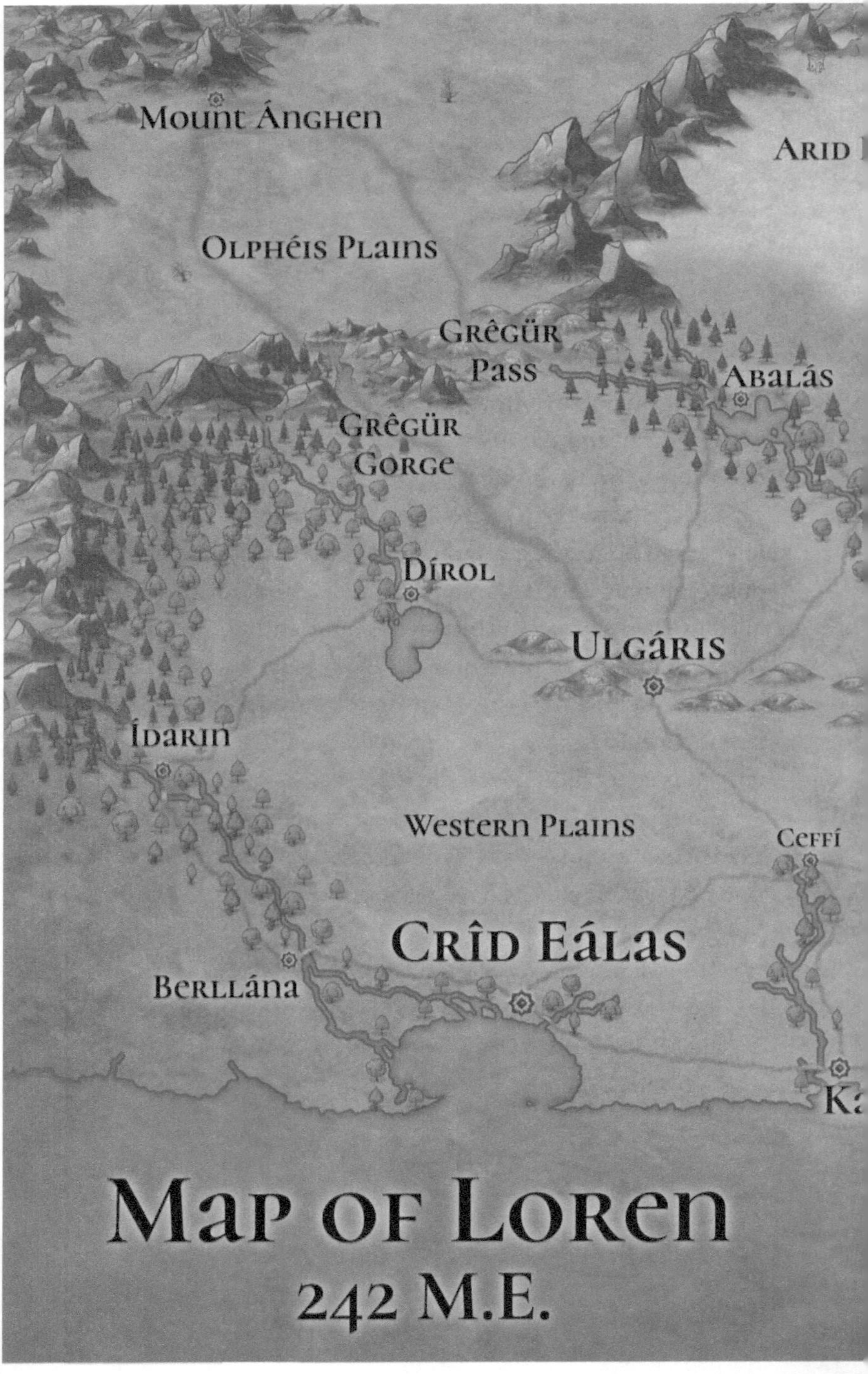

Mount Ánghen
Arid
Olphéis Plains
Grêgür Pass
Abalás
Grêgür Gorge
Dírol
Ulgáris
Ídarin
Western Plains
Ceffí
Crîd Eálas
Berllána
Ka
Map of Loren
242 M.E.

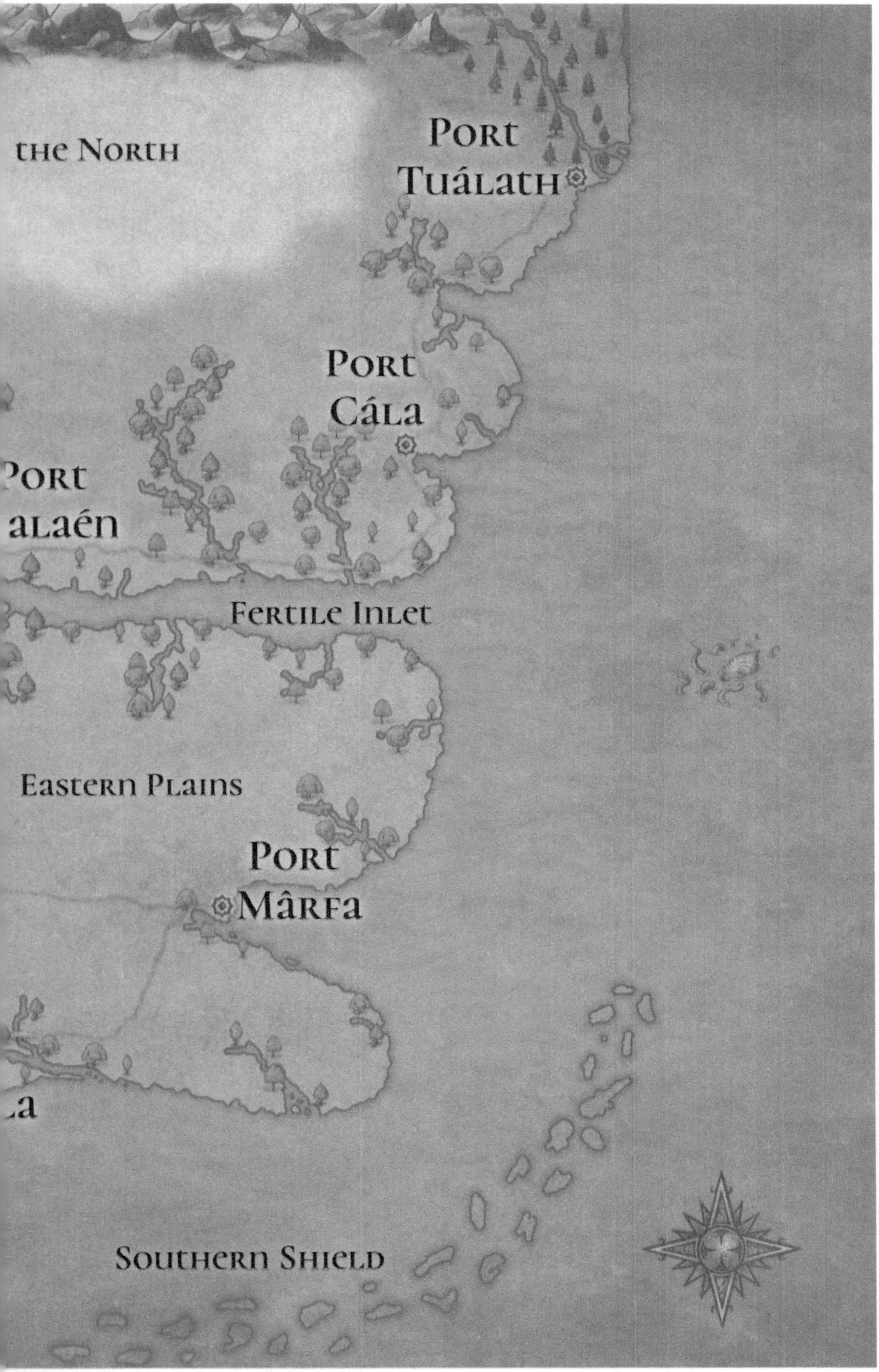

the North
Port Tuálath
Port Cála
Port alaén
Fertile Inlet
Eastern Plains
Port Mârfa
la
Southern Shield

242 Marian Era (M.E.)

The heat washed over her, falling in waves that pushed her deeper into the mud of the jungle floor. Keira drew a ragged breath, feeling the moisture of the air settle heavily in her lungs. *Any minute now.* A mosquito buzzed incessantly around her nose, and it took every ounce of her deeply held willpower to resist the desire to swat at it. Instead, she held perfectly still—muscles tensed and ready to strike.

She glanced at the Bellators that surrounded her—statues in the midday heat. Red cloaks abandoned and faces smeared with camouflaging mud, they crouched in perfect silence, awaiting a quarry that had yet to show its face. Her heartbeat thrummed in her ears; the familiar tang of adrenaline settled on her tongue. She let it wash over her, pushing down every thought and jagged memory along with it. There was nothing beyond this—the hunt. She reveled in it.

And yet still they waited, the lingering seconds stretching into even longer minutes. The marauders that had been terrorizing the Southern Shield for months had embedded themselves deep within its tropical jungles, carving out fortresses that were impenetrable to any outward assault. In truth, they had no reason to face the Bellatorio on equal terms, not when they merely had to wait.

The gentle cracking of a twig immediately grabbed her attention, and her ears perked to catch the spongy sucking sound of the muddy jungle floor, confirming her suspicions; someone was out there. Her fingers twitched toward the sword at her belt, but she resisted the urge. She couldn't give away their position until the last possible moment.

Keira could feel the tension in the air, a palpable thrill that coursed through her body.

This is it.

Slowly, ever so quietly, she allowed her fingers to inch toward her gilded hilt, the cold steel of its pommel firm under her curling fingers. Still more twigs snapped, and she felt the hairs on the back of her neck rise.

They're practically on us.

On instinct, Keira reached within herself to feel the pulsing ball of energy behind her stomach. She flitted on the edge, desperately wanting to send feelers out, to calculate how many of them there were and find out their strength. But an all-too-familiar sensation of panic bloomed in her belly, and she quickly released the ball of energy. *I can't,* she thought, *not without—*

She bit her lip. It didn't matter. Besides, her pneuma still required a whistle to guide it. To cast it out required sound, and sound was the one thing they could not afford, not yet, at least.

Another moment passed, and then a strangled roar emerged from her compatriot only a few yards away, quickly followed by the cries of the entire patrol. Keira surged to her feet, meeting the startled eyes of a frightened marauder, who barely had time to react before her blade pierced his chest and he crumpled to the ground.

From the corner of her eye, she noticed one young Tiro cry out as he stumbled, crashing to his knees. The marauder he'd been skirmishing with let out a strangled yell of triumph as he lunged toward the fallen Bellator.

Keira leapt over her fallen comrade, barely registering the sharp ring of metal as her sword collided with the marauder's blade. She was close enough to see his yellowing teeth, to feel his stale breath. Spittle flew from his mouth, and her stomach lurched as it struck her face. She ignored the sensation and disengaged, repositioning to come at him again from the side.

He parried, and she deftly twirled their blades through the air in a shearing clang of sliding metal—making a full arc before they released. She staggered back, trying to regain her footing as she glared at the hulking man.

A flicker of movement made her drop to a crouch as the whistle of an arrow hissed just overhead. Glancing around, she couldn't make out a likely source in the mayhem of clashing blades, the Bellatori patrol fully engaged now against the marauders.

Spinning back to her initial quarry, Keira found him gone, disappeared through the dense overgrowth of jungle. She swore and started after him.

She'd made it about three steps when the cry of a young Bellator drew her attention, and she watched as he collapsed to one knee, gripping a deep slice to his side as his assailant's blade arced up and over—coming in for the kill.

Keira's legs moved of their own volition, and she lunged forward, slamming her shoulder into the marauder. They tumbled to the ground in a heap, and Keira squirmed, desperate to disengage, before a crushing blow to her abdomen knocked the wind out of her. She rolled, dry-heaving her nonexistent breakfast as she scrambled to her feet. She barely got her sword up in time to parry as the man surged toward her.

Their blades met with a force that sent an ache through her arm, her fingers instantly going numb. She dodged to the side, aiming for his exposed flank, but he was too quick. He spun with her, forcing her back until she felt the press of gnarled bark against her spine. She let him advance, waiting for the last possible moment as a cruel side cut flew toward her. She dodged, letting his blade slice deep into the tree, where it lodged. It was just a moment before he wrenched it free, but it was one moment too long.

She slammed into him, thrusting her dagger into his belly once . . . twice . . . before he collapsed in a heap, blood gurgling from his throat.

Keira stood, chest heaving as she stared down at him, his eyes slowly dilating into the ghoulish surprise of death. But in her mind, she was seeing another body—face swollen and hair matted with blood . . . *Danny*.

Keira squeezed her eyes shut, willing the image to burn free of her retinas, and her breath came in shallow gasps. She forced her body into submission, breathing through pursed lips as she steadied her shaking hands on the tree beside her. When she had control, her eyes flickered open—darting around as she searched for whatever threat beckoned. But from where she stood, all the marauders lay dead—their bodies already being looted by the surviving Bellators. Whoever remained must have fled for safer ground.

"Th-Thank you."

She turned to find the young Tiro she'd saved staggering toward her, arm still gripping his side as he stared at her in wide-eyed gratitude. Keira felt a flush stain her cheeks, and she waved him off, turning to stalk away. His face fell as she slid past, but she kept moving. She felt her adrenaline fading and moved faster, desperate to outrun the hollow exhaustion she knew would follow in its wake. She pushed aside the underbrush until she could just make out the muddy tracks left by the fleeing marauders.

"They went this way!" she called, before taking off through the dense vegetation, not caring who, if anyone, followed her.

Branches tore at her clothes and hair as she pushed her way through the underbrush, leaping over snarled roots the size of her thighs that snaked up from the ground. Somewhere in the back of Keira's mind, she wondered if she was even headed in the right direction, or if she was only pushing deeper into the heart of the jungled island. She wasn't sure she cared. The adrenaline in her stomach burned out any doubt or worry before it could take hold as her legs carried her forward. She was beyond worry.

Crashing through a wall of foliage, Keira stepped through to dazzling tropical sunlight. She blinked against the rays that reflected off the white sands and shielded her eyes, scanning the horizon for any sign of the fleeing marauders.

There!

Footsteps trailed away from the jungle's edge, making for the port town of Albé. Cursing, Keira started toward the village, fighting the drag of her boots as they sank into the powderlike sand.

Reaching the edge of the town, Keira slowed to a walk, not wanting to attract undue attention, but she soon realized the effort was pointless. With her pale, sunburnt skin and blue eyes, not to mention the sword strapped to her hip, she couldn't have been more conspicuous. Keira kept her head down as she moved along the streets, but she could feel the islanders' dark eyes following her, narrowed and tense.

A figure crossed her path and Keira tensed, reaching instinctively for her sword. But it was only a middle-aged woman, slobbering baby bouncing on her hip as she looked Keira up and down scornfully. The woman eyed Keira's sword, and she quickly dropped her grip on its hilt.

Relaxing, the woman sidled closer, speaking in a hushed murmur. "The one you be looking for? He came tru' not ten minute before you, be making for the stables right off."

Keira glanced around eagerly. "Where are they, then?"

The woman pursed her lips and raised her dark eyebrows pointedly at Keira's waist satchel. Keira's eager grin twisted into a scowl as she fished out a handful of penarii, the copper coins that saw most business done on the islands. She dropped them into the woman's palm, who pocketed them with businesslike efficiency before gesturing to the west.

"You be following this road, but stop before you be reaching the blacksmith. The stables being just to the right."

Keira turned to thank the woman, but she'd already pushed past, baby still bouncing on one hip, her other arm firmly wrapped around a large basket. Tightening her sword belt, Keira set off at a near-jog down the road the woman had pointed to, hoping she wasn't already too late.

The stable itself was an airy building, built on strong balsané wood stilts to elevate it above the ever-present threat of flood. Keira peered past the half dozen horses tied under the three-sided exterior overhang toward the open door beyond. Inside, the stablemaster argued with a man whose back was to her. She froze. Though he wore a cloak with the hood pulled up, her gaze traveled down to his boots, to the thick jungle mud caked up the sides.

She broke into a run.

Maybe it was the sound of her footsteps, or the slide of metal as she unsheathed her blade, but the cloaked man suddenly turned and caught her gaze. It was him.

Shoving the stablemaster aside, he made for the row of horses tied under the overhang within the inner corral.

Oh no, you don't, Keira thought, veering toward a horse that stood tied outside a nearby building. Keira saw the marauder's knife flash as he unfettered the reins of a sorrel mare and leapt onto its back. Wheeling the horse around, he barreled toward the open side. Keira was still a few yards away from the nearest horse, but as she glanced toward the entrance to the stable complex, she felt the breath punch out of her in a whoosh.

There was only one way in or out of the corral, and a group of children crouched just beyond, their view of the marauder blocked by tall hay bales as they skipped smooth pebbles across a circle drawn in the sand that blew across the wood planks of the street. From the angle of the doorway, Keira knew there was no way the marauder would see them in time. She had a moment's indecision as she glanced at the waiting horse in the opposite direction. Then she was running.

The children shrieked as she came upon them, but she ignored their squeals. Scooping up the two smallest children in one arm, she yanked a slightly older girl to her feet, hauling them all out of the horse's path.

The two youngest came willingly enough, no doubt stunned by the shock of it all, but the oldest writhed and kicked as Keira dragged her out of the road.

"My necklace!" the girl shrieked, wrestling her way out of Keira's grip and dashing back toward the circle. She lunged for the glinting object that lay amid the stone as the marauder's horse came barreling toward her.

"What are you doing!" Keira cried. Dropping the squalling children, she lunged for the older girl—tackling her just as the sandy circle erupted under flying hooves.

It took a moment to disentangle themselves. Coughing, Keira shot a rueful glance at the marauder's back before rounding on the girl. Rising from the ground, the girl brushed sand from her dress and carefully peeled open her fingers. Cradled in the center of her palm lay a perfectly spiraled sea shell fixed to a broken piece of twine. Keira glanced at it, noting the speckled rose pink that stood out against the girl's warm brown skin. It was beautiful, Keira had to admit, remarkable in its perfect symmetry and the way the sunlight twinkled off the grains of sand embedded in its surface. But it was certainly not worth dying over.

"What on earth were you thinking?" Keira asked, glaring at the top of the girl's head, where strings of dark brown curls escaped her twin braids. The girl met her gaze, glaring right back with the most piercing eyes Keira had ever seen.

Keira blinked.

They really were extraordinary, their shade almost white-green, the color of seafoam or a choppy wave. They'd be a unique feature in any company but were striking among the Udánma, the native people of the Southern Shield. Keira knew they took pride in the dark warmth of their eyes, often ringing their lids with light hues to make them stand out all the more.

"You really should be more careful," Keira said, shifting awkwardly as she realized she'd been staring at the girl for a bit too long.

The girl glowered back, either not noticing the pause or else too used to gawking to care. She muttered something in the native language of the islands that Keira couldn't understand, although she definitely picked out the word *grelún* uttered with a surprising amount of condescension for someone who likely still had some baby teeth.

Keira was about to reprimand her again when the girl spun on her heels and scampered away, gesturing at the two younger children, who quickly chased after her.

Jaw clenched, Keira glanced back in the direction the marauder had gone but saw no sign of him. *Great*, she thought, *no doubt spreading word of our camp position.*

Keira stretched, feeling the adrenaline eking out of her muscles as a familiar wave of exhaustion washed over her. With it came the emptiness, that hollow void and accompanying panic she kept at bay through sheer force of will and the ever-present distraction of combat. She quickly shoved the feeling away. There was still a job to do, and she clung to that thought. She had to warn the Bellatorio. The next attack would be swift and precise. Pneumos help them if they were caught off guard.

CHAPTER

TWO

Night had fallen like a thick wet cloak over the jungle camp by the time Keira returned. The Bellatori camp itself was always a bustling hive of activity, especially in the evenings, when young women from the surrounding villages found their way to the gates in search of drink and merriment, but most of all coin. Not interested in any of the above, Keira pushed her way through the throng, ignoring the drunken shouts and averting her eyes from the tangles of limbs she glimpsed in the shadows between tentpoles.

She passed by the infirmary and saw the Bellatori healer, Argus, wringing bloody water from a pile of rags. She paused.

"Need any help, Argus?" she asked, ignoring the protest of her aching muscles. Ever since arriving in the Southern Shield, she'd naturally gravitated toward the infirmary. She helped the healer Argus in whatever way she could—determined to keep busy and remain useful. But she'd be lying if she said there wasn't a sense of familiarity in it, a tie to her old life in her own world, where she'd thought she just might end up a healer herself one day. But that was a long time ago.

"No, no, Keira. I appreciate it, but I'm almost done." Argus's smile shone as sweat dripped down his dark-skinned face. "Besides, from the looks of it, I'd likely end the night sweeping your raggedy bones off the floor. Go get some sleep, girl. You look like horse shite."

Keira snorted but waved a hand in acknowledgment. Pushing on methodically, she went in search of her tent and the waiting cot within but found herself waylaid by a tall figure.

Keira tensed instinctively, her fingers twitching toward her hilt, but paused when she registered the familiar face—the young Tiro she'd saved from an early grave in the afternoon's attack.

"Glad to see you made it back all right," he said, smiling shyly as he rubbed the back of his neck. "We tried to follow you but lost your trail in the overgrowth. Did you catch that last marauder?"

"No," Keira replied shortly, glancing over his shoulder. *So close,* she thought. Ten more yards, and she'd have been home free. She realized then that he was still talking.

"Sorry, what was that?" she asked, brows furrowing as she registered his rising tone. He'd clearly asked her a question.

"I was just wondering if you'd care to join us. Some other blokes and I've found where Cook keeps the good mead. Though if we don't hurry, I doubt Stanus will leave us any at all." He trailed off and shot Keira a half grin.

The brusque brush-off she'd been rehearsing caught in Keira's throat as she stared at him. As the lowest ranking soldiers in the Bellatorio, Tiros were generally close in age to Keira, but she couldn't help but think they all looked little more than boys—too young to be fighting an unwinnable war and far too young for the death that no doubt awaited them. This one was clearly a downlander, as evidenced by his arched syllables, olive skin, and dark features. He looked nothing at all like . . .

Keira closed her eyes, beating back the memories with all the strength she could muster, though she could feel the dam she'd built around the lapping waves of sorrow weaken. *He's not him,* she thought fiercely. *He's not.*

"I'm sorry. Have I said something wrong? I really just wanted to thank you. You know, for saving my arse back there."

Her emotions better controlled, Keira opened her eyes and gave the young Tiro another once-over. She remembered him from around camp, knew they'd been on several patrols together. But what was his name? Anton? Crispus? Maybe Jovian? She shook her head. In truth, she'd made a distinct effort not to learn any of their names. Why bother? Not when any of them could end up on the wrong end of a spear the next day. No, it was better not to get too attached.

The young man's brow furrowed now, and he shifted his weight awkwardly. Clearly, she'd taken too long to respond.

"You're welcome," she said finally. "And thank you. I appreciate the invitation, but honestly, the only thing I want right about now is to be horizontal."

Offering a small smile in apology, she turned then to go. He caught her arm, and she froze. His touch was light, but it brought with it no end of memories, and she slowly but resolutely pulled away.

"How about tomorrow, then? Breakfast, perhaps? One of the village ladies always brings a warm egg stew to sell in the morning—eases the headache after the night's merriment."

He offered another half grin that surely made all the village girls' hearts melt. Keira pressed her lips together in a thin line.

"No, thank you."

And without further explanation, she pushed past his confused expression and made for her tent and the solitude she craved.

Once inside, she leaned one hand heavily against the tent post, in a single breath releasing all the tension she'd kept pent up inside since the attack that afternoon. As she felt it leave her body, her shoulders slumped, and she collapsed onto the bed. In its wake, the weight of something else fell firmly into place— silence. Though she could still hear the revelry outside, inside her haven, all was still and quiet. The belongings she'd arrayed so precisely behind her lay exactly where she'd placed them. She was alone, and that was right where she needed to be.

One after the other, she kicked off her boots and placed them at the foot of the bed, arranged so she could slip her feet in at a moment's notice should she need them. Steely gray eyes flashed in her memory—Gaius Flavius's regimented precision as he arrayed every article of armor and weaponry at precise intervals around his cot. She shook the thought away and unstrapped the sword at her hip. Laying it across her thighs, she reached for the worn rag and began rubbing methodical circles into its surface, until it reflected her weary expression. Nazor's velvety, stern voice echoed in her memory, chiding, "A warrior is only as good as her worst-kept weapon." Keira swallowed and pushed the sword aside, rubbing her temples as if to burn the thoughts away. Then, carefully unstrapping each piece of leather armor, she eased it off her aching muscles. Reaching for the rough horsehair brush, she briskly cleared the dirt from each piece, chipping away the caked mud with her knife as she ignored the growing wave of nostalgia.

A toothy half grin. Soft, olive-green eyes looking up at her beneath a flop of sandy-blond hair. Danny.

Keira closed her eyes, forcing herself to breathe normally—

in through her nose and out through her mouth. But she couldn't fight the sting that came to the corners of her eyes or the burning in the bridge of her nose. She swallowed a choked sob. *Oh, Danny,* she thought. *Why did you have to leave? You promised you never would, promised you'd always be here.*

More memories flashed in her mind's eye. Elliott approaching her, face splintered by sorrow, speaking words she couldn't quite comprehend. The buckling of her knees as she sank onto icy flagstones, and Elliott's arms tight around her shoulders as the words she couldn't quite believe echoed in her mind. *He's gone. He's really gone.*

In the weeks that followed the riots that had first taken him from her, she'd known logically that the chances he'd simply wake up one day were growing slim beyond measure. But what currency had they been dealing in, if not slim chances and desperate hopes? So when Danny had finally slipped away, it had been like having all the oxygen sucked from her body. The tether that had for so long held her to this world had vanished in an instant, and she'd found herself adrift in a sea of sympathetic glances and unsolicited words of consolation. It was for the sake of her own sanity that she'd escaped on the first Bellatori transport ship leaving Crîd Eálas, barely waiting for Landry's hesitant permission to join his soldiers in their campaign against the marauders harassing the Southern Shield. All she'd known before arriving was that it was a way out of the capital—promising combat and no end of nights spent far too exhausted to dream. That was certainly enough for her.

Now, pressing the heels of her palms to her closed eyelids, Keira compelled her breathing to slow, forcing her head above the waves of grief, refusing to let it suck her down into its icy grip. Crawling under the thin blanket of her cot, Keira bolted the door against the memories that threatened intrusion and slipped into a fitful sleep.

THE NEXT DAY, Keira emerged bleary-eyed from her tent to find the camp already rolling into motion, wide awake despite the night's merriment. All around her, Bellators saddled horses and stoked fires. Keira spied Centus Arennius barking orders as he reviewed his troops. Shrugging on her own leather jerkin, Keira headed for the wiry Centus, who didn't bother looking up from the scroll he was reviewing as she approached. She cleared her throat.

"Yes?" Arennius asked, eyes still trailing one finger as he scanned the list of rations.

"Is there a patrol going out, sir?"

Arennius made a grunt of acknowledgment. "To Albé. After yesterday's attack, it seems unlikely the marauders came upon our position by chance."

"You think we'll find them hiding in the town, then?"

"Probably not," Arennius replied mildly. "The rats have all scampered back to their hollows by now. We'll not find them until they've had time to lick their wounds, reemerging only to bite our heels when we've stopped looking."

Keira's mouth twisted in distaste. "Then why are we going to town?"

Arennius finally glanced up, offering her a considering look. "Because the marauders must get their information from some-where. And the town is the most likely source."

Keira nodded, moving to grab her horse as Arennius added, "Well done yesterday. You've . . . done well here. I won't pretend I wasn't doubtful, bringing an untrained civilian along, but you've proved yourself a genuine asset on the battlefield, and Argus speaks highly of your work in the infirmary. We're lucky to have you here."

Keira blinked at him in surprise. She'd felt the wary glances when she'd first arrived—the unwelcome tagalong to the centurium. So she'd stayed out of the Centus's way, happy to do her job quietly and unobtrusively. "Thank you, sir," she said, feeling a blush creep over her cheeks.

Arennius cleared his throat, shifting awkwardly, and she spared them both further embarrassment, offering her excuses as she ran to saddle her own horse. She was happy to be thought useful, though. And despite herself, she was rather fond of the usually taciturn Arennius. In his stalwart way, he reminded her of her old friend Gaius Flavius, who she and Danny had accompanied to Mount Ánghen to retrieve now-Regio Landrianus. Landry had been little more than a spoiled princeling back then, but Flavius had taken his duty seriously—so seriously he'd died defending him when his own Centus betrayed them. She missed him. She missed all of them.

Wheeling her horse around, Keira considered Arennius's earlier statement. There was little doubt many within the local town would like to see the Bellatorio discharged from the islands altogether. After all, tensions ran deep between the military and the islanders. The Shield Wars were only a few decades past, and stories of the sickness and death that had resulted were still widespread. But side with foreign marauders raiding and pillaging their shores? Keira thought it unlikely.

Still, it was probably worth asking around town to see what strangers had ventured there of late. The islanders were naturally distrustful of outsiders, and a foreign marauder would not have gone unnoticed should they have ventured to market for supplies. Of that she had little doubt.

THREE

The Bellators weren't exactly well-received. Walking through town amid the rows of red-cloaked Bellators, Keira could feel the eyes of the people following them, some merely distrustful, others outright hostile. Though they'd dismounted, they still looked every bit the conquering army. Which, Keira thought, they sort of were. She ignored the grating feel of the thought and focused on observing her surroundings. Albé was a bustling port town, with the largest docks on the island of Tibolé—the largest island in the Southern Shield archipelago.

This town has prospered, she thought, remembering stories of the devastation wrought by the Shield Wars on what were then only small villages on these islands. Their fortunes were now tied to the trade that ran through this port. The marauders were a threat to that.

They couldn't possibly be feeding them information, she decided. No matter how much they might hate the Bellatorio, she suspected their self-interest would win out in the end.

A commotion at one of the market stalls caught her attention, and she turned to see a young, red-faced Tiro arguing with a shopkeeper, presumably over a price he felt was too high. The shopkeeper murmured something to his companion in the island dialect, and the two chortled.

"'Ey! What you sayin' then?" the Bellator demanded of the shopkeeper. He was one of the young Tiros, and an uplander by the look of his freckled face and copper hair—his cheeks were turning a matching shade by the second.

"Nothing, nothing! Only happy you being so hungry before even midday. But I'm sorry to say, my prices being set."

The shopkeeper smiled serenely as his companion hid a smile behind a hand. They clearly had had a laugh at the Tiro's expense. By then, the commotion had caught the attention of the other Bellators, and a small crowd had formed. The young Bellator's friends began egging him on, and Keira could see the tension building. She stepped forward.

"Is there a problem here, Tiro?" she asked. The young man looked undeterred but paused, eyeing her. Keira might not have had any formal rank in the Bellatori power structure, but her reputation preceded her, both for her actions in the capital and since arriving on the island. And if there was one thing Bellators respected, it was martial competence.

"No, ma'am," the Bellator said finally, his words cutting through the palpable tension. Then he turned back to the shop-keeper. "Damn clambacks," he growled. "Sneakin' snakes, all of you."

Keira pursed her lips at the insult but let the young man walk away, glad not to have had to break up a violent encounter. *Ironic*, she thought instead. An uplander, who likely suffered regular taunts from his Bellatori comrades for his own heritage, feeling entitled to degrade someone else for theirs. She shook her head.

Feeling suddenly exhausted, Keira turned and began making her way farther down the street. She'd stopped to admire a leatherworker's intricate designs when shouts drew her attention down a side alley off the main street.

Not again, Keira groaned inwardly.

But as she jogged down the road, she realized the noise was coming not from the Bellators but from a gaggle of islander children, who'd gathered around something hidden at their center. Their ages varied widely, but Keira spied at least a couple teenagers in their midst. As Keira pushed through the throng, the children parted easily, their jeers cut short in surprise at the sudden appearance of an outsider. When she finally made it to the center, she found two older boys—one holding a small girl and the other waggling a jeering finger at her.

"These other *grelún* be coming to take you back, eh, *grelún*? You glad to be going back to your proper home?"

The girl's head shot up then, and Keira was shocked to see light seafoam eyes staring back, white-hot in their fury as she leveled the older boy with a withering glare.

"At least I not being dumb enough to think the world be ending at shore's edge."

The older boy's cheeks flushed, and he took another menacing step toward the girl. To her credit, she didn't flinch. But Keira saw the flash of fear in her eyes and decided that was enough.

"All right, then, you've had your fun. Now get out of here."

The older boys spun toward Keira. They were a head taller than she, and there was a time when she would have been afraid of them. But she was a different person now. She leveled them with her best "You ought to be ashamed of yourselves" look of reproof, but the two of them didn't look anywhere close to abashed. The silence filled with loathing, and the two merely glared at her. It took a flick of her fingers toward her sword for them to take the wisest course of action and let the young girl go. Surprised, the girl crumpled to her knees.

"Come on," said the older boy, dark eyes haughty and cruel. "Leave the *grelún* with its proper family." The crowd of children laughed as they melted away up and down the alley on either side.

Keira turned then to help the girl up and found her already on her feet, tiny hands balled into fists as she glared up at her, eyes glinting with tear-filled fury.

"Why you be following me?"

It took Keira aback, and she was instantly defensive. "I'm not following you. In case you didn't notice, I saved your butt! Were you looking to be on the wrong side of a black eye? Or worse?"

"I didn't be needing your help," the girl said, swiping furiously at the tears that rolled down her cheeks.

Keira snorted. "Could have fooled me. You sure have a nasty habit of getting yourself into trouble."

The girl's lips pursed, and she glared back at Keira. Her appearance was striking; dark brown hair that displayed the golden highlights of a long-term affair with tropical rays fell in waves around her shoulders. The girl murmured something in the island dialect as she brushed the dirt off her bark-cloth dress.

"What was that?"

The girl's eyes shone with dislike, and her mouth kinked into a small smile. "I be saying it be just like a *grelún*, sticking her nose in where it not being wanted."

Keira's own eyes narrowed. "*Grelún*, huh? If I'm not

mistaken, that's exactly what those boys called *you*. What does it mean, anyway?"

The girl's grin twisted into a scowl. "It be meaning 'outsider.' And now, thanks to you, I being even more *grelún*."

Keira felt a seed of guilt twist in her stomach, and she pushed it down. She would *not* be manipulated by a little kid. "Why would they call you an outsider?"

The girl's shoulders slumped slightly, and she murmured, "It don't matter. Only fools and sloths be caring for such things, make themselves feel more important."

Her words held the authority of ones said by someone she respected, but a note of doubt crept in at the end. Keira crossed her arms, cocking her head slightly as she leveled the girl with one arched brow. "You're pretty smart for a six-year-old."

The girl's head snapped up. She straightened, drawing herself up to her highest height of nearly four feet. Her eyes narrowed.

"I'm eleven, thank you very much."

Eleven? Keira thought, giving the girl a quick once-over. From the girl's rangy limbs to the softness of her jawline, she certainly didn't look older than about eight. But returning to those impossibly bright seafoam eyes, tinged with a hardness Keira hadn't noticed before, she was inclined to believe that the girl just might be telling the truth.

"What's your name, anyway?" Keira asked.

"Oli'iraina," she answered. "But people be calling me Raina. What's yours?"

Keira smiled at the clear pride with which she pronounced her name. "I'm Keira. And where do you live, Raina?"

This time Raina hesitated, eyeing Keira with uncertainty. "I be living with Marné," she said. "She's my grandmother. My parents—" Raina paused, the hardness coming back into her eyes. "My parents being dead, five years gone now."

Keira pursed her lips. "I'm sorry. Mine too, I'm afraid."

Raina looked surprised, and the two stared at each other for a moment. Then Raina's expression turned to one of suspicion. "Why you be caring, anyway?"

Keira snorted. "Calm down, tiger. Why don't we just get you home? I'll come with you. Not—" Keira interjected, seeing Raina about to protest, "because you need help. But because I think your marné might not be so happy if you get that bully's blood all over yourself."

Raina glanced down at her bark-cloth dress before returning Keira's smile with a scowl, but nodded. Clearly, that line of argument was convincing. If this Marné was anything like her granddaughter, Keira suspected she was not a woman to be crossed.

Like much of Albé, the cluster of buildings Raina led Keira toward were all thatched, and while some benefited from the elevation of stilts to avoid the incoming tide, others simply had to make do with what they had. Young children played barefoot in the mud as they passed, while parents watched the two of them with narrowed eyes.

When they reached the last house on the street, Raina led the way up a set of stairs to the elevated front porch, where an old woman sat bent over a long stretch of felted bark cloth. Her fingers moved quickly, long-stemmed reed brush in hand as she sketched lightly over its length. Her milky eyes stared unseeing at a point far off in the distance. Keira approached her cautiously.

"Good morning, Marné," Raina said, bending down to kiss the old woman's twisted knuckles in the way Keira had seen many children address their elders. "This be Keira. She be coming with the red cloaks, but . . . she seeming nice enough."

Keira hid a small smile, thinking it wouldn't help her case. The old woman turned her unseeing eyes toward her and held out a hand. Not sure what the correct protocol was, Keira copied Raina and gave the woman's knuckles a quick peck. Neither seemed offended, so Keira took this as a good sign.

"Is it just the two of you here?" she asked.

Raina nodded, a slight furrow crossing her brow. "My brother, Akamu, used to be living with us, but he moved into the men's quarters last rainy season. He still be visiting, though," she added quickly.

This surprised Keira. She knew that the Southern Shield was a matriarchal culture. Such matriarchs often boasted sprawling family trees of descendants and held an elevated position within Udánma society. The woman turned her wrinkled, sun-darkened face to Keira and inclined her head slightly but said nothing.

Keira proceeded hesitantly, "It's a pleasure to meet you, ma'am."

Raina giggled from behind one hand, and Keira blushed. "You can call her Marné, Keira. Everyone be doing so."

Keira nodded, watching as the older woman's fingers never stopped moving over her canvas. Keira shifted her weight awkwardly. Had the old woman even heard them? She was about to ask Raina if she needed anything else before she left, when the old woman moved to grab Raina's wrist, her fingers trailing up the sandy length of her arm.

"I see we be getting ourselves into trouble," she mused. Her voice had the lived-in quality of old leather, but there was a warmth to its rasp, a kindness folded into its unyielding will.

Raina averted her gaze from the woman's unseeing milky depths and kicked her bare foot against the uneven planks of the porch. "They started it, Marné," she said finally.

The older woman made a contemptuous sound in the back of her throat. "You be paying them no mind, you hear, *dinué*?"

Raina made a noncommittal sound, and her grandmother's voice grew firmer.

"You being touched by Cála, child. Never forget that. Your eyes being a gift. Never be ashamed of them."

Raina looked abashed and quickly said, "Yes, Marné," before kissing her knuckles again. The young girl then hurried into the house, where Keira could hear the high-pitched squeal of a kettle sounding. She climbed the steps then, kneeling beside the old woman and watching as the ink brush danced over the bark cloth.

"Marné," she said hesitantly, "may I ask, how long has your family lived in these islands?"

The woman gave her a crooked smile, and Keira noticed several teeth missing.

"At least ten generations. Since Cála first created the islands from the waves, my people be living here. We be coming from the island and always been a part of Tibolé."

Keira nodded, then stopped, blushing as she realized that the woman had no way of seeing her, and said, "May I ask, are the islands very different from when you were a girl?"

Marné again turned those unseeing eyes to Keira, who had the distinct impression that behind their milky opacity lay a keen intelligence and a quick, still-agile mind. From the door, Raina emerged bearing a thin wooden tray laden with pewter cups and a kettle. She began pouring the tea but glanced up to hear Marné's answer.

"I lived many lifetimes and be seeing many powers come and go—seeing the chaos come from the water," the old woman began, "order and chaos in an endless cycle. I be seeing the likes of you, *Le'ena* . . . spirit-binder."

Keira froze, staring at her. Could she—could she really tell? How?

Cautiously, she asked, "What do you know of spirit-binders, Marné? Do you have many here?" Keira held her breath as she waited for the woman's response. Could it be that the Legion was not the sole source of pneumonancy in this world?

The woman inclined her head slightly before replying. "In the olden days we did, but they being long gone now. They protected our island, children of Cála who be preserving our island against the churning waves that always be seeking to swallow it whole. The spirit-binders be working their magic to keep us above the waves. They ordered the world and fought back the chaos of the waters."

Keira swallowed. *Children of Cála?* Wasn't that what she'd called Raina? Or was it *touched by Cála*? Was there a difference?

She glanced at Raina, who leveled her with that piercing gaze. Keira shivered. She opened her mouth then to ask another question, but stopped short at the long, low call of a horn in the distance.

"I think that being your signal," Marné said, sounding amused. "Your warriors be calling."

Keira nodded, downing the last of her tea and instantly regretting it as the scalding liquid coursed down her throat. She stood.

"Thank you for the tea, Marné. And . . ." She paused, looking at Raina, who behind her indifferent demeanor looked almost sad to see her go. "Take care of yourself, Raina," Keira finished.

She began making her way down the street toward the market, hoping she wouldn't get lost. At the end of the street, she paused and cast one final glance back along the row of thatched houses for the old woman and her granddaughter, who sat alone on the porch, watching her as she departed.

THE NEXT MORNING, Keira woke to shouts and braying horses. Emerging from her tent into the predawn light, she blinked the sleep from her eyes as she tried to make out the source of the commotion. It was then that she saw two litter-bearers moving across the yard, a crowd of Bellators in their wake. Pulling on her boots, she sprinted toward the infirmary. By the looks of it, Argus would need help.

Keira pushed past surprised Bellators as she went, the flap of their red cloaks splashing the ever-present mud of the islands onto her legs. She barely noticed. Reaching the tent flap, she wrenched it open to find a crowd already gathered. The hot, damp air of the Southern Shield filled the cramped space, while the smell of sweaty bodies and putrefaction lay heavy and oppressive. Keira pushed past the gawking onlookers to find the source of their attention. The young Tiro who'd waylaid her outside her tent now lay stretched out on a cot—mostly intact, but for the mass of mangled flesh where his right foot used to be.

The healer, Argus, was already hard at work, rinsing the leg with water from a clay bowl. Looking up at her entry, he said gruffly, "Good, you're here. Fetch clean bandages and prepare the wound cream!"

Keira let her eyes linger on the ghastly wound for a split second more before hurrying to the cupboard to fetch the supplies, quickly measuring the required herbs into the mortar. When she returned, she hastily ground the mixture with the pestle and turned to the nearest Bellator.

"What happened?"

"Damn clambacks littered the place with bear traps, of all things," growled a nearby Sergius, one of the senior enlisted soldiers. Keira glanced at him. While technically below the rank of officer, the Sergius often held more sway with the younger men.

"Is he one of yours, then?" she asked, her stomach turning at the sight of the trap's steel metal jaws, blood-drenched and forgotten in the corner. *I guess I know where the screams came from,* she thought, wincing. The metal must have been hellish to remove.

"Aye, he is. Curse the blockheaded fool." Despite his harsh words, Keira could hear the note of genuine concern that echoed through.

From the look of him, the Tiro had lost a lot of blood. He was shivering despite the oppressive heat. Sweat plastered sandy-blond hair to his forehead, and his teeth chattered so fiercely that he'd worn his poor lower lip ragged.

"What's your name, Tiro?" Keira asked as Argus lifted the bandage to inspect the wound further. Glancing at the boy's face, she was startled to find sky-blue eyes staring back at her.

Suddenly, the boy on the table was no longer a young Bellator but a little girl, in a village far from here, crushed by falling boulders and in desperate need of a healer.

Keira's eyes clamped shut, and she shook her head as if to shake away the apparition. She swallowed hard, forcing herself to return to the present. This was not then. This was *now,* and

Keira didn't do that sort of thing anymore. It was too dangerous without—

Deciding not to finish that thought, she took a deep breath and opened her eyes to take stock of the scared boy in front of her.

"E-Ewan, ma'am." His words drew her attention back to him. "Am I goin' to die? I-I don't want to die."

She stared at him, willing herself to give the false reassurances that lay on the tip of her tongue. But she didn't.

Armed with wound cream mixed into a thick paste, Keira moved to Argus's side and helped him apply it to the now clean wound. Tiro Ewan cried out, and Keira gestured to the Sergius to help hold him down. Argus had gathered the ingredients for the cream himself, under the careful instructions of one of the local healers, who swore it warded off infection and promoted healing. They'd had some success with it for minor scrapes and injuries, but this mangled limb was something else entirely. Keira could only hope it would hold long enough to get him to the Lorenan mainland.

They then wrapped the wound in fresh bandages, before Argus gestured for Keira to follow him. She did so, curious what needed asking out of earshot of the crowd of Bellators.

"There's little hope, I'm afraid," he murmured, confirming her worries as he sorted through the jars in his cabinet. "There's only so much herbs can do. That poor boy will probably lose his foot, if not his life. Unless . . ." Argus glanced at her from the corner of his eye, then turned to face her fully, dark eyes leveling her with a steely gaze. "Unless you intervene."

Keira stared at him, uncomprehending.

"If there's something I can do to help . . ." she began, before trailing off at Argus's knowing expression.

"I know what you are," he said. "Spirit-binder, pneumonancer, whatever it is you want to call it. I've heard the rumors from the mainland, and I know what you can do. You can help him."

Keira felt the ground beneath her feet suddenly become unsteady. Had he known all this time? "Look, Argus, it doesn't work like that. I don't—do that anymore." Argus crossed his arms, looking thoroughly unconvinced, and Keira hurried on, almost pleading now. "I need someone called a grounder, someone to pull me back if I go too deep. It's too dangerous without—" She cut off, searching for the right words. "I don't even know if I could do it. I've never even tried something like *this*." Keira imagined again the boy's foot, hanging on by the fragments of shredded flesh, and shivered. "I'm sorry, Argus, but I can't."

Argus's jaw tightened as he gave her a searching look. But then he nodded. Keira breathed out a sigh of relief and opened her mouth to ask how she could help.

"Go on, then," he said instead, catching her off guard.

"I'm sorry?"

"Go on. There's nothing more to do here. I'll clean up this mess. You go on."

Keira stared at him. Though his words weren't sharp, she couldn't help feeling wounded. But most of all, she just felt guilty. She bit her lip and gave him one last glance, but he'd already turned back to the jars in his cupboard, vainly searching for something, anything, to ward off the truth of what was coming.

Keira turned to go, avoiding the curious looks the other Bellators gave her. She pushed through the tent flap, ignoring the shouted questions of the crowd, desperate for news of their friend. Her own guilt was a crushing weight between her shoulder blades, threatening to drive her face-first into the dirt.

But she pushed on toward the well in the center of camp. With trembling hands, she rinsed the blood from her arms before leaning heavily against the stone and closing her eyes.

"I see you've been keeping busy."

Keira's eyes flew open to meet the amused gray gaze of Cyrus Flavius.

"What are you doing here?"

The words came out in a squeal, but at that moment, Keira couldn't care less. Forgetting the exhaustion from a moment before, she sidestepped the well and flung her arms around Cyrus's neck. She felt him stiffen in surprise before slowly relaxing and returning the embrace.

Keira held Cyrus at arm's length and saw the slow fade of his crimson blush. He flashed her a shy smile. "Why? Aren't you glad to see me?"

Keira rolled her eyes. "Of course I'm happy to see you! We just didn't get any word that you were coming."

Cyrus shrugged. "I'm here on official business, actually, recruiting representatives for the new People's Council. The Southern Shield has never been represented in the Lorenan government, and, well, the Regio wants to correct that."

Keira nodded, but a sudden thought occurred to her, and she asked, "Landry isn't here with you, is he?"

"No, even he isn't dumb enough to stroll into a war zone."

Cyrus paused, then shot Keira a pointed look. "Unlike some people."

Keira snorted and bent to pick up the bucket she'd dropped in the commotion.

"Is that why you're here, then, to lecture me? I can't imagine why. He's the one who sent me here, after all."

Though Gaius said nothing, his eyebrows nearly touched his hairline. Exasperated, Keira rounded on him. "Out with it. What's the matter?"

Slowly, Cyrus said, "You say Landry *sent* you here? The way I remember it, you nearly begged him to get you out of the city. But it's been months now, and you've sent no word!"

Keira's jaw tightened. "That's enough, Cyrus. You have no right to come here and chide me. I'm just trying to live my life. Haven't I *earned* that?"

Such a firm reprimand would have mollified the old Cyrus, but to Keira's surprise, he stood his ground.

"Is that what you're doing here, Keira? Living your life?" He gestured at the bloodstained ground and the spartan Bellatori camp. "Is this your life now?"

Suddenly self-conscious of the watching Bellators, Keira took Cyrus by the arm and steered him away from the infirmary. When they were safely away from prying eyes, Keira turned back to Cyrus. She was prepared to scold him roundly, but the look of abject concern on his face quickly dampened her zeal.

"Look, Cyrus, I'm doing a lot of good here. I mean, there's a war on, and these guys need as much help as they can get. The marauders aren't just going after military positions. They've embedded themselves in the jungle and are using their camps to launch attacks on local trade routes. It's basically an insurgency at this point." She searched his face for understanding but found only skeptical disbelief.

"And what about the Legion? Are you just done with them, then?"

At the mention of the Legion, Keira felt a sense of dread creep down her spine. She chased the feeling away with ridicule and snorted. "I doubt I'd get that lucky. No, I'm sure they're just biding their time before they send someone here to fetch me. But yeah, if I had my way, I'd be done with them."

"How can you say that?"

"They betrayed me, Cyrus! Betrayed Landry!" Keira's voice had lost all semblance of casual conversance by this point. She was practically yelling. "*They're* the reason Danny's—" Her voice cut off, and she swallowed before meeting Cyrus's sympathetic gaze.

His eyes tightened, and he cocked his head slightly. Then he said quietly, "I'm sorry . . . you know, about Danny."

Keira deflated, all of her righteous indignation whistling away on a breeze of grief.

"I know, Cyrus, but that's why . . . well, that's why I'm better off here, away from . . . everything."

Cyrus grimaced, and he shifted his weight nervously.

Keira eyed him with suspicion. "There's more, isn't there."

"Yes." Cyrus fiddled with the red signet ring he wore, a last gift from his father, before continuing, "There's trouble in the capital, Keira. The Council of Benadur and the new People's Council are already at each other's throats. Meanwhile, the crown's debt continues to balloon out of control—not helped by this war, by the way—which has led to tax hikes, and the people are absolutely furious. Meanwhile, the Cross-Sea Lands have officially withdrawn all diplomatic ties. It's an absolute mess, Keira."

His words immediately put Keira on edge, fear and concern warring with annoyance that he'd bring her yet more problems to solve. She shook her head, forcing down her own worry as she made her voice cold and measured.

"Aren't you his advisor, Cyrus? Then advise him. None of us thought Landry's transition to power would be easy. Do your job, and let me do mine."

Cyrus winced at her words, and she instantly regretted their sharpness. She was about to clarify when he replied, firmly, "I need your help, Keira, and I'm not ashamed to admit that. I've tried to talk to Landry, but he won't listen to me. He's got too many voices whispering in his ear, the Benadur most of all. But —" Cyrus paused, his eyes tightening as his voice took on a pleading tone, "he'll listen to you, Keira. He trusts you more than anyone. If you came back . . . you could help him. And he needs your help right now. Isn't that what you came to Loren for in the first place?"

Keira had been battling a rising sense of guilt, but at these last few words, she felt pure, unadulterated fury erupt. "You know what, Cyrus? I used to think that. I used to think that I had a grand purpose in all of this, that I was *destined* to fight chaos and put the world to right. And, by Pneumos, I did my best! And do you know what it got me? Nothing but pain and suffering. I lost everything, Cyrus, everyone who ever cared for me. First your father, then Sara, Nazor, and . . . Danny." Her voice caught on his name, and she put up a hand to stop Cyrus and the words of sympathy she knew would follow. "I'm done losing people, Cyrus, and I'm done following whatever grand plan Pneumos supposedly has for me."

Silence echoed between them, and Keira refused to meet his gaze, afraid of whatever sympathy she might find there, afraid it might undo her entirely.

Finally, Cyrus spoke, in a voice that was hollow and raw. "Keira, I know what sacrifice means. I've lost people too." She glanced at him, shame rippling through her as she saw him fiddle again with Gaius's red signet ring. He didn't stop, though, concluding, "But if we don't do something, we risk Loren falling right back into anarchy. Then everything we've done, everything we've *sacrificed*, will have been for nothing!"

"Look, Cyrus, I don't know what you want me to say. I have a job to do here. I can't just be running off to—"

"Then at least take me to the Legion!" Cyrus blurted, brow furrowed, with an expression of such intensity that she was taken aback.

"Why? How can they help?" She was genuinely confused, and Cyrus's raised eyebrows weren't exactly helping matters.

"You know as well as I do, Keira, the role that the Legion has played in Loren. Just look at your own actions only a few months ago. The Legion makes kings, and they can just as easily topple them."

"That's ridiculous," Keira replied. "They didn't even want *me* to get involved, and they worked against me at every turn —"

"Yes, and almost succeeded!"

A group of Bellators standing farther down the training yard halted their conversation to stare curiously at them. Neither Keira nor Cyrus said anything for a moment, both too taken aback at his outburst. Finally, he rubbed his eyes, looking suddenly more exhausted than Keira had ever seen him.

"Look, I'm sorry, Keira. I didn't mean to shout. It's just—it's been a difficult few months. Honestly, we could use all the help we can get. But—" He paused, shooting her one last hopeful glance before continuing. "But I understand if you've made your decision. I won't argue."

Keira bit her lip, searching his dejected face for any sign of the lighthearted young Bellator she'd met only a few months ago.

"Ok, I'll tell you what. I can't come with you, but at least let me help you find your representatives for the People's Council. I was in town yesterday, and I think I know someone who can help."

Cyrus inhaled before nodding. Disappointment laced his voice as he said, "That would be helpful, thank you. Now, if you'll excuse me, I believe there's a young Tiro who was going to show me to my tent."

Keira snorted. "Good luck with that. Honestly, he's probably off drinking with his buddies by now. Those not on patrol duty tend to get started early."

"Yes, well, either way, I'd like to unpack my things. Will you be free in a few hours?"

Keira nodded and, after a quick squeeze of his elbow, turned to make her way back toward her own tent.

"Oh, and Keira," Cyrus called after her. She paused. "I do hope that whatever it is you've found here—well, I hope it brings you peace."

Keira swallowed but continued on to her tent.

"IT'S JUST at the far end of this street," Keira explained, gesturing for Cyrus to follow her down the nearest alley. "I wasn't able to send word, so hopefully they're home."

"It's odd, really," Cyrus said. "My father was stationed here, a long time ago. Did you know that?" When Keira shook her head, he continued, "He never spoke much of that tour, but he called it a cursed place, with death and tragedy around every corner." Cyrus shivered slightly, then looked around the town of Albé, at the women chatting by the market stalls and the children playing with a leather ball in the street. "I wonder what he'd say if he could see it now," Cyrus said, almost absently. "Would he recognize it?"

Keira didn't know how to answer that. There was so much she didn't know about the grizzled old Millus—her friend and companion for far too short a time. She only hoped he was at peace, finally freed from the life of violence he'd seemed unable to escape, or perhaps unwilling to.

When they reached the house, Keira was surprised to see a young man reclining on the porch where Raina's grandmother had sat the day before. He looked up, brow furrowing at their approach, and Keira slowed, suddenly unsure.

"Who you be looking for?" the man called out, though since slowing their pace, they were still a house and a half away.

Keira clenched and unclenched her hands. "We're looking for the woman who lives here," she said finally. "We met the other day." At his doubtful expression, she added, "I'm sorry, I don't know her full name. Raina told me to call her Marné."

The young man's face split into a wide grin, and deep dimples appeared in either cheek.

"Ah, yah. Eh, Marné!" he called. "There being people here to see you, ah?" He waved a hand at them, gesturing them forward. "You must be the girl little Raina can't stop talking about. I'm Akamu, her brother." His smile turned apologetic. "I hope she not been bothering you. She never met a girl Bellator before. Ay, I mean, a woman Bellator," he amended, one corner of his mouth tugging upward as he looked her up and down appreciatively.

He was a charming one, Keira decided, though the smile

made him look younger. She realized he couldn't be much older than her.

"I'm not a Bellator," she clarified. "But I am helping them with the situation here."

Akamu's face darkened, and his mouth pressed into a thin line. "Yah, those sea devils be terrorizing our shores for months. I be happy to see them gone. And who be you then?" he asked, turning to Cyrus.

"Cyrus Flavius, official representative of Regio Landrianus. That's actually why we're here. I've been tasked with recruiting representatives from the Southern Shield to join the newly formed People's Council in Crîd Eálas."

Akamu leaned forward slightly, curiosity warring with wariness across his face. "And what power this Council be having, then?"

Cyrus shrugged. "Laws, taxes, diplomacy. All the business of state will be discussed by both the People's Council and the Council of Benadur. *That* was the agreement."

A thin voice came from the doorway, and they all turned to see Marné emerging from within. "And what of their decision?" she asked. "What be binding the king across the waves to act on the word of this Council?"

Cyrus shifted, bringing a hand to the back of his neck as he replied, "Well, nothing set in stone, as of yet. But the Regio assures me—"

"Yet again you be coming here from the land across the waves, seeking to subdue our islands. This time with words and promises to be joining your swords and threats." Marné had reached the porch by now, lingering in the doorway as she leaned heavily on her knobbed walking stick. She was balanced on the other side by Raina, who held her arm steady. Marné's milky eyes narrowed, and her lips pursed, but she graciously accepted a seat as Raina hurriedly brought one for her. She leaned forward, propped with her staff between her legs, like an ageless seer holding court.

Keira decided now was as good a time as any to step in, especially as she was apparently the visiting representative for all things swords and Bellatori. "We do not seek to subdue, Marné, only to protect these islands from marauders, to stabilize them and prevent the rise of violence and extremism."

"And what use we be having for the king across the waves? He never be stepping foot on Tibolé or any of her sister islands."

Cyrus cleared his throat. "Marné, I know the king across the waves, and he cares deeply for all of his people. That's why he sent me here, to better understand the Southern Shield—"

"That all we be to you," Marné interjected, "a shield, a human blockade against that which you despise and that be threatening *your* way of life. You be having no care for ours."

Cyrus didn't seem to know how to answer that, and Keira couldn't exactly deny the woman's logic. How many times in the history of her own world had great powers renamed things to better suit their own purposes? But Marné wasn't finished.

"Ever since your Shield Wars, some thirty years ago, our islands be knowing nothing but violence. You be saying you seek to bring peace, and yet every day you remain be serving only to stir up more violence and chaos. We lost Raina and Akamu's father to that violence. And my daughter to the sickness that soon followed." Marné's voice twisted slightly on the words, and she caught her breath before resuming. "If we be wanting your peace, we would been asking for it."

It surprised Keira to hear Akamu speak up.

"But Marné, if the Regio Landrianus really be forming this People's Council, then this could be our chance to be heard."

Cyrus nodded quickly, adding, "He truly wants to hear the

input of all his subjects and to understand how he can better serve you."

Keira glanced at Raina, whose expression looked torn, eyes darting between Marné's cold certainty and Akamu's hopeful optimism.

Marné cocked her head, considering Akamu even through cataract-filled lenses. "You would be leaving our islands? What self-respecting Udánma would be leaving their island?"

"One who be hoping to save it, Marné! That I might be bringing prosperity home with me."

"You are young," the woman said, shaking her head. "And I know you be meaning well. But I'm afraid there be much you not be understanding about this world."

The two stood in silence, Akamu's certainty having grown to parallel that of his grandmother. He turned then to Cyrus.

"I be distributing this message, and letting the Udánma know their voices are wanted, that we may be joining this People's Council. There will be a vote among the elders, but I be letting them know I wish to be joining this council myself."

"Wonderful!" Cyrus cried, reaching out and shaking Akamu's hand eagerly. Akamu looked startled but returned the gesture with the eagerness of a newly discovered game. "There's a ship in port. I was hoping to leave in three days' time. Will that be enough?"

Akamu nodded, his broad grin matching Cyrus's. His smile quickly faded when he saw Marné's scowl. "Please, Marné, I be having your blessing in this? I only wish to be seeing peace and prosperity for the Udánma. But every day, we be waking to more sea devils and empty market stalls."

Marné made a harrumphing sound. "It always being some-thing—in my day, it be 'insurrectionists'; today it be marauders.

Who say tomorrow it not be the Udánma themselves? Nothing good be coming from dealing with the king across the waves."

"Maybe, Marné. But what other choice be there? I not be content to live out my days hoping things be better tomorrow, not when I have a chance to be making change today."

A long silence settled then between them, before Marné finally spoke. "If this truly be what you must do, then I be giving you my blessing, Akamu. Only know that it be not always as easy to come home as it be to leave."

Akamu nodded to that and reached down, bringing the gnarled knuckles of Marné's hand to his lips.

While Cyrus continued to share his grand plans for strengthening the People's Council with a still-dubious Marné, Keira walked along the porch that ringed the circular thatched house. Leaning on the railing, she gazed out at the perfect turquoise of the ocean's waves as they lapped onto the shore. She was happy to help Cyrus recruit for the People's Council. It eased her guilt over refusing to take him to the Legion. She just wasn't ready. She wasn't ready to leave the small peace she'd found here and return to a reminder of all she'd lost, not when there was still a reason to stay.

It helped that Akamu seemed as eager as Cyrus. They'd make a good pair, she decided. And with Akamu ready and willing to cross the seas to a far-off capital, surely other young people in the islands would follow suit, risking the disapproval of their elders for a chance to improve their lot and have a say in the fate of the Southern Shield.

Voices from behind her made her glance around, through

the thin bark cloth that covered the window. Inside, Keira could see Akamu gathering the last of his belongings.

"Pleeeease, Akamu," a small voice begged. "Please be taking me with you."

"No, *dinué*." Akamu laughed. "You're too young, Raina."

"I am *not*, Akamu. I being smart and fast and—"

Akamu chuckled. "I not be doubting that, Little Sister, but your place be here, with Marné. Who be looking after her if we both be leaving, eh?"

From where she was standing, Keira could just make out Raina's face, twisted in an expression of yearning mixed with guilt. Then she shook her head. "She'll be *fine*, Akamu. There be old lady Soli down the street. She be having an entire house filled with children and grandchildren, and you know how much she be loving Marné. She be making them come and help."

Akamu didn't even look up from the articles of clothing he briskly stuffed into his satchel. "The mainland be no place for a little girl. It be dangerous, and—"

"If it being so dangerous, then who be watching your back, Big Brother? You need me to make sure those *grelún* be true-true." Raina's face had screwed up into a defiant glare, and Keira couldn't help but smile at the sharp angle of the girl's chin as she stood with arms crossed before her towering older brother.

Akamu finally turned around and crossed his own arms in exact imitation, looking down his long, chiseled nose at her. "I said *no*, Oli'iraina."

The girl seemed to shrink before him, as if the utterance of her full name had somehow deflated her. Her gaze dropped to the floor, but not before Keira spotted tears welling up in the corner of each eye. Akamu's expression softened, and he moved to kneel beside her. Placing one hand on her shoulder, he lifted her chin with two fingers to meet his gaze.

"You be very special, Raina," he murmured. "More than you know. Your dreams be too big for this island, and I believe you be leaving one day. You be catching the whole world in those hands of yours." He took her tiny hands in one of his and squeezed them for emphasis. His brow furrowed as he continued, "This world be cruel, Raina, and I be seeing the struggles you be having here. But you're stronger than all of that. You hear? You be having our mother's courage in your soul, *dinué*, and our father's loyalty in your heart." Akamu's fingers brushed the shell that Raina wore around her neck, and Keira could have sworn the shell grew brighter as it caught the late afternoon rays of sun that passed through the window. "I'll be coming back for you one day, Raina. I promise."

Raina collapsed onto him then, throwing her arms around his neck. He stroked the back of her head and made reassuring noises as she sobbed.

Keira blinked tears from her own eyes before turning away, suddenly embarrassed to have witnessed such a private moment. She strode along the porch, moving toward the front of the house and hoping they hadn't felt themselves watched. All the while, her heart ached for them, but most of all for little Raina. After all, Keira knew better than most what it was to be left behind.

FIVE

When Keira came back around the corner, she suddenly found herself alone with Marné. Cyrus apparently had abandoned his attempts to convince her and had retreated inside to help Akamu. Keira cleared her throat awkwardly. After all, she didn't want to sneak up on the poor lady.

"I hear you, *Le'ena*," Marné said loudly. "I may not be having the use of my eyes, but my ears be working just fine."

"Sorry," Keira said, coming to stand beside the old woman's chair. "He means well, you know. Cyrus, I mean. He's just a bit enthusiastic."

Marné snorted.

Keira was so surprised by the sound that she laughed aloud and was rewarded with a smile.

"I not be envying Akamu that long trip with a chattering bird like that—you either, for that matter."

"Oh, I won't be going with them," Keira replied. "There's still so much to do here. I'm needed, you see."

Marné's eyebrows rose, and her mouth twisted into a

knowing smile. "You be having a role to play in this, *Le'ena*. Marné be seeing that quite clearly."

Keira glanced into the milky depths of Marné's eyes and shivered, then felt guilty, suddenly glad the old woman couldn't see her. "I'm sorry, but my time meddling in capital politics is long over."

"You're a bridger of worlds, *Le'ena*. And the others like you, they may believe meddling be *precisely* what's needed."

"Then let *them* get involved," Keira said, exasperated. "I've done my part. I have a new job now, a new role here."

Marné shook her head, expression dark. "They who be having power over death itself may be easily corrupted."

"Look, the Legion may be strong, Marné, but even they can't fight death."

Marné leveled her with a long, low look. "And just how you be thinking you were brought here, *Le'ena*?"

Keira blanched, staring at her. *Does she mean what I think she means?* How was it that this old woman from the Southern Shield had so much information about the Legion? About how they came to be in Loren? So much for secrecy.

"H-How do you know all this, Marné?"

Marné made a noncommittal sound. "You be *Le'ena*, not of this world, a spirit-binder." She inhaled deeply, and her voice arched, morphing into the rhythmed cadence of verse. "*When rains do fade and waves be calm, then sun and moon be borne alike. Le'ena walk among the stromb, death be gone when Cála strike.*"

Keira stared at her. Could the Legion really have power over death? *I mean, that is how you got here*, she reminded herself. But when she'd asked him about it, Elliott had always painted their arrival in this new world as one of the great mysteries of pneuma, something unknowable and outside the Legion's control. But what if it wasn't?

"Marné, I don't even know how I would use pneuma in that way—conquering death."

"Those who be gone never truly be leaving us, Keira. Their essence, the spirit of them, remains, needing only to be bound in flesh. You be a healer, be you not?"

"Not really, not anymore," Keira replied, feeling a sharp pain in her chest. "I lost that ability when I lost my grounder."

Marné's lips pursed before saying only, "That which is undone may be reborn."

Keira gaped, searching the old woman's face, looking for a punch line that never came. Was she actually saying that healing pneumonancy could reverse death? She opened her mouth to ask for clarification.

"Come on, Keira!"

Cyrus's voice interrupted her musings, and she glanced up, startled. He and Akamu stood just outside the open front door, where Raina stood slumped against the frame, eyes still bloodshot and looking utterly dejected.

"I told Akamu we'd drop him off by the men's quarters. He's eager to talk to them."

Keira glanced back at Marné, desperately wanting to continue their conversation. But the old woman's eyes had closed, her breath lightening until it was a shallow pulse. Whether the sleep was real or feigned, Marné clearly intended the conversation to be over. Keira stood reluctantly and made to follow the others. Meanwhile, with every step down the road, Keira could feel Raina's eyes burning into her back, the intensity of her yearning palpable in the afternoon heat.

AFTER FINALIZING their plans with Akamu at the men's quarters, Keira and Cyrus made their way back to the Bellatori encampment. Their horses had fallen into a steady rhythm, and Keira was deep in thought over Marné's words.

"Are you sure you won't come with us, Keira?"

Cyrus's question startled her from her distraction.

"Even if you won't take me to the Legion," Cyrus continued, "I could still use your help in the capital. We're doing incredible work there. This new council could change everything, really make a difference in the people's lives."

Keira snorted, replying dryly, "Not if the Council of Benadur has anything to say about it. I can't imagine they're happy to be handing over power to the masses." She glanced up at the glimpse of sky she could make out through the canopy above, darkening far faster than she'd expected. They'd stayed too long in town, and Keira regretted declining to bring Bellators with them.

Cyrus seemed oblivious. "Yes, but this is the start of something *new*, don't you see? Landry will be the first Regio to govern with the true consent of his own people—not merely a ceremonial nod to hearing out their grievances, true consent!"

Keira smiled at his excitement. She imagined the concept of representation would seem truly novel for someone who hadn't sat through an entire year of ninth grade US history or experienced what true democracy actually looked like. She wished she could share in Cyrus's optimism. Of course, she was happy about Loren's newly more representative government, but those same history classes had taught her what often befell rapid changes in government power structures, and she didn't like their odds of avoiding all-out bloodshed. At least they didn't have guillotines here—yet.

A sudden movement in the underbrush to her left made her tense, and she felt the horse beneath her skitter nervously.

"Cyrus," she murmured, peering hard through the layers of foliage.

". . . and this is just the beginning. Soon we'll have established patterns of—"

"Cyrus!" she hissed, louder this time and with a decided note of fear. That stopped him, and he peered around curiously.

"What is it?"

Keira's eyes danced over the wall of green as her fingers tightened on the hilt of her sword. "We're not alone."

Cyrus said nothing, and she glanced at him. His normally olive-toned skin had paled, and his dark curls seemed plastered to his forehead in a sheen of sweat.

When was he last in a battle? she wondered nervously. Cyrus was a former Bellator, but he'd always been an artist at heart, caring nothing for blood and gore. Yet here he was, in the middle of a war zone. What had she been thinking? Why had she not asked for an escort? Asked for help?

Before she could verbalize her mental self-berating, there was a second movement—this time on the other side.

A figure darted onto the path before them, and their horses reared, screaming in shrill notes of fear. Cyrus cried out, and with horror, Keira watched him fall from his horse just as several dark figures flew from the shadows.

As soon as her horse's hooves hit the ground, they were off. Desperately, Keira gripped the reins, tearing at the horse's head to turn him about. But this only terrified him more. Peering over one shoulder, Keira could see Cyrus and the figures falling away.

A moment's hesitation, and the decision was made. Carefully slipping her feet out of the stirrups, Keira balanced on the careening saddle for just a moment before leaping from the horse's back.

She landed painfully in a mass of Loli bushes and rolled to her side, feeling as if every bone in her body had been rattled out of place. Pushing the sensation aside, she clambered to her feet.

She ran, listing dangerously to the side as she sought to catch both her balance and her breath. In the distance, she could see Cyrus, sword outstretched, as he spun to face each approaching figure. He was terribly outnumbered.

Hold on, she thought at Cyrus. *I'm coming!*

Two of the figures sprang toward him. He parried, lunging at one, who danced out of the way. Another figure came at his back, and he spun to meet him. *Too slow.* Keira watched as the figure's swing caught Cyrus across the side.

Then he fell.

She watched as if in slow motion as Cyrus's head hit the ground with a dull thud, his body crumpling at an odd angle.

"No!" she screamed. She pumped her legs faster, lungs screaming in demand of oxygen as she barreled forward. Her cry caught the attention of the four marauders, and they turned to meet her.

She slowed as she neared them. Now that she had their attention, she needed to find a better position, lure them away from Cyrus. He still hadn't moved from where he'd fallen. *Why hasn't he moved?*

Keira danced to the side of the road, the dense foliage at her back keeping them from encircling her. She hoped they didn't have any friends nearby. She'd never see them coming.

The first marauder lunged at her, and she deftly parried, circling his sword up and above him until he was slightly off balance. Then she ducked. Sliding beneath his arm, she grabbed for the dagger at her side. Spinning around, she plunged it into his exposed flank and saw him drop, shrieking in pain. She kept moving, and the next two met her in stride. She held her ground, watching her opponents for movement. One reached out with his blade, and she swatted it away with her own. He didn't move closer, though, didn't commit. They were close enough now that she could see their leering faces. They were toying with her.

The third man finally reached them, and Keira knew then that she was well and truly outnumbered, with no help in sight. Yet again, she cursed her stupidity at leading Cyrus into town with no backup. When would she learn?

A flash of movement to her right, and Keira got her sword up just in time to parry the thrust of the beady-eyed marauder. She let the momentum of the block carry their swords around in an arc. Then her eyes lighted on a gap in the men's ranks—Cyrus's crumpled figure was visible just beyond.

Keira seized the opportunity, twisting around until she had a clear angle to reach the gap.

A knife flashed, and she disengaged her sword just in time to bat it away. But the motion threw her off-balance, and she felt her foot slip. She staggered back, reaching for something, anything, with which to stabilize herself. Then something massive struck her left side.

She hit the ground, hard.

The taste of blood filled her mouth as she looked up into the smiling face of the beady-eyed marauder. Laughter filled her ears, and the icy finger of fear trickled down her spine. Was this it? Was this the end of her short second life? She was afraid, of course, but there was also . . . relief? Like the sudden exhale after a deep dive into freezing waters. The loneliness, the isolation, it was all over. She closed her eyes.

Move, Keira!

Her eyes snapped open, looking for the source of the voice, that impossible source.

You need to move, Keira!

Danny?

Move!

Keira rolled to the side just as a club struck the mud where her head had been. She staggered to her feet, fingers wrapping around the hilt of her sword, which had mercifully fallen within reach.

How are you here? she asked, incredulous. *Talking to me?*

To your left, Keira!

She staggered to the right, spinning just in time to avoid the downward swing of a war axe. Seizing the moment, she kicked the axe away, bringing her own sword forward in a lightning-fast thrust through the man's middle. He cried out, crumpling.

Wrenching the blade free, she turned to meet the next man, who bore the longest spear she'd ever seen.

Of course you'd have a spear, she thought acerbically.

It'll slow him down, though, Danny's voice said. *Keep out of range and wait until he overcommits. Then get in close and finish him, just like we practiced.*

A flash of memory—Danny and Keira practicing in the drill yard. Keira landing on her butt and them both laughing. Keira shook her head, trying to focus.

The spear flashed toward her, and she jumped back, keeping one eye out for the fourth marauder, who seemed to be checking for a pulse on the one she'd gutted.

The spearman advanced, mouth twisted in a sneer. He lunged, arcing the tip at the last possible moment. Keira staggered back, barely keeping out of range. She kept her gaze focused on his chest.

Good, Keira. Remember what I taught you.

She remembered—the long hours spent in the drill yard, the endless repetitions after Nazor had all but given up on her ever mastering the technique. But Danny never gave up on her. *"All movement originates from the chest,"* Danny had said. *"Keep your eyes on their heart. It'll betray them every time."*

The spearman lunged again, but Keira was ready for him.

She dodged to the side, grabbing the shaft of the spear with one hand as she yanked it back. Caught off guard, the spearman stumbled forward, where the tip of her blade stood ready to meet him.

Shaking the man from the end of her blade, Keira spun around in search of the final marauder—nothing. Keira cursed and briefly considered going after him. Then her gaze lit on Cyrus, and she ran toward her friend instead.

REACHING CYRUS, she knelt and felt for a pulse. One second . . . two seconds . . . there it was! Keira let out a breath she hadn't known she'd been holding.

"Cyrus? Cyrus, can you hear me?" She gently shook him and was ecstatic to hear a low groan escape his lips. Cyrus opened his eyes a sliver, then more. She thought she saw recognition in them.

Help him, Keira. I can ground you.

"You're not even here!" Keira screamed at him, not caring who heard. "How can you ground me?"

Trust me.

Cyrus smiled weakly at her, even as he grimaced with every

slight movement, sweat dripping down his brow. Pain clouded his steely gray eyes, but they still bore into hers, refusing to be lied to—his father's eyes.

Keira blanched, staring at him. In that moment, she couldn't help but remember the other Flavius, another friend she'd been unable to save when it really mattered. *Not this time,* she resolved. *Not again.*

Good, let's do it.

Though his external injuries seemed to be mere cuts and bruises, Cyrus was clearly bleeding internally; his rapidly diminishing pulse and the massive bruising that had blossomed across his abdomen were evidence enough of that. The deep cut to his left side revealed the likely culprit. Not for the first time, Keira cursed her own lack of medical training. She racked her brain for the fragments of anatomical knowledge she'd retained in the years since those stuffy college classrooms so long ago. *The spleen,* she decided finally. *It has to be the spleen.* It was the only solid organ on the left side of the abdomen, and certainly the only one capable of producing that much blood. Keira placed a hand gingerly on his abdomen, pressing in slightly and then releasing. Cyrus yelped in pain, clutching at his left shoulder, of all things. He was definitely bleeding into his abdomen, Keira decided, remembering how nerves of the abdominal wall often referred pain to the shoulders. But what to *do*? Keira felt the panic rise again. There was no tourniquet that could stop this bleeding, no small vessels she could cauterize with her pneuma. This was major surgery, she realized, the type of patient who'd be rushed from the emergency room to the operating table back in her old world. *And who am I?* she thought. Basically, a college dropout trying to play surgeon in a world with no antibiotics, sterile instruments, or even the most basic of imaging technology. *I'm insane,* she realized. *This is insane.*

This is his only chance.

Cyrus groaned again, louder and more insistent.

I'm going to do this, Keira realized, *because he'll die if I don't.*

Keira knelt and brought the rag to the wound. She could feel the blood coursing through her fingers and squashed the familiar sense of fluttering fear in the pit of her stomach. Forcing her heartbeat to slow, she reached for her pneuma. It took her a moment to find the ball of energy that lay just behind her stomach. She nudged it, and it uncurled, slowly, as if unsure. She felt it creep through her body, slow from disuse and neglect. She shivered at the familiar sensation. Then she let it go on a whistle too high for normal ears to hear. She waited for the familiar sensation of disembodiment, the accompanying panic of dissociation, but it didn't come. Instead, she felt something else. It was a warm, familiar presence in the back of her mind, a tether binding her spirit to herself.

You're here, she thought, tears pricking her eyes. *You're really here.*

I really am.

With a cry of delight, she felt her pneuma course through her fingers and into the trembling body of Cyrus Flavius. Inside, she found only . . . blood—and it was everywhere.

Focus, Danny said. *Find where it's coming from.*

As her pneuma spread throughout the rolling hills of bowel and blood, Keira searched in vain for a landmark, some point of reference by which to find her way as she scrambled for a hole to patch. *There!*

Just when she'd been about to give up, she felt more than saw the pulsing, corded mass. With each of Cyrus's heartbeats, the tissue expanded—*the aorta.* Feeling it, Keira knew every heartbeat was sending more of that precious crimson pouring out onto the already drenched floor. Shaking away the thought, she raced along the vessel's length until she found the major offshoot she knew would take her to the spleen. Slowing then, she searched along its length, looking for any injury, any hole she might patch. Nothing.

With a shudder, she realized that the injury must be to the spleen itself, that blood-filled bag of tissue ripe for piercing. Keira wanted to scream, wanted to just cut the damn thing out. People didn't really *need* a spleen, right?

Not a good idea, she decided, imagining the bloody mess that would result if she tried. But Cyrus would be dead within the hour if she couldn't stop the bleeding.

Then a thought occurred to her—why not just slow it down? Hadn't she learned something about techniques that stopped the bleeding from *inside* blood vessels? After all, if a clot in an artery could give you a heart attack, why not cut off blood to the spleen? But what if she was wrong? What if the bleeding was coming from somewhere else entirely? Keira shuddered before silencing the thought. There was no way to know for sure, no hospital or imaging at her disposal. But this was Cyrus's only shot, and by Pneumos, it was worth it.

You can do this, Danny said, voice warm with encouragement.

Buoyed by his words, Keira unsheathed the small knife at her belt and focused on the artery. Picking a spot basically at random, she let her pneuma seep into the vessel, feeling the liters of blood coursing past. With a mental shudder, she pressed the blade deep into her palm as she cast her pneuma to either side of the vessel, drawing its inner edges together as she slowly shifted the molecules that constituted them, letting them melt together in a slow burn. She watched with mounting excitement as edges came together, working down the edge until it covered the length of the vessel's interior. The larger it grew, the stronger the push of the blood became, speeding up as it forced its way through an ever-decreasing aperture. Then the clot sealed over the entire vessel, and no more blood passed through.

I knew you could do it.

Hesitantly, Keira loosened her pneuma, watching with trepidation for the vessel's seal to rupture, spilling an avalanche of blood toward her, but it didn't. She slowly withdrew her pneuma, sliding back into her own body. She sat with eyes closed for a long moment, not daring to open them. She was terrified of finding that her efforts were all in vain, that Cyrus had lost too much blood and had died anyway. Holding her breath, she cracked open one eye and then another to meet the sharp gray gaze of Cyrus Flavius—very much alive.

She sagged against him, barely holding back the tears that sprang to her eyes.

"Are you all right?" she asked.

"I-I think so," Cyrus rasped.

Keira eyed his normally olive-skinned face, now paler than her own.

"We need to get to the encampment. Can you walk if I help you?"

Cyrus nodded, and Keira helped him to his feet. Leaning heavily on her, Cyrus took one shaky step and then another forward. Slowly, the two of them trudged back toward the Bellatori camp.

How are you here? Keira thought, searching her mind for the presence she'd felt only a moment before. But there was no reply, and no sign of him. *Did I make it all up? Am I truly that desperate?* she wondered. No, she decided. Even if she could have imagined the voice, that presence grounding her pneuma as she healed Cyrus was unmistakable. Danny had been there. In the hour it took them to make their way back to the camp, Keira thought again of Marné's words. *"Their essence, the spirit of them remains, needing only to be bound in flesh. That which is undone may be reborn."*

Could this death-defying pneumonancy actually be learned? If so, there was only one place Keira could go to find it. Coming to this sudden realization, Keira said on impulse, "I'll take you to the Legion, Cyrus. To Port Galaén. That's where we'll find them."

"Really?" Cyrus replied faintly, exhaustion thick in his voice. "That's wonderful."

Keira said nothing as they trudged through the gate into camp, and she passed Cyrus off to the crowd of Bellators that greeted him. After seeing that he made it safely to the infirmary, Keira brushed off Argus's offer to tend her own wounds and instead trudged back to her tent, already going over plans for the journey.

I'll find a way, Danny, she promised silently. *I'll bring you back.*

SIX

876 Common Era (C.E.)

The echo of hooves and the quick stepping of feet rumbled through the earth as the army continued its slow, inexorable roll forward. As Danny looked out across the sea of faces, columns of soldiers arrayed in perfectly rigid lines, he couldn't help but feel a hum of excitement, a remnant, no doubt, of an earlier life. He'd never forgotten the feeling of being one among many within the masses of an army —that air of excitement on the eve of battle. He shifted slightly in his saddle, gazing down from the cliff where they overlooked the Bellatorio's slow advance. Beside him, Imperator Longus was in deep conversation with his second-in-command, Millus Rommel. Danny had traveled everywhere with the Imperator the last few weeks, ever since arriving at the Eastern Imperium's headquarters just south of Ulgáris.

Glancing up, he shaded his eyes against the slanting rays of the sun to better view the ancient city, looking just as regal now, 200 years before he'd seen it last. He shook his head at the strangeness of the thought.

The city had cloistered itself for weeks, according to their scouts, preparing for the siege they'd all known was coming—its high walls impenetrable upon the cliff ledge, a sheer drop of hundreds of feet off either side. The hill country's similarly ragged peaks rose on all sides of them, taunting in their obstruction.

There was only one way up to the city, a single narrow, winding road that could approach its gates. Danny knew they faced a mighty challenge, but he also knew from his history lessons with Elliott that they would ultimately fail. The holy city of Ulgáris would never fall to the invaders. It would surrender only when every other piece of Lorenan territory was firmly under Marian rule.

The sound of hoofbeats brought his attention back to the present as a black horse galloped up the ridge toward them. A small woman in leather armor rode astride, her long black curls tied up in a stiff bun at her nape. Her hazel eyes were sharp and penetrating—holding none of the softness or laughter that had always characterized her daughter's.

"Tammy," Danny said as she pulled up next to them.

She nodded in response but turned instead to the Imperator, clearing her throat loudly. "Scouts confirm it, sir. They've evacuated most of the countryside, sending the people into the city, with one exception—a small village to the northeast. From the sound of it, they seem to be a particularly stubborn bunch."

She looked like she wanted to say more but closed her mouth with a snap, waiting for the Imperator's response.

The Imperator didn't bother looking at her, continuing to survey the progress of his troops. Instead, Millus Rommel took her report, turning lazily toward her as he arched one eyebrow in a look of impatience. "And?"

Danny saw a familiar flash of annoyance cross Tammy's face, and he shoved down the sense of déjà vu that immediately dawned.

She's not Keira, he reminded himself for what must have been the thousandth time.

In truth, Tammy and Keira had very different personalities. Keira had always been open and hopeful—convinced she had some higher purpose in life. Meanwhile, Tammy was more closed off, suspicious of others' intentions and yet desperate for their approval.

Yet these differences in personality only made the spark of familiarity that accompanied the odd gesture, phrase, or flare of temper all the more jarring.

It had shocked Danny to find himself back in Loren. He'd been equally surprised to be met not by Keira but by her *dead mother*. A few stuttered questions later had demonstrated clearly that this Tammy had no memory of having a daughter and was in fact only eighteen years old. *Did the connection to the Legion run in families?* he wondered, making a mental note to ask Elliott the next time he saw him. *If* he ever saw him again. He shoved down a flash of pain at the thought, focusing instead on the more practical aspect of the equation.

But he couldn't explain it, couldn't unravel the nuances of time and world-skipping that Pneumos clearly facilitated. And yet, somehow he'd been reborn back in Loren, but several hundred years earlier, in the middle of the Marian Empire's invasion.

Danny had no idea what had become, or what *would* become, of the chaos gripping Loren back in his own time, where he supposed Keira and his family still were. Had they succeeded? Had Landry assumed the throne? Was there even a kingdom left?

Danny shook his head. It was no use fixating on questions he had no way of answering. *Besides*, he thought, *I've got my own brand of chaos right here.*

As if in answer to his thought, Tammy's voice cut through the air. "The Legion has warned you, sir, that this assault of yours will not end well." Tammy's eyes narrowed as she stared up at the Millus.

"Yes, yes, you have," the Millus replied impatiently. "In your cripplingly vague manner, you have indeed informed us of such. However, we have also been told that the assault will lead to the capitulation of the Lorenan peoples."

Danny watched Tammy bite her tongue against the retort she wanted to issue.

Just like Keira would have, he thought.

"True," Tammy said instead. "But we are here representing the Legion not merely to assure your victory but to ensure that there is as little chaotic fallout as possible from the effects of your *campaign*."

"Indeed." The Millus's eyes narrowed in a mirror of Tammy's. "Well, with this lone village not yet evacuated, I'd think that would be your first visit. We need to make sure these people are aware of exactly what they risk by choosing to shelter within the city walls rather than throw themselves upon the mercy of the Empire."

Danny eyed Millus Rommel carefully. He'd always been suspicious of the man's bloodier tendencies, suspecting a shifting moral compass that cared less for the decorum and standards of ethical combat than for the glories that victory might provide. Still, it was not for him to decide who led the Bellatorio.

He was there on behalf of the Legion, and the Legion was there to act in an advising capacity only, something they'd reminded him of *repeatedly* since his arrival. They were there to ensure order, as much as was possible in a time of war. He laughed silently at the hypocrisy of ensuring "order" in the middle of a war zone. Hadn't they learned that by now?

He was about to say as much when Imperator Longus turned to regard him and Tammy carefully. Danny had grown to like the man during his time with the Bellatorio. Careful and measured, he was a fair balance to his more hotheaded Millus.

"The village should be warned," the Imperator said, cutting Millus Rommel off short. Tammy grinned broadly in triumph as the Millus scowled. But the Imperator wasn't finished. "The Legionnaires will do it."

Tammy gaped, and even Danny's brows raised.

"That's your job, isn't it?" the Imperator said mildly. "To stave off the chaos and prevent unnecessary casualties?"

Tammy scowled, but even she couldn't argue directly with the Imperator. She and Danny both nodded, thumping forearms to their chests in the customary Bellatori salute before turning their horses to make for the village.

"IT'S COMPLETELY IRRESPONSIBLE!" Tammy ranted, gesticulating wildly in the air as they rode side by side away from camp. "I mean, who does he think he is? We're not his Bellators, that he can command as he sees fit. We're *advisors*—if he'd ever actually take our advice."

Danny rode on in silence, occasionally nodding and making agreeable-sounding grunts. He'd learned through prior experience it was best not to interrupt these tirades, and risk drawing wrath down on himself instead.

"And *you're* no help," Tammy continued, glaring accusingly at him.

"Me?" Startled out of his affable posture, Danny turned to give her his full attention. "What did I do?"

"Always so buddy-buddy with the Bellators, training with them, eating with them. You've completely lost all perspective!"

"Hey, there, I don't think that's fair," Danny replied, stiffening. "Sure, I get along fine with the men, but that doesn't mean—"

"It means you can't be objective!" Tammy's eyes burrowed into his. "We're here to do a job, Danny, which we can't do if you're too worried about offending your new friends."

Danny glared at her. "Look, where I come from, the Legionnaire's job is as much ally-building as it is *antagonizing*."

Tammy's eyes narrowed at his insinuation. "Ah, yes, this mysterious life you had that you've told me practically *nothing* about."

Danny bit back the retort that had immediately sprung to his lips. He'd already decided that the best course of action would be to tell Tammy as little as possible about the future he'd come from. He didn't know how the Legion's time travel worked, but he wasn't about to risk somehow changing things so that Keira was never born. And he certainly wouldn't be goaded into doing so by *Tammy*.

At his prolonged silence, she rolled her eyes, muttering, "Typical," before lapsing into her own tight-lipped interlude. They rode that way for a while, even as Danny could feel Tammy's discomfort at the lengthening silence. *So like Keira,* he thought. Then came the sharp stab of pain that always accompanied such slips in the mental wall he'd constructed. He pushed the thought away and rolled his shoulders to relieve the pinch of his armor.

"You do like it here, though, don't you?" Tammy said, peering at him curiously. It wasn't a question, but Danny considered it anyway.

"If you say so." He shrugged, then thought harder about her statement. "It reminds me of my old life, I suppose. Before the Legion, before . . . everything."

Tammy nodded, seeming to understand this. "Well, I suppose the Legion and the Bellatorio aren't all that different, when you come right down to it. The military life suits a lot of people, I figure. Everyone joins up looking for something: meaning, adventure, a family, escape. People will put up with a lot of shit to get those things."

Now it was Danny's turn to peer at her curiously. What had she joined the Legion for? From the little Keira had told her about Tammy's life, he figured "escape" probably ranked high on that list.

"I don't know," he said. "When I enlisted in the Army, it wasn't really for any of those things. I just . . . well, I just thought I ought to."

Tammy snorted. "Wow, what a patriot."

"I don't know if it was that so much as it was just . . . expected. Everyone I knew was signing up. I'd have felt I'd failed if I didn't, not done right by my family."

Tammy gave him a searching look, brow furrowed and eyes tight, before finally turning away. Danny was left to wonder exactly what it was she'd been searching for, and whether she'd found it. Her snort broke the moment's reflection. "That's right. I forgot you were an old World War geezer. Tell me, how does it feel to be a part of the *greatest* generation?" Danny rolled his eyes. She'd mentioned the term before, and it still felt odd to him, uncomfortable, even.

"Yep," she continued, "supposedly by the nineties—that's when I'm from, you know—the entire country's gone to hell in a handbasket, at least according to you old warhorses." She shook her head. "Frankly, I think the world's no shittier than it's ever been. People just get out more to see it. Still," she said, her tone darkening, "I'm glad to be rid of it."

"Well, I suppose it's a good thing the Legion found you, then," Danny said mildly.

"That means nothing," she murmured, eyes tense. "We've got no guarantees in all this." Seeing his confused look, she explained, "It's happened before. Someone broke the Legion's rules and ended up *discharged* from the Legion itself, cut off and sent back to where they came from." She shivered slightly. "I'm not about to give them any excuse for that."

"I don't know," Danny said offhandedly, thinking about all he'd left behind in his old world: his mam, his sisters, their little grocery in South Boston. "I think there'd be worse things than to finally get to go home when all this is said and done."

"No, thank you. I swear I'd rather die for good."

Startled, Danny replied, "Surely there must be some things you miss from your old life."

Tammy turned cold hazel eyes on him and said flatly, "No, there isn't."

Neither of them said anything as they rode on in silence. It was as they crested the last hill that Danny first smelled the smoke. With a shared look of alarm, the two of them heeled their horses to a hard gallop.

CHAPTER
SEVEN

242 Marian Era (M.E.)

Keira leaned against the ship banister, closing her eyes against the biting cut of the wind as the ship rocked from side to side. She inhaled the salty sea spray that flew up to meet her face. Opening her eyes, she watched the passing floodland as they sailed through the fertile inlet. Arable lands rose on either side, giving way to bountiful harvests of wheat and barley.

Almost there, Danny, she thought. *Just hold on.* Then she snorted, adding, *Can you even hear me?*

No response.

There'd been no word from him in the two weeks since they'd set off from the Southern Shield. She told herself she didn't expect there to be . . . obviously. But in truth, the disappointment stung. Half the time, she wondered if her mind had merely conjured him up out of fear and sheer desperation. But no, those memories were seared into her mind's eye—she knew what she'd heard. Cyrus was alive because of Danny's intervention; of that, she was certain.

"Ah, thought I'd find you up here."

The man in question strolled up beside her, the breeze ruffling his dark curls as he squinted those gray eyes against the sun.

"Morning, Cyrus."

"Enjoying the scenery?"

"Definitely." Keira smiled, inhaling the spicy scent of rhonían that wafted over the wave. She'd almost forgotten what it felt like to not be damp . . . and hot.

"Have you ever been to Port Galaén?" Cyrus asked, shielding his eyes as he looked out over the waves. Keira shook her head. The city in question was a mere speck off in the distance. But judging by the speed with which they sailed through the inlet's waves, Keira guessed they'd arrive before noon. They'd made good time traveling from the Southern Shield, mercifully avoiding the worst of the late spring storms.

"I've never even met the High Council," she explained. "And now I'm about to ask them for help. Hopefully they're feeling generous."

Keira felt familiar nerves churn in her stomach. *The High Council.* She knew little about the Legion's overall structure. But from what Elliot and Nazor had told her in the early years of her training, she knew that a council of elders presided over the Legionnaires who worked in each land. They were tasked with governing all the pneumonancers that found themselves there —ruling on strategy, policy, and even discipline. Keira shivered.

"I didn't exactly part on the best of terms with them, you know—the Legion," she said, thinking back on her last few days in the capital. She and Elliott had had their worst argument ever—him trying to reason with her as she furiously packed for the voyage to the Southern Shield. He'd wanted her to stay, to continue working for the Legion in the capital. She'd refused—claiming no interest in working for an organization like that. A familiar sensation of guilt wafted over her as she remembered the harsh words she'd thrown Elliott's way—words she hadn't intended or truly meant. What could he possibly think of her?

A silence fell over them, and Keira realized with a start that Cyrus had asked her a question.

"I'm sorry, what was that?"

He laughed. "Your mind drifted out to sea, I think. I said I managed to get my hands on a map of Port Galaén. I figured we ought to have a look and sort out where exactly this mysterious High Council might be located. It's in my chambers. Follow me."

Cyrus's ever-present grin widened, and Keira couldn't help but return it.

As they descended into the belly of the ship, Keira suppressed the familiar sense of claustrophobia, holding her breath against the smell of mildew as she glanced between the dank wooden boards that enclosed them on all sides. Their arrival in Port Galaén couldn't come fast enough.

Reaching the bottom of the steep stairs, Cyrus motioned her toward a small cabin off the side of the hallway. Keira was about to follow when a rustling sound caught her up short. She paused, searching the dark interior of the hallway for signs of movement.

Another rustling sound, and Keira spun just in time to see two eyes disappear between the slats of the stairs.

"Oh no, you don't," Keira said, darting around the side banister to the hide-a-hole beneath the stairs that the crew used for extra storage. Reaching beneath, Keira grabbed hold of one arm and then another, yanking the tiny interloper from their hiding place.

Seafoam-green eyes looked up at her from beneath a mop of dark hair.

"Raina!" Keira cried. "What are you doing here?"

The girl wiggled from her grasp and stood staring at her—chin angled in clear defiance, while a victorious smirk danced across her lips.

"I be coming to the capital with you."

Keira stared at her in shocked silence as Cyrus sputtered at her side.

"Wh-What? How—" he asked. Raina's grin grew wider.

"I knew I couldn't follow Akamu. He be spotting me for sure. But silly _grelún_, you all be easy to hide from."

"Clearly not easy enough. We found you, after all," Keira said, eyebrows raised.

"Yes, but only because I be trying not to laugh at you."

"Raina—" Keira started, but the sight of the girl's hopeful face caught her up short. "Raina, Akamu isn't here."

The younger girl stared blankly at her before a veil of confusion fell across her features. "What you be meaning by that?"

"I mean that Cyrus and I came alone with his ship and crew to Port Galaén because we have business here. Cyrus arranged passage for Akamu and the other two representatives on a merchant ship heading straight to Crîd Eálas, to join the People's Council there."

Raina's mouth fell open, and Keira saw panic flash across her face. "You mean, this Port Galaén everyone be talking about isn't in the capital?"

"I'm sorry, but no," Cyrus said, rubbing the back of his neck.

"Well, I be wanting to go to the capital," Raina said, crossing her arms over her chest. She looked every inch the defiant princess, but Keira eyed the slight tremble of her bottom lip. For a girl who'd never left her hometown, let alone her island, it must terrify her to find herself alone with strangers heading in the absolute wrong direction.

Cyrus shot Keira an alarmed look, and she sighed.

"Well, you'll just have to wait, little miss. We have business in Port Galaén, but soon enough, Cyrus will head south to the capital. He'll take you with him, and you'll find your brother there."

Raina shot Cyrus a dubious look.

"You not be going to the capital?" Raina asked, and Cyrus looked pleadingly at Keira, no doubt terrified at the thought of being suddenly responsible for an eleven-year-old. Well, that was just too damn bad, Keira thought. *Someone needs to figure out a way to get Danny back.*

"No," Keira answered, ignoring Cyrus. "With any luck, I'll be staying in Port Galaén. But don't worry," she added, smirking. "Cyrus will take good care of you. Just don't expect any help doing your hair."

Cyrus shot Keira a sidelong glare, and Raina pursed her lips in indignant outrage.

"I not be needing any help with my hair. I'm not a baby."

"Of course you're not. So be brave and stop acting like one." That shut her up, and Keira turned back to Cyrus. "You said something about a map?"

He waved her off, saying, "It can wait."

Keira turned back to Raina. "All right then, we'll be arriving in Port Galaén soon. You'll come with us, but you'll need to do exactly what I tell you to. I don't need you getting lost in the city."

Raina looked slightly green at the thought but quickly hid it with a confident nod.

All right then, Keira thought. *We're on our way, Danny.*

Port Galaén was every bit as Nazor had described it—lively, bustling, a true hodgepodge of humanity. From where Keira stood in the shipyard, she could see the city sprawling out in all directions. Arranged in a semicircular pattern around the shipyard itself, Port Galaén's cobbled roads formed concentric circles, with the major thoroughfares intersecting in a radial pattern that branched out from the shipyard at its core. Along these streets trundled endless lines of Tramorian caravans, merchant fleets, and the lone wagons of individual farmers. All brought their goods to and from the market that was based in the shipyard itself—the easier to transport the purchased product in or out of the city, Keira assumed.

"All right then," she said finally, looking to where Cyrus and Raina stood ready to depart. Heaving her own satchel onto one shoulder, Keira started down the gangplank of the ship. When they reached the bottom, the others looked at her expectantly. She glanced away, hoping they didn't notice her indecision. She didn't know much about the location of the Legion's headquarters, only what Elliott had told her the day of her departure for the Southern Shield. *"If you change your mind, I'll be in Port Galaén. Look for the grandest building you can find, ten o'clock sharp by way of the shipyard."*

Looking around, Keira figured that if the thoroughfare leading directly north from the shipyard was twelve o'clock, then ten o'clock must be the road that ran to the northwest. It was worth a shot, at least.

"This way," she said, gesturing down a road packed with uplanders bearing carts of fish from the riverlands to the west.

As Keira passed through the streets, she couldn't help but feel that familiar sense of excitement to be around people. After her time in the Southern Shield, she'd nearly forgotten that excitement that came with everyday interactions—buying, selling, neighbors congratulating and gossiping.

It was the simplicities of daily life played out on a massive scale that so intrigued and excited her. In Port Galaén, Loren's mixture of cultures was on full display—from the dark-skinned Tramors, with their head wraps and desert-colored cloaks, to the uplanders in the warm greens and browns of their riverland hues. Then there were the city-dwelling downlanders, dressed in fine Marian style—all gossamer fabrics and sky-high hair dressings. Keira even spotted Olphéis nomads, looking quite out of place without their wagon-like homes but easily identified by their colorful garments.

As they passed a group of Cross-Sea sailors bartering with a local merchant, Keira felt a spark of familiarity at the sight of the richly hued scarves they used to cover much of their faces, leaving only their eyes exposed. To her surprise, Keira found those eyes darting among the crowd, narrowed with hostility. They stood with tense stillness as their companion discussed terms, mistrust clear in their demeanor.

"I'm surprised to see them here," Cyrus murmured. "I thought most of the trade with the Cross-Sea lands had dried up at this point. These must be some stragglers."

"Dried up? I thought we were on better terms with them now. The war was so long ago."

Cyrus glanced at her, mouth pressed into a thin line. "We were," he said hesitantly. "But after Inaba Sara's death . . . Well, let's just say things have become quite tense."

Keira started at Sara's name. Memories of the Cross-Sea warrior who had accompanied their cohort to retrieve Landry came in flashes—her lyrical laugh, the bright hues of her scarves, her lethality on the battlefield. They had become friends on that journey, and Keira still felt a sharp pain at the thought of her. A familiar sense of guilt washed over her, and she managed to nod but picked up their pace until they'd passed the hostile eyes of Sara's countrymen. *And we thought we'd avoided chaos,* Keira thought. *How foolish.*

A half mile or so from the shipyard, Keira finally spotted what could only be the Legion's headquarters. Reaching the iron gate, she stood frozen, staring in awe at the massive stone building. Elliott hadn't been kidding, she decided. While far smaller than the skyscrapers she remembered from her old world, the looming walls of white stucco still dwarfed all the surrounding edifices. Like them, its exterior was a crisp white, the roof covered in terra-cotta shingles. But the comparison ended there. In every other way, the headquarters seemed more like a castle, complete with towers and what looked like a small rampart at the top.

"That be the biggest building I ever be seeing," Raina breathed, staring awestruck.

"Wasn't the Legion supposed to be covert?" Cyrus asked.

"It is," Keira said. Or at least, that's what she'd always been told. If this was the headquarters of the secret organization, what else had she been misled in?

"Don't get me wrong," Cyrus added. "It's lovely. It just seems a little . . . ostentatious."

Keira decided to try the gate and was unsurprised to find it locked. Seeing no one nearby to ask, she was left with few alternatives. *Well, here goes nothing,* Keira thought. *I hope you're listening, Danny, because I might need some help.*

She needn't have worried, though. After grounding herself as best she could to the earth, Keira sent out a clear whistle, her pneuma pulsing toward the lock, and found the path within its gears well-worn by others. *It's a test,* she realized. A lock that could only be opened with pneumonancy. Feeling for the pliable tumbler that so many had melted before, Keira felt her pneuma course through it, the molecules slowly rearranging until an audible click sounded, and the gate creaked open. Quickly reeling herself back into her body, Keira eyed the lock with satisfaction.

"How, by Cála's eye, you be doing that?"

Keira glanced at Raina and found her gaping—not at the building, but at her.

"It's called pneumonancy," she answered. "It's what we do, the Legion, that is."

"You really be *Le'ena* then?" Raina made the sign to ward off evil, her admiration quickly turning to suspicion.

Keira nodded. "I suppose. Although your grandmother seemed to have a bit of a different understanding of what that means than we do."

Raina was still looking at Keira like she might combust at any moment. Unnerved, Keira pushed past and through the gate, gesturing for them to follow. She climbed the stone steps to the imposing front door to find it unlocked. Pushing through, she found herself in a beautiful rotunda with curving staircases on either side, its ceiling decorated with a stained glass motif of swirling black-and-white strands.

Then a voice cut through the air.

"What in Pneumos's name are you doing here?"

EIGHT

"At the very least, you could have locked the gate behind you."

Before Keira stood a tall, athletic young woman with an olive skin tone. Her stick-straight black hair fell past her shoulders, and she regarded Keira with eyes narrowed in distrust.

"I-I'm Keira Altman," Keira said finally, recovering her composure. "I'm here to see the High Council."

The girl's eyebrows raised in surprise, and she scanned Keira up and down, looking decidedly unimpressed.

"Oh, well, but of course, if the great Keira Altman desires an audience . . ." The sarcasm practically dripped from her voice, and Keira felt Cyrus's and Raina's eyes on her. Her cheeks burned, and she stiffened.

"It's important. I wouldn't ask if it weren't. I'm not sure if there's some protocol I'm supposed to follow, so I'm sorry if I'm going about this wrong. But that's why I'm here."

The girl's jaw clenched, and her eyes narrowed even further.

"Of course you wouldn't know such a thing. Why would you? You haven't even undergone the rites yet."

Keira's stomach twisted, and her embarrassment fueled her anger. "Look, you don't even know me. All I'm asking—"

"Oh, I know you. You've been quite the topic of conversation around here, and not in a good way, in case you were wondering."

Keira stared at her as her stomach somersaulted. The Legion? Talking about her?

"Well, if you know all about me, then you know why I had to leave."

The girl snorted. "All I know is that in the middle of mass chaos, a complete change of government, you decided *your* needs were more important. Yes, I'm aware you lost someone," she added, seeing Keira about to interject. "Do you think you're the only one? We've all lost people. That doesn't give you the right to shirk your responsibilities."

Exasperated, Keira threw her hands up and looked at Cyrus, hoping for some support. Instead, she found him focusing decidedly at his boots, refusing to make eye contact. *Great,* Keira thought. *He agrees with this craziness.*

"Look, uh . . ." Keira paused expectantly.

The girl seemed to grow taller as she folded her arms over her chest, lips twisted in a smirk. "My name is Zipporah, Zipporah Mizrachi. And unfortunately for you, I'm on guard duty today."

"All right then, *Zipporah,*" Keira continued. "What is it going to take to get you to let us through so I can set up a meeting with the High Council?"

Zipporah's lips pressed into an impossibly thin line as she regarded Keira with cool detachment. Keira shifted awkwardly, refusing to look at Cyrus and Raina but feeling their eyes on her.

What would she do if Zipporah kicked them out? She had no other leads to bringing Danny back, and Cyrus was depending on aid from the Legion. This was their only chance.

"Wait here," Zipporah replied thinly, before turning and disappearing through a door in the far wall. Keira blinked after her. That was it?

The minutes stretched on, and Keira finally took to pacing the small rotunda. When she looked at Cyrus and Raina, she saw a nervous glance flash between them. She kept walking. Finally, after what seemed an impossibly long wait, Keira pulled up short.

Spinning on her heel, she announced, "I'm going to see what's going on."

"Keira, I don't think we're supposed to—"

Keira ignored him and made for the door at the far end. Reaching for the handle, she pulled, just as it sprang forward on its hinges. Keira stumbled backward and felt herself caught by strong arms. She looked up into warm amber eyes.

"Elliott?" she asked, shock warring with some deeper, unnamed emotion in her chest. He smiled down at her, and the tension escaped. She felt herself deflate in relief and laughed, throwing her arms around him in a hug. He chuckled and returned the embrace.

"It's good to see you too, Keira."

Stepping back, she looked up into his kind face and remembered the last time they'd spoken. She swallowed the shame that rose into her throat like bile and said, "Elliott, I'm sorry about—"

He put up a hand to stop her, smiling kindly. "It's all right, Keira. We both said some things we didn't mean."

He was being generous with that, she thought. They both knew that he'd been nothing but kind, while Keira had acted like a rabid banshee—crying and yelling all at the same time. She repressed the memory with effort and focused on the present moment.

"Zipporah tells me you've come to see the High Council," he began, "and that you've brought friends. Cyrus I've met, but this little one is a stranger to me. Care to introduce us?"

Quickly recovering, Keira gestured Raina forward. She lingered, looking Elliott's lanky frame up and down like he might strike at any moment.

"This is Raina," Keira said. "We met in the Southern Shield. Her brother, Akamu, will join the People's Council as a representative. She wanted to tag along but picked the wrong ship. She'll be heading to the capital with Cyrus when his business is done here." Elliott's eyebrows rose at the word *business*, but he didn't ask.

"It's a pleasure to meet you, Raina. My name is Elliott Hughs, but I would be delighted if you would call me Elliott." He waggled his eyebrows at her and was rewarded with a small smile, though she still kept her distance.

"Good to see you again, sir," Cyrus said, coming forward and offering a hand to shake. Elliott took it and replied in turn.

Raina, seemingly buoyed by this harmless encounter, squared her shoulders and stepped forward, offering her hand with such determined rigidness that Keira had to hide a snort behind a cough. Elliott's gaze held firm, though, and he solemnly accepted her handshake. Though, because of the size difference, he ended up waggling her fingers instead. Courtesies aside and neutrality established, Elliott returned to the task at hand.

"The council is already in session for the day, Keira. I can vouch for you and try to have whatever it is added to the agenda, but you'll have to tell me what this is about."

And here it was, the moment of truth. She knew he'd agree to let her present Cyrus's request for aid on behalf of the Regio. Elliott was as invested in helping him solidify power as she was. But the rest of it—truth be told, the real reason she'd agreed to come here was to learn the art of healing pneumonancy and bring Danny back.

Did she dare tell Elliott her real reasons? She remembered his and Nazor's reaction the last time she'd told him of her practice, when she'd healed the little girl, Anya Cuball, back in Abalás. It hadn't been good. They'd accused her of tampering with powers she didn't understand, risking her life and the balance of chaos and order. What would he think now? *I could offer to bring Nazor back*, she thought, then felt instantly guilty. She couldn't use Elliott's feelings for his old grounder against him. No, it was better he didn't know, at least not yet—not when the High Council might hold the answers to everything, if only she had the courage to ask.

"Landry needs our help," she said finally.

"It's true," Cyrus added. "The Council of Benadur is up to its old tricks again, stirring up discontent among the people. And there's even rumor of a new faction, more militant and hardline than even Neval Brennan's people. They say they're prepared to use violence if they don't get their way. We need the Legion's support, publicly, for Landry as Regio. If we had Legion representatives in the capital, then it would further bolster his claim to the throne. Anyone who opposed him would think twice before making a move."

Elliott nodded, considering. "They won't like it," he said finally. "The Legion has lived in hiding in Loren for generations. Not since the Marian invasion have they acted so openly, publicly supporting someone's claim to the throne. And even in those days, it was hard-won. It was before my time, but I'm told that many believed the Legion had no business meddling in the affairs of state. They believed our role to be more spiritual, almost cosmic, preserving the balance between order and chaos in our individual practice rather than on a macro scale."

"But this would preserve the balance," Cyrus argued. "If Landry falls now, the chaos would be even worse than last time. He has more support now, you see. The Bellatorio, for one, would be steadfast in his defense. We wouldn't have peace for a decade or more as various factions vied for power."

Elliott shook his head. "You don't have to convince me. It's the High Council you need to worry about. They'll have questions, and they won't be easy ones."

Cyrus nodded. "I'm ready. Show me where."

Elliott hesitated before looking at Keira. "Actually, you're the one who needs to speak to them," he said, glancing apologetically at Cyrus's crestfallen face. "He isn't a Legionnaire and so isn't permitted inside the inner sanctum. You alone must present his case."

Keira stared at him blankly. Her? She'd barely even agreed to bring Cyrus here, let alone argue his case for him. Besides, she had her own argument to make. Could she really ask for both? Was she that bold?

"I mean, I'm not a full Legionnaire," she mumbled. "I haven't undergone the rites."

Elliott shook his head. "But you're in training . . . technically," he added with a small smile. She had had no formal training in over a year, a point he was gracious enough not to point out.

Cyrus turned to her, clearly disappointed but determined as ever. "Go on, Keira. You know as well as I do how important this is. I know you'll be able to convince them."

The confidence he had in her only made her own guilt

harder to bear. She'd agreed to bring him but had never told him of her ulterior motive. Too late for that now.

"All right," she said, nodding. "Let's go."

And with that, she followed Elliott and Zipporah, who'd appeared behind him like a shadow, through the doors and into a dark passageway beyond—the light of the city framing Cyrus and Raina as they watched her go.

KEIRA FOLLOWED Elliott and Zipporah down a dark and twisting passageway that seemed to lead deep underground. With every step, Keira had the sinking feeling that she was being swallowed up by the earth itself, and the thought made her shiver.

When they finally emerged into a second rotunda, this one lit by torches along its circular length, Keira stared at a massive set of double doors, each standing twice her height. Elliott gestured for them to wait there as he strode toward a smaller door set within the larger and rapped briskly with a metal knocker before pushing it forward and stepping inside.

The door snapped shut behind him, and Keira stood alone with Zipporah, who insisted on eyeing her with an expression usually reserved for a puppy that had done something naughty on the carpet.

The silence seemed to swallow them whole, and Keira cleared her throat, pointedly avoiding Zipporah's narrow-eyed gaze. She fiddled with the hem of her tunic while feigning interest in the intricate designs that decorated the rotunda walls. But she couldn't ignore the feeling of eyes boring into her shoulder blades.

Just when she felt the tension in the air might snap at any moment, there was a deep rumble of the floor, and Keira staggered back from the walls in alarm. Turning, she saw the double doors slowly open, with only blackness visible on the other side.

In tight-lipped silence, Zipporah gestured for Keira to go ahead. Keira quickly dried her sweaty palms on her tunic before squaring her shoulders, drawing herself to her full height, and stepping into the darkness.

As the doors closed behind her with a rumbling shudder, they left Keira in complete dark. Then a brisk clap resulted in flames igniting within the torches that circled the room.

Keira gaped as rows of Legionnaires suddenly appeared before her. The stacked rows of their pews elevated them to the vaulted ceiling, leaving her with the distinct feeling of being a bug under a microscope.

A rough clearing of someone's throat brought her attention back to the high table before her, where seven Legionnaires sat in high-backed chairs, staring down at her. They ran the gamut of age—from a shriveled, elderly man, his white beard cascading down into his lap as he adjusted his spectacles, to an equally diminutive girl, who looked like she should still be in grade school but eyed Keira with an otherworldly adultness. This was the High Council of the Legion of Pneumos in Loren, frozen in time at whatever age they had passed from their old world into this one—all sworn to the battling of chaos and the preservation of order across worlds.

Keira shivered slightly despite herself.

A middle-aged woman with gray strands cutting through her chestnut hair was the first to speak. "You are Keira Altman?" she asked in an accented voice. She sounded European, but Keira couldn't quite place it.

"I am," Keira responded. "Uh . . . ma'am," she finished,

unsure of the correct title to address a council member. This had certainly not been in any of Elliott's lessons.

"You appear before the council today at the sponsoring of Elliott Hughs with a petition to put before the council. Do you concur?"

"I—uh, yes?" Keira's eyes darted around, looking for Elliott's affirmation but not seeing him anywhere. Where was he?

"Very well, proceed."

Keira blinked, sweat dripping down her spine as she felt the room's eyes fall on her.

"I—" Her voice came out in a croak, and she quickly cleared it before trying again. "I come bearing a request from the Regio Landrianus and his emissary, Cyrus Flavius. They ask for Legion support in the capital. There—uh, there's been rising discontent there, and the Council of Benadur is stirring it up. And then there's apparently division within the People's Council, with a separate faction threatening violence if their demands aren't met." Keira paused, waiting for some sort of reaction. She searched the faces of the council members, looking for any sign of their feelings on the matter. Blank faces stared back at her, and she swallowed. Keira racked her brain. What else had Cyrus said?

"He—uh, I mean, *they* ask for reinforcements from the Legion to travel to the capital. They need a show of support from us to quiet the opposition, to make it clear that the Regio has our backing and that we'll oppose any attempt to over-throw him." The last sentence came out in a rush and she ended, winded. But still they sat in silence, watching her. Was there some sort of signal she was supposed to give?

"That—uh, that's all."

The middle-aged woman leaned forward, the fingers of

both hands pressed together. "So you propose that a Legion cohort travel to the capital."

It wasn't a question, but Keira felt obliged to put in, "Yes, yes, that's right."

"And you would wish to lead this cohort, I presume?"

That took her aback, and she floundered for a moment, searching for the best response. Her eyes flickered across the room again—still no sign of Elliott. Good, well, that made this next part a little easier, she supposed.

"No. With all due respect, I'd like permission to remain here." She took a deep breath and dug her nails into her palms to keep them from shaking. Time for the moment of truth. "I've recently found a new way of using pneumonancy, and I humbly request use of the Legion's resources to explore it further."

Deafening silence echoed throughout the room as a hundred eyes bored into hers. She held her breath, waiting for someone to speak.

"And what, pray tell, is this supposedly new form of pneumonancy?"

"Healing, ma'am. I can use my pneuma to heal. In my training, I learned of the vast depth of the Legion's Library—its documents spanning millennia and worlds. If there is any wisdom to be gained from its depths, I would like permission to pursue it."

A low murmuring swept through the crowd at that, and Keira felt a thrill of excitement. *Maybe this will work after all.*

A swift rap on the high table brought the murmuring to an end as the old council member with the long white beard leaned forward to speak. "And how do you know this discovery of yours is truly the work of Pneumos?"

Keira felt her hopes for an easy victory deflate as the man continued.

"Séiro is cunning, and acts of destruction may be easily disguised in cloaks of good intentions."

Keira stood a bit straighter at that, jutting her chin out. "I know only what I've been taught—that Pneumos seeks order out of chaos, the healing of the broken. And that as the Legion, we are charged to build more than we break and heal more than we destroy. That is all I am asking to do—to use pneumonancy for healing." She paused, but the silence was a palpable weight, and she hurried on. Her voice grew more agitated as the words spilled out, trying in vain to fill the judgmental silence. "Besides, the Legion doesn't exactly have the cleanest record, you know. After all the damage we've done to this country, I think it's only fair we offer something to balance the scales a bit."

The murmurs erupted at that, this time crescendoing into anger.

"Insolence!" the European woman replied. "To think that you have greater foresight than those who have served for far longer than you."

Keira flinched at that, immediately regretting her harsh tone. Then, from the corner of her eye, she saw Zipporah smirking as she nodded in agreement. Keira clenched her teeth.

"I, for one, am seriously uncomfortable with this proposition," another council member pronounced. He was a younger man, dark-skinned and with an East Coast American accent that reminded Keira of old vaudeville films from the 1950s. "There is no study of pneumonancy that is complete without practical application. What guarantees can you provide us that all experimentation will be done under the strictest of ethical standards?"

Keira gaped at him. "Look, I don't plan on *experimenting* on anybody."

"Oh? Then what would you call your untethered forays into this area? You did say you *discovered* this area of pneumonancy, in the past. I presume that involved an actual injury of some sort. Did your subject consent to having their insides tampered with?"

Keira felt the wind get knocked out of her at that one. She had to work to control her breathing, to control the fury that coursed through her. "Look, I don't deny that I've tried healing before, but it was under some pretty dire circumstances! I was also in a difficult position, seeing as Legion policy dictates discretion in our actions. Tell me, how, exactly, do I ask for consent without revealing my intent?"

There was a murmur of agreement from the crowd, and the young man scowled. "Perhaps the answer, then, is to hold off rather than charge ahead in your pursuits."

"You could have brought your concerns to the council," replied a velvety-smooth voice from the far end of the table. Keira glanced over to meet the startling blue eyes of a man she thought must have been in his mid-twenties—with hair cut short and a well-trimmed mustache above his upper lip. His arch British accent reminded her of Elliott, and she felt a twinge of familiarity tug at the back of her mind.

"Well, after recent events, it wasn't exactly my first inclination to approach the Council for help or support—you know, after you basically betrayed me and the Regio only a few months ago."

Another disgruntled murmur echoed across the room.

"And what about now?" piped up a tiny voice from the opposite end of the table. The little girl sat up straight and clasped her hands on top of the table, her legs dangling comically from her chair as she eyed Keira with a wary appraisal.

"Will you accept the ruling of the council in this matter? Or will you continue to follow your own inclinations?"

Keira had to keep herself from laughing at the serious expression on the girl's face. She looked no more than seven or eight, but she spoke with the voice of an adult. The girl's eyes narrowed, and Keira sobered, hesitating. This would be tricky to maneuver.

"I trust that the Council will see the validity of my efforts and will support me in continuing to study the potential of these *gifts* Pneumos has given me," Keira said slowly. "To simply ignore them in the face of all the suffering in the world right now—some of which is of our own making—seems highly irresponsible. How could that possibly be Pneumos's plan?"

"Are you suggesting that you understand the will of Pneumos better than the council—you, a girl only just arrived a few years ago? Whereas many of us have sat upon this council for decades, if not centuries!"

"Of course not," Keira said, backtracking. "But I just don't see—"

"Of course you don't see!" the middle-aged woman put in. "You cannot possibly understand the true risks at play. If we venture into this territory of disrupting the human body, challenging its design and reworking it to our own purposes, then this would inevitably open a Pandora's box. For to assume the role of Pneumos herself would be to stretch far beyond our abilities, let alone our mandate."

"Oh, *please!*" Keira said, her annoyance finally getting the better of her. She ignored the shocked murmuring of the crowd. "Look, every time we place a bind on a person, we take control of their body. We sift through their memories and thoughts. You cannot tell me that *that* is any less invasive than fixing a broken leg! If anything, what I'm doing is far *more* respectful.

And if you would condemn me for this, or stand in the way of further study, then I suggest you take a hard look at the Legion's policies up until this point. Because to deny these abilities, you would first have to deny your *own* actions."

The low murmuring of the crowd increased in intensity, and Keira could see individuals in the pews arguing intensely among themselves. She glanced at Zipporah and practically crowed at the flash of uncertainty that crossed her face. A feeling of victory bloomed in Keira's chest.

After a chaotic moment, the mustachioed British man raised his hand, and the crowd fell silent.

"Your point is well taken, Keira Altman," he said, giving her a considering look. "You've given the council much to consider. This session is now adjourned."

Keira stared at him, feeling the lump of worry settle again into the pit of her stomach. A firm hand gripped her arm, and she looked up into the stone face of Zipporah, who firmly steered her out of the chamber. The echo of murmurs continued behind her before being suddenly silenced by the rumbling snap of the double doors.

I don't know, Danny, Keira thought. *I just don't know.*

She'd put everything on the table. She only hoped it would be enough.

CHAPTER

NINE

876 Common Era (C.E.)

As they crested the hill, Danny stared down at the small upland village below, his stomach clenching at the sound of screams and shouted protests.

The village itself was small, nothing more than a handful of houses clumped together around a single dirt road that curled between rolling hills. Even from this distance, Danny could see the plumes of smoke rising from thatched roofs, the bloodred capes of the Bellatorio in and among the people.

"What the—"

Danny didn't wait for Tammy to finish her sentence but heeled his horse forward, racing down the steep, rocky bank as abject fury bloomed in his chest.

When they made it to the village, Danny was enraged to find a crowd of Bellators gathered in the village center as a handful of men passed around meats and cheeses—no doubt stolen from local stores.

Jumping from his horse in one swift movement, Danny

stalked toward what looked to be a Sergius, the highest-ranking among the gathered men.

The man saw him coming and stiffened abruptly, turning to meet Danny's furious gaze with a defensive scowl.

"What is the meaning of this, Sergius?" Danny snarled. "Tell me, who authorized you to steal from locals and drive them from their homes?"

"And who might you be?" the Sergius asked, eyeing Danny with distrust. "I don't see any uniform."

"We are Legionnaires," Tammy said, appearing suddenly at Danny's shoulder. "Advisors to Bellatori high command. And you, Sergius, were asked a question."

The Sergius eyed her with barely disguised disdain and turned to address Danny. "It appears we're on the same side, then. We were just warning the locals that they'd best be on their way—what with the Bellatori advance to Ulgáris."

"Really?" Danny asked thinly. "Is this what you would call a warning?"

"Best kind of warning, I say," a young Tiro said, to the guffaws of his friends. "Show these Lorenan dogs what's what. I'd like to see them try to stand before the might of the Marian Empire."

Danny shot the boy a glare, which he returned with an upturned chin—his confidence buoyed, no doubt, by the support of his laughing comrades.

"This is *not* what we agreed to, and it certainly wasn't authorized by Bellatori high command," Danny said. "I *will* be reporting this to Imperator Longus."

The Sergius shifted uneasily, glancing at the barrels of salted meat they'd hauled from the storehouse. He turned back to Danny with eyes narrowed as he said calmly, "Of course you will. Just as I'll report how our scouting mission located some much-needed rations for the men. We'll make sure the Imperator knows *all* the facts."

Danny felt his cheeks flush with fury. He could still see the line of fleeing peasants headed for Ulgáris, the hilltop city that would soon be under siege. But realizing he would get nowhere with this tack, Danny turned and nodded to Tammy.

There was nothing more they could do here. And he'd see that the Imperator heard of the rough treatment his soldiers were giving the locals. This was *precisely* the sort of thing the Legion was there to prevent.

TAMMY SAID nothing on the ride back, but Danny could feel her eyes on him, watching and calculating something. He ignored her.

"What will you tell the Imperator?" she asked finally.

Danny clenched his jaw. "Exactly what we saw—his Bellators harassing the populace, in direct contradiction to his orders."

"I'm not sure they are, though," Tammy said, brow furrowed. "Contrary to his orders, that is."

"What are you talking about? Of course they are. The Imperator told us himself. We were to warn the locals to surrender before we put the city under siege. We're trying to *avoid* local casualties, not make them worse."

"That's true, but do you really think the Imperator would let food stores go to waste? Or worse, let them go to Ulgáris and make the siege run even longer? You know as well as I do that the smart move is to claim them for his own soldiers, especially with a long siege ahead."

"Not at the expense of driving people from their homes,

surely," Danny said. "They're trying to win over the local populace, not antagonize them further."

He could see Tammy's lips press into a thin line and sensed she wanted to say more, but she fell quiet, and they continued on in silence.

THEY FOUND Imperator Longus in his quarters back at camp—busy signing the paperwork his aid had brought him.

Danny and Tammy entered, briefly thumping their chests in the typical Bellatori salute.

"Come in, come in," the Imperator replied. "Be quick about it, though. I'm rather busy. We've got a new regiment in from the east to bolster our ranks before the siege. So we moved up the timetable. We'll catch the city by surprise, cut off any aid they may have sent for."

Danny's stomach turned at the thought of the line of refugees still making their way to the hilltop city. He wondered if they'd make it in time—wondered if they'd be better off inside or outside its gates.

He shook his head to clear his thoughts. "Sir, we're here with a concerning report from the village outside Ulgáris. As requested, we went to garner support and warn them not to undermine our efforts or flee to the city. Unfortunately," Danny continued, his voice adopting an acidic edge, "a small centurium, newly arrived from the western front, beat us there. They not only antagonized the locals so that they fled to the shelter of the city, but they then ransacked the village —taking its stores for themselves. If you don't mind my saying so, sir, we'll have a hell of a time gaining their trust now."

The Imperator glanced up at him, frowning. "I see. And what stores did they manage to—requisition, then?"

Danny blanched. "I'm not sure," he said. "We left before they finished the count. But *sir*, is it not more concerning that they've undermined our efforts? Shouldn't they at least get a stern talking-to?"

Imperator Longus sighed, dragging a hand across his face. "Legionnaires, I appreciate your concern. I simply cannot share it. Of course it would have been best for our campaign to be conducted without attracting undue hostility from the locals. But quite frankly, it's more imperative that my men are fed and clothed, *particularly* with this new timetable. We're stretched quite thin just now, and I worry about our ability to feed and equip the new regiment that will join us for the siege. We simply don't know how long Ulgáris will be able to hold out."

Danny stared at him. "Do you mean you *ordered* this looting?"

The Imperator's eyes narrowed. "I did not order any locals to be harassed. But yes, I ordered the requisitioning of goods and supplies from the local area—all they could muster. We have few options, as Cross-Sea pirates have disrupted much of Marian shipping. I've been told not to expect any more goods for the rest of the year, and Loren is still far from subdued."

Danny grimaced at the term, and the Imperator's eyes narrowed further.

"I understand that the Legion's affiliation in this matter is —complicated. But the surest way to minimize the casualties on both sides of this conflict is for it to come to a quick and decisive end. For that, I need supplies. But I am sorry if my men behaved unprofessionally. I will speak to their commanders."

Danny could practically imagine the weasel-eyed Sergius's triumphant expression, and the thought brought a bitter taste to his mouth. What he wanted more than anything was to tell this Imperator off, explaining to him how the Marian Empire had no real right to these lands and that even so, it wouldn't justify his Bellators' actions. He'd just opened his mouth to say as much when a sharp elbow in his ribs made him turn to meet Tammy's look of warning.

He paused, giving Tammy just enough time to say, "Thank you, sir. We appreciate your looking into this matter."

At the Imperator's nod, she turned on her heel, dragging Danny behind her as they exited the Imperator's quarters. "What is wrong with you?" she hissed.

"Me? What's wrong with *you*? Weren't you just complaining about the Imperator treating us like lackeys? You can't possibly be all right with this."

"Of course not," she said. "What those men did was inappropriate."

"Inappropriate? They were stealing! You don't think those people needed that food to survive the winter?"

"They'll take shelter in the city," she said. "You've got to have some perspective, Danny. The city itself is about to be under siege. Far more will die from starvation and sickness in the coming months than by some village looting."

"That doesn't make it all right," Danny said through clenched teeth.

"Of course it doesn't. But this is a war, Danny, and we're here to minimize the casualties."

"Exactly!"

Tammy rubbed the bridge of her nose in exact imitation of Keira, making him stop in his tracks.

"We have to tread carefully here, Danny, choose our battles. Whatever we may think of the invasion itself, it's already happened. And thanks to you, we know how it will end."

Danny grimaced, the familiar pang of guilt needling at the back of his neck. It was the first conversation he'd had with the Legion here, nearly a year before—newly arrived in Loren and only a few months ahead of the Marian Empire's invading ships. He'd told Tammy what would happen, half out of his mind with grief at the world and family he'd lost. She'd brought him to the Legion's nearby camp. They'd been seeking to prevent it, avoid the onslaught that was to come.

Danny had been the one to stop them. Who knew how preventing the invasion might change the timeline? He'd been terrified of what might happen to his family if history were changed so completely—Elliott, Nazor . . . and Keira. They might never come to Loren.

He needn't have worried. Rather than continuing to try to prevent the invasion, the Legion had considered his description of the Marian Empire's military dominance and quickly decided that success was inevitable. Their role would be to minimize the fallout—keeping chaos at bay.

"We can do more good from inside the Bellatorio than from outside it, Danny. You know that. If fighting the chaos means that some villagers have to give up their winter meat stores to speed along the siege, then that's what it means."

Danny grimaced, not at all sure he approved of such a utilitarian outlook. But he couldn't deny her logic. Besides, he'd grown to know and trust many of the men within the Bellatori ranks. Most were decent, hardworking men just doing a job and fighting for a cause they believed in.

The Marians truly thought that they were bringing law and order to Loren, even if the Lorenans had no interest in their version of it. But Tammy was right. Danny *did* know how this war would end. What right did he have to delay the inevitable, especially if it cost more lives in the process?

"Besides, it won't matter much longer." That surprised him, and he glanced toward her. "I've had word from the Legion, Danny. We're being reassigned. There's a camp to the south that's requesting aid. It's little more than a fishing village right now, but the Marians are hoping to turn it into some sort of capital. The Legion is sending several delegates for the official naming ceremony. They're calling the new city Crîd Eálas. Have you heard of it?"

Danny's eyes widened at the name, but he merely nodded.

"We leave in the morning—ahead of the siege."

Tammy's eyes searched his—no doubt curious at his silence, but Danny kept his face carefully blank. "I'd best pack my things," he said. There'd be no time for goodbyes or best wishes to the friends he'd be leaving behind once more. It was probably for the best. But despite all Tammy's arguments, a creeping doubt burrowed itself into the back of Danny's mind—flickering to life at her mention of his first conversation with the Legion months before. He couldn't help but think they'd been too quick to accept his story, too easily swayed by the vague prognostications of a stranger.

They already wanted to aid the Marians, a voice whispered in the back of his mind, sounding remarkably like Keira's indignant voice.

But if that were true, then what was the Legion's true role in all of this? What ulterior motives did they have for picking sides in this war?

Danny didn't know the answer to that, but he had a feeling that the ceremony in Crîd Eálas, and the Legionnaires it would attract, would likely be an excellent place to start.

CHAPTER

TEN

242 Marian Era (M.E.)

Zipporah spun to shoot an accusatory glare at Keira, arms folded over her chest and dark eyes narrowed. "That was not the proposition you put before Elliott."

Keira shifted slightly, eyeing the council doors that rumbled to a close behind them and swallowed. "I asked for support for the Regio—"

"Yes, but that was *not* your true purpose. You made a fool of your mentor after he agreed to vouch for you, made him look ignorant and easily manipulated—which, I suppose he was . . . by you."

The low rumble of guilt churned in Keira's stomach, making her feel nauseous. Zipporah was right. She had manipulated Elliott, given him only a half-truth so that he would take her to the High Council.

I did it for you, though, Danny, she thought. *I didn't have a choice.*

Keira shoved away the feeling of guilt and stiffened her spine, leveling Zipporah with a glare of her own.

"That's really none of your business, is it? This is between Elliott and me, and I don't recall asking for your input."

Zipporah's eyes widened and her lip curled. She opened her mouth then to issue a retort, when a soft voice came from behind Keira.

"She's right. Leave us, Zipporah."

An icy chill raced down Keira's spine. Reluctantly, she turned to face Elliott.

He stood leaning against the rotunda wall, arms crossed and amber eyes leveled at her.

Keira searched those eyes for any sign of anger, almost hoping for it, anything to ease the sickening feeling of guilt in her stomach. But she found only profound disappointment gazing back at her.

He had heard everything, those eyes told her, and understood the lie she had tricked him with.

Of course he did, she chided herself. *You think he would have left you to face the High Council alone? It's Elliott.*

The realization only deepened her guilt at betraying this man who had done nothing but care for and support her in the years since she'd arrived in Loren. In that moment, she hated herself, hated her own selfishness and how it always seemed to spill out, hurting those around her.

She searched in vain for the words that would make it better, that could take away the sting of what she'd done. But there were none.

"Your request has been approved," Elliott said finally. "Both of them."

Keira's mouth fell open, and she blinked in surprise. That had been a fast deliberation. She'd expected to be waiting around all day.

"Your studies will be overseen by Albert, the Englishman," Elliott continued.

This surprised her. She wasn't about to quibble, but she had one question. "Why can't you oversee me? You are my mentor, after all."

Elliott hesitated, considering her for a moment before continuing. "It was felt," he said, lingering over each syllable, "that I was incapable of *objectivity* when it comes to you. That another, less *invested* mentor would be better to oversee your progress and prevent any overstepping."

Keira stared at him. Another mentor? Was he serious? Elliott was the first friend she'd ever made in Loren, before Danny, even. He'd guided her, coaching her through the early days of learning pneumonancy, encouraging her when she fell short of her goals. Was he really so replaceable in the Legion's mind?

I did this, she realized suddenly. *I manipulated him, betrayed his trust, and now he's being punished.*

"Elliott, I—" she started, searching his face. "I'm so sorry."

His eyes softened then, losing some of the distance they'd acquired.

"My only regret, Keira, is that you felt you had to lie to me, that you thought I wouldn't understand."

His words brought tears stinging to her eyes, and she blinked furiously, willing them to vanish. If she started crying now, she knew it would be a while before she could stop. And Pneumos forbid Zipporah see her.

"Of course I understand your wanting to heal, Keira. I should have foreseen it. You were training to be a physician in your old life, after all. I should have expected something like this to be your calling."

More guilt, another lie. What he said was true, but it wasn't the whole truth. Keira briefly considered coming clean then, telling him about Danny, about everything. But something held her back, and she bit her tongue, only nodding instead.

"But Keira, I must tell you . . ." Elliott paused, and Keira was surprised to see him look nervously around. "About Albert . . . he's an excellent pneumonancer. But I—" Elliott rubbed the back of his neck.

"Elliott, what is it?" Keira asked. He was worrying her.

"I'd advise you not to put an inordinate amount of trust in him. The workings of Séiro really are quite tempting, and he and I . . ." Elliott trailed off, his eyes gazing at something far off in the distance. "Well, let's just say, he and I have had unfortunate dealings in the past."

Keira stared at him. Was he really saying this member of the High Council might have dealings with the Worshippers of Séiro?

"Of course, Elliott. I'll be on my guard," she assured him. She truly meant it, though at that moment, she'd have promised him just about anything.

"I know you will," Elliott said, a wan smile flickering across his face. "And I'll still be here, you know. Happy to help in any way I can. Even if the High Council *has* declared me unfit to be your mentor."

Keira felt like someone had punched her in the gut, but she nodded. There was just one more question she had to ask. "Elliott, can I ask—do you know anything about arrivals? The redoing, I mean?"

Elliott blinked, surprised, and answered slowly, "Why do you ask?"

This was getting into dangerous territory, and Keira chose her words carefully, trying to make them light, almost flippant. "I just thought it might give me a lead. Creating bodies for our pneuma to be reborn into must be related to the power needed to heal, don't you think?"

Elliott swallowed, and Keira thought she saw something flash across his eyes. She froze. Did he suspect? Did he understand why she was really asking?

But Elliott only replied, "I'm afraid I don't. I'd suggest looking in the library, though I wouldn't hold out much hope. Some things are meant to remain mysteries, you see; such is the way of Pneumos."

Keira nodded, hiding her disappointment behind a small smile. "Just thought I'd ask," she put in quickly. They stood in awkward silence then, something hanging between them that had previously been absent, though Keira couldn't have said what.

"Well, come along then," Elliott said finally, breaking the tension. "We had best fill Cyrus in on what the council's decided. It will take a week or two to organize the cohort, but then they'll be off."

Keira followed Elliott back through the passageway that led to the entry rotunda, every step out of the dank belly of the Legion's headquarters like a weight being lifted from her. As they emerged to daylight shining through the stained glass window of the upper rotunda, Keira knew that despite everything, this was a victory. *It'll be worth it, Danny,* she thought. *I know it will.*

～

KEIRA AND RAINA followed the councilwoman, who looked in every aspect like a girl younger even than Raina, though her thick, curly hair was pulled back in a severe bun. She'd introduced herself earlier as Zoya Melaku before leading them up a tightly twisting staircase that seemed to go on forever. Through the narrow windows that were spaced throughout their ascent, Keira could see the city of Port Galaén falling away beneath them, as off in the distance, the fertile inlet cut like a blue fissure through the earth.

"So—uh, how old you being, again?" Raina asked the councilwoman, who stood a few inches shorter than herself, with childlike features. Zoya turned to shoot Raina a daggerlike look, tilting her nose upward as she said haughtily, "I am four hundred thirty-six years old, girl."

Raina's mouth fell open, and she fell back to walk beside Keira.

"Do years be meaning something different to your people?" she whispered in Keira's direction. Keira stifled a snort as Zoya's hawklike eyes fell on her.

"Not exactly," she murmured when the councilwoman had resumed climbing. "We don't age like normal people. Whatever age we were when we died, back in our old world, we stay that way—forever."

Raina nodded warily. Keira had explained the basics of pneumonancy and how the Legion operated to her and Cyrus but had spared them the details. Still, when offered lodging in the headquarters themselves, Cyrus had quickly declined, claiming his representative duties on Landry's behalf required him to have easy access to the merchants and messengers of Port Galaén, which would have been more difficult locked behind the Legion's iron fence. Keira suspected he had no desire for the restless sleep he'd get sharing a roof with a host of pneuma-wielding warriors.

Unfortunately for Raina, she got little choice in the matter. Keira wasn't about to leave her unattended in a strange city, and Cyrus had begged off, claiming he'd be far too busy to look after her. So Raina would stay with Keira until the cohort was ready to depart for the capital. And though she grumbled loudly enough about not needing a babysitter, Keira suspected she was secretly intrigued by the Legion and its *Le'ena*.

Keira didn't mind too much. Though Raina certainly had a knack for getting herself into trouble, it felt surprisingly good to have someone else hanging around, even if she was a cheeky know-it-all.

When they reached the top of the staircase, Zoya directed them down a dark hallway, passing several doors before coming to one with a swirling seashell carved into it. Zoya unlocked it and led them into what turned out to be a bedchamber. The white stone walls arched up to a vaulted ceiling, and in the corner, a large wooden bed stood surrounded by a thick canopy of dark Oxford Blue drapes. The headboard was decorated with the same swirling mass of lines carved into its bulk—lines that seemed to move farther away the longer you stared at them. A massive stone fireplace took up the bulk of the center of the room, with two upholstered chairs standing before it.

"These are your quarters," Zoya pronounced. "The little girl can sleep in the adjoining room, through there." She gestured to a door on the far wall. "It's a walk-through, so she won't wander."

Raina bristled, first at the term "little girl" and second at the implication she couldn't be trusted with her own door to the hallway. Keira placed a hand on her arm and squeezed pointedly.

"It's perfect, thank you."

"You'll find the dining hall directly across from the study off the entry rotunda. Their hours are strict and nonnegotiable. I hope you enjoy your stay."

She said this last with a sticky sweetness that put Keira's teeth on edge, but she merely forced a smile and a nod as the girl turned and left.

Raina let out a groan of frustration. "I *not* be liking that one."

"Yeah, me neither," Keira replied, surveying the room. "Well, I guess this is it. Might as well unpack."

Raina nodded, heaving the tiny rucksack she'd ferreted aboard Cyrus's ship off her shoulder and dragging it behind her as she plodded toward the adjoining room. Keira opened her own larger, albeit still compact, bag and began unpacking everything into the small trunk at the end of the canopied bed. From the other room, Raina called out, "So what exactly is it you be looking for here?"

Keira paused. She'd been expecting this, but still her stomach tightened in a knot as she decided how much to tell the younger girl.

"I—I'm learning a new type of pneumonancy," she explained slowly. "Healing pneumonancy."

Raina's dark head poked around the corner, her seafoam eyes bright and curious. "And what is it you be needing here? A teacher?"

"Not so much that as the knowledge that's here. There aren't any Legionnaires living here who practice this type of pneumonancy—as far as I know. But the Legion's library is famous for its expansiveness, having gathered Legion knowledge from across all times and worlds."

Keira herself remembered Elliott's lessons on the matter—

describing the library with unadulterated wonder as Keira and Danny sat in rapt attention. Keira's chest tightened. That was so long ago it felt another lifetime entirely—before chaos, revolt, and death had ever touched their doorstep, back when they'd all been happy—and alive.

Keira shook her head, banishing the phantom memory and the quivering grief that accompanied it.

"What about you?" she called instead. "What are your plans for when you get to the capital?"

Raina's head again bobbed around the corner, bright eyes pinched, this time in confusion.

"I be finding my brother, and we be living together in this new city. What else?"

"Yes, but what will you do all day long—while Akamu's busy with People's Council business? Will you go to school, pursue a trade of some sort?"

Raina's lips pinched together at that, boldly declaring, "I not be going to school with no spoiled *grelún*. I not be having nobody else looking down at me."

Keira chuckled. "Well, you have to do *something*. It's a big world out there, Raina, and if you want a place in it, then you'll need schooling, or at least training. You don't want to be left behind, do you?"

Raina came fully into the doorway at that, arms crossed as she scuffed her feet against the doorframe. Finally, Raina's gaze shot up, and the intensity in her eyes surprised Keira.

"I not being left behind—not by Akamu, not by anyone—not again."

As Keira stared at her, taken aback by this declaration, she couldn't help but see the defiance in those eyes, an indomitable spirit to be sure, but something else as well—fear. Desperation and terror shone even among the boldness.

To be left behind, abandoned—again—*that* was Raina's worst fear.

Keira felt herself slump as she rubbed a wary hand across her face.

"Come here, Raina," she said, waving a hand to beckon the girl forward. Raina obeyed, plopping herself beside Keira on the end of the bed. She pulled each of her feet up and wrapped her arms around her legs, hugging them to her chest.

"Raina, I'm so sorry for all you've lost. First your parents, then your home—it's enough to make anyone angry . . . and afraid."

Raina's head snapped up at that as she leveled an icy glare at Keira. "I not being afraid."

Keira shrugged before pulling her own legs up onto the bed as she sat crisscrossed. "It'd be ok if you were, you know. Fear's just a part of life, Raina—as much as breathing. And people leave us—they just *do*. We can't let that control everything we do. We can't always be chasing them. At some point, we have to stand on our own two feet, live our *own* lives, not someone else's."

Raina turned glassy eyes to her then. "Who you be losing, Keira?"

Faces flashed before Keira's eyes in a swirl of memory—her mom, Gaius Flavius, Sara, Nazor, and . . . Danny. Keira's jaw tightened, and she willed the shaking in her breath to still. "Too many."

Raina nodded, clearly expecting as much. "I be thinking about what you say. Maybe—maybe school not be so bad."

Keira chuckled, giving Raina a light shove on her shoulder. "Those *grelún* won't know what hit 'em."

Smiling broadly, Raina opened her mouth to stay something, but then closed it and instead threw her arms around

Keira's neck. Startled, Keira froze, before hesitantly returning the girl's embrace. Raina stood then, looking as if her spirit was suddenly light as a feather, and practically skipped back to her room.

Keira stared after her, a gnawing ache growing in her belly. *This* was exactly why she'd kept to herself all these months. She was getting too close. Here she was giving advice about letting go of the spirits that haunt you, all while desperately chasing her own. She inhaled a shaky breath and leaned forward to grip her knees. It was *too much*. She was barely holding on herself. How could she afford to give this much of herself away, to *care* this much? Because Keira knew, better than anybody, that another loss might just unravel her entirely.

ELEVEN

This was their library? Keira stared in awe at the room before them. Like many in the Legion's headquarters, the room was circular, its shelves of books, scrolls, and seemingly random stacks of faded parchment arranged around its edges. The floor formed a spiral ramp that curled up toward the ceiling and wrapped down into the belly of the earth.

"All your libraries being like this?" Raina piped up from her side, looking equally impressed as she gazed over the edge of the banister toward the seemingly bottomless expanse of the library's core.

"Not exactly," Keira breathed. She stared at the immense quantity of books and suddenly felt tiny and unprepared. She didn't even know where to begin. There had to be some sort of organizational system, didn't there? If so, it certainly wasn't readily apparent.

She'd hoped that Elliott would have been able to accompany them, but he'd suddenly been called away on Legion business, leaving only a note that explained where to find the library, and nothing about how to use it.

Well, this ought to be interesting, Keira thought.

She glanced down to tell Raina they needed to find help first, when she realized the girl was gone. Yards ahead of her already, Raina strolled down the curved walkway, hand trailing lightly on the banister as she gazed admiringly up at the rows upon rows of books.

Sighing, Keira followed. Picking a tome at random from the first bookcase, she opened it to the first few pages. There was no sign of a title, table of contents, or any sign of exactly what she could expect from its yellowed pages. Instead, the text started at a seemingly random point, picking up halfway through a sentence and continuing on.

. . . that said, the ancient culture of the Cross-Sea Lands was such that any individual seeking recompense has only to challenge their opponent to a duel of the swords as well as the words to achieve satisfaction. The strict honor system within the Cross-Sea Lands demands nothing less . . .

Keira clamped the book shut and reached for another, hoping for better luck, or at least some recognizable thread of organization.

. . . and as descendants of the Etruscii culture, the Marian Empire took great pains to ensure that the lands it conquered came as willingly as possible. They absorbed the religions, holidays, and traditions of their subjects, shaping the . . .

"You find what you be looking for?" a voice piped up beside her. Raina gazed curiously at the thick tome, eyes alight with excitement.

"Nope." Keira shook her head. "I don't even know where to start with this. It's like there's no organizational system at all.

Books seem to start and stop wherever they please, and there are no titles or indices to think of. Whoever the librarian is here has a twisted sense of—"

"Can I help you?"

The voice was high and sweet and completely unexpected. Keira jumped, spinning around in search of its owner.

"Over here!"

Keira and Raina turned and padded up the spiral walkway, passing further rows of books, until they reached a tiny alcove carved into a wall. There a girl sat in a boxed window seat—pillows, blankets, and stacks and stacks of books piled around her. Out the window was a gorgeous, sprawling view of Port Galaén. The red and orange hues of sunrise were just peeking up over the horizon, leaving the city awash in their rays.

The girl herself was petite and sprite-like, her hair cut short in a pile of bright, unnaturally red curls that stood out against the warm tone of her skin. Her nose was pointed and angled up just at the end, and she met their gaze with a wide, welcoming grin. Keira spotted a single chipped tooth, the solitary imperfection somehow only adding to the girl's charm. Keira returned the smile, unable to resist.

"Hi there," she began, hesitant. "I'm Keira, and this is Raina. I-I didn't mean any offense . . . before, I mean," she added quickly, realizing this might be the very librarian she'd just insulted. "We're just having a hard time making heads or tails of the catalog. Uh—*is* there a catalog of sorts?"

The girl smiled serenely and hopped off her window bench, lithely avoiding the haphazardly stacked books.

"Of course. Come with me! I'm Martina, by the way, Martina Lucia Sosa, but everyone calls me Marti." When she hopped up, Keira could see she was a few inches shorter even than Keira, her limbs tiny and birdlike. Marti's voice was thickly accented, with a heaviness about the *r*'s and *h*'s that Keira couldn't quite place. She was curious about what had brought Marti to the Legion but bit her tongue, not wanting to be rude. Raina held no such qualms.

"Where you be from?" she asked boldly, ignoring the pointed look Keira shot her.

Marti only smiled, though. "From the shores of *el Rio de la Plata*, in a place very far away called Argentina."

Raina nodded, impressed despite surely having no clue where that was. A softness had entered Marti's voice at the mention of her home, and Keira thought she detected a wistful look in her eye, but it disappeared just as quickly as Marti bounced ahead of them.

She led them up the spiraling walkway of the library, ever closer to the stained glass window that constituted its ceiling—another swirling array of light and dark, Keira noted. The top of the walkway opened to a large space with yet more stacks of books and papers. But at its center stood a single marble basin. Keira approached it warily, drawn by a magnetism she couldn't quite name. From where she stood, she could see it was filled with a shifting metallic sand that rose up and out of the bowl in a hefting wave before collapsing back in. It was constantly moving, and as Keira neared, she saw images forming within it —but solely the negative imprint. Like the Pin Art board she'd had as a child, the tiny metal rods leaping forward to show an image of the hand or face pressed behind, these sands morphed and changed. Unidentifiable faces leapt out at sporadic intervals, and battles emerged across the sand's surface before disappearing, swallowed up by further waves of movement.

"What is it?" she breathed.

"We call it an amalgam," Marti explained, voice filled with an awe to match Keira's own.

"How does it work?"

"We don't really know," Marti said, shaking her head—not with disappointment but with wonder. "But it's a synthesizer of sorts, using pneuma to create order out of the universe of information that the Legion has gained, across all time and worlds. It never stops, creating book after book in an endless procession."

Keira strolled around it, admiring the simultaneous grace and ferocity of its movement. As she stared, an object seemed to appear from within its depths, the sands shifting away to reveal a thick, leather-bound tome that was suddenly flung from the dais, landing on the floor with a thud that made Keira jump.

With trembling fingers, she reached for the book, ignoring the buzzing in her ears and the queasiness of her insides as she neared the dais—a sure sign of pneumonancy at work. Thumbing through the first few pages, Keira again saw no indication of the book's subject. It merely jumped in, seemingly in the middle of a sentence.

. . . whereas the kings of the old worlds could not be satisfied within the bounds of their treaties and oaths, they set their minds to war and the terrible undertaking of empire . . .

"And what?" Keira asked, flipping the book shut. "It can't be bothered by inconveniences like titles or tables of contents?"

Marti laughed. "Such things would only be confining to the amalgam. It's compromise enough for the dais to work in the medium of leather and paper, to satisfy our puny limitations. No, the pneuma guides its unique sense of order and organization. The reader, too, must let pneuma guide their search if they're to weed through the expanse of the collection."

That knocked the wind out of Keira as she realized the true extent of the deep dive she'd need to take if she were to uncover whatever secrets of healing pneumonancy, not to mention the redoing, the Legion had gained over the millennia.

Marti must have seen her dazed expression, for she reached over and placed a hand on her arm.

"Lucky for you," she said, a mischievous grin dancing on her face, "you have an amalgamor to help you."

"An amalga-what?"

"*Amalgamor*," Marti corrected. "How do you think the books end up on the shelves? Magic?" The bell-like tinkle of her laugh echoed throughout the library, and Keira smiled at the sound.

Reaching for the book in Keira's hands, Marti practically skipped down the walkway, her fingers trailing in the banister with childlike delight as she called, "Follow me!"

Keira glanced at Raina, who was staring dubiously at the dais, arms crossed in obvious distrust.

"Well, shall we?" Keira asked.

Raina raised an eyebrow at her before looking pointedly after Marti. "You *want* to be following the crazy lady, then? Deep into the belly of this place?" She shook her head, and Keira couldn't help chuckling at this eleven-year-old's practical, no-nonsense outlook on things like magical daises and unsearchable libraries.

"*O-yoy*," Raina finally sighed as she turned to go after Marti. Keira quickly followed, smiling as Raina muttered, "Silly *grelún*," under her breath.

They caught up to Marti a turn and a half past the door they'd entered. She'd slowed, eyes closed as her fingers lightly traced the spines of the books she passed, a low hum on her lips.

Keira's eyes widened as she tasted the pneuma in the air. *She was serious, then,* Keira thought. Marti *actually* used pneuma to guide her through the immense athenaeum.

Marti's eyes suddenly flew open, and her fingers trailed to a stop between two other books.

"Here, I think," she pronounced. "The perfect mix of history, war, geography, Carnos, and political strategy." Hefting the tome with both hands, she squeezed it into the waiting space, which miraculously seemed to fit it perfectly. Turning back to Keira, Marti smiled broadly. "Now it's your turn."

Keira's eyes widened, but she nodded, feeling Raina's eyes on her. "How do I do it?"

"Just as you use your pneuma normally, although please try not to melt anything, yes? The amalgam gets very upset when it has to redo its work."

Keira blinked, a wave of nerves settling in her stomach, but Marti continued.

"I find it easiest to channel pneuma in this way when actually touching the books themselves." Marti shrugged, grinning. "Call me old-fashioned. But the key here is to hold your question in your mind, let your pneuma flow through it, immersing it, and then just walk. You'll know when you've reached your destination."

Keira nodded, moving to the nearest row of shelves and placing her finger lightly on a spine. Then she hesitated, doubt suddenly creasing her brow, and she turned back to Marti.

"I don't need a grounder for this?" she asked. "I won't lose the tether?"

Marti shrugged. "It's always possible. But no, I rarely need grounding for this. You're not really letting it get away from you, you see. It stays right at your fingertips." Seeing Keira's still-doubtful expression, Marti took a new tack. "Think of the pneuma as a balancing scale. An unanswered question, it's like a little seed of chaos, yes? Blurring all that surrounds it. An answer brings order to your mind, helps you see clearly and make sense of the world around you. Your pneuma knows how to seek order from the chaos. Let it guide you."

Keira nodded, swallowing hard. Then she closed her eyes, feeling a little silly as she reached deep within herself to nudge the ball of pneuma at her core. She found it easily enough and gave a low hum—lower, more controlled than her usual high-pitched whistle. She did *not* want this getting away from her, not without a grounder nearby.

Her pneuma responded almost immediately, unfurling and flowing through her body and toward her outstretched fingers. When she felt her fingertips grow warm, she slowly let go of the pulsing ball at her core and focused her attention on a single question.

How do I bring him back?

It wasn't the question she'd asked the High Council, or even the one she'd told Elliott, but it was the single burning question within her—the weight of its unknowing seeming to carve out a chunk of her soul. This was the piece of pulsing chaos in her heart that kept her mind ablaze with swirling thoughts and fears, day and night.

She let her pneuma entwine with the question, imagining it flowing in and between the letters of it, pulsing as it absorbed the chaos that sprang from it—and then it was off.

The pneuma was like a pulsing thread, urging her onward, and with an effort, Keira put her legs into motion. She'd never performed pneumonancy while moving before, and even a small action such as this left her feeling off-kilter and untethered, each step conveying a sense of unsteadiness that left her feeling queasy. But still she pushed herself onward, guided by the tiny, pulsing thread that promised order and understanding.

As her fingers moved lightly over the leather spines, images flashed through her mind. Her pneuma acted as a sieve—sifting through the contents, searching for the orderly answer her question demanded.

With each book she passed, the tug of the thread grew more insistent—as if growing stronger from the information absorbed and discarded, more sure of its path.

Keira's speed picked up, her legs growing used to their wobbly detachment from the floor, until she was practically jogging. Excitement bubbled within her as she felt the thread's tug grow ever stronger, and she barely noticed as she completed not three, but four rotations down the walkway, the starry stained glass growing farther and farther away as she descended ever further into the library's depths. As she went, the images that shot through her mind grew stranger—creatures she'd never seen and landscapes that looked so alien they might have been in another world entirely. *Maybe they are*, she thought, and the realization sent another bolt of excitement through her.

The thread was practically throbbing now, and Keira had to slow to a walk as she concentrated on remaining upright, placing each wobbly foot precisely and surely. They were close —that much she knew.

Suddenly, the thread stopped as her fingers floated across an unassuming bookshelf, and she felt the pull of it angle upward. Reaching for the wheeled ladder that ran on tracks from one shelf to the next, Keira slowly climbed, one hand firmly adhered to the tether as it guided her up to a single leather-bound tome, which she gripped with trembling hands. Slowly, she climbed back to the floor.

The book itself looked quietly inconspicuous, no real difference to distinguish it from its neighbors. Keira let the thread pull her fingers to a single page about two-thirds of the way in, and she slowly parted the pages.

. . . *the grieving process is a tricky subject, as it may vary from person to person. Individuals may vary in their progression through the stages of grief, with many alternating between denial and bargaining, searching for some way, any way, to bring their loved one back—*

Keira snapped the book closed, anger boiling inside. *Nice,* she thought acerbically at her pneuma. *Very nice.* Then she sighed aloud. She should have known this was all too easy, and yelling at an inanimate force was probably not going to help matters.

"Not quite what you were looking for?" an airy voice asked from her elbow, and Keira jumped. Marti shot her a toothy grin before pondering her. "It all comes down to the question you choose, and the answer your pneuma thinks will put the chaos in your mind back into order. You must also get to know your own pneuma as well to better understand how—um—*literally* it interprets your questions. You may find your pneuma even has a bit of a sense of humor! Although I suppose that may speak more to the user than the force itself—a philosophical question for another day," she added quickly, likely seeing Keira's defeated expression.

Keira sighed, feeling absolutely drained, and the weight of her disappointment dragged her down to a nearby bench, where she sat kneading her temples.

"This is going to take forever," she muttered, staring at the seemingly endless array of books as they stretched deeper and deeper into the earth.

"The pursuit of knowledge is never-ending," Marti murmured. She surely said the words as a consolation, but the note of excitement Keira detected in her voice put Keira's teeth on edge. Keira enjoyed learning as much as the next person, but there simply wasn't *time*. What had Marné said? *"When rains do fade and waves be calm, then sun and moon be borne alike. Le'ena walk among the stromb, death be gone when Cála strike."*

The more she'd thought about it, the more convinced she was that the first line referred to the equinox, when the sun and moon shared equal time in the skies. Looking back to her own arrival, she felt sure she'd arrived at or around the autumn equinox. They were less than a month away from the spring equinox now. If Keira was going to bring Danny back, it had to be soon. There was, of course, the autumn equinox, but who knew if the connection she still felt with him, his voice in her head, would fade the longer they spent apart? As it was, she'd yet to hear it again since the marauders' ambush. She squelched the panicked feeling in her stomach. No, she had to find an answer sooner rather than later.

"I could help you, if you'd like," Marti said suddenly, shaking Keira from her internal monologue. "We may have more luck with two searching."

"Me too," piped up Raina, and Keira spun around, feeling guilty. She'd completely forgotten Raina was there. "You know," Raina continued, looking abashed, "the normal way."

Keira hesitated. She hated asking for their help—hated that sense of indebtedness that always seemed to accompany the favors of others. But in this case, she didn't really see any other way. Finally, she nodded.

"I'd appreciate that. Thank you."

THEY SPENT the next several hours combing through shelves, carried on wild goose chases by the fickle qualms of their pneuma. But eventually, Keira realized her stomach was growling, and the light from the ceiling mosaic had all but faded.

"I think it's time we went in search of some dinner, yes?" Marti asked, stretching her tiny fingers out in front of her. Raina immediately snapped her book shut with an eagerness that suggested long-suffering silence. A twinge of guilt nibbled at Keira. She'd had the poor kid poring through dusty old books all day, and with very little to show for it. Keira had stumbled across a few promising leads, references to the use of healing pneumonancy in some war or other, but no details. She sighed. This was going to be more difficult than she'd thought.

She climbed to her feet and followed the others up the winding walkway that cut the path up to the surface. Keira watched in amusement as Raina pestered Marti with question after question about her life here in Loren and this mysterious place called "Argentina." Keira searched Marti's face for signs of annoyance, ready to redirect Raina's curiosity if needed, but Marti only smiled serenely and answered each question in a measured manner, as if considering her answers with the utmost care. When the line of discussion turned to Argentina, her face practically shone, a glassy hue entering her eyes as she regaled Raina with tales of gauchos, tango dancers, and the warm taste of empanadas straight out of the oven. Raina absorbed it all, wide-eyed and excited. The sight brought a bittersweet smile to Keira's lips as she thought of her old world and all the places none of them could return to.

As they emerged through the great double doors that led into the library, the swift sound of footsteps on flagstone met them in the hall.

"There you are," a warm voice murmured. "Have you spent the entire day in the library again? I swear, if you . . ."

The voice trailed off as Keira's wide eyes met the equally surprised look of Zipporah.

Keira immediately stiffened. "What are *you* doing here?" she asked, remembering their furious argument the day before and not feeling inclined to be polite.

Zipporah looked equally tense, and she regarded Keira with the disdain one usually reserves for insects. "I was *looking* for Marti. It's well past dinnertime." Zipporah's previously teasing tone had turned to one of pointed annoyance.

Keira's cheeks flamed. "Well, it's not my fault, if that's what you're implying. Marti offered to help." She glanced between the two other women. "Are you two *friends*?"

Great, Keira thought. *And just when I was starting to like Marti.*

Marti sighed. "*Tranquílan*—calm down, you two. There'll be plenty left to eat. And yes, Keira. Zipporah is actually my grounder."

Keira's mouth fell open, but she snapped it shut at Zipporah's look of smug satisfaction. Her *grounder*? The two of them couldn't have been more dissimilar. Whereas Marti was kind, sweet, and helpful, Zipporah was churlish, condescending, and rude. Keira shook her head. She supposed no one really *chose* their grounder. Even so, to be such complete opposites . . .

The silence hung heavy, and Keira shifted awkwardly as she wondered what to say. She saw Marti shoot a pointed look at Zipporah and was reminded of the secret glances Elliott and Nazor used to share, at once unassuming and yet heavy with meaning.

Zipporah cleared her throat, shot Marti a reproachful look, and then said, "Well—um, shall we go to dinner, then?"

Keira blinked, utterly at a loss for words, but was saved the effort by Raina's too-cheerful agreement and her insistent tug on Keira's hand as the five of them made their way toward the dining hall.

Ahead of them, Keira watched as Marti jauntily looped her arm through Zipporah's, looking like a rag doll beside the other woman's towering frame.

Keira shook her head. She really never would understand this place.

CHAPTER

TWELVE

Keira's research efforts continued in starts and stops over the next few days. Marti's help was invaluable, as she seemed to know every nook and cranny of that immense holding. She had an infectious, bell-like laugh that Keira couldn't help but warm to, even if she did have terrible taste in grounders. Mercifully, Zipporah spent little time in the library. Marti explained that the place made Zipporah antsy, and she much preferred guard duty, where she could remain free to roam out of doors. Even Raina's initially dubious appraisal of Marti's eccentricities had turned into something more akin to worship—which Keira found herself surprisingly jealous of.

Every day they toiled, following their pneuma as it chased down lead after lead. Most of what they found was of purely historical significance, but they had stumbled upon a couple books that explored the nature of pneuma itself. Keira had tried her best to dig into the massive tomes, hoping they might give her more information on how the healing pneumonancy actually worked, and therefore how it could be expanded upon. But the reading was slow and convoluted, something more akin to five hundred pages of philosophical musings than a practical how-to manual. It would have been a cumbersome study on her best day. But as the days ticked closer and closer to the equinox, with few results to show for all their efforts, Keira grew more impatient, often finding herself reading and rereading the same paragraph with no comprehension of its meaning.

One day, as Keira made her way back toward the library, she found herself deep in thought. Was this really the best way to be going about this? Even an amalgamor as skilled as Marti seemed to have difficulty navigating the library's immensity. And though she seemed unbothered with the effort, insisting that research just took time, Keira alone understood that the time she had wasn't exactly abundant. Should she take a new tack? Was there maybe somewhere else the Legion stored its records? *Someone* else she could ask for help? So transfixed was she by the conundrum that she nearly ran smack into a tall figure as she rounded a corner.

"I'm so sorry," she blurted, stumbling backward.

"It's quite all right," the robed man replied in an arched British accent, his thick mustache twitching in a smile.

"Albert," Keira stammered, recognizing him from the council room. "I'm sorry, I wasn't paying attention." Elliott's warning flashed in her mind. *He and I have had unfortunate dealings in the past. The workings of Séiro really are quite tempting.*

Scanning him quickly, Keira had to admit that he didn't look like a Worshipper of Séiro. There were no tattoos to speak of, and he submitted to her survey with clear amusement.

"Not at all," he said, voice light and curious. "I understand you've been researching this new healing pneumonancy you spoke so passionately about. How are things coming along?"

Keira hesitated, wondering how much to tell him. She

decided that the truth was likely the safest, especially seeing as he was unlikely to glean anything useful when they themselves were stumped.

"Honestly, not too well," she said. "I'm still getting used to the amalgam, and it's been pretty slow going."

Albert's mouth twisted into a sympathetic grimace. "I never could make heads or tails of that device myself. Any question I had, the amalgam always seemed to twist into the most absurd formulations. I did find that the more specific I could be, searching for a particular individual's research, for example, the better. Give the damn thing fewer ways out, I say." He chuckled, and Keira offered a small smile in return.

"Thank you. I'll definitely try that."

"I am curious, why isn't Elliott helping you?"

Keira blinked, then replied, "He's out of town."

"Hmm," Albert replied. "Very interesting. I would have helped you myself, you see, since the council appointed me overseer, but he was quite insistent that I keep my distance."

"Elliott talked to you?"

"Oh yes. I'm not exactly his favorite person, as I'm sure you've probably gathered." Albert's smile broadened, though with a self-deprecating twitch at the corner of his mouth.

"I did get that sense," Keira admitted. "And why is that?" It was a bold question, and Keira regretted it as soon as it left her mouth.

But Albert didn't look offended. "Well, it's at once a timeless story and also quite short. The usual thing, honestly—two men in love with the same woman. Never ends well, I'm afraid."

This caught Keira up short, and she gaped at him. In love with the same woman? Did he mean—he couldn't possibly mean *Nazor*, could he?

"Yes, Chinazor was quite the woman, as I'm sure I don't

need to tell you. It broke my heart to hear she'd passed on." Albert's eyes were soft, almost glassy in appearance.

He really loved her, Keira thought. She could only nod blankly, mentally recalculating everything she'd thought she'd known about her mentor, the tall, imposing Nigerian woman who could no doubt make an entire Bellatori centurium's knees buckle simultaneously. She'd betrayed Keira, in the end, but ultimately redeemed herself by saving her and trying to save Danny. *Too late*, Keira thought darkly.

"Elliott—he said you two knew each other, from before, I mean."

Albert nodded, considering her. "We were students together at Oxford, and then both became professors later on—he in physics and I in the classics. Neither of us came from the elite background most of our classmates could claim, and we became fast friends. We were incredibly close. But that was also a *very* long time ago, I'm afraid." He smiled sadly at her, and Keira couldn't help but believe he meant it. Her head was still spinning from this newest revelation, and she opened her mouth to ask more, but nothing came out.

Albert seemed to sense her difficulty and added, "Tell me, has our research at least provided you with a good starting point?"

Keira could only stare blankly at him, and Albert's curious expression morphed into a frown.

"Elliott *did* share our research with you before he left, did he not? It seems like it would apply to your current line of inquiry. Your focus is on healing pneumonancy, of course, but our work into the nature of arrivals and the redoing certainly seems—"

"Your research into *what*?" Keira blurted, eyes going wide.

Startled, Albert replied, "The redoing—in which arrivals

from other times and worlds are reshaped into bodies to live in this one."

Keira's mouth opened and closed, her mind racing between plausible explanations. That was exactly the question she'd asked Elliott her first day in Port Galaén. Could he have misunderstood? Maybe she'd been too cautious in her phrasing, hoping he wouldn't catch on to her true aim—rescuing Danny. Then she remembered the startled look he'd given her, the curious expression that had flashed across his face. Keira felt her cheeks burn as she realized there was no alternative to the inevitable truth—Elliott had lied to her. She'd asked him point-blank. Wondered if there was any connection between arrivals and healing pneumonancy. She'd asked him if he'd known anything, and he'd lied to her face. Keira's breathing was shallow, and her hands shook with rage. She forced them into fists, letting the bite of nails into her own palm bring her back to the present.

Albert stared at her expectantly, clearly having asked her a question.

"I'm sorry, what?"

Slowly, he repeated himself. "I asked if *I* could be of any assistance? As I mentioned, I have some experience in this area. We could work together, you see."

Keira tensed, remembering Elliott's words of warning not to trust his old friend. *Well, you said I could trust you,* she thought angrily. *And look where that's gotten me.* Still, Albert was a stranger, and she wasn't about to let her guard down. She regarded him warily before replying, "That's very kind of you. There are a few of us looking, though, and I'm not sure how helpful too many more would be . . ." Her voice trailed off, and she shifted awkwardly, darting a glance his way.

Albert laughed. "I assure you, I have no interest in combing through old books. I'll leave that to you all, to be sure. No, my preferred methods of learning are far more—practical. I say *doing* beats *reading* about doing any day. If you'd care to join me, we could test the limits of this new healing pneumonancy ourselves. You've done it before, after all." He offered her a knowing smile, and Keira felt her own lips twitch in answer, almost of their own accord. She couldn't argue with logic like that. Still, Elliott's warning sounded in her ears, and though she gritted her teeth at the memory of his concerned look, she wasn't ready to dismiss his advice out of hand—not yet, anyway.

"That's definitely tempting," she admitted. "If I have to read one more dusty old book detailing shipments of medical supplies, I might scream. I'll think about it, all right?"

Albert smiled broadly, throwing up his hands in easy acquiescence. "Of course, think it over. But do have a look for that research I mentioned, will you? I think you'll find it most—stimulating."

With a small dip of his head, Albert continued on down the hall then, not looking back once.

You can bet your ass I'll be looking into it, Keira thought grimly, not sure what, exactly, she was hoping to find. Proof of Elliott's innocence, or possibly the very answers she'd been looking for. Either way, she was going to find out.

DETERMINED to sort through this newest revelation, Keira spent the rest of her lunch hour poring through old archives of thesis research by Legionnaires-in-training, searching for something, anything, that might help her understand the nature of the redoing. But if she was honest, there was a part of her that hoped desperately to fail. After all, if no such research existed, then Elliott had been telling the truth. She'd know then that Elliott was still on her side, that he really wanted to help her.

A few hours later, Marti found her sitting cross-legged amid several massive stacks of books that encircled her. Keira flipped through each of them, having neither the energy nor the patience to summon her pneuma to guide her. She just wanted to *know*.

"Well, you certainly have been busy," Marti said. "What has you all in a *frenesí*?"

"Someone tipped me off to look through old Legionnaire research. A friend of a friend said I'd find something on arrivals and the redoing—mentioned it might help . . ." Keira's voice trailed off as she remained transfixed on the text before her, blinking rapidly as the lines of ink blurred together.

"Really?" Marti exclaimed. "Well, you're in the wrong section entirely! They keep all of *our* students' research at the very top—the better for their authors to crow of their own achievements, yes?"

Keira blinked at her before snapping the book shut and tossing it to the side. Scrambling to her feet, she made a beeline up the twisting walkway and past the double-door entrance. Marti quickly caught up with her and led her to a finely decorated shelf midway up the ascending walkway. The spines of the books on this shelf were ornately decorated, though still with no visible titles. *Ridiculous*, Keira thought. But she closed her eyes, formulating in her mind's eye the most specific question she could muster.

Where is Elliott and Albert's research on arrivals and the redoing?

Her excitement grew as she felt the coiled pneuma in her stomach unravel. Placing two fingers lightly on the nearest spine, Keira felt the tiny thread of an answer begin to form, tugging her forward as her fingers traced over the gold embossing of the unnamed tomes.

Her fingers finally settled on one of the smaller books, and Keira's eyes fluttered open. Her breath hitched as she stared at the book, and there was a tightness in her chest, but whether from excitement or dread, she couldn't say. *Well, here goes nothing*, she thought, sliding the book from its dusty moorings and flipping through the first few pages.

As her eyes danced over the first few lines, the tightness grew until she could barely breathe, but still her eyes flicked compulsively over the words, barely comprehending their meaning.

"Well?" Marti asked.

Keira met her bright eyes with her own blank stare and swallowed.

"Is it what you were looking for?" Marti pressed.

Keira could only nod as the book's meaning sank in. This truly changed everything.

CHAPTER

THIRTEEN

876 Common Era (C.E.)

"Legionnaire," Tammy growled, eyeing the young man across the table with menace, "drop the roll."

Her companion laughed and went to toss it to her before yanking it back at the last second, taking a large bite from its side. Tammy lunged for him, and they both ended up in a heap on the floor, drawing curious stares from the rows of Bellators lining the makeshift mess hall.

Danny snorted, shaking his head, though he eyed the two with growing interest. Fitz was a Legionnaire who'd arrived with a larger group the week before in anticipation of the capital's naming ceremony. Tammy and Fitz had become fast friends, on account of their shared love for mocking the many oddities of the Bellatorio. Between his English sensibilities and her California sentiments, their mocking left no Bellator unscathed. But glancing over at their laughing tangle of limbs, Danny couldn't help but wonder if there was something more growing between them.

He quickly cast his gaze back to the bowl of stew in front of him as Tammy met his searching look with narrowed eyes. Something told him she wouldn't take kindly to his observations.

They'd been in the capital, still little more than a run-down fishing village, for over a week as they waited for the supposed naming ceremony to take place. They'd arrived to find Legionnaires from across the country already gathered. Unfortunately, the crown prince and future Regio Magnus's ship had been detained by weather and the threat of pirates off the southwest coast. So, in the interim, they'd had scant little to keep themselves occupied. As if to punctuate that sentiment, Tammy and Fitz suddenly broke into a loud argument on the merits of rye versus wheat bread.

Danny took that as his cue to go to bed.

"So, Danny, is it really true you arrived from the future?" Fitz's voice was casual, but the gleam in his eye betrayed a keen interest.

Danny hesitated before nodding.

"I've never met a Legionnaire who'd traveled between times in the same world. Quite intriguing."

"It's apparently pretty rare," Danny muttered, shifting uncomfortably under Fitz's scrutiny. He didn't enjoy talking about the future, especially not with Tammy listening intently to every word. "The High Council just said there must have been something drawing me to this particular time, something Pneumos needs me to do. But whatever it is . . ." He shrugged. "I got nothin'."

Fitz nodded, rubbing a hand thoughtfully across his chin. Danny seized the opportunity to get to his feet—bowl in hand. "Well, I'd best be off. Early day tomorrow. And I promised the

Imperator I'd act as secretary for his meeting with some Marian politician."

Fitz snorted. "Excellent use of your skills, I'm sure."

Danny shrugged. In truth, he'd been going a bit stir-crazy and so had jumped at the chance to do something—anything other than sit around and listen to Tammy and Fitz's flirtatious bickering. He waved a hand. The two of them barely acknowledged him, though, already onto a new debate—this one seemingly about the martial merits of Bellatori unit formations versus Cross-Sea lone operators.

It was as Danny was depositing his dishware in the collection bin that he saw her. She was tall for an uplander, her flaming red hair tied back in a low bun as she cleared the empty tables. When she glanced up, her freckled face caught the light, and suddenly she was someone else.

"Maggie," Danny breathed.

And suddenly he was moving toward her. It wasn't her. He knew it wasn't her. His youngest sister had been barely fourteen when he'd left home, but he still remembered those green eyes of hers filling with tears as she buried her face in his shoulder. He shook his head to clear it.

The girl didn't see Danny approach, but he watched with wry amusement as she pocketed the leftovers from the abandoned, still half-full plates.

"Pretty hungry there, are we?" he said mildly.

The girl nearly jumped out of her skin, rounding on him with the look of a rabbit caught in a snare, eyes darting to the side as she rolled onto the balls of her feet. Danny quickly raised his hands in what he hoped was a reassuring gesture. "I'm not here to get you in trouble," he blurted. "I just want to talk."

Clearly mistaking his meaning, the girl stiffened. The look she gave him was one of abject fear mixed with steely resolve.

She was clearly ready to fight him if she had to. But Danny could see the sharp angle of her cheekbones, the way her dress fell loosely over her narrow shoulders. She really was hungry— too hungry. As she inched away, Danny felt a rising sense of panic bloom in his stomach. Reaching into his pocket, he scooped out the cloth-wrapped sweetmeats he'd been saving for later and offered them to her. She eyed them suspiciously.

"Please," Danny said, hating the pleading note in his own voice. "Take it. I know what it is to go hungry."

The girl's eyes flitted from the food to Danny's face, an unmistakable gleam of yearning there, and Danny could practically hear her stomach growling.

Slowly, ever so gently, the girl reached for the sweetmeats, keeping her eyes fixed on Danny as she did. He stayed absolutely still, careful not to spook her further. Her fingers brushed his as she took the cloth bundle, only for an instant, but Danny felt a shiver race up his spine. He stepped back reflexively, and the girl's pale green eyes narrowed in suspicion, her fingers squirreling the food away into the hidden pockets of her dress. She glanced up at him and then away, shifting her weight awkwardly. Danny stared at her, watching as a stray copper-colored lock of hair fell from her low bun. He'd swear he'd never seen this girl in his life, but there was something about her that seemed so familiar.

"It's not for me," the girl murmured, glancing around the mess hall. "It's for my mother and my little brother. They've not 'ad a proper meal in weeks, not since . . ." Her voice trailed off and her freckled cheeks flushed crimson, clearly realizing exactly who she was speaking to so boldly. "Anyhow, I thank you for your kindness, sir," she said crisply.

Danny shrugged, finally clearing the knot from his throat. "I know what it is to stand by with nothin' to do but watch those you love starve." Danny shook his head, thinking about those lean years when the Depression first hit Boston, not long after his father's death. It had been up to him then, to leave school and work in his uncle's grocery so his mam and sisters could eat. He knew all too well the hunger that could drive someone to thievery. "I wouldn't begrudge anyone the unwanted scraps from a table."

The girl continued to stare at him, her eyes still narrowed in suspicion, but with something else flitting under the surface, a curiosity churning up questions she likely didn't dare voice. He couldn't say exactly what it was about her, why he felt so drawn to her, so protective. Maybe it was because she reminded him of the girls he'd grown up with, back in Boston's South End. Something in the eyes, filled with a scrappy boldness that came from hard times and gumption.

"Here," Danny said finally, pulling a few coins from his pockets. "Make sure everyone's got full bellies for the night." He dropped the coins into the girl's outstretched palm, watching as the whites around her eyes widened and she glanced between the coins and him before stashing them in her pocket.

"And next time, I'd focus on the flagstaff mess—that's where all the highest-rankin' Bellators get their grub. There'll be roasted meats and puddings galore sent back to the galley barely touched." Danny shrugged. "Their loss, I say."

The girl shook her head in disbelief. "Hobnobbed downlanders. I'll never understand 'em." She glanced up at Danny warily then. "No offense intended, sir."

Danny waved a hand breezily. "None taken. I'm not from around these parts, so you certainly won't offend me. I'm Danny, by the way, Danny O'Leary."

The barest hint of a smile crossed the girl's thin lips, and she responded. "I'm called Moira, Moira Foléan."

Danny smiled broadly, feeling lighter than he had in a long time. "Well, it's a pleasure to meet you, Moira. I have a feeling we're gonna be great friends."

Moira cocked her head at him slightly, frank curiosity warring with something far more mischievous. "Maybe so, Danny O'Leary . . . if you should be so lucky."

Danny laughed outright, and Moira's smile widened. "I must be goin'," she said, "but I thank you for the coin, and the advice. I'll surely be taking it."

Danny nodded in acknowledgment, watching as she turned to finish gathering up the used dishes and headed for the galley. He could feel a warmness spreading through his breastbone as she left, leaving him happier than he'd been in days.

"ABSOLUTELY NOT."

Imperator Titus Longus's eyes narrowed, and Danny felt himself tense as he felt the Imperator shift almost imperceptibly, squaring off against Mauricen. To his credit, the diminutive diplomat ignored the gesture, merely circling around the desk to riffle through the stack of papers that lay there—clearly refusing to be intimidated.

"The Emperio has made his wishes perfectly clear," he declared in a voice that brooked no dissent. "The young prince Magnus's wedding is set for the spring, and His Imperial Highness is determined that Loren's new Regio—and his favorite son—have a ruling seat of power before then. Construction on the royal palace will move ahead *as scheduled*."

"We're *trying* to fight an insurgency here," the Imperator growled. "It's bad enough with this horse-and-pony show of a naming ceremony, but you want to give them another target? And a lucrative one, at that."

"What's wrong, Imperator? Can't handle a rowdy bunch of peasants? I expected more from the Empire's legendary Eastern Imperium."

Danny caught the burn of red creeping up Titus's collar, and he quickly intercepted. "The Vindolum will attract the Empire's wealthiest and most powerful leaders, not to mention foreign dignitaries. You're just asking for an attack if you move ahead with this plan."

Mauricen snorted. "*Wealthiest and most powerful?* Please, boy, we're still talking about the Lorenan backwater here. It will be some years before they're attracting anything of the sort. No, the Marian Empire will not be cowed by a lot of sniveling river people. They will submit to our rule, or they will be punished."

Exasperated, Danny shot a glance to Titus, who was gritting his teeth, a muscle working in his jaw. Danny opened his mouth to try again, but a quick shake of Titus's head warned him off.

"Very well, sir," Titus said through clenched teeth. "I'll see to the needed security detail."

Mauricen smiled smugly in reply, eyes shining at the surprise victory as he bent to gather up his things. Straightening, he leveled them with a beatific smile. "I knew I could count on you, Titus. Oh, and one more thing. The Imperial Librarian has arrived from the capital and is requesting aid unloading his supplies, a security detail . . ." His voice trailed off with a wave of his hand, as if the details of such things lay far beneath his concern.

"A librarian?" Titus asked in disbelief.

"Why, of course. The Empire takes the education of its citizens to be a top priority—even barbaric river people. Perhaps especially them," he added, wrinkling his nose toward the uplander boy who pushed open the door to clear the plates. To his credit, the boy didn't flinch, didn't even raise his gaze from the dishes he gathered, but Danny felt his own lip curl as his ears burned with anger.

"I'll leave you to it then, Titus," Mauricen said finally. "Long live the Empire!"

"Long live the Empire!" Titus replied, thumping his forearm to his chest in salute as Mauricen swept from the room in a flurry of robes. Only his thick perfume lingered, curdling in Danny's nostrils.

"A library," Titus said, shaking his head. "Because that's *precisely* what you build in a war zone. Spare me from the idiocy of politicians, O'Leary. I swear they'll be the death of me." The disgust lay heavy in his voice, and Danny nodded in agreement. It had surprised him to hear the Imperator was to be recalled back to the capital. But apparently the formalities of a naming ceremony were of more pressing concern to the Empire than the siege against the last Lorenan bulwark of Ulgáris—the conclusion of which they'd already deemed inevitable.

"I'm getting too old for this," Titus muttered, heaving himself into the chair with an audible groan. Danny surveyed him curiously. The Imperator couldn't have been over forty, but already he moved with the stiffness of an old man. The long years on various campaigns and battlefields had clearly taken their toll.

"Do you ever—" Danny hesitated, weighing his words. He liked the Imperator well enough and enjoyed working with him, but the sting of his harsh practicality back in Ulgáris was still fresh. "Do you ever wonder if it's worth it? The fighting, I mean. Is the Marian Empire any better off? Why not just leave countries like Loren be?"

Titus's eyes narrowed as he considered the question.

"Just between us, O'Leary, I often wonder the same thing."

Danny blinked in surprise, taken aback by the Imperator's candor.

"But you and I are cut from the same cloth, O'Leary. Duty, honor, loyalty. Those things are paramount. Without them, who are we? No one. And all we've done, the sacrifices we've made, they mean nothing."

Danny swallowed, watching as Titus rubbed a weary hand over his face, bloodshot eyes staring deep into the flickering flames of the fireplace. A long moment passed, and Danny searched for something to lighten the mood, to ease the burden he saw painted so clearly on the Imperator's face.

"I'll handle the library detail, sir. I'll gather the men, and we'll build the best damn library the old goat's ever seen."

Titus blinked at him in surprise, then chuckled. "Good lad, O'Leary. One less thing for me to handle."

CHAPTER

FOURTEEN

242 Marian Era (M.E.)

It was several more days before Elliott returned to the Legion headquarters. Raina broke the news to Keira.

"He came in last night," she explained, nervously fiddling with her shell necklace. "We only be hearing the news this morning."

By "we," Keira knew she meant herself and Marti, who Raina had taken to tailing the last few days whenever Keira refused to leave the library. Keira often spied the worried glances they shot each other when they thought she wasn't looking. She refused to be bothered by it, though, not when she still had so much left to do.

Keira snapped shut the thesis she'd read cover to cover twice and got to her feet, hands resting on the mahogany desk before she straightened and turned to leave. This conversation was long overdue.

She found Elliott in the main study, just off the entry rotunda, and wasted no time in striding up to him. She was

139

practically shaking with anger, and she had to focus on holding her voice steady as she asked, "Can I speak with you, Elliott?"

Elliott, who'd beamed when he'd seen her enter, waving her over excitedly, now wore a look of confusion, his brow furrowed in worry at her expression.

"Of course, Keira. Whatever's the matter?"

"You—you lied to me," Keira forced out through gritted teeth. "*That* is what's the matter."

Elliott's face blanched. Nodding slowly, he gestured to an open side door. Working to keep her breath steady, Keira obliged, feeling the weight of curious eyes on her back as she left.

Elliott closed the door gently, leaving them alone in a small antechamber to the study, its walls lined with books and ancient oil paintings. The scowling faces depicted would have intrigued her if not for the boiling rage that threatened to overflow from her chest. She rounded on Elliott.

"Well? What do you have to say, then?"

Elliott tucked his hands in the front pockets of his green robe as he regarded her coolly. "I take it you spoke with Albert." A note of bitterness crept into his voice at the name, and Keira crossed her arms, staring him down.

"I did. Apparently, my new mentor is more truthful than my last."

Elliott gaped at her, looking as if she'd slapped him. Keira shook off the twinge of guilt. *It's true*, she thought. *And he deserves it.*

Elliott sighed, rubbing his face with one hand, and Keira couldn't help but note the deep shadows under his eyes and the haggard look that hung from the hollows of his cheekbones. She wondered briefly what he'd been up to these last few days but didn't feel inclined to inquire.

"You have to understand, Keira. The research that Albert and I conducted was a long time ago, and quite frankly ill-advised. Nothing good came of what we found, and it only fueled further obsession. Albert took that bit of knowledge, twisted it for his own purposes, and—"

"What are you talking about?" Keira demanded, appalled. "Is this about Nazor? Albert told me about the three of you, how you were both in love with her. Is that what fueled this absurd rivalry between you two?"

Elliott snorted. "Is that what he told you?" His words turned bitter as he added, "I don't doubt his feelings, though. Albert always did want whatever was just out of reach. But to suggest we had any sort of rivalry . . . He's just trying to manipulate you, Keira."

"Honestly, Elliott, the only person I feel manipulated by is *you*." Keira watched Elliott flinch, and then the words came out all in a rush. "I've read through it, Elliott—twice. And it's incredible! You detailed exactly how you believe the redoing occurs—how it must take place at either the spring or fall equinox, when day and night are balanced and the space between worlds is thinnest. You talked about ancient artifacts acting as conduits for pneuma, taking the place of grounders to channel whatever chaos surrounds it into the highest form of order—a human person! How can you say that's nothing?"

With every word she spoke, Elliott seemed to deflate, until finally he sank into a chair, holding his head in his hands. She stared at him, unable to understand how he couldn't see the value of what he'd contributed. With this knowledge, she could bring Danny back! She *knew* she could. All that remained was to find the location of this conduit and find a way to implement the channeling techniques before the equinox.

"Keira," Elliott murmured, steepling his hands around his

mouth and nose, "our *research* only peddled in theories, vague suspicions buoyed by ancient texts with unclear translations. We thought we knew *how* the redoing could be channeled—summoning the arrivals when chaos was at its peak. But we had no idea *why*."

Keira blinked at him. *Why?*

"Arrivals come to join the Legionnaires in their fight against chaos," she recited slowly, the familiar words sliding into each other as she watched Elliott shake his head sadly.

"That is why the Legion exists, why it does what it does. That does not answer why certain people are chosen to be redone, why they arrive one place and not another—honestly, why they come at all!" Elliott exhaled sharply and hurled himself out of his chair, striding to brace his hands against the windowsill.

"In your reading of that book, Keira, did you happen to notice that nothing was said of the Legion having any control over the matter?"

Keira's mouth snapped shut, and she gritted her teeth, refusing to give him the answer he already knew.

"The redoing occurs with no effort on our part, Keira. So the question remains, *why*. If none of us incited the redoing, then it must have been a power far greater than our own, Pneumos even, and she must have a *reason*."

"Does it matter?" Keira demanded, striding around the chair to face him at the window. "Who cares why these things occur naturally? What matters is how we *use* what we know!"

Elliott turned to face her, arms crossed and a glint in his eye. "And how, exactly, do you plan to use this, Keira? *Healing*?"

From the angled way he said the word, Keira knew he didn't believe it for an instant. She opened her mouth to reply, but nothing came out.

"Now who's been lying to whom?" he asked quietly, giving her a look of such utter sadness and disappointment that she had to look away. Staring at the ground, Keira focused on her breathing, squeezing her eyes shut to fight the stinging sensation.

"You can't bring him back, Keira," Elliott said quietly.

Her eyes snapped open, and she leveled him with a glare. "Says who?" His lips pressed into a thin line, but she barreled on, ignoring him. "I've had it up to here with the Legion telling me what I can and can't do, Elliott. Where were they when Gaius died slowly and painfully, when Sara was murdered, when Nazor died to *save* me, when Danny—" Keira's voice broke, and she blinked away the blurring of Elliott's face. "I've lost too many people to give a damn what the Legion or *Pneumos* or anyone else wants. Danny was the best of us, Elliott, and he deserves to live. So if there's a way that I can bring him back, then *nobody*—not you, and certainly not the Legion—is going to stop me."

Elliott gazed at her with a contorted look on his face, an odd mixture of grief, pity, and something else entirely—*fear*, maybe? The look made icy fingers race down her spine. But she didn't back down, leveling him with the same determined glare she reserved for every barrier that had ever stood in her way.

"You really are *so* like him . . ." Elliott murmured quietly, his voice sounding far away, as if lost in a sea of memory.

Keira blinked, no idea which *him* he was referring to but determined not to give him the satisfaction of asking.

Elliott blinked then, rolling his shoulders as if shrugging off something heavy as he offered her a pinched look. "I know you're hurting, Keira. We've all lost so much. If this is what you're determined to do, then I won't try to stop you." Excitement bloomed in Keira's chest at his words but was quickly extinguished as he continued, "But this path you're on is not one in which I can join you. And it hurts me, Keira, it *kills* me even, because if it ends where I think it will, there will be no one left to save you from your fate."

The icy fingers of dread caught hold of Keira, and she stared at Elliott's grief-stricken face. She swallowed hard before opening her mouth to reply.

The sound of shouts and scraping chairs caught them up short, and they exchanged a confused look before racing through the study and out into the entry rotunda. There Keira found Cyrus, Raina, and Zipporah, all looking grim.

"I'm here to speak to the High Council," Cyrus said, his usually laughing eyes turned the steely gray that reminded Keira so much of his father. "There's word from the capital," he continued, "and it's not good."

THE FIVE OF them hurried to the dining hall to find the High Council already seated at the head table—the normal dining tables having vanished to make way for the crowd of Legionnaires that had already gathered. This was where they received guests from the outside world, those who were barred by custom or formality from entering the inner sanctum. A hushed murmur fell over the crowd as they found their seats, all eager not to miss whatever word had come from the capital. Keira shared their anticipation but couldn't help the kernel of dread at the thought of what it all might mean.

Was Landry all right? Had the People's Council fallen already? What if Junia had returned?

Questions raced through her mind, and she searched

Cyrus's face for any clue but was met only by his grim-eyed determination.

A High Council member banged a gavel, and silence descended like a cloak across the room. All eyes turned to Cyrus, and Keira watched as his Adam's apple bobbed nervously. He cleared his throat.

"Members of the High Council of the Legion of Pneumos, I come before you today as a representative of Regio Landrianus, the last reigning monarch of the Marian Empire, who seeks your assistance on a matter of some urgency." He paused, seeming to gather his thoughts, but was interrupted by a high-pitched voice.

Though Zoya's feet dangled a foot off the ground, the glint in her eyes was that of a world-wary adult. "Yes, yes, we know of the threat of chaos that has risen in the capital. We're assembling a team as we speak to assist. They should be ready by the end of the week."

"With all due respect, my . . . lady . . ." Cyrus blinked furiously, no doubt very confused that a child would speak with such authority. "But I'm afraid the threat has grown even since Keira last briefed you. We've received word from our intelligence network that there is now a credible threat against the life of the Regio—a plot to assassinate him that is already underway." Cyrus ignored the hushed murmuring that echoed around the room. "I'm afraid we don't have until the end of the week. I'll be leaving at first light tomorrow and humbly ask that Legionnaires be prepared to accompany me."

Silence fell as all eyes turned to the High Council, who turned to discuss quietly among themselves. Keira's mind raced. *An assassination attempt? Against Landry?* Her stomach roiled at the thought, and her chest tightened. Finally, the High

Council members straightened, and Zoya leaned forward to speak.

"Upon deliberation, we have concluded that it is impossible to move up the timeline of our planned cohort of Legionnaires. Too many of them are still out in the field and have yet to arrive."

Beside her, Keira felt Cyrus deflate. Her fingers twitched, itching to grab his hand, but she refrained, not wanting to make him seem weak before the council.

"And yet," the girl paused, eyes narrowing at Cyrus, who quickly straightened at the words, "we understand this matter to be of some urgency. Therefore, we are prepared to authorize a Legion escort for you, Master Flavius. They may begin the investigation and assist you by whatever means necessary until our cohort arrives. Councilman Albert will lead this escort but will need volunteers who wish to accompany him."

Keira's eyes shot to Albert, who looked serene at the end of the table, and she felt Elliott stiffen beside her. Albert leaned forward slightly, asking, "Do I have any volunteers?" Albert's gaze met hers and he smiled slightly, an open invitation. Keira glanced from him to Elliott, whose eyes were full of warning.

Indecision warred within her. Albert had offered to train her and clearly knew enough about the redoing to help her get Danny back. Meanwhile, Elliott had said himself that he refused to get involved. Yet though she was still furious with Elliott for deceiving her, she couldn't shake his warning about Albert. Could she trust him? And then there was Cyrus, whose eyes she could feel boring into the back of her skull. He needed her help, as did Landry. But was she really ready to return to the viper nest that was Crîd Eálas? Beside her, Raina looked thrilled —clearly delighted at the prospect of seeing her brother. Keira's chest tightened further at the thought of saying goodbye to the girl, and she decided she wasn't ready just yet. She'd see Raina safely to the capital and into her brother's care.

"I volunteer to join the escort," she announced loudly. At her words, she saw Elliott's eyes close and his shoulders sag. Though guilt pricked at her, she ignored him. She'd made her choice.

"As do we," announced a low, silky-smooth voice—Zipporah. Beside her stood Marti, and Keira wondered briefly where she'd come from. She was pleased, though, happy to not have to say goodbye to her new friend, even if it meant tolerating her obnoxious grounder.

"Very well," the councilwoman said. "The three of you will accompany Councilman Albert to the capital as escort to Master Flavius, there to begin your investigation and await further instructions from the arriving cohort. I suggest you ready your things for departure at first light."

Her words had an air of dismissal, and she banged her gavel in further confirmation, releasing the gathered Legionnaires, who erupted in excited murmurs as they filed out of the room. Yet instead of leaving, Albert made straight for them, smiling serenely at Elliott as he said, "Good to see you, old friend. Though I daresay you have looked better. Tramors acting up again, I suppose?"

Elliott leveled Albert with a narrow-eyed glare but said nothing.

Chuckling, Albert turned to Keira. "Glad to have you join us. I daresay we'll have plenty of time to get to know each other on the journey—and much to be *learned*, I'm sure."

Keira's eyes darted between her two mentors, not knowing what to say and feeling torn. She was saved from answering as Albert pivoted on his heels, fluttering a hand as he announced, "See you tomorrow, then!"

Keira turned to Elliott, searching for something, anything, to say but coming up woefully short. It was Elliott who said only, "Travel safely, Keira. Take care of each other, and trust in Pneumos. She *will* guide you."

Keira opened her mouth to thank him, to apologize, to reconcile, but before Keira could respond, he, too, turned and departed, leaving her with only his words and the gnawing sensation of guilt. But there was something else as well—a blooming excitement in her chest. *I'm coming, Danny,* she thought, and for the first time, he seemed truly within her reach.

CHAPTER

FIFTEEN

Keira and the rest of Cyrus's cohort had been traveling for two days before she finally got up the nerve to talk to Albert. She couldn't say why she was avoiding him, only that Elliott's warning still rang in her ears, curse him. She couldn't help but be on her guard around the older Legionnaire. For his part, Albert didn't push the question, not once bringing up his earlier offer to help her train.

But by the third day, Keira was determined to make the most of the opportunity. So, steeling her resolve, she kneed her horse forward to ride beside Albert.

"So—umm, I found that research you mentioned."

Albert turned bright eyes on her, a broad smile on his face. "Oh, really? Well, I do hope you found it helpful."

"It was *really* helpful, actually. I—I was wondering if I might ask you a few questions about it."

"Of course! I'm happy to share what I remember. Although it *was* quite a long time ago, you know."

Keira nodded, steadying her own excitement as she racked her brain to decide where, exactly, she should even start. "So, from reading, it definitely sounds like the arrival process is connected in some way to healing pneumonancy." Albert nodded intently, eyes locked on hers. "So does that mean that someone has to physically *construct* the arrival—their body, I mean?"

Albert's lips pursed, and he regarded her thoughtfully. "I had the very same question myself. But in all our investigations, we could find no one in the many Legion headquarters that stretch across the countries of this world who would admit to doing so. They could be lying, of course." He shrugged, clearly unsurprised by the idea. "People lie—it's just their way. But in this case, it's hard to imagine what motivation they might have for hiding the truth. So we concluded that the most likely explanation was that the process was performed by someone *outside* this world."

"Like Pneumos?" Keira breathed, voice catching in her excitement.

Albert snorted before offering her a wry smile. "If you believe in that sort of thing."

Keira blinked at him, surprised. Elliott and Nazor had always spoken of Pneumos with such reverence. While Keira couldn't say if Pneumos was so much a *person* as a *force*, she'd assumed that everyone in the Legion held similar awe and respect for the deity.

Albert must have seen her shock, because he chuckled. "These days, Elliott puts a lot of stock in old stories meant to scare children into knowing right from wrong. I, however, still maintain *my* scholarly standards. I believe in facts and logical explanations." He pursed his lips. "Are you familiar with Occam's Razor, Keira?"

She nodded slowly. "The simplest explanation is usually the right one."

"Exactly. Now, you tell me, which is more likely, that a magical deity exists above all worlds, dabbling in the most minute happenings of our daily lives to hold the universe in some divine cosmic balance between order and chaos? *Or* that there is merely someone within the Legion or another organization who uses something akin to healing pneumonancy—a skill we already know to be possible, thanks to you—to save someone from death and grow the ranks of our beloved Legion?"

Keira shifted awkwardly at his sarcastic tone, not knowing how to respond, or even where her opinion fell on the question she had posed. She was a scientist, yes, but since her arrival in Loren, so much had caused her to question her most basic assumptions that she sometimes wondered if the universe truly was as knowable as she'd always assumed. She shook her head, deciding it wasn't worth the mental effort.

"I honestly don't know, Albert. I just want to learn these skills and how to better control them. You know, so I can—can help people," she finished lamely, catching herself just in time.

Albert arched a single eyebrow, regarding her with amusement. "Don't you mean so you can save your grounder—Danny, I think his name was?"

Keira's mouth fell open, and she quickly snapped it shut, panic welling within her. How had he known? Would he try to stop her? Had she really just given herself away, after coming so far?

Albert laughed aloud at her expression. "Calm yourself, dear girl. I've had my suspicions for a while, you know. It's not every day someone stumbles across healing pneumonancy and then immediately barrels their way into Legion headquarters, desperate to learn how to use it, merely to *help people*." He waved a hand vaguely in the air. Then his eyes softened, and he added, not unkindly, "I'm not a fool. I know what you've lost, what serving the Legion has cost you. I do not blame you for wanting to recover just a piece of the happiness you once had."

Keira swallowed the lump that had been building in her throat and blinked away the stinging that had come to the corners of her eyes.

"Elliott said it was *unnatural*," she said, voice twisting around the word. "That the effort would destroy me and everyone I care about."

Albert snorted. "Again, Elliott pays too much heed to nonsense fairy tales, holding ridiculous concepts such as *fate* and *destiny* in far too high regard. He *used* to be a scientist, you know." Albert's tone had taken on almost a sneering tone but then turned morose. "But again, that was a very long time ago."

He gave her a half smile then, and Keira felt something inside stir at the kind look in his eyes. "I don't think there's anything *unnatural* about what you want, Keira. In fact, I think it's the most natural thing in the world to yearn to save those we love."

They rode on in silence, a buoyancy filling Keira's chest that she hadn't felt in months. *This could really work,* she thought. *I can really bring him back.*

As THEY RODE through the central plains, Keira couldn't help but admire the surrounding landscape—the vast expanse of open prairie with the sea far to the east and the epic Lorenan mountain range sprouting across the horizon to the west, its snow-capped peaks shining in the midday sun. Raina rode beside Keira most days, quickly becoming used to the horse that had at first made her eyes go wide. She'd certainly seen horses before, but riding them was another matter entirely. While the islanders of the Southern Shield traded in horseflesh, mostly to the Bellatorio and foreign traders, most individuals still preferred the sure reliance of their own two feet. Raina had bravely squared her shoulders, though, letting Keira help her onto the animal's back even as her face paled at the shifting of the saddle beneath her. Two days later, and she already looked like a pro.

"Tell me more about the capital, Keira," Raina begged again, eyes shining in delight at the thought of her new home.

Keira couldn't help a small smile at her excitement, though she snorted aloud. "I've described every nook and cranny to you by this point. What more is there?"

"True-true," Raina conceded, "but tell me more about the people—what they be like. Be they waking up every morning with smiles and hope or dragging themselves through each day? Be they—" She paused, uncertain, before barreling on with a look of determination. "Be they hating those who be different —just because?"

Keira's eyes softened as she gazed over at the girl, still only eleven, though she looked even younger. Her impossible hopes gleamed like live coals in her eyes. Keira sighed, thinking about the uplanders and downlanders and their centuries-long feud.

"Raina," she began, mind churning as she sifted through how to break the news. "Wherever you go, there will always be people who can't see past the differences. Whether it's skin color, where you come from, the clothes you wear, the way you speak, or yes—even your eyes, there will always be those who try to separate and those who try to unite." Though Raina had let her hair fall in a curtain over her face, Keira could see her eyes blinking furiously. "But that's not on you, Raina. All you can do is be the best version of you, and everyone else can honestly go to hell."

Raina nodded, still staring at her saddle, and Keira reached over to grab her hand, squeezing it lightly. To her surprise, the usually prickly Raina squeezed it back, finally meeting her eye with a watery gaze and a small smile that was like thorns digging into Keira's heart. She quickly let go, careful not to let her own smile falter.

"All right then, *dinué*, go bug Marti for a while. Tell her it's been ages since she told you a good Legion story."

Raina nodded, spurring her horse to a trot, and Keira couldn't help but snort as the girl bounced about on its back, clinging to the saddle like a lifeline.

A low chuckle from behind her made Keira jerk around to see Zipporah's mount amble into place beside her own. Keira tensed, ready for whatever insult Zipporah deigned to cast her way. But the taller girl only looked bemused as she watched Marti and Raina—already engaged in animated conversation. The diminutive Marti sat little taller than Raina, but the sun's rays seemed to reflect off her short, bright-red curls—flounced about by her horse's gait. From the looks of it, Marti had willingly complied with Raina's request and was now engaged in an animated rendition of some ancient Legion legend—no doubt gleaned from Marti's long hours spent digging through the amalgam's reserves.

"They're well-suited, you know." Zipporah's silky voice beside her made Keira start, and she glanced over to see Zipporah still watching Marti and Raina. "They've both lost so much and yet still cling to the joy in life with a fervor. It's really quite remarkable."

Keira's brow furrowed as she watched Marti, with her

bouncing red curls, seemingly so light and carefree. What had she lost? What pain did she carry buried deep within her?

"What happened?" she asked, not expecting Zipporah, of all people, to tell her anything of the sort.

To her surprise, Zipporah met her gaze with a sharp look of her own and cocked her head, considering. "Marti told you she was from Argentina, didn't she?" Keira nodded, blushing slightly as she realized exactly how *little* she knew of Argentina's history.

"She lived—and died—during the period known as the Dirty War, in the early 1980s, I believe. It was *well* after my time, you see. Her sister was one of the *desaparecidos*, those made to 'disappear' by the government for their dissenting political beliefs. Well, naturally, Marti tried to find her. She was a budding journalist, you see, though one who belonged in a library rather than on the streets of a fascist state. They killed her for her efforts, and the rest of her family." Zipporah said this all so matter-of-factly that Keira couldn't help but gape at her—eyes darting between Zipporah's stone-eyed stare and Marti's ready grin, her head thrown back in peals of laughter at something Raina had said. Raina, too, smiled brightly, despite all she'd lost—her parents, her grandmother, and her home. And still she seemed—happy... most of the time, at least.

"I-I didn't know," was all Keira could think to say.

Zipporah shrugged. "You wouldn't. Though I suppose you could have asked."

Keira's throat tightened as she realized how little she'd really gotten to know Marti, happy to accept the benefits of friendship with none of the true familiarity. *I'll do better*, she thought. When they made it to the capital, she'd get out of her own head and focus on the people around her. It's what Danny would do. He'd always been quick to make friends, caring deeply about each and every person he met and the story of their lives. Heat crept up from Keira's collar as she thought about what a terrible friend she'd been. What would Danny think of her if he could see?

"Before, you gave Raina some excellent advice," Zipporah observed mildly, breaking Keira's internal monologue.

Keira blushed, realizing she'd already broken her resolution to get out of her own head. "Did I?"

Zipporah's eyes were cool as she observed, "You told her she shouldn't concern herself with the limitations of feeble minds, but focus solely on that which is within her own power."

"Well, I'm not sure I said it *quite* that eloquently," Keira muttered, more heat rising from her collar.

"Regardless, you were right. Perhaps it's time to take your own advice." She said this with a slight arch of her eyebrow that immediately put Keira's teeth on edge. With an effort, she put her temper in check and waited expectantly for Zipporah to continue.

"We have all lost much, Keira. And I am not unappreciative of the pain you must feel for your sacrifice for the good of Loren." Zipporah said this stiffly, and Keira stifled a grin at her obvious discomfort. Compliments surely did not come easily to this warrior woman. "But the fact remains that it is time to put away your own self-indulgence. There are people relying on you now—people *I* care about. And I *refuse* to let them come to harm because you were too absorbed by your own self-inter-est." This came out in a half-snarl, and Keira was taken aback by the ferocity of Zipporah's statement. Her cheeks flushed, and she glared back.

"*I* care about these people too."

"Not as much as you care about *him*." Zipporah's eyes narrowed, and Keira felt her fingers go numb. Did *everyone* know about Danny? About her plans? So much for being covert about it. She started to argue, but Zipporah cut her off.

"Do what you must, Keira Altman, but do not sacrifice the family you have for the chance of saving the one you long for."

And with that, Zipporah spurred her horse forward to join Marti and Raina, leaving Keira behind to gape openmouthed at her retreating form.

THERE WERE times when Raina hated being small and going unnoticed, thought too young or too little to be worth listening to. But as she quietly slipped into the darkness around their camp after a long day of riding, she realized that being small may have its benefits after all.

The others wouldn't notice her absence, she felt sure. They were too busy whispering about the Legion's plans in the capital. Only she and Cyrus, as the lone nonmembers, had been excluded. He didn't seem to mind, happy to read his books and scratch away at whatever correspondence he was always working on. Raina had been angry and hurt to find herself on the outside of whatever plans and preparations they were making. But she'd quickly used the distraction to her advantage.

Silly grelún, she thought to herself as she silently slipped between the low-hanging branches.

She'd spotted the flashing light as they'd set up camp. Even in the dimming twilight, she'd been just able to make out the soft twinkle on the grassy knoll to the west of their camp. Raina had gripped hold of the shell on her necklace, feeling its warmth trickle in through her fingers, along with a nearly overwhelming sense of . . . peace, stability. There was something there, and she *had* to find out what it was.

As Raina slithered through the long grass that rose nearly above her own head, she remembered back on Tibolé when she'd asked her grandmother about the necklace. Marné had smiled that distant look she always got when asked about the various mysteries that seemed to encircle Raina's life—the way the village children looked at her, how they taunted her for the seafoam eyes that to them marked her obviously as *grelún*-born, how she'd learned to slip past them into shadow. How many times had she returned home sobbing, collapsing into Marné's lap as the old woman gently stroked her hair, crooning softly? She'd demand stories of her parents, then—her mother, who she could remember only in fractured images and half-forgotten lyrics, and her father, who she had no memory of at all. To her relief, Marné had assured her again and again that they'd both been one of the Udánma, and that she belonged there. The necklace itself had been her mother's, and Marné assured her it would never lead Raina astray.

She'd never parted with it since, and its presence warmed her, as if her own mother's beating heart pressed against her own. Whenever she was afraid, it reassured her. And when she was angry, it tried to calm her—though with limited success. Unfortunately, it also had led her into some less-than-ideal situations, as she'd followed its pulsing heat into trouble time and again. In fact, it had been the necklace that had led her onto Cyrus's ship—instead of the one Akamu had been ready to sail on. Raina shook her head. Whoever or whatever spoke to her through the necklace, they sure had a sense of humor.

As she neared the base of the grassy knoll, Raina's footsteps slowed, and she moved purposefully, careful to avoid the various holes and mounds that made up the hill's base. Using foot- and handholds she knew others could never see, Raina scrambled up the hill, ignoring the flecks of dirt that showered onto her face. At the top of the hill, she paused, taking in the surrounding landscape, painted deep shades of blue and purple by the settling dusk. There was no sign of the flashing light she'd spotted earlier, and she absently squeezed the shell necklace, reassured by its continued pulsing heat.

What you be wanting me to see? she asked it silently.

The sound of skittering rock behind her made Raina spin on her heel, mouth falling open in terror at the leering face before her.

"And who do we have here?" the man asked. His voice was cracked and rough, as if the words were barked through sandpaper rather than vocal cords. But that wasn't what terrified Raina. Her fear sprang solely from the spiraling tattoo that curled in an arching diagonal across his face and the milky, opaque eye that shone from amid the blackness.

Raina screamed.

CHAPTER
SIXTEEN

242 Marian Era (M.E.)

"It's not worth it," Zipporah snarled quietly.

Albert didn't flinch from the biting words, only steepled his fingers thoughtfully, regarding the parchment before him, the letter he'd been crafting to send back to the Legion.

"I understand your concerns," he murmured, "but if the Legion's forces aren't able to reach the capital in time, we may find we have no other option."

For once, Keira kept her mouth clamped shut, eyes darting between the two of them. They'd been at this for an hour already, debating back and forth precisely how best to incorporate the promised Legionnaire reinforcements in the capital—how to support Landry without making it look like a hostile takeover.

While Zipporah favored a clear and decisive message, Albert was far more concerned with the chaos that such a show of force might yield. If so many already doubted Landry's good-

160

will in establishing a People's Council, the sudden arrival of pneumonancers to enforce his edicts would hardly help matters. Keira sighed, rubbing her eyes in exhaustion. She'd barely been able to sleep since first starting on the road, her thoughts racing between how best to help Landry and the mysteries of healing pneumonancy and how she might use it to bring Danny back. With every day that brought the equinox closer and every mile they took toward the capital, she seemed to feel his presence more strongly, the steady warmth of his tether beckoning her ever onward. In the end, though, these buzzing thoughts hadn't exactly lent themselves to restful sleep.

"We're limited by the agreement the High Council made with the Marians. We can't simply waltz—"

"That was centuries ago, Albert. Times have changed."

As Albert opened his mouth to argue once more, Keira heaved herself to her feet. They'd circled this wagon twice already, and she doubted they'd be making any more progress this evening. Zipporah and Albert barely noticed her leave, but Keira felt Marti's eyes on her—no doubt as exhausted as she by the back-and-forth.

Keira knelt by the bucket of water they'd fetched from the stream and ladled some of it onto her plate, scrubbing it down with practiced efficiency. She'd spent months in a Bellatori camp, after all. She was nothing if not field-trained. Her thoughts turned to the Southern Shield, and she wondered how the centurium was faring in her absence. Had they run into any more trouble with the marauders? She suspected—

A piercing scream cut through the night air, and Keira froze, her muscles locking before instantly propelling her to her feet, sword at the ready. Spinning around, she saw the others scramble for their own weapons. As her eyes scanned over them, something about the mental calculus didn't add up. Someone was—

Raina. Raina was missing.

"Raina?" Keira called, hearing the panic in her own voice. "Raina, where are you?" Icy fear slid down her spine as nausea twisted in her gut. She saw the others spinning around, looking for the young girl and whatever attackers loomed nearby.

Another cry—this time laced with pain as well as fear.

Then Keira was running.

Sprinting through the trees that surrounded their camp, Keira shoved away the branches that slapped at her face, her fingers inching toward the sword she'd mercifully kept strapped to her hilt.

"Raina!" Keira called, not caring in the slightest who—or what—else heard her. *Please be ok*, Keira's mind chanted. *I'm coming.*

There was no answering cry, so Keira angled herself toward where she thought she'd heard the scream. She wove through the tall grass, making for the hill that suddenly rose before her. Her aching muscles protested at their sudden use, but she squelched the sensation, some mixture of panic and adrenaline fueling her onward.

Distantly, she heard the others behind her, calling her name this time. She didn't stop.

Finally, reaching the base of the hill, Keira drew her sword with the singing trill of metal on metal. Scanning the hillside, she saw no one. Then her eyes suddenly lit upon scattered dirt and uprooted grass—signs of a struggle.

Deep grooves were cut into the hill's side, as if tiny heels had dug obstinately into the earth as they were dragged away. *Raina.* Whoever or whatever it was would take her somewhere less exposed, Keira decided. Human and animal alike knew the threat of exposure. So, slowing her breathing, her blade at the ready, Keira stalked around the hill.

The world was silent, even the birds having gone quiet, as if sensing the danger that lurked in the night. Keira felt beads of sweat trickle down her neck. Her eyes scanned the night, but there was no sign of Raina. Another wave of panic buoyed within her.

Where are you? she thought, desperation coloring the words in a silent plea.

And then she wasn't alone.

There's only one way to find out, Danny's voice replied.

Keira had no time to be surprised or feel relief at his sudden reappearance. Instead, she clenched her teeth, shaking her head at what he was proposing. *I can't. Not without you. I-I won't be able to get back.*

Yes, you will.

I'll leave my body vulnerable. Anything could sneak up on me.

It's the only way.

Though her bones sang out in fear at the idea, Keira knew Danny was right. It was the only way.

So, setting her mouth in a firm line, Keira crouched in the dirt. Digging her fingers deeply into the loose soil, she did all she could to ground herself, to form a tether that would guide her back. In the back of her mind, she felt Danny's pneuma wind around her, adding his calm reassurance to the grounding. She closed her eyes and found her pneuma, that tightly coiled ball of energy that lay just behind her stomach. She barely nudged it and felt it spring to life. *I missed you*, it seemed to whisper. *Where were you?* Keira smiled grimly to herself. *Lost.* Then she let out a long, high whistle and felt herself rise—up, up and out of her very body.

She was careful, keeping a tight grip on the willowy tether, so much looser than she remembered, even with Danny's spectral grounding. She couldn't think about that, *wouldn't* think about that. Instead, she surveyed the surrounding land, looking for any sign of that familiar spark of life, of Raina. At first, she felt nothing, and icy dread made her lips feel numb. Then a tiny glimmer caught her attention, nearly opposite her location on the far side of the hill.

It was too far to see, too far to know for sure. So after giving that tether a trembling tug, she pushed herself toward that glimmering spark. And as Keira's pneuma flowed over the hill, the scared girl took shape on its other side.

Raina was there, bound and gagged amid a camp of figures cloaked in black. There were at least ten, and Keira strained to get a better look, the tether to her body growing taut and thin. Then the face of one figure turned toward the fire, and Keira realized exactly who they were dealing with. If her pneuma had had a stomach, it would have dropped at the realization that these figures were, in fact, Worshippers of Séiro.

I thought they were gone, she thought. *Taken to the seas and the mountains after Junia fled and Landry took the throne.*

Apparently not all of them, Danny answered, his voice tense, and Keira sensed what felt like fury leaking off him.

There were too many, she realized. Too many for her to attack with just her pneuma alone. They were likely pneumonancers themselves, or whatever you could call their distortion of the Legion's practice. She couldn't risk it, couldn't risk getting trapped outside her body, leaving Raina alone.

So, making note of their position, Keira began reeling herself back into her body, ignoring the feeling of nausea that accompanied the motion, that sensation of having all the air squeezed out of her as she watched Raina's terrified eyes grow farther and farther away.

Keira slammed back into herself with a snap, barely catching herself before face-planting directly into the dirt. She sprawled on hands and knees for a moment, just catching her breath and letting relief wash over her. *I did it*, she thought. *I pulled myself back.*

You certainly did.

Then, remembering what she still had to do, Keira lumbered to her feet, bracing herself against a nearby tree as she let her eyesight adjust to her dark surroundings.

Sudden rustling to her right made her spin around, dropping into a slight crouch, blade at the ready. The rustling grew louder, footsteps pounding the ground, until a figure suddenly emerged from the darkness, steel-gray eyes glinting.

Keira sagged slightly. Cyrus.

"Did you find her?" he asked urgently, eyes scanning the clearing, as if Raina might be stumbling around just out of sight.

Keira nodded, gesturing to the other side of the hill. "Directly opposite our position. Looked to be at least ten of them. They—they're Worshippers of Séiro."

Cyrus's normally olive skin paled slightly, and he nodded once, not bothering to ask how she knew this. Instead he turned, placing two fingers in his mouth as he let out three quick whistles, two low followed by one high. A moment later, they were joined by the others, Zipporah, Marti, and Albert all bearing drawn swords and grim expressions. Keira quickly repeated her findings, and Zipporah was the first to speak.

"We split up, approach from both sides of the hill and one from above. We'll have a better shot of overpowering them that way."

Keira nodded, for once glad of Zipporah's confident air, realizing it had eased her own nerves. She turned to Albert. "What are Worshippers of Séiro still doing in these parts? And what on earth do they want with Raina?"

Albert only shook his head, expression dark and brooding. "There's no telling. We chased out the bulk of their forces after the revolt, but it would seem some slipped our grasp. As for what they want?" He shrugged. "It could be Raina merely happened upon them and they feared exposure."

Keira scowled. "I'll wring her neck if we get her back in one piece," she muttered, unable to hide the note of fear in her tone. Thankfully, the others didn't point it out.

Albert merely grimaced. "Zipporah and Marti, you take the route to the left. Keira and I will go around to the right. Cyrus, you take the top."

Cyrus nodded, readying his bow, fingers twitching toward the quiver of arrows on his back. Zipporah and Marti, too, nodded, and Keira could have sworn she felt the tether of pneuma between them strengthen as Zipporah's hand slipped around Marti's, their fingers interlacing. A shard of pain cut through Keira at the memory of her own grounder's steadying grip, the way Danny's calloused hands had squeezed her own, sending strength and encouragement as well as pneuma through the bond they'd shared.

I still can, Danny murmured. *We'll get her back, Keira.* She felt herself flooded then with a warm presence, the familiarity of it nearly bringing tears to her eyes.

The feel of another's gaze on her quickly snapped her out of her own thoughts, and she turned toward Albert, nodding.

"I'm no grounder," he said quietly, leveling Keira with an unsettling look that made her wonder precisely how much he knew. "But I can certainly provide some sort of tether if we run into trouble."

Keira nodded, grateful, and turned back to the others.

"Let's go get her."

THE COOL BLANKET of darkness settled even further as Keira and Albert slipped into position, crouching low behind the tall grass that obscured their side of the camp. Her initial scouting had been correct. There were indeed ten cloaked figures, and the firelight reflecting off their tattooed faces confirmed them to be Worshippers of Séiro.

Keira took a deep, steadying breath, remembering the last time she'd come face-to-face with their ilk, back in Gregür Gorge, and the ambush they'd walked straight into. Back then, the rogue pneumonancers had been hunting Landry, hoping to throw the realm into chaos by assassinating its fledgling heir. What could they possibly want here? Now?

Keira shook her head. There'd be time enough for those questions later. She scanned the camp, searching for the real reason they'd come. Then she saw her. Raina was bound and gagged, placed against a tree near the campfire—no doubt to ensure she didn't make a run for it. Not that she'd make it far, Keira thought, noting the thick ropes tied around her wrists and ankles. Keira's jaw tightened, and she fought down the raw fury that bubbled up within her as she saw the streaks of tears that cut a path through Raina's dirt-covered cheeks, her green eyes wide and terrified as they flitted between each of her captors.

Hold on, Raina, Keira thought fiercely. *We're here for you.*

A light touch on her elbow brought her attention back to Albert, who motioned toward the two cloaked figures nearest them. One stood, shaking out his legs as he warmed himself by the fire, while the other sat hunched over a bowl of gruel. His eyes drifted closed time and again, and he nearly face-planted twice into his food. Keira knew what to do.

Reaching toward the ground, she rooted herself as tightly as she had before, feeling a second, thin tether of pneuma spin off from Albert, latching onto her. He was right. Albert was no grounder, and the tether was far weaker than the firm binding Danny had always lent her—her partner, her grounder. Keira shook off the memory, focusing on the task before her as she gently nudged the ball of pneuma in her stomach, releasing it on a high-pitched whistle that coursed through the air. She felt herself rise—up, up, up, until she was hovering near the branches at the top of the clearing. She focused her keen mental eyes on the cloaked figure who stood near the fire and, with a swift change in tone, shot toward him.

Her pneuma hit him with a force like a battering ram, and she scrambled to find a foothold in his mind, careful to avoid that coursing stream of consciousness, lest she be dragged under.

He felt her presence immediately, and his own pneuma bucked and twisted beneath hers. She was out of practice, and the shock of impact, combined with his immediate resistance, threatened to dislodge her entirely. But she clung to him, sending tendrils of power deep within his body, swiftly binding those key bundles of nerves until, finally, she felt his muscles lock up as he crumpled to the ground.

Satisfied, she withdrew, only to feel chaos unfurling around her. All eyes had turned to the crumpled man, even as Albert leapt from the shadows, sword drawn and quickly buried in the back of the seated figure.

Flames immediately leapt from the hands of the eight remaining figures as objects exploded around the clearing.

Panicked, Keira reeled herself back toward her body, quickly respooling the tendrils of pneuma even as she heard Raina's terrified yet muted cry. Keira's pneuma met her body with a force that sent her sprawling backward in the grass. She scrambled to her feet, sword drawn in an instant as she charged forward.

Marti and Zipporah were already there—Zipporah's blade was drawn as she fought hilt-to-hilt with a tall woman, angling her body to shield Marti's crouched, muttering form. Marti's fingers grazed the dirt as earthen barricades shot up to shield Zipporah from the flames arcing toward her. In an instant, Keira was transported to another clearing, almost a year ago, when Elliott and Nazor had fought with similar unity, cantor and grounder in a lethal dance of blade and fire.

Keira shook her head, sprinting for the tree, where she saw Raina trying to crawl from the clearing, hands and feet still bound tightly. Keira was about ten yards away from her when she caught a lick of flame out of the corner of her eye. She turned just as a fireball barreled toward her.

She dropped. Her body pressed hard into the ground as the flames roared just above her.

She rolled—angling herself behind a boulder as she scrambled to her knees enough to spy two figures stalking toward her. Her gaze flitted to Raina, who had seen Keira sprinting toward her. Raina's eyes widened slightly, glassy with fear and still-unshed tears. Keira gritted her teeth, readying herself to sprint to the nearest tree.

But a motion to her left made her flatten to the ground as another inferno battered the boulder before her. She covered her head with her hands and cursed. She racked her brain for any memory of the earthworks Elliott had tried to teach her, the ones Marti had so clearly mastered. Keira had never been good at them, even with Danny's steadying presence. Still, it didn't look like she had much choice.

Keira dug her fingers deep into the soil, summoning the last of her strength reserves and funneling them deep into the earth.

A rustling to her left made her eyes flare open, to see Albert sprinting toward her, just as another fireball struck the boulder—the heat of it singeing her skin, even from her hiding place behind it.

Then Albert was there—not beside her, where he, too, could shelter, but in front of her, in front of the boulder she hid behind.

Keira sprang up, lunging for him—fully prepared to drag him down beside her. But the sight of an oncoming fireball made her freeze. Not run, not hide—freeze. And she knew this was it. Her number was up. As the fire barreled toward her, she thought only of Danny, of those green eyes that sparkled when he laughed, the sandy-blond hair always flopping into his eyes.

And then Albert was there, stepping in front of her, even as the fireball slowed in its arcing descent. Albert's arms were outstretched, and every muscle in his body tensed with effort as the flaming object seemed to cave in on itself, its flames curling and fizzling out until the branch or whatever it had been fell lightly to the ground.

Keira gaped at Albert. "H-how—? What—?"

He only shot an exhausted glance at her, and she could see the sweat dripping down his face.

"No time," he answered, gesturing behind her. "Get Raina!"

Keira swallowed and nodded, spinning on her heels as she sprinted toward the tree. But another figure stepped in her path.

Keira tensed, fingers gripping her sword more tightly as she slowed to assume a guard stance. The tall, powerfully built man in front of her was clearly not a pneumonancer—or else he'd spent all his power in the early minutes of this fight. No, his easy stance and grip on his two-handed longsword told her his skills were far more suited to the physical realm.

Keira glanced around at the other members of the cohort, all clearly engaged in fierce fights of their own. No, she was on her own this time.

Good, she thought. It had been ages since she'd had a good sword fight, and she could already feel the rage she'd kept tightly bottled up bubbling to the surface.

Easy, Danny murmured. *Remember why you're here.*

Keira shot a glance toward Raina, still trying to inchworm her way out of the clearing. Raina's wide eyes met hers, and Keira gave her a tiny nod of encouragement. *Get out of here*, she warned with her eyes. Raina's eyes again brimmed with tears, but she obeyed, using her bound feet to propel herself backward. Drawn by the motion, Keira's opponent's eyes flitted toward Raina, as if he might follow. Keira lunged forward. She'd draw his gaze, make him focus on her. But she drew up short as she blinked at the space where Raina had just been—no, where she still *was*. But where Raina had been inching away only moments before, there was now only a smudge of color, as if the light from the campfire had shot toward her and then somehow *bent*. Keira blinked furiously, but Raina didn't come back into focus. There was just that smudge, still inching backward across the ground.

"What on earth—" Keira didn't have time to finish that sentence as she glanced back to her opponent, just in time to see him lunge forward, sword jutting out in a skewering thrust. She barely managed to stagger back, batting his blade away even as she quickly recalculated the reach he had with that massive weapon. She'd have to be *very* careful—keeping out of his range while also getting in close enough to reach him with her much smaller blade.

Keira rolled her shoulders, dancing her feet slightly as her muscles readjusted.

You're out of practice, Danny said thinly, his judgment and annoyance flooding her mind.

She snorted. *Not exactly the time, Danny.*

He said nothing, but Keira could feel his worry simmering, almost *see* him sizing up the opponent before her.

She was too, eyeing his every move as he sent a few testing strikes her way—sizing up his speed, his strength.

He's slower than you, Danny said tersely. *Stronger, too, but if you can get around that blade—*

"Oh, is *that* all?" Keira hissed through gritted teeth as a particularly well-placed thrust made her lurch to the side, her blade arcing up just in time to parry the overhead cut. Her teeth chattered and arms went numb at the impact of the man's sword, and Keira staggered back, instantly on the defensive as he pressed forward. She sent a side slice curling up and over her head as the high-pitched shear of metal made her grind her teeth. Sensing she'd caught him off balance, Keira pressed her advantage, lunging forward only for the man to quickly sidestep her advance, the hilt of his blade coming down hard on her knuckles in a bone-crushing brace.

Keira cried out in pain as her blade went flying and a heavy fist caught the side of her jaw. She fell flat to the ground, only to have her head crunch against a rock that jutted up, knocking her neck back in an impact that sent her eyes rolling backward in her head. Darkness curled in from the edges of her vision as she rolled off the rock, now slick with blood—*her* blood. But still the darkness came, a warm, lapping wave that threatened to pull her under.

Get up, Keira. Get UP!

She could hear the panic in Danny's voice, even as she blinked against the stars that danced before her eyes. Then the cloaked man's face appeared, too close to her own—his ugly tattooed mug leering down at her as he raised his blade for the killing blow.

"Get up, Keira! *Please!*"

That was Raina's voice, somehow freed from the gag that had held her. Raina's voice. And she *needed* her.

Keira rolled.

She lurched toward her assailant, not away as he'd expected, and he stumbled slightly in his surprise. Her blade was gone, but she was far from defenseless. Hooking one arm around his leg, she curled her bruised and bleeding body around him, bringing a leg up and directly between his legs.

He doubled over, wheezing, and she hooked the other leg around him, forcing him to come crashing to the ground flat on his back.

Move! Danny's voice cried.

Keira cursed as she saw her assailant had managed to hold on to his sword, and she tried to obey, tried to roll out of that blade's lethal reach. But her limbs had been trapped in his fall, too tangled up in his to be easily extricated now, when she needed it most.

Then a meaty fist caught hold of her hair and yanked her still-throbbing head back. Tears sprang to her eyes, and she clawed at him with her nails. She threw an elbow into his side, a punch to his kidneys—anything and everything she could think of to escape, to get to Raina.

But his fingers only tightened, and from the corner of her

eye, she saw him raise his sword. In a panic, she grabbed at her pneuma, ready to throw whatever kind of bind she could at him, grounding or not. She'd face the undoing, if that's what it took. But the very thought brought her throbbing pulse battering against the inside of her skull. Her pneuma slipped between the formless fingers of her scrambled mind, even as she tried to mold it, to shape it into the form she needed.

The sword arced toward her, and a part of her welcomed it, welcomed the end of the throbbing pain in her body.

Don't you dare *stop fighting*, Danny snarled. And Keira could feel his fear intermixed with her own, his fury and rage at his own powerlessness, trapped as he was in her mind. And suddenly she knew. She knew what she wanted, and it wasn't to end up on the wrong side of a blade. She wanted to live.

Then came a whistle, a low thud, and the fingers in her hair loosened. Not waiting for an invitation, Keira yanked herself free, kicking and rolling away until she knelt on all fours, staring back at the man. Her vision danced in time with the throbbing of her head, and the ground seemed to roll as nausea flooded over her. Keira vomited, hurling up every piece of the dinner she'd had not an hour before.

A cool hand on her back made her flinch.

"It's all right," a voice said quickly. "It's just me. They're all dead, it's over."

Keira blinked, bringing Cyrus's worried gray eyes into focus. Then her gaze shifted to the now-still man sprawled on the ground before her—an arrow sticking out of one eye as the other stared unseeing straight at her.

Keira shuddered, and her stomach rolled again.

"I guess that makes us even," Cyrus said, voice grim with a weariness that echoed the exhaustion quickly filling her own body. Cool fingers grazed her temple, and Keira turned slightly to see them come away bloody.

"Are you all right?"

A ridiculous question, but Keira nodded anyway—instantly regretting it as the motion sent shards of glass piercing through her brain.

"I'm fi—Where's Raina?"

The thought made her head shoot up, and she scrambled to her feet, braced slightly by Cyrus as she staggered precariously.

"She's fine, Keira. Marti's seeing to her."

Sure enough, Keira spied the rest of their cohort crouched beneath the tree as Marti untied the last of the ropes from around Raina's ankles.

Keira lurched toward them, and the others made way as she approached.

"Keira," Raina's tiny voice whispered. "Keira, I'm so sor—"

Before she could finish, Keira dropped to her knees and wrapped Raina in a bone-crushing hug, trying not to think of how the girl's body trembled slightly in her arms even as she clung to her. They sat that way for a while as the others made themselves busy elsewhere. Finally, Keira pulled back, staring at the girl as a mounting wave of rage rushed through her.

"Are you hurt?"

Raina blinked at Keira's suddenly bitter tone, eyes widening slightly. "N-No."

"Good," Keira said, sitting back on her heels as the anger built and built inside of her—her head throbbing with every staccato heartbeat. There was anger, yes—but tinged with fear and guilt, and a whole host of other emotions that it gave Keira a headache to parse through. Finally, it exploded.

"What the hell is wrong with you?"

Raina's eyes widened further, and her lower lip trembled.

This seemed to only add to Keira's anger. "You could have been *killed*," Keira said, voice low and trembling. "You could have gotten someone *else* killed."

"I-I know. I'm sorry, Keira. I just be wanting to—"

"I don't care what you wanted, Raina! You never wander off by yourself, *especially* not at night, and *especially* not without telling someone—*anyone*—where you are!"

Fat tears rolled down Raina's cheeks, and she wiped them away, further smearing dirt in streaks across her face. The motion almost undid Keira, and she felt her anger loosen, threaten to come untied altogether. But then Raina's expression hardened, and she glared back at her.

"I said I was *sorry*," Raina spat. "I just be wanting to see—"

"You keep telling me you're not a baby, Raina, that you can look after yourself. Well, this is a hell of a way to prove it."

"You're not my mother, Keira! I don't be owing you any sort of—"

"And thank Pneumos for that," Keira snarled.

Raina looked like someone had slapped her, and Keira instantly regretted her words. But she'd come too far to back down now. "And what the hell was that, by the way? That *thing* you did, when he came toward you."

Raina blanched, mouth settling into a firm line. But Keira remembered. Her head throbbed with every thought, but something had *happened*.

"It was almost like the light bent somehow, curving around you, *hiding* you." With every word, Keira's voice grew more and more frayed. It was too much, all just too much. But Raina just stared at her, eyes stubborn and chin tilted to that obstinate angle that made Keira's blood simmer.

"She must have manipulated the photons, somehow."

Keira spun around, head protesting sharply at the motion,

to find Albert standing close behind. His eyes were bright and held a gleam as he regarded Raina intently.

Raina's fists clenched and unclenched as she worried at her bottom lip. "It be nothing, a trick—to escape the bullies back on Tibolé."

"Similar to our pneuma and its effects on atoms," Albert continued, ignoring her protests. "But this is her first life—she can't possibly be a Legionnaire. But could she be trained?"

Raina's mouth twisted into a firm line. "I don't be wanting any such *training*. I just be wanting to go to the capital, find my brother." Raina's words were firm, even as she shifted her weight, like a spooked deer prepared to bolt at any moment.

Keira glanced uneasily between the two of them, settling on Albert's too-interested gaze. On an impulse, she stepped between them and addressed Albert. "How are the others? Anyone hurt?"

Albert blinked quickly, as if suddenly pulled from his musings. "Yes. But Zipporah, she needs your help."

Keira nodded and followed him as he turned, but on an impulse threw one final glance at Raina—trying and failing to figure out what, exactly, had happened in those last moments before Keira had nearly gotten herself skewered. The girl's expression told her she knew exactly what she was talking about but had no intention of explaining anytime soon. Keira's nails bit into her palm as she glared right back.

With a sigh, Keira turned away, allowing herself to focus on this fresh problem. She was instantly alert, instantly tense.

"What happened, Albert?"

CHAPTER

SEVENTEEN

It was her leg, Albert explained quickly. Zipporah's leg had been crushed by a rain of falling boulders that a pneumonancer had sent exploding off the hillside at their backs. Zipporah had seen it first and lunged for Marti, pulling her out of the way, but not before her own leg was trapped in the rain of rubble.

As they approached, Keira saw the sheen of sweat across Zipporah's brow and the grimace that twisted her mouth. Her knuckles blanched as she clutched Marti's hand. Then Keira saw her foot.

It was twisted at an odd angle that made Keira's stomach churn. Memory flooded her as she recalled the image of a screaming Bellator, his own mangled limb far worse off after being caught in a bear trap back on Tibolé. Guilt nipped at her, chilling her fingers. *You can't help him,* she'd told herself that day, content to drown herself in her own misery and pain, too afraid of her own gifts to even try. But she'd helped Cyrus, saved him, even. Could she not have saved that poor boy's foot?

She banished the memory as she realized the others were

staring at her expectantly. She swallowed, the motion settling a hard lump deep in her stomach.

"Well?" Albert asked. "I warned you I favored a more *hands-on* approach to training."

Marti shot Albert a reproachful look as Zipporah tried to shift herself into a more comfortable position, grimacing with the effort.

"Go on, then, Keira, savior of Loren," she murmured, fixing Keira with a challenging look. "Let's see this healing pneumonancy you keep going on about. If I lose this foot, I just might have to kick your arse." Behind her bravado, Keira saw a flash of fear cross Zipporah's face. That settled it.

Brow furrowed, Keira knelt to lightly place a finger on the top of Zipporah's twisted foot, ignoring the hiss that escaped the girl's teeth. No pulse. She tried again, this time at the spot just behind her ankle. Nothing.

An icy finger of dread dripped down Keira's spine, and her eyes met Albert's. The look he gave her was calm, sure, as if he'd known all along it would come down to this. Keira inhaled sharply and turned back to the limb.

"What do I do?"

Albert made a noncommittal noise, and she glared at him.

"You tell me. Your instincts seemed to serve you well enough with Master Flavius here."

Keira's eyes shot to Cyrus, who'd appeared at Albert's side. Her cheeks flushed at his confused expression, and her eyes drifted of their own accord to his side, where she knew he still bore bruises from that encounter with the marauders back on Tibolé. His hand drifted to it, his eyes widening slightly, and she glanced away. Though she'd briefly recounted the experience to Albert in their early discussions of healing pneumonancy, she'd never told Cyrus the details of what had happened, content to let him think he'd merely had a lucky break.

"That was just blood," she muttered, still eyeing Zipporah's foot. "I've stopped bleeders before. Bones, though . . ."

Keira rubbed her sweating palms against her pants before daring a look up at Albert. He had a pensive look on his face as he regarded her carefully.

"I think the principles should remain relatively constant. Like does flow deftly unto like, after all. By shredding already half-destroyed tissue, you can channel that energy into knitting the blood vessels back together, or clotting the flow, as it were. Very well, I can help guide you through the anatomy side of things. Luckily for you, I've become quite well-read over the centuries. Will you allow me into your mind?"

Keira balked, eyes widening slightly at the thought. She'd never willingly allowed any pneumonancer into her mind before.

Except me, Danny added. She could practically hear the grin in his voice.

Keira gritted her teeth. *Well*, you *didn't exactly give me much choice in the matter.* He laughed, and she felt her cheeks warm. *You better get out of here, though,* she warned. *Back to wherever you go most of the time. If Albert finds you, we'll have some* other *questions to answer.*

She felt him fade almost instantly and started as she realized Albert was still staring expectantly at her. *This is for Zipporah,* she reminded herself, and nodded.

"Very good. You'll feel my presence off to the side, but I won't intervene at all."

Keira nodded, tensing as she felt his pneuma flow into her, staying, as he promised, off to one side of her mind. Closing her eyes, Keira felt for her own pneuma. In her mind's eye, she kneaded it, feeling it ripple and roil with potential. Remembering her training, she sent it first coursing down through her legs, feeling it tether her solidly to the ground, rooting her to body and soul. Then she tensed, and with a sharp whistle, cast it out. Her skin fairly buzzed with the thrill of power as she felt the pneuma flow steadily through her fingers and into Zipporah.

She kept her pneuma thin at first, trailing just under the surface of her skin, seeking the bundle of nerves that conveyed sensation. She found them quickly, and with the deft fusion of her pneuma felt the bonds between them sever. It was temporary, she knew. Nerves were resilient and, since their position had been unaltered, would reform those connections quickly. But at least Zipporah would have some relief, even if only for the next few hours. Even in her dissociated state, Keira could have sworn she heard Zipporah sigh in relief.

She then turned her attention back to the injury itself and allowed her pneuma to sink deeper, through flesh and bone, surveying the damage that had been done.

Definitely fractured, Albert murmured into her mind. She felt a flicker of satisfaction as he looked in awe at the images before them. *Incredible*, he said. *Absolutely incredible.*

She had to agree with his assessment, though. Even with her limited medical training, she could see that the large leg bone seemed to have broken cleanly through, but the smaller bone had shattered into several pieces.

Keira hesitated.

You'll have to be careful, Albert said. *Bones are tricky things.* She could feel him recall a passage from a textbook, and she gleaned the basics from their shared minds. Bones really were tricky. Tightly woven matrices of rock-hard calcium gave their interior an almost spongy quality that was hard to imitate.

They had to be simultaneously solid and flexible. Too solid, and they would shatter on impact; too flexible, and they'd crumple under the weight of the human body.

Thanks for the pep talk, she shot back at him.

Remember your training, was all he said. *Like flows deftly unto like.*

How many times had Elliott told her that? How often had he waxed poetic about the nature of pneuma, how it could never be created nor destroyed . . . only transformed? With a jolt, she realized she had an idea. Cautiously, she opened it up to Albert and felt him warm with approval.

Yes, yes, I think that might work quite nicely. But you'll need to set the leg first.

Keira nodded and withdrew her pneuma enough that she could regain control of her hands as she firmly wrenched Zipporah's foot and leg back into alignment. Zipporah winced at the cracking sound but didn't cry out. Good—the nerve bind was still working, then.

Keira then turned her pneuma back toward the largest leg bone. She could see the fault line that spiraled around the bone shaft. One wrong move, and it would displace again. Meanwhile, there was little that could be done for the nearly crushed smaller leg bone.

In her old life, Keira had shadowed surgeons who'd described harvesting the smaller leg bone and transplanting it elsewhere in the patient's body—replacing a jawbone or part of the spine. Since it bore little of the weight in the leg, these patients did pretty well afterward. Could she do something similar here?

It was worth a try, she decided. Moving quickly, she easily isolated the shattered bone fragments and began morphing her pneuma to fit their exact molecular makeup. Once fused, she then intensified the energy, veritably rattling the molecules apart until she could feel the material coursing with unformed potential.

This done, she angled the pneuma toward the larger leg bone, working her way along the chasm as she channeled the harvested material and began fusing the rift. She kept her pneuma light, clinging to the very outer layers of bone, which she knew to be the most solid, as she fused her pneuma with the bone. She felt the material take shape as the molecular bonds slid slowly into place, a knitted bridge across the bony chasm. With any luck, she'd lain the material far enough away from the bone's spongy interior. Hopefully that would be enough for it to heal normally. Slowly, Keira withdrew and surveyed her work with a growing exhilaration.

Like flows deftly unto like.

She blinked to find four sets of eyes staring at her, faces slack with surprise and awe. Heat flooded her cheeks, and she glanced away, back down to Zipporah's foot. Had realigning the bones been enough to decompress the artery? With a trembling hand, she reached forward, gently placing two fingers across the top, and waited, barely daring to breathe. And there it was —a pulse.

Keira exhaled sharply in relief as the others let out their pent-up emotion with barks of laughter. Marti quickly wiped tears from her eyes as she leaned over to plant a kiss on Zipporah's cheek, who blushed crimson as she stared with molten eyes at her cantor.

Cyrus clapped Keira on the back, and she turned to find Albert beaming at her—pride, and something else . . . excitement filling his face. But when Keira looked around to find Raina, the younger girl was several yards away, arms crossed in a look of sullen hostility. Keira swallowed and looked away.

There'd be time enough to deal with Raina's anger later. For now, she simply wanted to sleep.

Everything hurt.

As the cohort rode away from their makeshift camp and the site of the night's activities, Keira could feel every bump and shift in her horse's gait as a rattling shock wave through her aching bones. She knew she looked as bad as she felt, a quick glance in the nearby stream confirming that a violet bruise had crept over her jaw. Zipporah had grumpily informed her that her eye looked like a cranberry—filled as it was with several busted blood vessels. For her part, Zipporah had been swearing up a storm all morning as she limped about her activities on her makeshift splint. The numbing bind Keira had placed the night before had faded, and in her usual show of stubbornness, Zipporah had refused to let Keira place another. She preferred instead to limp around, cursing at every person and object that dared cross her path. Marti had merely rolled her eyes when Keira had asked her about it, clearly content in her own long-suffering tolerance. Keira gave up after that and just steered clear.

So that was how she found herself riding beside Raina, with a cloak wrapped tightly around her against the early morning chill. The younger girl had barely said a word all morning, but the guilty look she kept shooting at Zipporah's limping, cursing frame told Keira enough about her friend's feelings. While Keira's own annoyance at Raina's escapades hadn't exactly faded, there were more pressing things to discuss.

"So, about last night," she began, catching Raina's wary look. "Do you know *how* were you able to do that?"

Raina blinked. "Do what?"

"You . . ." Keira searched for the right words. ". . . disappeared."

Raina shrugged. "I not so sure. But it's been happening since pretty much always. Be it the same as what you and Marti be doing then? This *pneumonancy*?" she asked, suddenly eager.

"I'm not sure," Keira replied cautiously. "In the Legion, we have cantors and grounders. But you—I don't think you're either. And the fact that you can practice in your first life . . . I honestly don't know what to make of it."

Raina rode silently, staring at the ground before replying, "It's *not* my first life—not really."

Keira gaped at her but, seeing the younger girl tense, quickly adopted an assumed nonchalance. "Oh? And when, might I ask, did you die?" She grinned over at her, but Raina didn't return the expression.

"Marné says I be little more than a babe when I be wandering too close to the ocean. I slipped, and a strong current be pulling me out. I barely be remembering it—can't, really. I only remember the feeling of water rushing over my head and then just sinking . . . Well, my mother, she be diving in to save me, but by the time she be pulling me out, I'd stopped breathing." Raina shrugged. "I don't really know the details, but Marné says my mother be special, that she had—abilities— unlike any others she'd seen. Anyway, somehow I came back, and be throwing up all the water from my lungs."

Raina paused again, and Keira saw her throat bob. "But— my eyes. Marné says my eyes be what the sea refusing to give back—a sign that Cála would always be with me. Ever since, I've been able to—hide. Whenever I being chased by the bullies, I be feeling my necklace grow hot. I don't really know how it be working, but somehow their eyes be just—slipping past me."

Keira started to reply, but a voice from behind her beat her to it.

"You're able to bend the light itself, nudging the photons slightly out of order so that they slip past you."

Keira turned to see that Albert had moved up to ride beside them. His face showed frank interest, and something about the expression made Keira wary.

"Does that be making me like you all? *Le'ena*?" Raina asked.

"I'm not sure, but I believe the other council members would be very intrigued to learn of your *abilities*. You'll have to return to Port Galaén with us once we've sorted out this mess."

Raina's eyes immediately shuttered at his words. "I don't think so. I being here to find my brother, and that's it. I don't be having time for magic." And with that, she spurred her horse forward to ride ahead with Marti and Zipporah.

Albert chuckled. "She's a plucky one, isn't she?" Keira said nothing, only stared after Raina, trying to decipher who, exactly, the young girl was who'd followed her all the way from the Southern Shield. Keira and Albert rode in silence for a while before he said mildly, "It seems your bond with your grounder remains strong as ever."

Keira started, eyes widening slightly as she turned to him.

He smiled at her expression and continued, "Yes, yes, I caught a whiff of Mr. O'Leary's presence as I helped you last night. I must say, I had my doubts about this scheme of yours, whether you could *actually* bring him back. But—" Albert shrugged. "I must admit, I'm impressed. With a bond that strong, I think it just might be possible."

Keira flushed with pleasure and pride at his words. But she couldn't help feeling the tug of fear at what it might mean.

"He—he talks to me, you know. Even grounds me. Do you—do you know *how* he's able to do that?"

Albert looked taken aback and was silent for a moment, staring far off into the distance as he considered her question. "You share a bond, as cantor and grounder. I've known many who could communicate whole conversations without uttering a word. But as for how you can communicate after death . . ." Albert shrugged. "I've honestly never heard of such a thing. But I suppose the two of you are connected through your pneuma itself, something that transcends your living bodies. After all, in the place between life and death, that's all any of us are— pneuma waiting to be breathed into life. Is it just him, or do you hear others?"

Keira started at the question. How many times had she heard her mother's voice over that long journey from Abalás to the capital? When she was angry or doing something foolish? How many times had her mother whispered warnings in the back of her mind?

"This is different," she said finally. "I can talk with him, ask him questions, and he *answers* them. And it's more now. Back in Port Galaén, I could barely feel him. But every day since, it's like his voice is getting stronger."

Albert nodded, an intrigued look crossing his face. "It's true, we are approaching the equinox, the time when the barrier between worlds is thinnest. And as we near the capital . . ." At this, Albert's voice trailed off, and he shook his head again. "I wish I could be more helpful. I never had a grounder, you see. I know little of what such a bond is like."

Keira stared at him. "Really? I just assumed everyone . . ." She trailed off then, blushing with embarrassment.

Albert smiled sadly. "Unfortunately, there are many of us, arrivals who find ourselves alone in a strange world. I spent centuries waiting for my grounder, but the process is far from scientific. There was a time when I thought, maybe . . ." His voice trailed off and he laughed. "But that's ancient history. I've learned to make do. And while remaining ungrounded has surely placed limitations on my pneumonancy, I've developed certain *workarounds*."

Keira gaped at him, and Albert laughed at her expression. "My dear, you didn't think there was only one method of practicing pneumonancy, did you?"

She blushed. That was exactly what Keira had thought, but she wasn't about to say that now.

Albert continued, nodding to Raina as he added, "Just look at our friend here. Completely untrained and ungrounded, and yet still able to bend light to her will. Look at your healing pneumonancy. Both your skills are more along the vein of cantors, but there are rumors of others whose unique abilities work off of grounding principles. It's even said that one can become so grounded that they can actually cancel out the pneuma of others, like lightning rods funneling energy into the earth." Albert shook his head, his tone turning bitter. "The Legion would like to claim it has a monopoly on the practice of pneumonancy in this world, Keira. They don't."

Keira shifted in her saddle, unsure what to say. She wanted to ask him more about these new abilities, and especially his particular vein of ungrounded canting. But his words drifted dangerously close to a line Elliott had taught her never to cross. And there was something else stopping her, something about the way his eyes had gleamed when he'd stared at Raina—like she was a puzzle he looked forward to unraveling.

Albert eyed her furrowed brow and chuckled. "Listen to me, rambling on about rumors and theories. Never mind all that. There will be plenty of opportunity for training once we arrive in the capital."

Keira nodded, but her mind was elsewhere, watching as

Raina rode ahead of them in sullen silence. Even now, Marti was trying to coax a smile from her as only she could, regaling her with stories and observations in that buoyant way she had. Raina barely looked up from her saddle. Keira knew she must feel awful, terribly guilty over what had happened—what *could* have happened.

You've been there before, Danny murmured.

Yes, but I had the good sense to admit when I was wrong.

Danny snorted, his choked laugh filled with disbelief, and Keira gritted her teeth, not dignifying that with a reply.

"Tell me, what is your goal in all of this, Keira? Besides bringing Danny back and rooting out the Regio's would-be assassins, that is. Will you return to the Legion? Open your own hospital with your newfound skills and abilities? Or do you have some other goal in mind?"

Keira stared at him, honestly lost for words. She'd thought little beyond Danny, beyond getting him back. The task itself seemed monumental enough that she'd never thought to think beyond it.

Albert's keen eyes missed nothing and softened at her furrowed expression.

"I know it must seem a pointless exercise, with all that lies before you. I do regret I could never meet your grounder, Keira. From the glimpses I saw of him in your mind, he seemed like a wonderful person."

Keira swallowed the lump that suddenly threatened to choke her. "He was."

Albert turned then back to the road before him, his expression pensive as he surveyed their surroundings. "It is intriguing, isn't it? The nature of this world? Of our place in it? On one hand, we're told our arrival is random, and on the other that we serve a purpose, fulfilling some role in the cosmic battle between order and chaos."

Keira stared at him, wondering where he could possibly be going with this. Albert fixed her with an unflinching stare.

"You once asked me to what extent we could control who comes and goes from this world. Well, from what I saw today, I do believe you're ready to hear the answer." Keira felt a sudden tightness deep in her chest and didn't dare breathe as he continued, "I believe that there is an object of immense power in the capital itself, a conduit through which you could bring back your grounder. If I could find it, would you be interested in trying to learn to use it? It would be dangerous," he added quickly, no doubt seeing Keira's eager expression. "As far as I can tell, it hasn't been used in . . . centuries, at least. But if I could . . ."

Albert trailed off, seemingly lost in thought, before leveling Keira with an unflinching gaze. "I ask about your plans because, if you go through with this, if you use this object of immense power for your own gain, even to save someone you love, then I'm afraid you'll likely never be welcomed back to the Legion."

Keira stared at him, thoughts racing. For once, Danny remained quiet, so still within her mind she wondered if he'd gone. Could she do that? Give up the Legion? They were the only family she'd known since arriving in this strange place nearly six years ago. Could she give up her place there—for Danny? Keira swallowed, remembering Danny's warm eyes, the solid feel of his embrace, the absolute faith he'd always had in her. Yes, she decided. Yes, she could.

CHAPTER

EIGHTEEN

876 Common Era (C.E.)

Danny had surprisingly little difficulty finding the library that Titus had mentioned, though *library* wasn't exactly the word he'd use. It was, in fact, little more than a tent, its sides built up by rough-hewn timbers to keep out the worst of the cutting wind that blew off the ocean. Danny didn't bother to knock as he pushed in through the open tent flap, waiting for his eyes to adjust to the relative darkness within.

He blinked.

The tent was filled from floor to ceiling with stacks of books lining nearly every available space. As Danny moved inside, he had to clamber over massive trunks overspilling with yet more books, scrolls, and leaves of parchment. Curious, Danny stepped to a nearby stack and scanned the nearest spines.

"What is it you're looking for?"

The voice caught him up short, and Danny spun around, eyes scanning the shadowy interior. From the far corner, a

191

shape emerged from the darkness. Danny blinked to find a wiry old man crawling out from underneath a table, of all things. He scrambled to his feet, brushing the dust from his pant legs as he took Danny in with a look of definite interest.

"I-I'm Danny," Danny stammered, taken aback by the sudden appearance of the man. "Danny O'Leary, that is, and I've been assigned to help you move your—uh, library." Danny's voice trailed off into muted incredulity as he again took in his haphazard surroundings.

"Oh, I know precisely who you are, Legionnaire. I'm Cato, the librarian." Cato reached out an ink-covered hand that Danny eyed in surprise. Seeing Danny's split-second hesitancy, Cato chuckled to himself before pulling out the filthiest handkerchief Danny had ever seen to wipe his hands with.

"Legionnaire," Cato murmured thoughtfully, chewing on his lip as he eyed him up and down. Danny squirmed under the tiny man's searching gaze. He racked his brain for something friendly to say, but Cato's eyes suddenly widened, twinkling with some undisclosed mischief. "I have just the thing!"

And with that, he dove for the nearest trunk and began yanking massive tomes from its depths with an alacrity that took Danny aback.

"I must say," Cato continued, "the new capital is a fair bit— smaller than I'd imagined."

Danny smiled wryly. "You didn't think you should wait for an actual, you know, library?"

Cato shrugged, suddenly switching trunks in search of the unnamed object. "What is a library, but a space where knowledge is gathered and shared? What do you think we're doing here?" Finding the book, he clambered to his feet and began eagerly flipping through the pages. "Any space is a space in which to read, you know. But—ah! Here you are!"

Danny glanced up to find Cato brandishing a stack of tightly rolled scrolls, bound together by several leather thongs. He deposited the stack unceremoniously into Danny's arms, looking altogether far too pleased with himself.

"What, uh, is it?" Danny asked, trying not to appear rude as he eyed the stack of paper.

Cato sighed, gazing at the stack with indulgent fondness. "A misplaced thesis attempt, I'm afraid, from back in my university days—far too little to go off of. But a scintillating probe nonetheless! I think you'll find its contents equally intriguing."

Danny eyed the papers dubiously. The last time he'd done any sort of research was for tenth grade social studies, and even then, Polly Hammond had let him use most of her notes. "What's it about?"

Cato didn't bother turning back as he riffled through another stack of papers. "Why, the Legion of Pneumos, of course!"

Danny gaped from Cato to the massive stack of rolled scrolls. Sure, the Bellatori high command had accepted Legion guidance in their Lorenan campaign, but that was a far cry from someone doing *thesis* research on them. What had happened to secrecy?

Cato must have seen or sensed his surprise, because he chuckled. "Secret organizations rarely remain so for long, dear boy. You should remember that and know a bit about where you come from." He said this with a waggle of his finger that left Danny feeling abashed.

"Look, Cato, I'm just here to set up a security detail and help move all . . . *this* to the new library once it's built."

"Yes, yes, well, it isn't built yet, now, is it? So you might as well take a look, as I have no other tasks to occupy you. That is, unless you happen to be well-versed in the Delphinian categorization system?" Cato glanced up from his labors with an eagerness that made Danny's ears burn. He shook his head, abashed, but Cato merely shrugged and returned to his work.

"Then have a seat. I'll let you know as soon as I need anything slashed or gutted."

Danny snorted at that but obeyed, moving to what looked to be the only free stool in the tent as he carefully edged a scroll from the tightly bound stack.

"The Birth and Rise of the Marian Empire," he read from the top of the scroll, before glancing curiously toward Cato's hunched back. "The Legion was involved in the early days of the Empire?"

"Of course!" Cato replied, glancing toward Danny before yanking an oddly square-shaped book from its crevice and tossing it onto the table. "Legend has it the first Emperio was birthed by a she-lion who could level city walls with a roar and build mountains from nothing." Cato shrugged. "More contemporaneous sources report this she-lion to actually be a prized advisor, and some say even the Emperio's lover. Now, whether she could level walls and build mountains . . . " Cato's eyes twinkled as he shot Danny a knowing grin. "Well, I have my own suspicions."

"A Legionnaire?" Danny asked incredulously.

"Perhaps. You have in your hands my painstakingly gathered research on the subject. You'll have to decide for yourself."

Danny turned back to the scroll with a renewed excitement as he scanned its pages. With every line, his fascination grew. How had Elliott and Nazor told him nothing of this? Had they even known?

He shook his head. But one thing was certain—he'd been right. The Legion *had* had a reason to favor the Marians in their invasion of Loren, long before any confirmation on his part. And if so, what were their intentions now?

Thanks to Cato, he just might have the answers he'd been looking for.

~

Danny's days passed in a blur—filled with long hours of training and laborious meetings that seemed to lead nowhere. His nights he spent in the library, combing through dusty tomes detailing the outcomes of ancient battles and tenuous treaties. But every once in a while, he'd glimpse the Legion's handiwork —an anachronous name, an unspecified political *consideration*, or the sudden arrival of much-needed reinforcements from an unnamed ally.

He noted each of these instances in a logbook—tiny threads teased loose from a hidden tapestry Danny was only just beginning to unravel. The Legion had been pulling the strings of power in this world for centuries. But to what end? Surely the Legion had some ultimate goal, but the answer to this question proved far more elusive.

"What are you readin'?"

Danny started in his chair, glancing around to meet the curious green-eyed gaze of Moira Foléan. She stood, mop and bucket in hand, as she surveyed the small tent Cato had set up for his temporary library.

Danny blushed, scooping up the stack of papers that had somehow sprawled across the length of the desk, clumsily shuffling them into some semblance of order.

"Brutus Idonicus's account of the First Grumaérian Campaign in 553 C.E. Sorry for the mess," he added. "It's normally just me here after hours."

"Cato asked for the floors to be cleaned. Seems *somebody* tracked mud in from the training field," Moira explained, cocking one eyebrow at the dried mud caked on his boots.

Danny grimaced. "Sorry about that."

"Well, I didn't mean to disturb you. I'll let you get back to your readin'."

Danny sighed, dragging a hand across his bleary eyes as he stifled a yawn. "It's fine. I'm having trouble with this correspondence, anyway. It's written in some script I've never seen before."

Moira leaned over the desk, her long copper braid brushing against his arm. He stiffened slightly as a whiff of something floral wafted over him. When was the last time he'd been this close to a girl? He shut that thought down quickly, shifting in his seat as he watched her brows scrunch together.

"It's Ancient Lorenan, rarely spoken these days, except by the elders in the villages. The passage you have here has to do with the *Galaéna*—spirit-binders, we call them today." She chuckled, shaking her head. "An old fairy tale to scare the children."

Danny gaped at her. *Galaéna?* As in *Port Galaén?* He knew it didn't exist yet, but it would. And it would hold the Legion's future headquarters. This had to be it, proof of the Legion's early activities in Loren. But none of that would make any sense to Moira.

"You can *read* it?" he asked instead.

She straightened, brushing down the front of her dress, her eyes shining. "My grandmother taught me, when I was just a winnie, wanted to keep it alive in the family, I 'spose." She shrugged. "I'm far from fluent, but I can well enough—"

"Help me," Danny interjected, grabbing her hand on

impulse. She yanked it away, stepping back as her eyes shuttered, clouded by suspicion.

"Why?"

"I'm just trying to find out some information," he said. "The spirit-binders this text talks about, the *Galaéna*, they have this habit of cropping up every time something nefarious goes down—an assassination, a betrayal, even a treaty." Danny shook his head. "Whenever the tides turn, in war or in politics, they never seem to be far behind. I'd like to know what they're up to now, which means figuring out exactly how we got here."

Moira's eyes narrowed as she searched his face for something. "You're saying the *Galaéna* are, what—real?"

Danny swallowed, holding her gaze before nodding. "Afraid so."

Moira blinked, then stepped close to take another look at the parchment. She shook her head. "This'll take me at least an hour, and I've got mopping to do."

Danny jumped to his feet. "Here, let me. You translate, I'll mop."

Moira snorted, brows raised in disbelief. "*You're* goin' to mop?"

Danny grinned broadly. "My mam taught me well. Not a speck, Scout's honor."

Moira laughed. "Scout's what?"

"Never mind." Danny waved her off. "Just leave this to me."

So while Danny swept and mopped every inch of the small library, Moira pored over the ancient Lorenan text, quill scratching away to the side as she made her translation.

Finally, she sat back, thumbing through the pages in her hand as she waved him over. "Here you are, then, O'Leary. Seems your spirit-binders have been busy. This text details how they acted as liaisons between the Bellatorio and the

Grumaérian high command in the First Campaign. Sounds like they 'ad people on both sides, if you ask me. Only when the negotiations didn't pan out, they used their contacts to destroy the Grumaérian forces from within. Lovely stuff."

Danny quickly scanned the pages, taking in line after line of Moira's neat script, detailing the story of how the Legion turned the tide of yet another war. How many times had they picked out the winner? Given an unfair advantage to one side or another when the sands of fate seemed to shift in a particular direction?

"There's more, Moira, so much more. And if I'm to figure out exactly what the Legion's been up to, I'll need some help."

Moira's eyes narrowed. "You make it sound like they're still runnin' about."

Danny chewed on his lip, searching Moira's face. Did he tell her? Risk it getting back to the Legion? They'd be furious if they knew he was spilling their secrets and dredging up old scores. But he had to figure out what was going on if he had any chance of getting back to his old time—to Keira. He had to try. "They are, Moira. They're still around, and they're very powerful. I think—I think they picked a side in this invasion. And I think they might still be pulling the strings."

Moira's eyes narrowed. "You should be pleased, then. You serve in the Bellatorio. It must be nice knowin' you 'ave spirit-binders as allies."

Danny gritted his teeth, giving her a wry look. "I like my wars like I like my baseball—straightforward and free of this devious nonsense. There's no honor in this."

Moira snorted, shaking her head. "You should know better than that, Danny O'Leary. When it comes to war, honor has nothin' to do with it." Danny had nothing to say to that, only waited patiently as Moira gazed thoughtfully at the stack of pages.

"All right then, Danny O'Leary. I will help you, but I'll be needin' somethin' from you as well."

"Name it," Danny replied easily, still running his finger down the lines of translation she'd committed to parchment.

"It's my father," she said slowly, hands twisting in her lap beside him. "He was captured, about a year ago now. I-I need information, you see—about where he might be."

Danny glanced up at her, brow furrowed. "As in a prison camp?"

Moira shook her head, mouth twisting as she explained, "The Bellatorio uses prisoners as camp slaves. I was told by a young Tiro I befriended that my father was assigned to the Eastern Imperium. If I only knew where they were, I could get a message through, find a way to make payment. They let prisoners go, you see," she added, a steely glint in her eye as her gaze met his, "for the right price. It's all off the record, of course, so I can't exactly go through the normal channel of appeals to find out who I should contact and where they'd be."

Danny sighed, running his hand through his hair. This was serious business, he knew. If the Bellatorio got wind that he was giving out information on troop movements, well—it wouldn't be pretty. He glanced at Moira, her eyes wide and hopeful as her hands continued to twist in her lap. She just wanted her father back. Hadn't she said she was supporting both a mother and younger brother? Danny knew better than anyone the strain of such responsibility.

He nodded. "I'll see what I can do, Moira. Meet back here tomorrow night?"

A bright smile slowly spread across Moira's face, and she

blinked against the glassiness that suddenly filled her eyes. Then, to his surprise, she threw her arms around his neck.

"Thank you. Thank you so much," she whispered. And then she stood, wiping at her eyes as she gathered up her mop and bucket. "Tomorrow, then, Danny O'Leary."

Danny waved goodbye as he turned back to gather up the stack of parchment. He felt buoyant, hopeful, even, for the first time since the siege of Ulgáris. He was doing something, making progress, and helping a friend in the process. Danny ignored the leaden ball that had sunk in his stomach, the sense that he was walking a very narrow path indeed and the realization that a sharp breeze might push him off into the chasm beyond.

242 Marian Era (M.E.)

After a week of travel, Keira and the rest of the cohort stood on the top of the Northern Hill, looking down on the bustling port capital, Crîd Eálas. Keira's breath caught as she spied the massive stone fortress of the Vindolum rising above the tossing waves—remembering the last time she'd seen it. She could still see Lady Junia's sneering snarl and shivered despite herself. From what Cyrus had told her, there'd been no word of Landry's traitorous sister, who'd fled after her failed coup, before her brother's coronation.

From this distance, the city looked peaceful, almost serene, in the midday sun. But Keira wasn't fooled; she knew what tension seethed just below the surface in a city split along fissures of blood—the uplanders and downlanders living in strained proximity in a capital that hadn't even existed a couple hundred years ago. This city had been the last place she'd seen Danny's sparkling green eyes, heard his laugh, felt his reassuring steadiness. She'd have gladly lived a happy second life far from its alabaster walls. But it seemed that wasn't meant to be.

"It's so . . . big," Raina breathed beside her, staring wide-eyed at the cityscape below. "This be the capital?"

Keira nodded, trying to ease the roiling in her stomach. "It is," she said finally. "The den of vipers itself."

Raina's lips pressed together, and her eyes fixed in determination upon the capital below. She had no intention of leaving her brother to any vipers, those eyes said.

"Are you ready?" Cyrus asked, guiding his horse over to her, eyes dark with a mixture of worry and determination. Gritting her teeth, Keira nodded, spurring her own horse forward as they descended the winding mountain road toward the city.

THE NOISE of the city swelled around Keira, and she wrinkled her nose at the scent of humans living in too-close proximity. They passed through the outer city quarter with little incident, avoiding the sharp-eyed glares of its uplander inhabitants—leveled mostly at Cyrus in his emissary's robes, with his dark hair and olive skin marking him clearly as a downlander. The tension in the air was palpable, and Cyrus urged them onward. Keira shared his worry, somehow certain that to linger would be to invite unwanted attention.

Standing before the ascending stairs to the mighty Vindolum's great double doors should have brought a sense of relief. But memories haunted this place as well—with the massive plaza, now empty of its once revolutionary occupants.

Cyrus led them forward, and after a brief word to the guard, their horses and belongings were escorted away as they moved forward into the vaulted marble entry hall.

The temperature immediately dropped ten degrees inside the stone interior, the sun's rays reflected by the alabaster limestone that made up the fortress's exterior. Keira welcomed the reprieve from the midday sun but shivered despite herself as she embraced the familiar sensation of being swallowed alive by a massive stone beast. Cyrus led them through the entry hall, passing by the courtyard and its mesmerizing reflective pool and into the throne room.

Inside, a near-empty hall met them, its buttressed ceiling soaring high above as they made their way to the raised dais at the far end. Landry was nowhere to be seen.

Cyrus murmured a few words to one of the watching sentries, then turned back to them. "They'll notify the Regio of our arrival."

The five of them shifted awkwardly as they waited for Landry, all but Albert, who gazed around the room with furrowed-browed intensity—searching, though for what, Keira couldn't say.

The echo of footsteps and the loud clang of a door being thrown open brought them all up short. Following Cyrus's lead, they each quickly took a knee before the swirl of robes that signaled Landry's arrival. Keira glanced up through the curtain of hair that fell before her face to see Landry standing on the dais's edge, surveying the bowed supplicants with a broad grin.

Unable to help herself, Keira lifted her head, and she shot him a smirk. "If I didn't know better, Your Majesty, I'd say that power suits you."

A curtain of silence fell across the room, and Keira heard Cyrus make a strangled noise in the back of his throat, no doubt aghast at her boldness. She kept her eyes fixed on Landry, though, and the muscle twitching at the corner of his lips as he tried and failed to stare her down.

Finally, he let out a loud guffaw and skipped down the steps of the dais, gesturing for them all to rise. Keira clambered to her feet, only to be swallowed in a crushing hug. Laughing, she quickly returned the embrace.

"I have to say, Your Highness, this throne room is certainly more impressive than your last, though perhaps with fewer *distractions*."

Landry snorted, no doubt also remembering the gaggle of fawning girls that had entertained him back at the monastery on Mount Ánghen.

"Yes, well, perks of being Regio, I suppose. And please, call me Landry, at least when court isn't in session." From the corner of her eyes, she could see Cyrus's mouth open and close, like a fish gasping for air. Landry ignored him, though, instead cocking his head at Keira, eyes searching hers. She resisted the desperate urge to look away, suppressing the instinct to run and hide from that probing gaze, lest he see all she'd meticulously stowed away. "It's good to see you, Keira," he said finally. "It's good to see all of you. Things have certainly become more *complicated* in the capital of late."

Cyrus tensed, his jaw tightening as he regarded Landry closely. "I received word of the threat, Your Highness. Is the prisoner still with you?"

"He is," Landry said, adding for the rest's benefit, "We got wind of the assassination attempt after we'd caught a servant sneaking about my private office."

"No doubt looking for information to track the Regio's movements," Cyrus said darkly. "We'll sort this out, Your Highness, I swear."

Keira saw a softness cross Landry's eyes, and he laid a hand gently on Cyrus's shoulder, squeezing as he said, "I know you will."

"Promises are all well and good," a steely voice murmured from behind them. Keira turned to see Zipporah standing with arms crossed. "But how, exactly, do you propose we do that?"

Cyrus opened his mouth to reply, but a quiet, almost bored-sounding voice beat him to it. "Clearly the prisoner requires further . . . interrogation." Keira glanced over at Albert, who stood with hands tucked into his pockets as he continued to survey the throne room.

"The prisoner's already been interrogated," Cyrus interjected, brow furrowed. "That's how we found out about the assassination attempt to begin with."

Albert regarded him coolly, refusing to rise to Cyrus's annoyed tone. "Not by our standards, he hasn't."

Keira felt Albert's eyes on her, no doubt expecting her to speak up on behalf of the Legion and their methods, but she refused to meet his gaze. She shivered, remembering the last time she'd attempted to interrogate someone with pneumonancy, the slippery coils of Marek Largaen's stream of memory. Albert's eyes continued to bore into the side of her head. She looked resolutely away.

She was saved from responding by Cyrus's brusque dismissal. "That would be a waste of time. We already know there's a radicalized faction forming within the People's Council. Our best chance is to appeal to the council directly, make them aware of the threat to the Regio's life, and ask for their help. If we want this new government to be legitimate, Your Highness, we have to empower it to make decisions and trust it to discipline itself. Or else our critics are right when they call it only a token gesture of representation."

Landry pursed his lips, thoughtful.

Albert scoffed, a mocking sound that made Keira blink in surprise. "Do you honestly expect a lot of miserly sycophants, accountable only to the restless masses and their own thought-less self-interest, to put all that aside in favor of some grand ideal of communal welfare? Particularly when that hinges on the survival of a Regio whose family relegated them to the lowest class for centuries?" Albert raised one eyebrow in disbelief. "I think not."

Cyrus gritted his teeth, glaring at Albert with undisguised dislike. "Well, we'll never know unless we give them the chance, now, will we?"

"Yes, and how much time do you suggest we waste on this endeavor?"

"As long as it takes."

"Ah, well, I hope you've lined up your successor then, Your Majesty."

Cyrus emitted what almost sounded like a snarl from the back of his throat.

Landry suddenly put up a hand, silencing both parties. He regarded Keira coolly and dispassionately. "And you, Keira? What do you suggest?"

Keira hesitated, glancing between Cyrus and Albert where they stood, squared off, on either side of Landry, both eyeing her expectantly. She took a deep breath.

"I'm sorry, Cyrus. I appreciate representation and democracy as much as the next person, but I'm not about to trust Landry's life to a council full of people that threatened outright revolt just a few months ago."

Cyrus's lips pursed, and Keira saw a muscle working in his jaw. Keira glanced at Albert, seeing a look of triumph flicker in his eyes, and something churned in her stomach. Remembering the last time she'd entered someone's mind unwanted, Keira felt herself break into a cold sweat.

"B-But I don't think we should interrogate the prisoner again—not yet."

The triumph vanished from Albert's eyes, replaced by an icy rage that bored into her. She blinked, startled by its intensity. But when she looked again, it was gone, so quickly she wondered if she'd imagined it, replaced only by pursed-lipped disapproval.

"Then what," Landry began, drawing her attention back to him, "do you propose, Keira?"

Keira swallowed, feeling all eyes on her. At that moment, all she wanted to do was get away. She wanted to run far from these people and their expectations, those piercing eyes that followed her every movement. She'd started this quest on her own, and by Pneumos, she'd finish it that way. She cleared her throat.

"I think I'd like to pay a visit to our friend Neval. Seems to me if anyone would know what's going on, it'd be him. If one of his people really is plotting this assassination, he would know."

"And what if he's actually the one behind all of this?" Cyrus asked icily. "You'd be handing him the advantage, practically giving him all the information we have."

Keira gritted her teeth, remembering the smirking tavern hand she'd met that day so long ago in Rabonéis, the boy who'd turned out to be the leader of a revolution. "Leave Neval to me," she said thinly. "If he's the one behind this, then I'll deal with him myself."

Landry cocked his head, eyes tight as they considered her.

"Leave us, will you?" he said suddenly to the others. "The attendants have already seen to your belongings. You'll find your rooms ready in the West Wing."

There was a quick shuffle of feet, until Keira realized it was just the two of them remaining. Landry's eyes traced the length of her, and Keira shifted uneasily under that gaze, fingers curling into fists under the inspection.

"You look thinner," Landry finally said. "Bellatori cooking leave something to be desired?" His voice was light, but his worried look belied the airy question.

Keira snorted. "Nah, nothing I like more than soggy bread and twice-baked gruel." The subject broached, her eyes suddenly registered Landry's own appearance—the light stubble on his jaw and the gray shadows under his eyes. He looked almost haggard, far from the rosy-cheeked prince she'd seen coronated less than a year ago. She started to ask how he'd been holding up, but he quickly interrupted her, as if registering the direction of her thoughts.

"So you—enjoyed your time in the Southern Shield?"

Keira hesitated, glancing at him. "I'm not sure *enjoyed* is the right word. But it was—I mean, I felt . . . useful there. I needed that," she finished, searching his eyes for some glimmer of understanding.

He nodded, muscles working in his jaw as he clearly wrestled with something deep inside himself. "After you left, I—I worried if I'd done the right thing—sending you away. I wondered if it would have been better . . ." His voice trailed off as Keira briskly shook her head.

"You didn't send me away, Landry. I wanted to go—practically begged you, if I recall. You were being a good friend." She offered him a weak smile, and he returned it, though the expression didn't quite reach his eyes.

"I miss him too, Keira."

Keira's breath caught in her chest, and she fixed her eyes on a crack in the flagstone floor, consciously willing her heartbeat to slow. Landry said nothing, merely watching and waiting for her to catch hold of whatever emotion had her caught in its crushing clasp. Slowly, she let the breath go through pursed lips, eyes fluttering closed and then opening again as she raised a single eyebrow at him. "He hated your guts."

Landry laughed at that, a loud, full-bellied sound that belied his exhausted appearance. Keira couldn't help the grin that cracked open the solid lines of her face, and she laughed with him, marveling at how wonderful it felt. *When was the last time I laughed?*

Landry's laughter faded, but a smile remained, and he nodded.

"Yes, I suppose he did. But he was one of the first to ever challenge me, to not take any of my princely crap—after you, of course."

Keira snorted, remembering all too well her first encounter with the self-centered prince in a throne room not too different from this one. He'd come a long way, she decided, eyeing the easy way he held himself now—confident but not overly so, secure in both the power and the responsibilities that he held.

"So you really want to do this?"

Keira nodded, leveling Landry with a determined look that brooked no further discussion. "You know he has to know something about what's going on." *Hell, he might even be a part of it,* she thought darkly. But she refrained from saying the words aloud, remembering the shaky friendship that had formed between the hunted prince and the charming rebel leader. It had taken all their combined abilities, not to mention a bit of luck, to see Landry safely on the throne and the People's Council formed alongside him. Could Neval really have turned against them after all that?

Keira remembered the flirting smile of Neval the tavern hand back in Rabonéis—so quickly morphed into the screaming leader of a rebellious mob. She shivered. Neval had spent time in a Marian prison for leading just such an insurrection only a few years before. He had every reason to despise the Marian Empire, regardless of what use he might have for them in the short run. *Yes*, she thought. *Neval could absolutely have turned on us.* Regardless of all they'd been through, she couldn't forget that *he'd* been through far worse.

"Well, I see I won't be able to convince you otherwise," Landry said, shrugging. "Go ahead, then. And be sure to say hello to Neval for me."

"Have you two not been keeping in touch?" Keira asked, shooting him an inquisitive glance. "When I left, you two seemed the best of friends—overhauling the government together, talking sports and girls." Perhaps Landry wasn't so easily convinced of his old friend's veracity, after all, she thought.

Landry shrugged, rubbing the bridge of his nose with one hand. "He's the leader of the People's Opposition Party—newly formed," he added, seeing Keira's confused expression. "And I'm—well, I'm me. I represent everything they hated about the old system, the system that oppressed them for centuries. He can't exactly be friendly. I understand."

His words were dispassionate, but as Keira glanced sidelong at his tense stance, she realized he was anything but.

"It'll get easier," she murmured. "It has to."

Again, Landry gave a noncommittal shrug. "Perhaps, but that day certainly seems a long way off." He shook his head quickly, as if to clear it of things far beyond his own control. He leaned forward, giving her a light shove. "Go on, then, go save the day again, Keira Altman. But—I am here . . . if you need me."

Keira swallowed, offering a smile that twisted partway into a grimace as she turned and made for the door, leaving the powerful Regio all too alone in his massive stone hall.

Keira hurried down the corridor, mind already racing with questions of how exactly she'd find Neval—and what she'd say to him once she did. Absorbed by these thoughts, she nearly missed the figure perched half-hidden on a bench inside a shadowed alcove in the wall.

"Keira Lone Warrior strikes again," a low, silky voice murmured.

Keira froze, then half pivoted on one foot to face the voice—searching the shadows, though for what, she couldn't imagine. The figure shifted, and Zipporah's smirking face emerged into the light.

Keira crossed her arms over her chest, glaring at Zipporah's seemingly innocent expression. She was *not* in the mood to hear whatever fault Zipporah seemed to find with her now. "What exactly do you want?"

Zipporah gave a half shrug, eyes still fixed on the tip of her knife as it cut tiny, curling slivers of wood from an emerging figurine. "Why, nothing at all. I assume our fearless Regio capitulated to your pleading wiles?"

Keira's jaw clenched. "Landry didn't *capitulate* on anything. And I certainly do not have wiles!"

Zipporah chuckled softly, infuriatingly calm in the face of Keira's mounting frustration. Worse, she seemed to sense it. "So off she goes to save the world, all on her own—the indomitable Keira Altman. Pneumos forbid she ever go along with someone else's plan."

"What are you talking about?" Keira asked, honest confusion intermingling with her frustration.

Zipporah's eyebrows shot up nearly to her hairline as she finally looked at Keira directly, the ghost of a smile on her lips.

"You can't even see it, can you?"

Keira glared at her, refusing to give her the satisfaction of asking exactly what "it" was. Zipporah seemed more than happy to inform her anyway.

"You can't see how you must constantly be in control, off on your own quest rather than dealing with any sort of interpersonal conflict." Keira opened her mouth to argue, but Zipporah continued unabated, "Nope, the moment things get tough and a decision needs to be made, Keira Altman is out the door."

"Maybe," Keira squeezed through gritted teeth, "that's because the decisions I make have a nasty habit of getting the people I care about killed."

She expected to see regret and maybe even embarrassment color Zipporah's cheeks. Instead, she snorted. "Oh, please. That has to be the worst excuse for someone's personal control issues I think I've ever heard."

Keira gaped at her, mouth opening and closing—unable to articulate the swirling chaos of thoughts in her own brain. Finally, she recovered.

"What is your *problem*?" Keira demanded. "You don't even know me! You have no idea what goes on in my head, what I've had to deal with. How dare you judge me?"

Zipporah arched a single eyebrow at her, undeterred. "Oh, but I do, Keira. I surely do. And I've known others exactly like you." She shook her head, face cold. "Someday, Keira, you're going to have to take a stand and actually rely on those around you. You'd better hope there are still friends around you when you finally do."

Keira stared blankly. She'd known she wasn't exactly Zipporah's favorite person. But this was on a whole other level. This woman actually *hated* her, and she had no idea why.

"Let me make one thing perfectly clear," Zipporah said,

taking a menacing step forward. Keira braced herself, refusing to flinch even as Zipporah's dark eyes flashed—a foot above her own, as the woman towered over her. "I will not allow your foolhardy hero tactics to put the people I love in harm's way."

By "people," Keira was pretty sure Zipporah was speaking exclusively of Marti. And though every inch of her itched to point this out, if only to put the other girl's teeth on edge, Keira ruefully kept her temper in check.

"I'm not planning on putting anyone in danger, *Zipporah*," Keira breathed, fighting to keep her voice steady.

The taller girl's dark eyes narrowed down at her, thick with suspicion. "We'll see about that." Then, as quickly as she'd appeared, Zipporah's back was to her as she departed, looking for all the world like she'd merely been out for a stroll.

Keira clasped and unclasped her hands, watching as Zipporah sauntered off down the hall. Just when she'd been thinking they might actually be friends . . .

She shook her head. That hell hound was not worth her worry, and certainly not her regret. Turning in the opposite direction, Keira hurried for the West Wing of the Vindolum and the waiting supplies. Whatever Zipporah had to say about it, Keira knew in her gut that Neval had the answers they needed, and she'd be damned if she let anyone stand in the way of her getting them.

The shadows of the rising cityscape grew longer as Keira hurried through the back alleys of Crîd Eálas's notorious South End—the growing dusk sending a shiver down her spine. She'd gone straight to Cyrus after speaking with Landry, ignoring Raina's pleas to come with her, and demanded to know where she could find Neval. After Keira brushed off his own offer to accompany her, Cyrus had reluctantly given her Neval's address. Keira was surprised to hear he'd never actually left his old haunts. With a tremor of fear, she remembered her and Danny's harrowing trip to the Miller's Plow and the surprise ambush that had awaited them there. Keira's fingers curled more firmly around the hilt of her sword as her eyes danced over each shadowed entryway of the stoops she hurried past. She could feel eyes on her, catching a glimpse every once in a while—a rustle of movement behind a curtained window or the quick disappearance of eyes around a corner.

Keira's heart hammered, and her mind went immediately to the coiled pneuma in her belly. She could send it out—curling around corners and fishing for the eyes that held her in their grasp. She cursed mentally. *Don't be ridiculous*, she thought. *There's nobody here to ground you.* Healing pneumonancy was one thing, when she could put her hands on the other person, with three points of contact firmly rooting her to the ground. She'd avoided most other canting since—

She swallowed, remembering what else had happened only a few short months ago in these very twisting alleys. A Bellatori charge, the flash of hooves, Danny diving to save a little girl, then the crunch of bone on stone as he crashed to the ground, the scream of a horse as it reared, hooves flashing before they crashed down on top of—

Keira gasped, collapsing against a wall as she pressed the heels of her palms into her eyes. *Go away*, she begged. *Please stop.* But the onslaught of memories was merciless—Danny's face, swollen and pouring blood, his chest barely rising and falling in that awful, lopsided fashion that indicated far too many broken ribs. The panic bubbled up, and Keira's breath came faster, tearing from her in waves that made her throat sting and chest ache. *I can't do this*, she thought, *not here, not again.*

Breathe, Keira.

She froze.

This is here, not there. It is now, not then.

"Danny?"

Keira felt a sob tear from her chest as her memory morphed away from his broken body and back to his lopsided smile and those twinkling olive-green eyes. She focused on the memory of those nights so long ago in the little farmhouse near Abalás, during the early years of their training. Danny would awake in a cold sweat, crying out as he relived his own nightmares of a war long gone, and she'd often wake up herself. Though her room lay on the other side of the house, she somehow always knew when he needed her. Dancing across creaking floorboards in stocking-covered feet, she'd slip into his room, crawling into his bed to curl around his massive frame. With her arm around his waist, they'd lay like that. *This is here*, she'd whisper, *not there. This now, not then.* Her own face pressed into the hard planes of his back, she'd hold him until the shaking stopped, until he'd slipped back beneath the unforgiving waves of restless sleep. And then she'd leave, never to speak of those nighttime excursions in the light of day.

"Danny," she sobbed then, eyes squeezed shut as she sagged against the alley wall, "I can't do this anymore, not on my own. I need—"

The soft clatter of rolling pebbles made Keira stiffen.

Thrusting herself off the wall, she spun to meet whatever threat had sneaked up on her practically unheard. The steel of her blade whistled as she unsheathed it and settled into a guard stance, her heart hammering in her ears and her mouth suddenly going dry. *Fool, idiot, sloth,* her brain chanted, imagining every insult Nazor would have hurled at her if she'd been there to witness this particular bit of foolishness. A movement in the shadows to her left caught her eye, and Keira shifted slightly to square off.

"Who's there?" she called. "Show yourself now or be off, unless you feel like eating some steel tonight."

The ferocity of her words belied the blood rushing in her ears as she remembered the last time she'd been caught unawares in these very alleys, when she and Danny both had been caught like rabbits in a trap of their own making, hauled before Neval himself just before the city imploded around them. She did *not* feel like repeating the experience.

She'd just opened her mouth to threaten her formless

follower when a tiny voice echoed in the darkness. "I just be wanting to see the city."

All the tension vanished from Keira's body, and with her legs now the consistency of jelly, Keira yet again collapsed against the nearest wall.

"Raina," Keira growled at the wide-eyed face that now peeked around the corner. "I *told* you to stay at the Vindolum. It's too dangerous—"

"Not too dangerous for you," Raina muttered, arms crossed and chin pointed at an obstinate angle. Keira squashed the seething heat that rose to her face, clenching and unclenching her jaw until she thought she had a hold of her voice. "One of these days, Raina, you're going to follow your own damn inclinations right off a cliff, and I won't even feel bad for you."

Raina looked stung at that but quickly hid the hurt as she asked, "How far being this Neval person's house?"

Still stewing, Keira pinched the bridge of her nose before glaring at the conniving eleven-year-old. "Just a few blocks up. And you're lucky, too. If we weren't so close, I'd march you right back and lock you up in that fortress."

She spun on her heels then and stalked up the alleyway toward the waiting tavern. "It would serve you right," she muttered to no one in particular, "sneaking up on people like that. Lucky you didn't get skewered."

"*You're* just mad you not be catching me sooner," a smug little voice murmured at her elbow.

Keira's jaw clenched, but she refused to give Raina the satisfaction of a retort. It *was* fairly impressive she'd been able to tail Keira all this way. Even if she had been a tad—*distracted.*

"This could be tricky, Raina. You'll have to come inside, since it's not safe for you to wait alone. But Neval, he's—unpredictable—his friends even more so." Keira felt another twist of nerves in her gut and felt her legs move faster, until Raina was practically jogging to keep up. "You stay quiet and let me talk to him. But if I give the signal—" Keira halted so suddenly that Raina smacked into her and stumbled backward. Keira caught her arm, steadying her, and then squeezed it purposefully. "If I give you the signal, Raina, you run like hell. You hear me?" Raina's eyes were the size of saucers as she gave two quick nods. Keira released her, turning back to see the glowing windows of the Miller's Plow. She let out a breath she didn't know she'd been holding as the familiar icy wave of adrenaline washed through her.

And again it begins, she thought.

Here we go again, Danny's voice agreed.

Keira walked to the door, Raina close in tow as they slipped into the warmth and light inside.

THE INSIDE of the Miller's Plow seemed just as she remembered it—warm firelight gleaming on the long wooden tables filled with laughing patrons, the floor covered with sticky ale that sloshed over the sides of tankards. Keira quickly scanned the room, searching for the mousy brown curls she remembered so well. Not seeing him, Keira made for the bar, gripping Raina's hand to tow her along. Raina's eyes danced around the room, her head whipping back and forth to take it all in.

The barmaid glanced up from the glasses she'd been drying with an old rag as soon as they reached her. Her brows raised in surprise as she took in the two of them. "You fink this is the best place for li'l ones, do ya?"

Keira ignored the question, focusing on her own instead. "I

think that we're looking for someone, and I'm pretty sure you can help us find him."

The woman's smirk remained, even as her brows raised higher. "An' who might that be?"

"Neval," Keira murmured. "Neval Brennan."

The woman's jaw clenched, and her eyes narrowed.

"Can't help you. Never 'eard of 'im."

Now it was Keira's turn to snort. "I find that hard to believe."

"Can't help that, can I?"

Letting go of Raina's hand, Keira placed both of hers against the bar as she leaned forward, eyes fixed on the woman in front of her, who stiffened at her approach.

"Look, I'm a friend of Neval's. Know much about what went down in Capital Plaza?" The memories quickly flitted across Keira's own mind—Junia stationed before the Vindolum, flanked by the Council of Benadur, about to wrest power into her own hands, before the supposedly dead Prince Landry emerged, the rebel leader Neval Brennan by his side. Together, the two had declared the institution of a new order, a People's Council, and an attempt to right the wrongs of the past.

From the look on the barmaid's face, she'd been there that day, or had heard enough stories to feel like she had.

"Well, I was there too," Keira murmured, "unseen but just as involved as Neval himself. Now I'm telling you," she hissed, "that I need to talk to him. So I suggest you figure out where he might have gone."

The woman's lips pursed as indecision warred within her eyes. For a moment, Keira thought about what it would be like to slip in through those eyes, letting her pneuma curl and unfold amid the stream of memory and pluck out exactly what she needed. Keira blinked—a feeling of nausea and horror at the thought churning in her stomach. No, she would not do that again. If this woman refused to help her, she'd just have to find another way.

The woman merely blinked slowly for another agonizing minute. Finally, she nodded curtly, and Keira let out the breath she hadn't known she was holding.

"Wait 'ere," the woman ordered before disappearing up the spiral staircase to the right of the bar. Keira rubbed her neck, trying to release the tension that had stiffened it.

"It worked!" Raina piped up beside her, a wide grin pasted across her face. Keira felt a smile tug at her own lips but forced them instead into a scowl.

"For now," she muttered, eyeing the stairway for any sign of the woman's return. They waited for a few long minutes before, exasperated, she pushed off from the bar and strode to those very stairs, gesturing for Raina to follow her. "The hell if I'm waiting here," she muttered. She took the stairs two at a time, hearing Raina scrambling up behind her. Finally reaching the top of the stairs, Keira had to pause a moment to let her eyes adjust to the dim hallway light. At the far end, light spilled from an open doorway, illuminating the barmaid as she muttered something to the room's occupant. Gritting her teeth, Keira strode toward them. Hearing her footsteps, the woman spun to face her, sputtering in rage, "I—I told you lot to wait downstairs!"

"It's all right, Martha dear," a voice like liquid honey murmured from inside. "It's pleasure enough to be seein' Miss Altman."

Keira turned to hug the wall as the barmaid stomped past her. When she turned back, Neval was leaning casually against the doorframe, arms crossed and a sensuous smirk across his lips. Keira swallowed quickly, staring at him. He'd certainly changed in the months she'd spent trying to forget the world in the Southern Shield. The young tavern hand she'd met back in Rabonéis had been gangly, with sinewy muscles hard-won from a scrappy life on the streets, but with a thinness that spoke of many evenings spent with not enough food. The young man who stood before her now was anything but gaunt. His skin had tanned to a golden hue in the seaside sun of Crîd Eálas, and his face and shoulders had filled out. His mop of brown curls still flopped into his eyes when he talked, but even they had lost their lackluster mousiness and were now a rich shade of umber. And there was something about the way he held himself, a confidence borne of trials won and buoyed by the trust of others. He looked . . . handsome, Keira decided, shifting awkwardly at the realization.

She caught his eye then and watched a knowing look tease at his mouth. Keira's ears burned, and she quickly forced a smirk. "Seems political life is treating you well, Neval."

"Like what you see, do you?"

Keira snorted, pushing past him to hide the color she knew had come to her cheeks. She surveyed the room. Richly decorated in warm hues and fine fabrics, it practically glowed with the new wealth Neval no doubt possessed.

"Seems you've gotten an upgrade from your last lodgings—you know, the ones you tried to have me killed in," she added thinly. *Let him be put off guard for once*, she thought.

But Neval merely chuckled behind her, striding past to offer a chair with an exaggerated flourish. "Kill you? Why, I never. If I remember correctly, it was merely a teensy misunderstandin'."

Keira rolled her eyes but went to take the chair anyway. As she reached him, Neval's eyes widened with a twinkle as his gaze fluttered to the doorway. "And who is this pretty sprite of a thing?" Keira glanced backward, flushing to realize she'd forgotten Raina, who shifted uneasily in the doorway.

"That's none of your business, now is it?" Keira snapped before quickly realizing her mistake. Neval's eyebrows waggled with piqued interest as he glanced between them. Keira sighed and quickly backtracked. "Neval, meet Raina, otherwise known as the royal pain in my backside. You may know her brother from your *lovely* People's Council."

Neval's eyes danced but he didn't ask any further questions, merely bringing over a third chair and offering it to Raina with the deepest bow Keira had ever seen. Keira snorted, and a tiny smile came to Raina's mouth as she sidestepped in through the door and cautiously joined them at the table.

"I think I've met your brother, Miss Raina," Neval said, taking his own seat across from Keira. "We were all quite excited to see representatives arrive from the elusive Southern Shield. Your people are rarely keen to leave their islands, as I understand."

A flush of pride and excitement colored Raina's cheeks, and she nodded, quickly adding, "You know where my brother be staying?"

Neval nodded. "He and the rest of the Southern Shield delegates took up lodgings here in the South End, not far from where we are now. I could certainly show you if—"

"Look, there'll be time for all that later," Keira interrupted, shoving down the flurry of nerves in her stomach while ignoring the look of annoyance Raina shot her. "We have other business to discuss."

Neval's eyebrows rose, and he steepled his fingertips together as he leaned forward, a glint in his eye. "Indeed? And what business might that be?"

Keira made an exasperated noise in the back of her throat,

and Neval's eyebrows rose still further. "Don't play dumb with me, Neval. I don't believe for a second you haven't gotten wind of what's going on, the threats that are being made against Landry's life."

Neval's face went blank, every smirk and smile gone in an instant as a mask of passive interest settled in its place. "Is that right? And I take it you think I have somethin' to do with it?"

There was an edge to his voice that belied his calm exterior, but Keira ignored the warning tone and barreled ahead. "Well, you *are* the leader of this People's Opposition Party now, aren't you? Tell me, what exactly are you *opposed* to if not Landry himself? No matter he used to be your *friend*."

Anger flashed in Neval's eyes as they narrowed. "Well, I'm not sure, Keira dear. What could we *possibly* have to complain about in the world now that the good Regio has *deigned* to award us a council of our own? Could it be the taxes that still cripple the poorest among us? Or perhaps the fact that uplanders are still treated as second-class citizens in our own country? Or, I don't know, maybe it's my own damnable village, still sittin' under a foot of water from that blasted dam?"

Neval's voice had steadily risen, until he was practically shouting. By the end, his words hung in the air, coloring the silence in hues of pain and outrage. A stone had settled in Keira's stomach, and though she opened her mouth to speak, nothing came out.

"To tell you the truth, Keira dear, I have no desire to hurt our poor Regio, so out of his depth among the vipers that surround him. Though as for his being my *friend*, you know as well as I that there can be no true *friendship* with the one that holds your chains." Neval was breathing heavily, staring at her before finally adding, "But no, my attentions are very much directed *elsewhere*."

Keira stared at him, not knowing where to begin or what she could possibly say in the face of such anger. She knew what he was talking about, of course, saw the injustices every day. To her left, Raina sat frozen in her seat, eyes fixed resolutely on the gnarls of wood-plank table before her. But in her eyes, Keira saw a muted echo of the fire in Neval's. Raina understood what it was to feel an outsider. But murdering Landry was certainly not going to solve anything. No, it would only lead to more chaos.

Keira sighed, pinching the bridge of her nose before again meeting Neval's eyes. "If not you, then who? Who's behind the assassination attempt? Where and when is it planned for?"

Neval's gaze met hers, and she saw a muscle working in his cheek. "I don't know."

"That's crap," she barked, slamming her hand on the table. Raina nearly jumped out of her skin, her eyes wide and scared. "I don't believe you, Neval. Tell me what you know about whatever this faction is and what they have planned for Landry."

Neval's eyes narrowed further, and he leaned forward, fingers splayed on the wood planks of the table. His voice was smooth as honey and barely above a whisper as he murmured, "Believe me or not, Keira dear, I don't know any such details. All I know is that there is a splinter faction within the People's Council who feel the current methods of making change leave something to be desired."

"So rather than work within the system, they'd rather burn the whole thing down." Keira let out a bark of laughter. "Nice people."

Neval gave that infuriating half shrug before replying, "It can be hard to get buy-in to a system that has never worked in your favor, Keira dear."

"Then at least tell me who they are."

"So you can barge into their homes? Terrify their children? Demand answers they'll never give you? Or just tell that pet of yours—Cyrus Flavius. With his Bellatori connections, I'm sure he could arrange a casual search and seizure." Neval's mouth twisted into a smirk. "I think not." Then his eyes narrowed further. "And what of you, Keira dear? If you've returned to grace us with your presence, I take it your mysterious Legion has decided to get its hands dirty. Tell me, what are they plannin'? A hostile takeover? Or will they simply disband the new People's Council as soon as it makes a decision they don't particularly fancy? What happens, Keira, when your Legion realizes true change can get a tad *chaotic*?"

"They wouldn't do that."

"No? Then what are their plans?"

Keira's lips pressed into a thin line, her eyes narrowing. She didn't owe Neval anything, and if he really was working with this fringe group, then he could go to hell for all she cared.

Neval chuckled. "Now who's bein' tight-lipped?"

Keira's jaw clenched and unclenched as she glared at him. Her steadily growing fury churned in her stomach until she wanted nothing more than to send him flying into the back wall. The violent thought raised the hair on the back of her neck, and she sprang to her feet instead, breathing heavily as she fought to keep her voice steady. "Fine. Have it your way, Neval Brennan. But don't blame me when this whole damn country falls down around your ears. You say your people have been treated unfairly? I seriously doubt they'll fare better under whatever Council of Benadur member steps forward to take Landry's place after this country tears itself apart trying to decide who will rule it."

And with that, she turned and strode for the door. Behind the pounding in her ears, she distantly heard Raina scramble from her chair and hurry after her. But Keira didn't slow her pace, not until she was outside the Miller's Plow, inhaling the crisp night air and willing her heartbeat to slow. She stood that way for a long while, Raina beside her, as she listened to the sound of the city settling in for the night ahead.

Finally, a small voice beside her asked, "Do you—do you think Akamu be part of this faction, Keira? The one that be wanting to kill the Regio?"

Surprised, Keira glanced down at Raina, whose entire face was pinched in worry. Keira felt her expression soften, though fury still bubbled within her stomach. She sighed. "I don't think so, Raina. Whatever it is they've been planning, it's been stewing for a very long time."

Raina nodded, relief evident. What Keira didn't tell her was that she suspected the uplander faction's own prejudices would keep them from granting any of the delegates from the Southern Shield access to their inner circle. Revolutionaries they might be, but she suspected their tolerance extended no further than those they considered their own—fellow citizens be damned. And what would befall the Southern Shield, even if these revolutionaries did somehow wrest power from the Council of Benadur? Nothing good, Keira suspected, shivering slightly.

Glancing down, she saw Raina's relief had twisted back into a frown, no doubt at the look on Keira's own face. Keira forced a small smile before taking Raina's hand and leading her back up the alley they'd come down.

"We be going back to the Vindolum, Keira?" Raina asked, voice hushed amid the long shadows of the buildings that rose on either side.

Keira nodded, her free hand tightening into a fist. "It turns out I have some business there after all."

CHAPTER
TWENTY-ONE

By the time Keira and Raina made it back to the Vindolum, the moon had well and truly risen, basking the sleeping city in a warm glow. Wearily, the two of them heaved their aching legs up each step of the twisting spiral staircase that made up the back entrance to the West Wing. Similar to the Legion headquarters, Keira and Raina shared adjoining rooms, though to Raina's infinite glee, she had her own entrance and exit this time.

"Head to bed, kid," Keira said, tilting her head toward the waiting doorway even as she made no attempt to enter herself. Raina paused, previously bleary eyes now sharpening into daggerlike assessment.

"You not be sleeping, then?"

Keira shook her head, rubbing a weary hand across her eyes.

"No, I still have some—things to attend to."

"What things?" Raina asked, arms crossing her chest. Any second now, Keira knew that chin would jut out at that impossibly obstinate angle.

She quickly replied, "Nothing to worry about—Legion business."

Raina paused, and Keira saw something churn behind those seafoam eyes.

"I changed my mind," Raina said finally—chin finally reaching its apical inclination. "I want you be training me, Keira. Teach me to be *Le'ena*."

Keira froze, mentally cursing Albert for even suggesting such a thing. She was no teacher, especially not now, not after—

"Raina . . ." Keira said slowly. "When Albert mentioned training, he was talking about the Legion's training, not mine. I'm no mentor, not even a full Legionnaire yet. I *can't* train you."

Raina's lips pressed into a thin line as her eyes hardened.

"I be seeing what you can do-ah," she murmured, her lilting Islander accent thickening with every fury-filled word. "I want *you* be training me, not some Legion—you."

Keira let out a barking laugh. "Me? You want me to train you? Can't you see what a *mess* I am, Raina?" Keira could feel the bitterness in her own voice, the scoffing look she knew played on her lips. But she was too upset to care . . .

"Maybe that was a possibility once," she continued. "Before I lost—" Her voice cut off, mind flitting to a long-forgotten memory—it was a dream, really—of her and Danny, grounder and cantor, surrounded by their own mentees in a farmhouse so like their old one near Abalás. Together, she and Danny would have taught them to wield their pneumonancy, to fight, and to trust each other with their lives—as they once had.

Keira squeezed her eyes shut, willing that image to disappear into the smoke of forgotten memory, where all impossibilities belonged.

Finally, she opened her eyes to find Raina staring at her,

eyes soft with concern despite her continued stubborn stance. "I can't train you, Raina. If you want me to take you back to the Legion after this is all over, then fine. But I can't be the one to train you."

Raina's eyes turned hard again as she glared at Keira. "Don't bother," she spat. "I didn't really want to be training with no *grelún*, anyway. Keep your Legion, and your powers. I came here to find Akamu, and that's what I be doing."

Keira opened her mouth to reply, but Raina had already disappeared inside her room, the door slamming shut with enough force to rattle its hinges. Keira massaged her temples, silently apologizing to her mother for every infuriating bout of temper that had left many a door in the Altman house creaking on its hinges.

She considered following her, to explain, to try to put into words the hollowed-out feeling that he'd left, the fear that nearly crippled her every time she tried to use her pneumonancy without him—without his immovable steadiness, the tether that always pulled her back, no matter how far out she strained. But she didn't. That was a story that every exhausted fiber of her body rebelled against telling. And from the loud bang of drawers being opened and slammed shut, Raina was in no mood to hear it. Groaning, Keira turned and made her way into her own room. Rifling through the saddle bags that had been carefully arranged by the bed, she tugged out a leather-bound folio from wish she pulled a sheet of parchment, its already addressed heading standing in lone contrast to the otherwise blank page. With a sigh, she smoothed it against the hard wood of the desk and reached for a quill pen. This partic-ular correspondence was long overdue.

⁓

Keira awoke to sunlight piercing through the cracks of the curtain-covered windows. She groaned, throwing an arm over her face as she rolled over again, willing herself back into the heavy weight of sleep. A moment passed, then another. Realizing sleep would continue to evade her, Keira flung off her covers and stared in annoyance at the frothy canopy above. She couldn't have gotten more than a couple hours of sleep, tossing and turning as she remembered yesterday's events—Neval's words, Raina's anger, and Cyrus's foolish plan. Keira groaned again before rolling over and sliding her legs off the bed. She sat there for a moment, rubbing sleep from her eyes, before shuffling over to the dresser and filling the bowl there with water from the pitcher. Splashing water onto her face, she could finally open her eyes fully, or at least enough to see the matted tangles of her curls flying every which way in the mirror before her. She groaned again and ran brutal fingers through it, forcing the curls into submission so she could tie a leather thong around the bulk.

Might as well get this over with, she thought. Amid her tossing and turning the night before, she'd decided to apologize to Raina, explain why it would be so hard to train her, and see if they could come to some sort of compromise. Hell, maybe even Albert could help.

She shuffled over to the door that connected her room to Raina's and quickly rapped on it. She waited, her nervousness mounting.

Nothing.

She rapped again, her nerves now tinged with annoyance.

Still nothing.

Frustration overcoming her nerves entirely, Keira pushed the door open.

The room was empty, some drawers left open, as if its occupant had packed in a hurry. Something else pricked at Keira now—fear. She quickly scanned the room, looking for any sign of what might have happened. There was no note, but also no sign of a struggle. Quickly, Keira racked her brain for memories of their conversation the night before. What had Raina said?

I came here to find Akamu, and that's what I be doing.

Keira sagged slightly, relief taking the edge off her fear but leaving something else in its wake—regret. Keira had known Raina would remain in Crîd Eálas, stay with her brother. That had always been her intention. But it wasn't until that moment that Keira realized how sad that actually made her. She'd never had a little sister. Never experienced the squabbling brand of love that so often accompanied such a relationship. The closest thing had been her cousin, Molly.

Keira swallowed, squashing memories of the last time she'd seen Molly, of the car crash that had ended both their lives.

No, she thought. *Raina is fine. She's just with her brother. I'll see her again.*

But the truth was that Keira already missed her, missed those bright, shining eyes and her ready laugh, even missed her infuriating stubbornness.

Keira gritted her teeth. *It's better this way,* she decided. *I have too much to do here. Raina would only have gotten hurt, or gotten in the way.*

Nice try, Danny's voice murmured.

Keira ignored him, heaving herself to her feet and striding back into her own room. They would appear before the People's Council the next day and so had a seemingly infinite number of preparations to make. Besides, she still had to brief Landry on what Neval had told her, or rather, *not* told her. She didn't have time for tagalong little girls with noses for trouble. There was simply too much at stake.

"Raina's gone," Keira announced abruptly, flinging herself down onto the too-soft cushion of one of the chairs at the breakfast table. Marti blinked at her, the words taking a moment to register after her attention was yanked from the small book she'd been so engrossed in moments before.

"And where'd she go?" Marti asked, brows raising.

"To find her brother. Neval told her he was staying with the rest of the Southern Shield delegation in the South End."

"But why now? She was so excited to join us at the People's Council tomorrow."

Keira shrugged, feeling color rise to her cheeks. She swallowed, forcing her eyes to meet Marti's all too clear-eyed gaze. "I said I wouldn't train her," Keira muttered. "I just—can't. I offered to take her back to Port Galaén, to find her a real mentor, but she wouldn't be swayed. She said she would find her brother, but I—I thought she would at least say goodbye."

Marti placed a tiny yet surprisingly warm hand on hers and smiled sympathetically. "She's just a kid, Keira, and a headstrong one at that—not unlike someone else I know," she added, eyes twinkling.

"Maybe I should try to find Akamu myself," Keira said, chewing on her lip.

"You have a lot on your plate right now, Keira, without running all over the city in search of the Southern Shield delegation. We meet with the People's Council tomorrow. I'm sure we'll run into Akamu there."

Keira nodded. Marti certainly had a point.

"And who knows?" Marti continued. "Maybe Raina will even tag along. We both know how much she enjoys . . . drama."

Keira snorted. *You got that right.* Marti was right. Raina could take care of herself. She'd been running around Tibolé on her own since she could walk, after all. Still, this was a new city and a lot bigger than the Southern Shield. Keira would feel better once she'd talked to Akamu, made sure Raina had gotten there safely.

"Geez, Marti," she said finally. "I sure know how to piss people off, don't I?"

Marti's eyes softened, and she glanced downward. "I heard what happened with Zipporah, how you two—"

"She hates my guts," Keira said flatly. "Always has, always will. I was stupid to think that after all this"—she waved her hand vaguely—"we might actually become friends. Hell, I'd have settled for tolerant acquaintances."

Marti grimaced, rubbing at her own face with one hand. "You have to understand," she explained, "Zipporah came from a world of utter self-reliance, where to trust a single living soul was to be mocked and thought weak. And she believed it, too. It wasn't until she saw that attitude destroy everyone and everything she ever cared about that she saw it for what it was."

"And what was it?" Keira asked, curious despite herself.

"A crutch," Marti said simply. "A means of protecting yourself against anyone who might hurt you, who might betray you. What many called strength, Zipporah finally saw to be what it was—crippling weakness."

Keira swallowed, feeling heat flush her cheeks.

"She's wrong, though, Marti. About me, I mean. It's not that I think I'm somehow better than everybody else. I just—" Keira's mouth felt dry, and she had to clear her throat. "I can't let anyone else down—let other people get hurt because I made the wrong decision, the wrong call. I just can't. Not again."

Marti's eyes held hers, no judgment, anger, or anything else clouding their surface. "I understand, Keira—truly, I do."

Keira remembered then the story Zipporah had told her on the long ride from Port Galaén—about Marti's family and the terrible time she'd lived through. Marti did know, Keira realized, maybe even more than she did.

"But Keira," Marti continued, drawing Keira's thoughts back to the present, "that's not your decision."

Keira blinked, not understanding. "Marti, surely you of all people would have done anything to save—to take care of the people you loved."

A flash of pain cut across the girl's face as a corresponding wave of guilt churned in Keira's stomach.

"Maybe I would have," Marti said quietly. "But that was never my decision to make. People are free to do as they will, to love who they will, and to make their own decisions, Keira. You cannot protect everyone, and you should not try. To sacrifice for another . . ." Marti swallowed, staring at her hands as they twisted a napkin in her lap. "It is the greatest show of love one can give. You cannot deprive people of that, and they will only resent you for trying."

Keira bit her lip, willing her stomach to stop its churning. How had she managed to screw everything up so badly? Landry's life was in danger, she was no closer to bringing Danny back, and now neither Zipporah nor Raina could bear to be in the same room as her. She opened her mouth, about to ask Marti for some advice, when a quick rap on the door was followed by the entry of a finely clothed footman bearing a small note of parchment on a silver tray.

"What is it, Daryn?" Marti asked sweetly, turning her head toward the sandy blond–haired footman, whose mouth seemed to have gone suddenly dry.

"A-A note, my lady," he finally murmured, addressing Keira. "From Lord Albert."

Keira dropped the apple she'd been about to bite into and reached for the note. She scanned it quickly.

Join me for a training session this morning. We have much to discuss and even more to practice. South Tower.

Keira hesitated. She really would rather check up on Raina first, but there was something about Albert's insistence that made her pause. And why send a note? Couldn't he have just come down to breakfast?

Careful, Danny's voice cautioned, distant but with a note of urgency in his voice. Keira swallowed before turning to Marti. "Seems I have some training of my own to do this morning. I'll see you at dinner? For the strategy meeting?"

Marti nodded, already turning back to the small leather-bound book she'd laid to the side, engrossed in whatever tale she'd slipped back into even as her long, dainty fingers idly picked at the berries on her plate.

Keira rose, trying to suppress the growing trepidation she felt blooming in her stomach. *It's just Albert,* she thought. *He's a friend, right?*

Danny didn't reply.

~

The South Tower was one of four that spiraled above the ramparts of the Vindolum—Crîd Eálas's mighty fortress and home to its Marian rulers for the past two hundred years. Keira was reminded of the fortress's immensity as her legs began burning on the fourth flight of steep stairs. Her pace slowed to a shuffle as she dragged herself up the remaining ten.

I really have gone soft since the Shield, she thought. *Too much mindless travel and long days in the library.*

This was greeted by a chuckle and a tsk as Danny replied, *Just terrible. What would Nazor have to say?*

Though too exhausted to reply, even mentally, Keira imagined the rudest hand gesture she could think of.

She was rewarded with Danny's rumbling laugh.

Breathing heavily, Keira finally emerged into an airy tower room, light spilling through the arched lancet windows to fill the space with midmorning light. Though she welcomed its relief, the cool breeze on her damp skin made Keira shiver. Outside, seagulls flew on a level with the tower's wide windows, and Keira gaped, awed by the expansive view of the capital that sprawled below her. Keira dared a few hesitant steps toward the open archway opposite the stairs, its open space stretching floor-to-ceiling and wide enough for three to stand abreast at the ledge. Her stomach twisted unpleasantly at the sheer drop to the sea-facing cliffs below, and she stopped several feet from the edge. She never had liked heights.

"Lovely, isn't it?"

Keira started, spinning to find Albert leaning casually against one arched pillar, gazing out that same wide archway.

Keira nodded, slowly taking a few steps back from the ledge as she turned to face him.

"Got your message," she said, shifting slightly as he watched her with those keen, all-seeing eyes. "You said you had something to show me?"

"Indeed," Albert replied, but made no move to shift from his position. Instead, he continued to gaze out the window, eyes narrowed as he surveyed the city.

"So close," he murmured. "This city came so close to utter destruction. Only to be saved by you, Keira. You kept it from imploding into its own chaos. It survives because of you."

Keira again shifted awkwardly, hand coming up to rub the back of her neck. "I had a lot of help," she muttered. "Landry had to face down his sister, Neval had to convince his followers, and Danny—" Keira swallowed, unsure how to put into words all he'd done for her. Instead, she finished, "I had a lot of help."

Albert inclined his head slightly. "Perhaps, but you rallied them to the cause, put the right people together in the right place, and . . ." Albert made a gesture with both hands, indicating all that surrounded them.

Keira said nothing, unsure how to respond or where he was going with this. Albert moved then, a few steps bringing him closer, until he was just behind her. Keira's eyes shot instinctively to the deadly ledge, and she wiped her now-damp hands on her pant legs.

"I was here, you know," Albert murmured. "I could feel the chaos brewing in the city and thought to channel it. An . . . assignment of sorts. We can manipulate order and chaos on the micro level, so why not on the macro as well?"

Keira stared at him. "And?" she breathed, her heart suddenly hammering in its chest, though from the conversation or her nearness to the ledge, she couldn't say.

Albert only stared at her, his eyes boring into hers. Then he shrugged, and the spell was broken. "It dissipated before my experiments were complete . . . thanks to you, no doubt. A good thing, of course," he added. "A little longer, and the chaos may have been unleashed in its entirety."

Keira scowled at him, arms crossing. "You mean to tell me

that instead of actually helping me to *stop* the chaos, the Legion sent you here to, what? *Study* it?"

Albert flashed a grin before patting her gently on one shoulder and leaning in to whisper, "I never said it was the *Legion's* assignment, Keira."

She gaped at him. But before she could bark out any of the questions that suddenly flooded her mind, Albert spun on his heel, gesturing for her to follow as he strode toward the far end of the tower room. There, Keira was surprised to see a raised platform had escaped her notice, drawn as she was by the windows and the sickeningly long drop to the cliff face below. But as Albert led her up the platform, Keira was surprised to see it occupied by a single ornate marble basin. It was into its shining depths that Albert now gazed.

Keira's footsteps slowed the closer she got to the object, as if lulled by something just beneath the surface of her understanding. It wasn't power she felt as she approached the marble dais. No, it was something else. Almost like a void of power, something that would draw her in and siphon her away if she got too close.

"The stories are unclear about how it came to be here," Albert murmured, running a hand lazily across the basin's rim. Keira shuddered at the image, the idea of even touching this object making her stomach flip-flop. "Was it the Legion? The Worshippers of Séiro? Or some other group entirely that brought it to the newly formed capital of Loren? But whoever it was, they convinced the Marians of not only its power but also the danger it presented. So they locked it away, high above the city itself. It lay safe and sound behind walls of stone and the impenetrable shield of forgotten memory—until now."

Keira took another hesitant step toward the basin, ignoring the churning in her stomach and the hair that rose on the nape of her neck. From this distance, she could see that the marble itself was decorated in a swirling pattern of light and dark. As she stared at it, Keira was instantly reminded of the stained glass window in the foyer of the Legion headquarters back in Port Galaén—of the swirling mass that symbolized the ever-present struggle of order and chaos. Peering over the lip into the bowl itself, Keira was surprised to see solid glass where water might have been, and beneath its swirling depths, a massive pearl larger than her fist sat at its very base.

"The pearl," Albert breathed. "A single grain of sand, an irritant that suddenly finds itself where it does not belong. Tossed and turned by time and forces beyond its understanding, until it emerges something else entirely, creation formed from destruction, pristine order emerging from churning chaos."

"This is the object," Keira whispered, wide eyes turning toward Albert's steady gaze. "You said there was an object of immense power, a conduit for the chaos, powerful enough to bring Danny back."

Albert nodded once, twice, then held her gaze.

"How do I use it?" Keira's fingers itched to touch the smooth surface, but something held her back, a tug on her subconscious that she had to fight to suppress.

Albert's eyes were bright as they shot between her face and her outstretched fingers. "That's what we need to find out. We have less than a week before the equinox. I hope that tether of yours is still strong," he murmured. "This may be the one chance you have of bringing your grounder back."

Keira swallowed, tugging gently on that tether connecting her mind to Danny's, and felt his reassuring response. "It is."

"Good, because we have a lot of work to do."

CHAPTER
TWENTY-TWO

The Night Before

"Selfish *grelún*," Raina huffed, hauling clothing from drawers and stuffing them into her satchel. One of the invisible servants must have unpacked their things while they'd been busy with all their plotting and planning. Well, it was now time to *un-unpack* them. It had been a mistake to linger so long in this place. She should have left to find Akamu as soon as they'd arrived. But it didn't matter. That slimy fellow, Neval, had told her all she needed to know. Her brother was in the South End with the Southern Shield delegation. They couldn't be that hard to find.

Raina didn't bother closing the drawers after herself, though she made a show of loudly slamming a few. *Let Keira be worrying about where I've gone*, Raina thought, *if she even would.* Keira clearly didn't care enough to train her, didn't want her as part of their precious Legion. Well, that was just fine. Raina didn't want to join their club, anyway. She may not have known what her flickering ability to bend light meant, or understood the warmth that flooded from her mother's necklace, but she certainly wasn't about to wait around for some *grelún* to explain it to her.

Her satchel packed, Raina heaved it onto one shoulder and blew out her candle. Then, ever so quietly, she undid the latch of the door and slipped into the hallway beyond. A quick glance under Keira's door told her she'd put out her own light and gone to bed. Raina quickly spied the servants' staircase at the far end of the hall and made a beeline for it. If there was a sure-fire way to make it to the bottom floor as fast as possible, that would be it.

Sure enough, the staircase opened onto the kitchens below the first-floor entry, and from there, it was easy enough to slip out the servants' back entrance into the crisp nighttime air of the capital city.

Raina knew the way well enough. They'd just come from the South End, after all, and Raina decided that retracing her steps to the Miller's Plow was her best chance of finding someone who knew exactly where the delegation was staying.

Too easy, she thought proudly. Keira may think her no better than a baby, but Raina had grown up taking care of herself, free to run around the island of Tibolé as she pleased. Why should the capital be any different?

Well, it was a good bit bigger, for one thing.

No sooner had the buildings rose to cut off her view of the Vindolum's towers than Raina suddenly found herself turned around. All the buildings looked the same to her and were tall enough that they partially obstructed her view of the night's sky—her usual means of navigation. Raina's heart hammered in her ears, and she forced herself to breathe slower. *Think*, she ordered herself. *Just think.*

From where she stood, Raina could just make out a circling

flock of seagulls to her left. There, she realized. The ocean must be there, and the South End should be near it. Excited at her discovery, Raina quickened her pace, aiming for that cloud of seagulls until things started to look more familiar.

As she approached the waterfront of the South End, the buildings themselves changed. They seemed older, more cramped together, and streaks of terra-cotta stretched from the roofs down their sides, no doubt from the salty sea air. One more turn, and she was staring down an alley that led straight to a tavern, the pooling light of the Miller's Plow spilling into the darkness as raucous laughter lit up the night.

Relief flooded through Raina as she reached for the handle and slipped inside. She was greeted by the familiar smell of bread fresh from the oven and something sharper, like the fermented sáve her brother and his friends used to sneak when Marné wasn't looking. Her mouth watered as she remembered they'd skipped dinner that night. Ignoring the rumbling in her stomach, Raina made her way toward the barmaid they'd spoken to before. The woman's eyes lit up in recognition, and she waggled a wooden spoon in Raina's direction.

"What you still doin' 'ere?"

"I-I be looking for someone—my brother," Raina said, slipping onto a stool at the bar and trying not to stare at the massive cauldron of stew that hung behind it, its intoxicating aromas making her stomach groan.

"That right?" the barmaid replied, one eyebrow shooting up. "It wouldn't be you're tryin' to get some free grub? Lookin' all pathetic like that?"

"N-No, ma'am," Raina quickly said. "My brother, he being part of the Southern Shield delegation to the People's Council. That one"—Raina looked pointedly up the stairs, a gesture met by the barmaid's scowl—"said they be staying here in the South End. I just be wondering if you know where?"

The woman's lips pursed, and she crossed her arms. "If *he* told you that, why not just ask *him*?"

Raina remembered Neval's furious expression as he and Keira had argued and quickly added, "I-I don't want to be bothering him. I'm sure he being real busy."

The barmaid snorted. "Clever girl." She sighed then and began ladling stew into a small pewter bowl. Raina's heart beat faster, and she almost sighed aloud when the barmaid placed it in front of her.

"Listen, I don't know anyfin' about no delegation, but I might know someone who would. Wait here, and I'll be right back."

Raina nodded furiously and managed to murmur, "Thank you, ma'am," in between spoonfuls of the best-tasting stew she'd ever had.

The woman then turned and bustled upstairs as Raina made quick work of the bowl's contents. She sighed and turned then, surveying the room around her. She'd been in taverns before, or rather, had snuck in with Akamu after Marné had gone to sleep. And while the taverns back on Tibolé were raucous enough, they were nothing compared to this one.

All around her, men and women were drinking themselves silly, their voices rising in volume even as their movements became more stilted and clumsy. Raina squirmed on her barstool, pushing her hands under her legs so she was sitting on them, if only to hide their shaking.

She was just about to run after the barmaid when the sound of low, serious voices came from the curtained entryway to a back room. Raina probably wouldn't even have noticed amid the din of the tavern, were it not for the names she knew all too well.

"... they'll be speaking in two days' time, then, that Marian tyrant Landrianus and his Legion lackeys."

"That's fast. I 'eard they only just got in today. Could be they—"

The voices were drowned out amid the indignant shouts accompanying an overturned flagon of ale. Before she knew what she was doing, Raina was sliding off her stool and creeping toward the back room. The curtain hid its occupants, but their voices carried beyond it. Raina pressed herself against the wall, trying not to breathe too loudly as she listened.

"So it's decided, then. We'll make our move during the Regio's address. There're only two ways out of those chambers. They'll have nowhere to run."

"And what of our people, mixed in among them?"

There was a pause, and Raina struggled to listen over the hammering of her own heart in her ears.

"For the cause . . ." another voice murmured lowly. "We'll bring down the whole damn building if we have to."

Raina pressed off the wall, heart hammering. She had to go back! Keira and Cyrus, they'd be joining Landry at that speech. She'd heard them talking about it earlier. And Akamu—

Raina's stomach flip-flopped as she realized her brother would likely be there too.

She had to warn them.

Raina turned. No time to wait for the barmaid, she decided. She'd run straight back to the Vindolum to warn the others. Finding Akamu would have to wait.

But as she slipped back around the corner, heading for the main tavern room, Raina darted smack into a dark-cloaked figure. She panicked, stumbling backward as she reached for the shell necklace at her neck. Ready to run, to hide. But before she could disappear, viselike hands wrapped around her arms, pinning them to her sides.

Raina struggled, twisting and kicking, bucking with every panic-stricken fiber in her body.

Her squirming was met by a low, rumbling laugh.

Raina glanced up to meet the most beautiful face she'd ever seen. His skin was smooth, jaw cut from river rock and yet with a delicateness she couldn't quite place. His hair was jet-black, and his deep-set eyes swirled like honey. A smile played on soft lips that Raina couldn't help but think were wasted on a boy.

"What do we have here?" he murmured in a silky tone, shifting slightly so Raina's face was brought into the light. "You're certainly not from around here, are you, little bird?"

Raina spat at him, mouth twisting into a vicious grin when he jerked back.

"More like a pit viper, I see." His lips pressed together in a thin line, and his eyes swept her coldly in a way that made shivers run down Raina's spine. "Well, since you seem so interested in my friends' discussion, why don't we all have a chat?"

Raina's fingers suddenly felt numb, and her heart was again a staccato gallop. But before she could call for help from any of the tavern drunks, she was being hauled into a back room, where half a dozen faces glanced up in surprise at their arrival.

Surprise quickly turned to anger as every eye latched onto her. Raina felt the blood drain from her face as the man shoved her roughly into a chair before the gathered men. Raina sat on her hands to keep them from trembling and steeled her face into something she hoped looked brave—like Keira would.

"So, then," the silken voice murmured from just behind her, "which one of you is missing a little birdie?"

A few of the men crossed their arms over their chest, and several nostrils flared as they took her in.

"No one?" the silken voice crooned. "Well then, little bird, it seems you were not invited. Tell me, then—" Fingers dug painfully into Raina's shoulders, and she had to grit her teeth to keep from yelping. "Who sent you here?"

"I-I . . . no one. No one sent me," Raina stammered. "I just be looking for—" She stopped herself before she gave them too much and finished weakly with, "for my friend."

"Oh, a friend," the man crooned. The surrounding audience laughed cruelly. "Well, if you're in need of friends, I'm sure we can find someone to oblige you."

More laughter, and Raina dug her nails into the seat. She didn't dare reply, not when she could feel the tears building in her eyes. *What would Keira do?* she wondered desperately, eyes darting around the room for some chance of escape.

"That's enough, Lisander," a familiar voice intoned from the back. "You'll scare the poor thing half to death."

Raina's gaze shot up, and her mouth dropped open to see a mop of brown curls as Neval Brennan emerge from the darkness.

"You—" Raina whispered. "How could you? Keira, she—" Raina stopped, realizing the other men were listening eagerly. Still, she couldn't tear her eyes away from the man who'd smiled so easily not three hours earlier, who'd teased her and promised to help her find her brother. *All lies*, Raina realized. Her hands balled into fists, and she leveled her most sneering look at him.

Neval's lips pressed together in a frown, but Raina saw something harden in his eyes. She'd seen that look before—like a jaguar moving in for the kill. He was a hunter, and she was now prey.

"Raina dear, you couldn't have just stayed away, now, could you?

TWENTY-THREE

876 Common Era (C.E.)

Acool, salty breeze whistled in off the ocean as Danny moved in and around the dark tents of the camp. *You have every right to be here*, he chided himself. *Just act normally.* But his hammering heart wasn't so easily convinced.

You're a traitor.

I'm not, he told himself, hand flitting to the folded parchment shoved deep in his pocket—the parchment filled with detailed troop movements, illustrating the exact path of the centuriums of the Eastern Imperium's movements across the Lorenan uplands over the coming weeks.

Moira was just looking for her father, Danny reminded himself. She'd insisted as much over the long nights they'd spent combing through Cato's archives. She'd told him story after story of her father, a fisherman who'd been drafted to Loren's defense when word of the invasion first arrived. He was an innocent—a bystander. He didn't deserve to rot away in chains, building the fortresses of his enemies.

She claimed she needed all the centuriums' movements because she wasn't sure which detachment he'd been assigned to. How else was she to get a message through to each Centus, pleading her father's case? It wasn't as if carrying letters for Lorenan peasants was high on the Bellatorio's priority list.

Danny had run through these arguments a thousand times, waffling on exactly what was the best course. But he kept coming back to the realization that Moira had lived up to her end of the bargain, painstakingly combing through ancient Lorenan texts with him every night. It had been worth it, though, as Danny learned more and more about the Legion's activities.

From Elliott's history lessons, he'd always assumed the Legion had arrived in this world after the Marian invasion, a means of keeping the peace under a new world order and preventing its collapse into chaos when that empire inevitably fell. But these texts told a very different story, that of a Legion deeply embedded in the various ruling powers of this world for hundreds if not thousands of years, carefully pulling the strings of power, manipulating the outcomes of wars, treaties, and insurrections. But to what end?

Danny had always believed the Legion's end goal really was order, above all, keeping the chaos at bay to create a better world for everyone. But what he found was an organization of flawed people, ones who picked sides and often chose wrongly, generating more destruction than healing in their wake. But still the question remained—why was *he* here? What confluence of chaos and order had drawn his pneuma to this place? Because if he could figure that out, maybe, just maybe, he could fulfill it and return to the life he'd left. It was a fool's dream, he knew, but a dream he clung to—to return to his family: Elliott, Nazor . . . and Keira.

One thing was for certain, though. He wouldn't find the answers he sought while schlepping about with the Bellatorio. He needed Moira's help to uncover the answer, no matter what she might ask in return.

He'd have offered to deliver her letters himself, but his work with Imperator Titus had quickly become all-consuming as the official Crîd Eálas naming ceremony and Magnus's coronation as Regio approached—now only two days away. Titus had handed him most of the security responsibilities for the event, and Danny now spent long hours every day reviewing protocols and troop listings. But despite the work, he'd found he actually liked the Imperator. There was a kindness to him, despite his rigid military demeanor. And though they'd likely never agree about the excesses that had occurred in the capture of the uplands, Danny felt sure that things would be better going forward.

Danny was just thinking about the stack of equipment orders he still had waiting for him when he rounded the corner to find two figures huddled in the alley behind Cato's makeshift library—now sporting four walls and a roof thanks to Danny's efforts in his limited free time. A flash of red hair caught the moonlight, and Danny raised a hand to Moira in greeting. Had Cato decided to join them in their research that evening?

His hand lowered slowly as he realized the other figure was too tall to be Cato, and he moved with an intensity that far outstripped the aging librarian's hovering excitement.

Danny's pace slowed as he continued toward them, a growing trepidation making his mouth go dry. He could see Moira's arms wrapped tightly around herself, her eyes darting from side to side as she murmured in a low voice to the stranger. Something about the jerkiness of her movements made Danny's senses narrow, a heightened awareness raising the hair on the back of his neck.

He swallowed, shaking out his hands as he strode toward her. He was being ridiculous. No doubt she was just gossiping with another uplander servant. They were a nervous lot, and for good reason. He pasted on a smile and raised a hand in greeting as he approached.

Moira's eyes widened slightly, but she quickly returned his smile and wave. A few murmured words to her friend, and he headed off back down the alleyway, but not before Danny glimpsed coppery hair and the glint of creased amber eyes beneath the boy's hood. He felt a chill race up his spine, and he rolled his shoulders, easing it.

"Who's your friend?" he asked, nodding toward the retreating figure.

Moira rolled her eyes. "Arlan's feeling unappreciated again. He's a server in the mess hall, and apparently the cooks have been bullying him." She shrugged. "He'll get over it. What about you? I thought Titus had you working late today?"

"He was, but I put some of it off for tomorrow. Titus has decided to do a full review of the troops personally the morning of the ceremony, so that's gone and tripled the amount of work I need to do—what with added security. Plus, the future Regio would like a full audience present . . ." Danny trailed off, eyeing Moira as he swallowed. "But I did stumble across some . . . information."

Moira's eyes widened, and she gently bit her lip, looking heartbreakingly hopeful in the darkness. "Did you—is he—"

Danny nodded, fishing the folded parchment from his pocket. His fingers moved slowly, a numbness creeping into them, though he forced them into action. As he deposited the paper in her hand, he felt a sharp twist in his gut.

Traitor.

He shoved the thought away, focusing instead on the tears that suddenly sprang to her eyes. She gazed up at him with an awe bordering on worship, and he felt a warm sensation creep into his chest. She wiped the tears away, slipping the parchment into her own pocket.

"Thank you, Danny. You don't know—you don't know how much this means to me."

Danny rubbed a hand across the back of his neck, offering a strained smile as he shrugged. "I know what it is to lose a father. I'd have wanted someone to do the same for me. Don't worry about it. Just—find him."

Moira nodded, and Danny thought he saw a tenseness leave her shoulders, and she seemed to stand taller.

"You ready to get to work then?" she asked, nodding toward the library. "I had an idea about the Grumaérian translations. They keep using the word *saléina*, which would normally be translated to *helper* or *friend*. But since the context is political, it's got me thinkin' that it might actually be closer to an ally of sorts. Could be the Legion's ties with the Grumaérian tribes were even tighter than we realized."

Danny nodded, only half listening as he followed her into the library. He was being overly suspicious. He knew that. No doubt on account of his own guilt. Moira was his friend, one of the few friends he had here, what with Tammy spending all her time with the beguiling Fitz. And she was a good person, just looking out for her family in the face of a war she didn't ask for or deserve. Helping her find her father was the least he could do.

～

MAGNUS MARIAN'S arrival was met with as much pomp and circumstance as a Lorenan backwater could muster. The prince was young, around Danny's age, and he wore a bored expression that put Danny's teeth on edge. He'd just plunked his arse down on his plush settee, fanning himself in the coastal heat as courtiers, military leaders, and dignitaries all waited in line to pay their respects.

Tammy and Danny stood with Imperator Titus, a symbol of the Legion's support for the Empire's siege on Ulgáris. They moved as one to kneel before the prince.

You're as much an arse as your great-great-great-grandson, Danny thought bitterly, eyeing the young prince from beneath hooded eyelashes as the royal yawned theatrically and waved for them to rise.

They moved off to the side, and Danny felt his blood continue to boil as yet another crowd of Legionnaires knelt before him. Here they were, the most powerful organization to walk this world, and they were giving mock fealty to a boy-king. All the better to mislead and manipulate him, Danny supposed. He watched as Fitz pronounced honeyed words of admiration and Magnus practically crowed with pleasure. The sight made Danny sick.

"I can't believe the Legion is swearing loyalty to this spoiled princeling."

"It's just for show," Tammy said from the side of her mouth, eyeing their surroundings to ensure they weren't overheard. "He'll be crowned tomorrow, and then they'll be rejoining the rest of the Legion."

"He's got no clue who he's even getting into bed with."

"Why does it bother you so much?" Tammy asked, eyeing him curiously. Danny pursed his lips, giving her a long, considering look. She gazed earnestly back, brow creased with worry.

"You can tell me, Danny. Whatever is going on with you, I can help."

Maybe it was her earnest expression, or the way her dark hair fell in curls around her face—so like Keira's. But he realized then that he *wanted* to tell her.

Gently, he took her arm and steered her away from the crowd and into a side alley between two half-constructed buildings.

"Seriously, what's going on with you, Danny? You've been sneaking out at all hours of the night, spending all your time in that weird library. And who is that uplander girl who keeps hanging around?"

Tammy leveled him with her best no-nonsense look, arms crossed and brows raised expectantly.

Danny sighed, dragging a hand across his face before saying, "Research. I've been doing research."

Tammy looked dubious as she pressed, "What kind of research?"

"Research into the Legion, Pneumos—hell, the history of this whole damn world. It's all connected, Tammy. The Legion has been pulling the strings here for centuries, and I think they decided the outcome of this invasion a long time ago."

He sighed at her confused expression and started from the beginning, telling her about the legendary origins of the Marian Empire and its ties to the mysterious Legionnaire "she-lion." He described the Grumaérian campaign and a half dozen other cases he'd found in which the Legion had intervened on either side of a conflict.

"But the question is why?" Danny asked. "What is their stake in all this? And *don't*—" he interjected, seeing Tammy about to respond, "give me some crap about chaos and order and the greater good. They were ready and willing to let me believe they turned on a dime because of what *I* told them. But Titus let slip just the other day that the Marians had been in communication with the Legion for well over a year before the invasion even happened. Which tells me they're basing their intervention on something other than foreknowledge about this so-called 'inevitable' outcome. I don't know if it's power, or influence, or just good old-fashioned corruption, but they've got their own reasons for getting involved, and I, for one, want to know why."

He was breathing heavily by the time he'd finished, and Tammy stared at him with some strange combination of annoyance and genuine sorrow.

"Is it worth it?" she asked.

Danny stared blankly at her. "Is what worth it?"

"The truth. Is it really worth risking everything? Who cares why things happened as they did? They happened. The Marians are here. This war is all but over. I just—" She stared back at the crowd of people gathered before the new Marian ruler of Loren. "I think some things are best left unknown, Danny."

Danny didn't know what to say to that. He'd lived his entire life, all three of them, in fact, firmly believing that all the fighting and killing was for a reason, for some higher purpose. To give up? To accept that there really was no rhyme or reason to the universe was more than he thought he could bear.

He started to tell Tammy as much, but her next words caught him up short.

"I'm leaving, Danny."

"What?" He stared blankly at her.

"I've received orders to help with the founding of a new headquarters for the Legion—here in Loren." She was babbling now, her eyes flitting to and from Danny's face as she fiddled with the hem of her tunic and continued to fill his shocked silence.

Tammy was leaving? She was the first friend he'd made in this time. The only connection to Keira he had left. He swallowed, trying to focus on what, exactly, she was saying.

". . . they're placing it at a key shipping port to the north, calling it Port Galaén or some such thing—"

"Port Galaén?" he suddenly asked in surprise.

The tense look on Tammy's face eased, and she shrugged, chuckling. "Don't ask me where they got the name."

"It's from Ancient Lorenan," Danny muttered, mind still racing. "It means *spirit-binder*. A bit on the nose there, don't you think?"

Again, Tammy shrugged. "I didn't pick it. Besides, isn't that old tongue all but dead? I can't imagine there are many who would make the connection. So why not let something of it survive in that city? Let it conjure up awe and inspiration, even if the people who hear it can't quite say why."

Tammy's smile faded as Danny continued to gnaw on his lower lip.

"Orders?" he asked suddenly. "From who?"

"From the Legion," Tammy said. Then she paused, glancing nervously at him. "I—well, I sort of requested them."

At his surprised look, she launched into yet another frenzied explanation. "I don't belong here, Danny. Not like you do. You have your work with Titus and with the new library. You always seem to be busy. Now that you've told me about your work with that uplander girl, I understand why. But still, my place is with the Legion. So with Fitz and the others heading back . . ." Her voice trailed off, and she searched his face with a worried expression. "Are you angry?"

Startled, Danny met her creased eyes. "Of course not," he

said, finally coming back to the present. He sighed. "I was just thinking how much I'll miss you, Altman."

Relief flooded her face, and she nodded. "You too, O'Leary. Don't worry, though, it's just for a while, a year max. I asked about your joining us, but Imperator Titus has asked for you personally to remain as his liaison to the Legion. Seems he likes you."

Danny snorted. "Can't imagine why. Seems all I do is argue with the old goat."

"Maybe he needs that," Tammy said, shrugging. "Everyone needs someone to call them on their crap."

"Even you, Altman?"

Tammy laughed. "Especially me."

As their laughter faded, they settled into a sad silence, neither really knowing where to go from there.

"Take care of yourself," Danny said finally, pulling Tammy into a tight hug.

"You too, O'Leary."

WINTER'S BITE had reluctantly released its stranglehold, but the early spring morning still held a biting chill as Danny joined the Imperator's review of the troops. They walked along the lines, inspecting the orderly rows of Bellators bedecked in their polished armor and stiff-flowing red cloaks. Titus barked sharp corrections as they went—a poorly shined breastplate, the trace of stubble on a jaw. Nothing but perfection would do for honoring the new Regio's coronation.

Danny shivered slightly in the predawn dew, glancing around the empty training field. In just a few hours' time, it would be filled with cheering spectators newly arrived from the

Empire's mainland, eager to take their place in the Empire's newest holding. They had made the training yard itself spotless, and as Danny glanced around, he couldn't help but note an eerie stillness that fell between the neat rows of identical tents. Something just felt *off*.

"That's all of them," Titus said, startling Danny out of his brooding thoughts and gesturing for them to return to the main command tent. Danny nodded, feeling an irrational relief to be moving out of the open. He turned to follow, casting a sympathetic glance at the young Bellators who'd been corrected, each now being bawled out by their respective Sergius. It was bad enough to violate standards, worse to do it in front of the Imperator.

The two of them ducked beneath the awning to enter the command tent. "Such foolishness," Titus said, rubbing a hand across his face.

"Sir?" Danny asked, startled.

"This whole facade," Titus said, gesturing out at the training field and its ornate decorations. "We're a war camp, not a coronation hall."

Danny said nothing, though he silently agreed.

Titus eyed him for a moment before adding, "I haven't notified high command yet, but I thought you should know that this will be my last command."

Danny blinked in surprise. "You're leaving the Bellatorio?"

Titus sighed, running a hand across his face as he leaned against the desk. "I'm tired of the games, the politics. I joined the Bellatorio to serve and protect the Empire, not play show pony for scheming politicians and pampered princelings."

Titus's eyes darted to Danny and away before he gruffly cleared his throat. "Not that—well, I don't mean to imply . . ."

"I understand, sir. I feel the same way."

Titus gave Danny a measured look before nodding slightly. "You've been a great help to me, O'Leary. Not just with all this nonsense, but in the campaign as well. You're a reliable soldier and a team player. I don't know how these things work in your Legion, but know you would have made an outstanding Bellator."

Danny swallowed the lump that had arrived in his throat as he stared at the battle-worn soldier—his lifetime of service coming to an unceremonious end.

"Thank you, sir," Danny said, surprised at this sudden show of affection and unsure how to return it. Though they were from different times and held differing opinions, Danny couldn't help but admire the older man's leadership and the high esteem his soldiers held him in. "It's been an honor to work with you as well," Danny said, and he meant it.

Titus grunted in acknowledgment, no doubt equally uncomfortable with such terms of endearment. He pivoted to the stack of paperwork already awaiting his attention for the day.

"Brewed mogda, sir?" a quiet voice asked as a server arrived with breakfast tray in hand.

"Yes, yes, thank you," Titus said, almost absently, still scanning the roster for the day's events.

"And you, sir?"

Danny glanced up and blinked as his eyes registered copper hair and creased amber eyes. It was Arlan, the friend Moira had met in that dark alley two nights before. Arlan seemed to recognize Danny at the same moment, and his eyes widened a fraction of an inch.

"No, no, thank you," Danny said, brow furrowing as he noted the beads of sweat on the boy's brow.

Arlan nodded sharply, turning and striding away almost too quickly.

Odd.

He turned then to find Titus staring into his cup with a curious expression.

His throat bobbed in a brisk staccato, and his nostrils flared. He stood that way for a long moment, just gazing into the cup.

Then he started choking.

Titus staggered out the tent flap and Danny lunged for the older man, catching him just under the arms as his knees buckled. Titus sagged against him, his breath coming in gasps.

"Get a medic!" Danny screamed at the gaping Bellators outside. Then his eyes met those of Arlan, who'd glanced back at the commotion. And in those amber eyes, Danny saw unabashed triumph. He decided in a split second.

"Stop him!" he cried, pointing at Arlan. The boy broke into a run but was seized by two young Tiros standing nearby. Danny's attention was again drawn back to Titus as he lowered the man to the ground, rolling him onto his side as the man heaved violently into the dirt. And then Titus's entire body contorted, limbs going rigid as they extended, his wrists and fingers bending backward at a painful-looking angle. Titus's neck jerked, extending back as the veins bulged and his face turned a beet-red. Titus's eyes widened, staring at Danny in terror before rolling backward in his head. Then his entire body began shaking.

The seizure stretched on for what seemed an eternity as Danny stared in helpless horror at the man he'd worked side by side with for almost a year. This noble warrior, reduced to a squirming animal, no longer in control of his own body. Indeed, as the muscle spasms increased, every bodily function was slowly wrested from the Imperator's tight grip—first movement, then breathing, and even the loss of his bowels.

Danny could do nothing but hold him through every violent contortion and indignity until the shaking slowly abated and Titus grew all too still.

Danny held still before realizing that the shaking now came from him alone. He swallowed before easing Titus onto his back. Titus was limp, his eyes dilated and the whites slowly filling with the slow trickle of blood. Hands trembling, Danny felt for a pulse at the Imperator's neck. Nothing.

With a shaky breath, Danny stood and wrenched his gaze from the Imperator's horrible death grimace. He felt . . . numb. The world around him seemed far away, and even his hearing seemed muffled.

Imperator Titus Longus was dead. No, he'd been assassinated.

A commotion from across the yard drew his attention, and Danny turned to find Bellators dragging the squirming Arlan before him. Danny stared down at the boy's defiant glare.

"Why, Arlan?" Danny asked, his mouth painfully dry. "Who made you do this?"

The boy spat at his feet.

"Death to tyrants," Arlan snarled. "And long live the tree from which liberty springs! Red—"

At that moment, a whistle of an arrow coursed through the air, striking Arlan directly between the eyes. He crumpled to the ground in a heap, eyes wide in death as blood dripped down his face.

Danny staggered back, adrenaline flooding his veins as he spun in place.

"Who shot that?" he demanded, furiously searching the faces of the gathered Bellators. They shook their heads, swords already drawn as they ran to search the surrounding darkness for the arrow's source. Danny dragged breath into his lungs, fighting every instinct he had that said *run, hide.*

Instead, he left the search to the others and knelt next to Arlan's body, trying and failing to swallow the ball that had caught in his throat. *How did they know?* he wondered. *How did they know Titus would be here?*

And then a voice in the back of his mind whispered back.

You know how.

Danny shook his head, the violence of the motion sending his hair flopping into his eyes.

You told her precisely where he'd be and when. Who knows what else she's passed along.

It wasn't true. It couldn't be true. Moira was his friend. There had to be some other explanation.

Glancing down at Arlan, Danny spied the twisting curls of ink peeking out from under one sleeve. Hands shaking, he rolled back the fabric to see the curling fronds of a willow tree twisting deftly around Arlan's arm. Danny swallowed.

He'd seen that tree before.

CHAPTER
TWENTY-FOUR

242 Marian Era (M.E.)

The People's Council Chambers were far larger than anything Keira had seen before in Loren. She wasn't sure what she'd expected, but this certainly wasn't it. From where she stood with Landry and Cyrus on the balcony that stretched in a half-moon around the amphitheater-like seating, she could take in a full view of the proceedings.

There must have been over a hundred chairs and desks arranged around the room, with the top rows blocked off for visiting audiences. Before all stood a high table at the front of the room, where Keira could see Neval and the rest of his presiding council members trying to keep order among the raucous bickering that ensued. Well, some of them were trying to keep order. From what she could see, Neval looked as if he were about to fall asleep.

Keira snorted as a rotund gentleman to Neval's left slammed a book down abruptly in front of him. Neval jumped and shot the man an incredulous look. But his companion,

263

whose blazer fit snugly over his protruding belly—a sure sign of his merchant-class status—merely ignored him.

Neval must have sensed her gaze, for he suddenly caught her eye, fingers fluttering in hello as his brows waggled suggestively.

Keira rolled her eyes, pronounced enough that he surely couldn't help but notice, and turned back to her companions.

Landry was dressed in his usual regal finery, lips pressed together thinly as his eyes roved over the parchment detailing his planned address. Meanwhile, Cyrus leaned heavily on the bannister, rumpling his dark blue emissarial robes. His entire body was tense and his fingers rolled rhythmically against the wood in a feverish staccato.

"Relax, Cyrus," Landry intoned dryly as he flipped through the papers before him. "This isn't exactly my first public address, you know."

"Of course, sir," Cyrus said thinly. Keira spotted a muscle working in his jaw and quickly smothered a smile.

This is very serious business, Keira. Try to have some sense of decorum.

Keira turned back to the council chambers just as a gaunt-looking woman at the high table rapped the dismissal for a short recess.

And when have I ever given two hoots for decorum, Danny?
Touché.

Albert had seemed similarly bemused by her general disregard for rules during the training session they'd had yesterday. After a long and very convoluted explanation of exactly what the conduits were and all the legends that surrounded them, they'd finally gotten down to the business of actually practicing. It had been grueling work, using her pneuma to break down objects and slowly rebuild them. And by objects, she definitely meant fruit. And while Albert had seemed intrigued by her unique healing pneumonancy, his interest had quickly turned to poorly disguised annoyance. While the conduit helped channel her power and served as a grounding force, it didn't make the actual task of reconstruction any easier. It was absolutely humiliating to find herself woefully incapable of even the most basic tasks. And what had she expected, really? She'd barely touched her pneuma in months, terrified of using it without Danny's grounding tether, lest she be unable to reel the power in.

Still, she had no idea how she'd possibly be ready in time. The equinox was only a few days away, and though her connection with Danny still seemed strong, she knew that it would fade as soon as the opportunity passed. The thought made her insides clench. She couldn't lose him again, even this tiny thread of him that she clung to. She couldn't. And yet, when Albert had suggested they might move on to living things, small rodents mostly, for *motivation*, she'd balked—unable to banish the vision of the small pomegranate before her exploding in a shower of juice and seeds. The thought made her physically nauseous. So she'd left. Begging exhaustion, she'd fled that tower room and in doing so had no doubt sealed Danny's fate.

It's not your fault, Danny murmured quietly.

Keira squeezed her eyes shut, forcing herself to breathe slowly. *Then whose is it?*

There was no answer.

To her side, Cyrus had launched into a whispered tirade about the narrow line that Landry had to walk in his upcoming speech.

"So the ones you really need to worry about are the working class. It's from their ranks that this violent group is likely coming from, so they'll naturally be defensive about it. Be careful not to make too many implications. Just focus on all you've done for them so far and all you plan to *keep* doing. Whereas, you most likely already have the merchants' support. They loathe instability, after all, and your death would certainly be a power vacuum. Now, you don't need to come right out and say that, of course, but a few subtle hints certainly wouldn't be amiss."

"So reassuring to hear my impending assassination would be *inconvenient* for everyone," Landry murmured dryly, but Keira felt him shift his weight nervously.

Keira squeezed his arm and was about to offer some awkward words of encouragement when she suddenly spied the Southern Shield delegation clustered together, heads bent in urgent discussion.

Finally. "I'll be right back."

Ignoring their looks of surprise and incredulity, Keira slipped out of the balcony box and down the stairs, toward the front of the chamber. Weaving between council members, who oscillated between annoyance and surprise at her sudden appearance, she aimed for the tall, broad-shouldered back that could only be one person.

"Glad you made it here in one piece, Akamu."

He turned then, and warm, laughing dark eyes met hers. Akamu looked much the same, though his tightly curled dark hair had been gelled into submission, and he sported the brightly colored sash unique to the Southern Shield delegation.

"Well, if it didn't be the Lady Bellator—or should I say, Lady Legionnaire?" Akamu dipped into a deep, flourishing bow that Keira couldn't help but laugh at. "I be hearing much about you here in the capital, Miss Keira Altman. I think you be holding out on us, back in Tibolé. You be quite the celebrity round here."

Keira snorted and rubbed the back of her neck, pointedly ignoring the frank stares of the other council members.

"Well, don't believe everything you hear. Your own sister has certainly had me on the runabout these last few weeks. By the way, did she find you all right? I swear, she scared the crap out of me, disappearing like that."

Akamu's brow furrowed at the question, his head tilted at an angle. A feeling like lead settled in Keira's stomach.

"Raina be here? In Crîd Eálas?"

Keira stared at him, searching his face for any sign that he was joking, having a laugh at the poor *grelún*'s expense. But there was nothing, only confusion and a growing fear to match her own. The room suddenly sounded muffled as she heard herself say, "She was—is . . ."

Keira stared at him, and the complete story poured out. Her words grew faster and more panicked as the hard truth hit her like a sledgehammer. She'd lost his sister. She'd lost Raina. How could she have been so stupid? Raina might seem old beyond her years, but she was still an eleven-year-old girl who'd spent her entire life on an island no more than ten miles wide in any direction. And she was lost—lost and alone in a strange city, and it was all Keira's fault.

As Keira explained, she saw Akamu's eyes gradually widen as tears pricked at her own. ". . . we'll find her. I promise, Akamu. As soon as this session is over, we'll track her down. I'm so sorry."

Something hardened in Akamu's eyes, and his jaw clenched as he replied coldly, "To hell with this session, and your damn People's Council. I be going to find my sister—now. Come if you like, but I being through with this simpering bunch."

Keira could only nod and moved to follow him. But the harsh bang of a gavel interrupted her as the entire room came to attention and Landry moved to take the lectern before them all. Keira twisted her head to meet Akamu's eyes and mouthed the word, *After*.

He seemed torn, glancing between Landry and the rest of his delegation, but grudgingly nodded. They'd leave as soon as Landry's speech was over, and they'd find Raina.

A sudden idea came to Keira, and she searched the high table for Neval. Perhaps Raina had doubled back after they'd spoken to him that night. He might have some idea where she'd gone. But as her eyes roamed over the high table and its finely dressed inhabitants, spotting his seat beside the rotund merchant, she was surprised to find it empty. A quick scan of the room confirmed her suspicions.

Neval was gone.

~

"I DO HUMBLY appear today before the People's Council, who from these hallowed halls of ancient order do enshrine a new age of peace and equity to all the citizens of Loren."

Though Landry's language was formal, it lacked the stilted edge the words often invoked. For him these words had meaning, were born of strife and sacrifice. These were words he truly believed. Keira swallowed, blinking away the sting of tears as she thought about how happy Danny would have been to see this—Danny, who had chafed so angrily against the plight of the uplanders in Loren. Keira looked around the room, hoping to take in the enormity of their accomplishment. But something made her pause as she noted more and more empty seats around the hall. Neval wasn't the only one missing.

". . . there are those who seek only to destabilize, to crush the . . ."

As Landry launched into his carefully rehearsed address, Keira did a quick mental count. Twenty, at least twenty council members were missing. And from their seat placement, most hailed from the poorest of districts and regions—the South End, the waterways, and the outer slums of the North End.

Where *were* they?

"...a fragile peace we have built here. To those I..."

Slowly, Keira's eyes drifted up to the balcony section that wrapped around the length of the chambers, and a shadow of movement caught her eye. With a sickening lurch of her stomach, Keira registered the glint of light off steel.

"...up to each of us to..."

"Landry, get DOWN!" Keira cried, launching herself to her feet just as the whistle of an arrow hissed through the air. She was too slow and much too far away to do anything as Landry stood blinking at her, blissfully unaware of the lethal steel that hissed toward him.

Luckily, Cyrus was quicker.

In a clatter of falling furniture, Cyrus tackled the young Regio, rolling him under the protective ledge of the high table, pinning him to the ground as he further shielded him with his own body.

Cries of surprise and shouts of fear echoed around the chamber. Keira spun, glancing up just in time to see multiple hooded figures emerge into the light of the balcony. Their bows were all raised.

"Take COVER!" Keira screamed, launching herself at a gaping Akamu, forcing him behind the seat ledge, just as a full barrage of arrows rained down on the unsuspecting council.

Screams engulfed them.

Keira tried to squelch her rising panic at the sound of

running feet, whistling arrows, and cries of fear that morphed into screams of pain.

"We have to get out of here," she said to Akamu, yet again pushing him to the ground when he tried to rise in aid of a fallen council member. He glared at her, and she glared right back. "We have no weapons, no first aid supplies, and they have the high ground here. We have to make it to the exit. Once there, we'll regroup and come back for them."

Akamu stared at her for a moment longer, and for a second Keira thought he might flat refuse, call her a no-good coward who would leave innocents to die in addition to losing his sister. Then he nodded, though the look he gave her said clearly, *We'll have this out later.*

Keira swallowed. No time to worry about that now. She gestured behind him, and slowly they began crawling toward the exit, partially shielded by the high-backed chairs of the chamber itself.

Who could have done this? she thought. *Why attack the entire council? What could they hope to gain?*

Not important just now, Danny growled, the steel edge of his voice no doubt an instinct honed by years of danger. *Keep. Moving.*

"Hurry," Keira said aloud. She glanced back in time to see that the half-moon curve of the council chambers was bringing their path into the direct line of sight of multiple archers. The screaming and crying grew louder, and Keira gritted her teeth with the effort of ignoring it. She was no good to them until she could get a weapon in her hand. Suddenly, Akamu stopped, and she nearly crawled right into him.

"What is it?" she hissed at him.

"A gap," his voice said thinly. "Nothing to shield us ahead."

She glanced around him, cursing when she realized he was

right. To cross the aisle that led down to the front of the hall, they'd be in full view of the archers from all sides.

"You'll have to make a run for it," she breathed. "I'll draw their attention, try to give you a head start."

Akamu's eyes bored into hers with an intensity she knew all too well. The family resemblance was certainly clear. "I'll not be leaving you."

Keira's mouth firmed into a thin line. "Go for help. Raina—you have to find her, Akamu, no matter what." Keira matched him look for look. His nostrils flared, and for a moment she thought he might still refuse. But then he nodded curtly and turned back to the open aisle.

This is a bad idea, Danny said tersely. *What,* exactly, *do you intend to do?*

Keira's brain hadn't gotten that far. But as she surveyed her surroundings, a particularly terrible idea suddenly occurred to her. She shifted from her crawl into a crouch, careful to keep her head below chair level. She took a steadying breath, then a second. Then she leapt from her hiding place, reaching for the chair back in front of her as she swung her legs around, vaulting over it. "Hey!" she cried. With any luck, she'd draw the archers' fire away from the escaping Akamu and his friends.

Keira landed hard on her knees, sending a sharp pain radiating up her leg. She ignored it, scrambling forward as she tried to put distance between her and the site of her inglorious vault—just as the first volley of arrows rained down over her head.

Get DOWN! Danny roared in her head.

Keira flattened herself to the floor, covering her head with her hands as she tried to squeeze herself as far under the row of seats as she could. Her fingers shook, and she laced them tightly together, focusing on her breathing and not the whistling thud of falling arrows.

Finally, the arrows slowed to a trickle. Her heart still hammering in her ears, Keira rolled out and began crawling quickly away. A quick glance through the slats between rows told her she was still several rows away from the high table, where Landry and Cyrus were hopefully taking shelter. What she planned to do when she reached them, she had no idea.

Steeling herself, she again vaulted over the next row of seats, landing this time in a crouch as she scurried forward, shielding her head as more arrows rained down on her. She vaulted two more rows in a similar fashion.

This might actually work, she thought.

Danny said nothing, but she felt his rumbling tenor of displeasure and fear.

Glancing through the slats, she saw she was only two rows away from the high table now. The screams and crying had even died down. Keira refused to think about what that meant, focusing all of her attention instead on the task ahead. She readied herself to take the next vault. It was only after she'd leapt into the air that she realized what a decrease in targets might mean. As her eyes met the two hooded figures that stood before her with bows drawn, she realized her mistake all too late. The archers had moved.

The world seemed to slow as her eyes met theirs and she waited for the sting of metal striking her body. Then a shadow moved behind them, and Cyrus emerged, dagger in one hand and what looked like a coat of arms in the other. He lunged, stabbing one archer in the back as he used the shield to batter the other to the ground. The first archer fell to his knees, bow dropping with a clatter as he shrieked in pain. The second stumbled under the impact of the shield, releasing the arrow from its bow with a hiss as it sailed directly toward her.

Keira tried to twist out of the way, but she wasn't fast

enough. She slammed into the ground with a cry as pain coursed through her side. She put a hand to her stomach and blinked in shock as it came away slick with blood. Then rough hands were hauling her to her feet as Cyrus half dragged her behind the high table, just as another volley of arrows assaulted their position.

They collapsed in a heap, panting as the thud of arrows persisted against the wood that surrounded them. Keira's head spun as she stared up at that solid oak underside, and she clutched her side, groaning loudly. Landry's worried face swam before her vision, and she felt hands shaking her gently. She blinked, trying to steady her vision, even as the pain burned deep into her core.

"Keira," Landry murmured. "Keira, let us take a look." Gentle hands peeled her own fingers away from the wound, and she clenched her teeth. Cold water splashed onto her side, and she couldn't help the strangled yelp that split from her throat.

"It's not too deep," Cyrus murmured. "And I don't think it caught anything vital. Though I'm sure it hurts like hell." Keira shot him a glare, and he grinned back. "Come on, Legionnaire. I thought you lot were supposed to be tough." Though her fingers trembled, Keira made a rude gesture, and he actually laughed aloud. "Yeah, I think she'll be fine."

"It's nothing," she agreed through gritted teeth. "But I can't say any of us will be fine unless we get some help, and soon."

"Can't you—" Landry hesitated, glancing toward the two council members sharing their shelter. Keira hadn't even noticed them before. "You know—use your *gifts?*"

Keira let out a breath through pursed lips, struggling into a sitting position, even as her abdomen felt like it might split in two. She shook her head. "It's risky. I don't have anyone to ground me, and being injured, it would be hard to—*focus.* Even harder to get back. I suppose I could try . . ." Keira's voice faded, and she gently nudged Danny with her mind.

Care to give me a hand?

He didn't reply, but she could feel disapproval radiating off of him. No, he had no intention of intervening, of helping her try something so risky.

Cyrus and Landry both looked grim but shook their heads. "No, we'll wait. There are guards posted all over the capital. Someone must have gotten word to them by now."

Keira's mind shot to Akamu and the rest of the Southern Shield delegation. Had they gotten out? Had they been able to get help?

For all they knew, the rogue faction had staged a second wave of attackers just outside, ready to mop up any survivors. They had to get out of here, Keira thought. Raina needed them, was no doubt scared and alone. Keira simply *refused* to die here.

So, taking a deep, steadying breath, she reached for the pneuma that lay just behind her stomach.

Don't do this, Keira. Danny pleaded. *It's too risky. You're too weak.*

She ignored him, focusing only on her breathing and the pulsing energy at her core. She had just reached out to nudge it into life, when the slam of doors could be heard from outside, followed by shouts and the pounding of feet on stone.

Keira's eyes snapped open just as the door to the chambers burst open. She poked her head out from under the table to see rows of Bellatori guards streaming into the chambers. She sagged with relief.

Then another thought had her scrambling to her feet with a groan, even as she leaned heavily on the table—her other hand clutching her side.

As Landry moved to meet with the Centus in charge, Keira scanned the room. The cloaked figures were gone. From the hall, she could hear search parties being ordered, while inside the chambers, medics tended to the wounded. Then her eyes lit on the lone cloaked figure remaining. He was clawing his way up the aisle, a knife still sticking from his back. Around him, two Bellators jeered.

"Your friends leave you behind?" said one young Tiro.

"Let us put you out of your misery, eh?" cajoled another.

Keira lurched toward them as the second drew his blade. The cloaked man didn't beg, didn't plead—only stared up at his executioner with cold defiance.

"Stop!" Keira called, leaning heavily on the rows of seats as she passed. "Bind him, but leave this one for us."

The Bellators jumped to attention before reluctantly obeying.

She gazed coldly down at the cloaked man as she reached them. He turned wary gray eyes on her, and she stared back, unblinking. There was something about the tiny smirk that graced his lips as he gazed up at her, familiarity and amusement etched into the tiny lines around his mouth even as he grimaced in pain. He *knew*.

"Where is she?" Keira breathed.

The man's brows rose, and he cocked his head slightly at her. Though the wound in his back bled freely, he said nothing, only returning her stare with casual indifference.

"Where is Raina?" Keira asked again. "The little girl from the Southern Shield. Where *is* she?"

The man's smile only grew wider, even as his eyes glazed with pain. Keira felt her own fury building, an unstoppable wave that she'd like nothing better than to unleash, wiping that unholy smirk from this snake's lips. A hand on her arm stilled her, and she turned to find Cyrus, eyeing her warily as he motioned for the nearby Bellators.

"Take him away," he said. "Get him some medical care, then deposit him in the nearest cell." Keira's eyes narrowed as she watched the Bellators muscle the man out of the room. "He'll answer our questions soon enough," Cyrus said slowly, still not releasing his grip on her arm. "Come on, let's get you back to the Vindolum."

Keira shook off his arm but followed him from the chambers. This wasn't over—not by a long shot.

I'm coming, Raina, she promised silently. *Just hold on.*

TWENTY-FIVE

The world around Keira swirled chaotically as she gritted her teeth against the sting of the medic's balms. Arriving Bellators had organized search parties to locate the fleeing assailants, while the prisoner was dragged off to the dungeons under strict guard, no doubt to a harsh interrogation. The Centus in charge had briefly mentioned they'd been tipped off by fleeing council members, but though Keira scanned the crowd, she saw no sign of Akamu or the rest of the Southern Shield delegation. Waiting only until the gash above her hip had been bandaged, Keira ignored the medics' strict instructions to rest and follow up at the Royal Hospital. Instead, she headed straight for the Vindolum.

Upon arriving, she had a brief word with a servant, who pointed her in the direction of the library at the far end of the West Wing. Keira headed straight there, wincing with each step up the twisting staircase, her knuckles going white as she gripped the banister. A quick rap on the door to the library, and Keira let herself in, her eyes quickly adjusting to the pale light from the fireplace. The library itself was two stories tall; a narrow walkway enclosed by a banister made up the second floor, and great wrought-iron chandeliers hung from the ceiling. She found Albert where she'd expected, nose deep in a book and quill scratching away on parchment as he took notes. A memory flashed through her mind, that of Elliott back in their little farmhouse near Abalás, fingertips smudged a dark black as he scratched away furiously with quill and ink on some research into herbs and plants. Those days seemed so long ago. What would Elliott think if he were here? What advice would he give her? Keira shook her head. Something told her she wouldn't like it, whatever it was.

Albert glanced up at the sound of her entry, and his lips pressed into a thin line. "Keira, I'm glad to see you on your feet, but you really should be resting."

She waved a hand at him, dismissing the idea out of hand. "I take it you heard what happened?"

Albert nodded, and Keira pressed on.

"They have Raina," she breathed. "The prisoner wouldn't tell us where she is, but I'm sure he knows." Keira couldn't help the note of bitterness that crept into her voice, or the fury that continued to claw at her stomach.

Albert nodded, clearly suspecting as much, but said only, "What do you wish to do now, then?"

He wanted her to say it, she realized. Wanted her to think it was her own idea, not the point he'd been deftly arguing only a few days ago—another prisoner and another question, but the same point. She felt her lips press into a thin line as she locked eyes with Albert, watching as a slow, steady smile spread over his features.

"I want to interrogate this prisoner."

∼

THE COOL DAMP of the prison walls pressed in on Keira as she and Albert slowly descended the steep staircase to the dungeons. Though it was still within the Vindolum itself, with every step Keira felt herself slip farther and farther away from the world of air and sunlight, into the belly of darkness and damp. The dungeon walls, glittering with the trapped dew of the subterranean levels, seemed to press in on her, and her breathing became shallower the deeper they went—as if the air itself sought desperately to escape the grip of blackness.

When they finally reached the bottom, Albert led her through the twisting corridors. Keira kept her eyes trained straight ahead, not daring to look too closely at the thick wooden doors of the cells they passed—lest they be occupied.

Finally, they came to the lone cell at the end of the hall, a massive lock bolting it closed. Keira glanced to Albert, listening to the high-pitched whistle he emitted, far too high for normal ears to hear. Yet there it was, and Keira felt it twist and curl around the metal of the lock. As the atoms that composed the metal shifted, becoming ever more excited, the lock itself glowed red—emitting heat and light from the energy Albert unleashed as he nudged each atom into a slightly more disordered state. With a click, the lock unhinged, and Albert carefully undid the latch.

With a shudder somewhere between fear and excitement, Keira followed him into the dank cell beyond. The man before them shivered—dressed only in tattered rags against the bone-chilling cold of the dungeon cell. At their entrance, he glanced up at them, eyes still glassy with remembered pain. They widened as he took in the two of them, and beads of sweat suddenly appeared across his upper lip.

"Please—" the man choked out.

Keira's fury was like a dark curtain settling over her senses.

"What," she demanded, "did you do with her?"

"Please, I-I don't know anyfin'."

"I said," Keira continued, forcing the words out through gritted teeth, "what did you do with her?"

"N-Nothing. I don't know who you're talking about."

Keira's jaw clenched, and Albert tsked at her side as he deftly relocked the door behind them. "Well, that certainly won't do." He paused, and Keira could feel his eyes on her—watching, surveying.

You don't have to do this, Danny murmured. *You can find another way.*

Behind her, Albert held perfectly still, content merely to watch and wait. He knew she was well and truly out of options.

There's no time, she told Danny curtly. *This is the only way.*

She took another step toward the man, and he tried to inch away from her, his movements hampered by bound feet and shackled wrists.

Albert tsked again. "No amount of distance will save you, I'm afraid." Turning to Keira, he asked, "Would you like grounding, or are you content to try yourself?"

Keira's lips pressed together, and she nodded once, reaching a hand out in wordless request. Albert's cool fingers slipped around her own, and she repressed a shudder before closing her eyes. She reached deep within herself, toward that ball of energy she knew so well. Maybe it was just her imagination, but its response seemed sluggish, uncurling slowly as if unsure what she truly intended.

Keira pursed her lips, emitting a high-pitched whistle that guided the pneuma out through her fingers, coursing through the air toward the prisoner. Despite every inch he tried to put between them, no amount sufficed to evade her pneuma's furious intent.

She felt the tendrils of her pneuma curl across the man's skin, seeping through his pores until she could feel the rush of his consciousness just below the surface.

She hesitated, flashes of her own memory intermingling with glimpses of his. Marek Largaen's face swam before her mind's eye. *You've done this before,* she reminded herself. *You can do this now.*

Gently, she eased herself into the biting cold of the prisoner's stream of consciousness—*Finn's* consciousness. The man's name was Finn Nolan, and he'd lived through some terrible things in his brief life. Remembering her mistake with Marek, Keira fought to keep herself from snagging on any of the memories, glancing at them sidelong before letting them flow past her. She certainly didn't need any more nightmares keeping her up at night. Still, she caught glimpses—violence, abuse, life on the street, begging, stealing, fighting for survival in a city that couldn't be bothered to lend a helping hand. It was no wonder he fell in with the first radical group that promised change and a step up from the life he'd been born into.

Keira let the memories flow by quicker, searching for any glimpse or hint of Raina and where she might be. As she reached memories of the last few days, she slowed so as not to miss any, letting them slip through her pneuma like water through fingers. Meetings, plans, Neval's face—she hesitated on that one, her own fury pulsating like a second heartbeat that threatened to choke her with its wrath. He'd betrayed them, even after everything—luring them to the People's Council and then disappearing just as the carnage began. But there'd be time to deal with him later, time enough to wipe that smug smirk from his face. Keira turned back to the task at hand, searching the memories for any sign of Raina, ignoring the shift and roil of Finn's mind as he tried to fight off the bind. Keira latched on, refusing to be shaken loose as she dug her talons deeper into the muddy banks of his stream of consciousness. She fought the rising nausea at the sensation of being flipped and rolled with each pulsing eddy. Then she saw them—seafoam-green eyes widened as Raina gazed up in fear from a chair at the far end of a table.

Keira's stomach lurched, and she leapt for the memory, loosing the firm hold she'd taken on the mental stream as she scrambled to reach it, tossed and turned amid the roiling waves of recollection. She seized onto the memory and with a jolt realized it had taken place at the Miller's Plow. Raina had clearly returned later that night, no doubt looking for information about her brother. She watched as Raina was hauled before a circle of conspirators, then bound and gagged and dragged off to—

The image suddenly went fuzzy, and with a jolt, Keira realized Finn was fighting her, his memories tossing and turning with a force that threatened to displace her tenuous hold on Raina. Who'd taught this poor street kid how to evade a mental bind? She didn't have time to dwell on the question as the force of Finn's resistance intensified. Keira gritted her teeth, mind straining with the effort of keeping him in check.

Subdue him, a smooth voice whispered into her mind. *He'll throw you off if you're not careful.*

Have any helpful suggestions? Keira seethed silently.

Albert paused, as if weighing his words carefully. *All humans respond to the same thing, Keira.*

She waited, barely daring to breathe lest she lose her focus on the tether she'd lashed to Finn's memories.

Pain.

Keira blanched. Was he serious? She'd already invaded this man's mind, combing through memories as one might sift blades of grass. Did he actually expect her to torture him as well?

It's the only way, Albert murmured. *You'll lose her otherwise.*

Keira tensed but realized immediately that he was right. Already the memory of Raina was fading, the grip of the pneuma flailing as the memory grew ever more transparent. Panic welled within her.

No, no, no, she thought. *I can't lose her, not Raina, not her too.*

Albert waited, and Keira caught the faint air of triumph wafting off him. He knew she had no other options, but still he waited, never rushed, always content to let *her* come to *him.* And with a deep breath, Keira felt herself nod.

Show me.

Without a moment wasted, Albert sent an image into her mind, an image of bone and sinew, a diagram of pain and the places upon which to inflict it. Keira shuddered, her stomach rebelling at the thought.

I can't, she thought. *I can't do that.*

You're a healer, Albert replied smoothly. *You have the knowledge, and that which is made can always be unmade.*

Keira took a deep, shaking breath. She forced herself to remember that this man had done terrible things. He'd tried to kill her, kill her friends, had tried to destroy the peace and order they'd so painstakingly built. But ultimately, there was only one thought that compelled her forward, one thought that allowed her to slowly unravel a tendril of pneuma and send it coursing toward the prisoner's knees. It was that thought that held her steady as she unraveled the atoms that held the ligaments in place, and one thought quieted her mind amid the screaming.

This is for Raina.

~

IT TOOK ONLY TEN MINUTES. Ten minutes for the answers to come, ten minutes for the images of memory to be released, with an eagerness brought on by desperation. It took only ten minutes, but Keira could have sworn she'd aged a century as she stood in the hallway outside the cell, waiting for Albert to finish locking up the weeping, crumpled man inside.

Keira's hands shook, and she balled them into fists to halt their quivering. She squeezed her eyes shut, but there was no refuge in darkness. The man's screams had wormed their way into her mind, painting the walls of her inner self in shades of bloodred that she knew could never be wiped away. It was clean torture, she thought remotely. She'd repaired everything she'd broken. But in her soul, she felt his blood on her and knew she'd never feel clean again. How many lives had she taken? How much suffering had she inflicted? But this, this was different. This was an unarmed opponent, incapable of doing her further harm. And what she'd done—

She'd used her own knowledge—healing knowledge—to inflict pain. She was disgusting, less than a worm, and undeserving of any happiness or goodness in this life—not after what she'd done.

"You did well," Albert commented mildly. "Crude, but the finesse will come."

Keira opened her eyes and stared at him, mouth falling open in incredulity.

"How are you feeling? Up for another, or do you need a rest first?"

Keira's mouth opened and closed, gasping for air and being offered only more water with which to drown herself. Albert didn't seem to notice but rather busied himself peering at a scrap of paper he'd pulled from his pocket.

"What are you talking about?" she managed weakly. Her voice was rough, as if she'd been the one screaming.

Finally, he looked up, and his eyes softened at her expression. "It gets easier, Keira, I promise."

"I-I don't *want* it to get easier. I never want to do anything like that ever again."

His eyes hardened at her words, and a muscle worked in his jaw. "You did what you set out to, Keira. You've learned Raina's location, and we now have the information needed to find her, not to mention the rest of those would-be assassins. But there's still more information to be gleaned. The first prisoner, the one caught sneaking around the Regio's offices, he knows more than he's let on. There's a piece to this puzzle of the conduit that we're still missing. After all, the power needed to reform a person from their pneuma must be immense. I suspect he may know the secret to how such power may be channeled. There are only a few days before the equinox, Keira—likely your only chance at bringing Danny back. Are you really prepared to give up on that?"

Keira stared at him and wondered why she'd never noticed the way his eyes burned like molten steel, the hard, cruel lines that marked his face. She finally closed her mouth, gritting her teeth as she stared him down.

"No, Albert. I'm done. Done with torturing people for information. I-I'll find another way to save Danny."

Albert scoffed, a cold, cruel sound that reverberated off the dungeon walls, echoing in harsh condescension.

"There is no other way. You know that as well as I do."

Keira shook her head. "It's wrong, Albert, wrong to do this. I can't use *healing* knowledge to cause *pain*."

"Don't play pious with me, you stupid girl," Albert sneered, arms crossing as his eyes narrowed. "Don't pretend you didn't know what you were doing. You knew what would happen, knew what the cost of saving that little girl might be. And you gladly paid it. You *made* that choice."

Keira swallowed, blinking away the burning that stung her eyes. "I did, and to save Raina, I-I'd do it again. I'm the one that put her in danger, and if that was the cost of saving her—fine. But not for this crusade of yours, Albert. I won't torture for a shot at some information that man may or may not have."

"Indeed. And what of your grounder? Do you really feel you're *blameless* in his death?"

His words hit her like a bludgeon to the gut, and Keira felt the air physically knocked out of her.

"O-Of course not," she whispered. "But Danny—Danny knew what could happen. He followed me." There were those tears again, and she didn't even try to stop them as they filled her eyes, overflowing onto her cheeks. She roughly shoved them away. "But he wouldn't want this, would never condone torture, even if it signed his own death warrant."

Of that Keira was certain, more certain than she'd ever been of anything in her life. Danny was a soldier through and through, and he'd never forgive her if he thought she'd used torture to save him. But worst of all, he might never forgive himself.

"No, Albert, I'm done." She turned then and ascended the stairs out of the dank dungeon, the walls of which threatened to collapse in on her. "Raina needs help, and I'm going to find her —one way or the other."

Albert's words floated after her as she quickened her pace. Every inch of her yearned to escape that dark abyss even as her teeth gritted against the sharp pain in her side.

"The time will come, Keira. You have the knowledge now, and it will never loosen its grip on you."

Keira shuddered, bracing herself against the wall as she pressed a hand to the bandaged gash above her hip. She blinked down in muted surprise as the hand came away crimson. She swallowed the burning sensation in her throat and forced her legs to resume their heavy-laden ascent.

CHAPTER

TWENTY-SIX

It really was an insane plan. The rational, saner part of Keira knew that, knew nothing good could come of leading her friends deep into the heart of Crîd Eálas's seedy underbelly.

And yet here they were, gathered outside the sewer entrance in the South End, about to do exactly that.

"You're sure this is where they took her?" Zipporah asked. She'd made an extra effort to be nice ever since hearing of the trap they'd all but walked into, no doubt out of guilt that she and Marti had remained safe in the public market, trying to gather information about the faction's contacts in the city. Or maybe Marti had had a word with her. Still, the dubious look Zipporah gave the wooden door, which was practically falling off its hinges, made her thoughts on the current plan perfectly clear. The cobwebs strung from the ceiling certainly didn't look like they'd been disturbed anytime recently. Keira hesitated for just a moment before nodding.

"Positive. I saw the whole thing in the prisoner's head. They dragged Raina here from the Miller's Plow, just up the street."

Zipporah still looked doubtful and opened her mouth as if to argue, but Marti quickly interjected.

"It makes sense, really. Where else would you keep an underground organization, except—well, underground, yes?" Marti's grin faltered at her poor attempt at a joke, but Keira made an effort to return it. She appreciated the effort, even if her insides felt like jelly.

"I suppose Albert won't be joining us, then?" Cyrus shifted his weight uneasily, and he scanned the empty alleyway around them, as if half expecting armed assailants to emerge at any moment.

"He's—uh, busy, at the moment."

Now it was Keira's turn to shift awkwardly. She'd given them only cursory details of what had transpired in the Vindolum's dungeon, leaving out the gritty details of exactly what she'd done. A cord of guilt twisted in her stomach as she remembered the prisoner's screams. In the end, it had been the only way of getting the information she'd needed to find Raina. But Albert's reaction—as if nothing at all had occurred, or at least nothing of consequence—made Keira shudder. No, there was a reason she hadn't asked Albert to join them—why she wasn't at all sure she'd be asking him for anything ever again.

Keira ignored the sidelong looks her friends flashed each other, busying herself instead with securing the sword at her hip.

"I'll take lead, with Cyrus just behind," Keira said. She held his eyes, noting the determined set to his mouth. "Be ready to surge forward if we encounter heavy resistance, though. Zipporah, you'll guard our rear, and be ready to ground Marti and me if things get dicey."

Keira swallowed, trying to suppress the swell of nausea at the thought of canting pneuma in such a small space, not to mention letting Zipporah get that close and personal. Hopefully, it wouldn't come to that. As long as the enemies came one at a time, she'd gladly remain secure in her own skin, thank you very much.

They all nodded, faces filled with a trust that made Keira's knees feel weak. Still, she turned and began the long, dark descent.

For Raina, Keira reminded herself. *They're doing this for Raina.*

But even she didn't believe that lie. No, if things went south, it would be on her. Whatever blood was spilled in this venture, it would be because she'd led her friends into danger.

The stairway was narrow, and if she lifted her elbows to either side, she could feel them graze both walls. Her feet moved quickly, her steps as quiet as she could make them in the echoing blackness. She stared ahead, willing her stomach to unclench as only blackness gazed back from beyond the faint rim of light her meager torch offered.

Down and down they went. Finally, after what seemed an eternity, flat ground emerged ahead of her torch's light. Keira exhaled sharply between clenched teeth as she flattened herself against the curved stairwell, signaling for the others to follow suit. Passing the torch back to Cyrus, Keira slowly inched her head around the curve, her fingers latched securely on her sword hilt as she willed her eyes to pierce the thick curtain of dark.

Nothing.

With a quick wave, she signaled to the others as she slowly eased down the last few steps. Her footsteps pattered against the thin layer of stagnant water that had seeped into the hall. Beside her, Marti wrinkled her nose in distaste. The smell was certainly on a whole other level.

"Through here," Keira breathed, leading them forward.

In reality, Keira didn't know most of what lay beyond. The images of Raina being dragged down here had abruptly ended, as the prisoner, Finn, had gone down a different side hall.

There. Up ahead, that was the fork in the hall she'd seen.

Not too bad for someone with an otherwise hopeless sense of direction, she thought wryly.

Danny didn't answer. He hadn't spoken to her since before Finn's interrogation. In fact, she'd barely sensed his presence at all. Was he angry? she wondered. Or was this severing of their bond inevitable the closer and closer she got to the equinox? Something turned unpleasantly in Keira's stomach at the thought. She was no closer to figuring out a way to save him than she had been back in Port Galaén—her few failed attempts at reconstructing pomegranates notwithstanding. And now, with Albert furious with her . . .

Keira pushed the thought away. *Raina first,* she reminded herself, letting out a slow, unsteady breath through pursed lips. *Then we save Danny.*

A low thump echoed down the hall, and Keira froze.

Barely daring to breathe, she quickly signaled for the others to halt as she slowly unsheathed her blade. They obeyed, shifting seamlessly into defensive positions. Keira fingered the hilt of her sword, savoring its reassuring heft as she slowly inched forward. She scanned the hallway, eyes straining to see into the murky blackness as she quieted her breathing, alert for any evidence of movement.

And there they were. The soft pattering of footsteps drew closer, getting louder and gaining speed with every second. Keira backed up slightly, fully entering the ring of light from Cyrus's torch as she settled into a defensive position—feet apart, legs slightly bent—as she braced to meet whatever was about to emerge from the dark. She heard a small gasp beside her but didn't dare look at Marti, focusing all her attention on the attacker before them.

Light suddenly reflected off the sheen of metal, and Keira lunged.

"Wait, it's—"

Keira heard Marti's words, but it was far too late to reverse course now. She brought her sword up and over, aiming to the right of that blade's deadly sheen. With any luck, she'd catch their neck—where no armor could save them.

Her blade caught metal, and she moved with the sword's momentum, letting it spin her to the side as the metal slid along in a shearing sound that made her cringe. She came fluidly back into a defensive position and prepared to attack again.

"Keira, wait, it's not—"

A face suddenly emerged in the blackness, and it took Keira a moment to register it.

Akamu's laughing eyes were somber now but still twinkled with grim amusement. "If you be wanting me dead, *Le'ena*, you need only have left me back with the council."

Keira sagged slightly, her adrenaline ebbing as quickly as it had come. She smiled sheepishly back. "Sorry about that," she murmured. But her jaw tightened as she added, "What are you doing here?"

Akamu's eyes narrowed, and Keira saw his fingers tighten on the blade—no doubt stolen from a faction member, by the look of its curved length, its tip dipping into a sharp point.

"Same thing as you, I think," he growled, face contorting into one of sheer fury. "I be getting my sister back from these mainland rats now."

Keira resisted the urge to shudder at the look of murderous

intent in his eyes and nodded grimly in agreement. Then a thought curdled her stomach.

"H-How did you know she'd be here?"

Akamu merely shrugged. "The South End be not so good at keeping secrets, even among its rats."

A wave of nausea coursed through her then. She'd been so sure that interrogating the prisoner had been the only option, the only way to find out where Raina was being held. It had all been for nothing. Keira lightly placed her fingertips against the slick wall and willed the room to stop spinning. She really was a worthless worm.

Feeling concerned eyes on her, she forced her spine to straighten and infused her voice with as much normalcy as she could muster. None of that changed the task at hand. Raina still needed help.

"All right, then. We better get moving. Whoever you beat *that* out of will be found eventually," she said, nodding toward the sheen of Akamu's sword.

They continued down the hall and Keira refused to meet Marti's worried look. She didn't deserve such concern. At her shoulder, Akamu nodded at the side entrance he'd entered through and the sprawling tangle of limbs of the guard who'd made the mistake of intercepting him. They hurried past, and Keira felt her breath quicken as the sewer curved deeper still. The thin layer of water at their feet deepened as they descended further, until they were wading through dark, stagnant pools that came up almost to Keira's knees. She kept her eyes fixed straight ahead, not wanting to think about what all floated through its murky depths.

Finally, they reached what appeared to be a cellblock.

"Spread out," Keira murmured. "Search each cell, but be on the lookout for any guards." That they'd encountered no resistance thus far sent a simmering cord of electricity through Keira's veins. *This was all too easy*, a voice in the back of her mind told her. *Much too easy.*

Most of the cells were empty, Keira quickly found. And those that weren't yielded bleary-eyed prisoners who stared blankly at the walls of their cells, indicating neither the desire nor inclination to rise and claim their freedom. The sight gave Keira the chills.

"Come on, Raina," she muttered. "Where are you?"

But there was no sign of her, not in that cellblock, nor in the one that followed. Keira cursed.

"Where is she?" she asked when the five of them had regrouped. Zipporah shook her head darkly. "There's no telling. They could have taken her anywhere. No doubt Neval could see she was important to you. It stands to reason he'd keep her somewhere safe, for use as a bargaining chip later on."

Not for the first time, Keira cursed her own stupidity—not only for ever trusting that slimy weasel but also for not turning straight around the moment she'd caught Raina following her. Instead, she'd let her tag along, and in doing so put an eleven-year-old girl's life at risk. How on earth could she have been so stupid?

Keira opened her mouth to reply, but her words were cut short by the echo of loud conversation and footsteps approaching. Keira saw Zipporah blanch, and Marti's eyes widened to the size of saucers.

Thinking quickly, Keira scanned their surroundings. "In here," she hissed, pushing open an empty cell. The others hurried inside, and Keira gently closed it, mentally willing its hinges not to squeak. She nudged it shut as much as she dared, leaving a crack between the ledge and the sill.

Keira barely dared to breathe, and she closed her eyes, listening intently to the voices as they passed.

". . . 'bout time, I say," a deep male voice growled. "Riskin' our necks like that, we deserve a bit of celebration."

His companion murmured something Keira couldn't quite make out but was met by cursing from his friend, who from the sound of it had stumbled roughly into a stool at the far end of the cellblock.

"Well, we don't 'ave to *trust* the bloke, now, do we?" the man replied after a moment, clearly regaining his balance. "He's got people and resources, and clearly enough ale to keep even me 'appy."

The voices faded as they made their way past and through to the adjacent cellblock. Keira let out a sigh of relief and gently eased open the cell door. She glanced to either side and, seeing the path clear, gestured for the others to follow her.

She aimed for the direction the two guards had come from, all the while ruminating on their words. Who was this "bloke" they had mentioned? Their leader? And why did he feel the need to ply them with ale to keep them in line? Perhaps this radical faction was far less principled than they seemed. Keira was still racking her brain for answers when they reached the door on the far side of the hall. Maybe it was Keira's distraction, or the fact that Marti was too shaken from their close call to cant ahead, but either way, Keira opened the door without thinking and suddenly found herself face-to-face with a room filled with at least thirty rebel guards.

Keira froze.

There were arrayed throughout the room, and mercifully, every one of them seemed to be fast asleep. Barely breathing, she quickly scanned their surroundings. The room was circular, with tables and benches surrounding a center fire. Food and ale overflowed from the edges, and men slumped over them, many falling nearly completely off. They slept deeply, unnaturally so. Keira watched as Akamu went to investigate, holding her breath as he gently nudged a man in the ribs. Keira watched in horror as he rolled slightly, flopping off the bench with a thunderous crash that should have woken the dead. The five of them tensed, watching and waiting for the others to come to. But there was nothing.

The room of men slept on, oblivious to all in their surroundings.

"Drugged," Akamu muttered, rubbing his chin in contemplation as he scanned the room.

Keira shook her head. "Time enough to figure this out later. We need to keep moving. Raina *has* to be here somewhere."

The others nodded and followed her as she led them toward the door at the far end of the circular room, weaving in and around sleeping figures as she went. She reached for the handle but staggered back as it swung forward of its own accord and she came face-to-face with Neval Brennan.

"You," Keira snarled, steel whistling as she unsheathed her blade, matched in tune by four others.

Neval's mouth pressed into a thin line as he surveyed the room and her waiting friends, but he made no move to either run or fight.

Then a small dark head bobbed into sight as she peered around the edge of the door, green eyes glittering.

Raina.

"Keira!" she squealed, surging forward. Keira staggered a bit as the smaller girl barreled into her, wrapping her arms around her waist. Confusion coursed through her as she stared down at Raina's dark head in disbelief. She was really here.

Raina's head shot up then as she spied Akamu's tense smile from where he stood in the corner.

"Akamu?" Raina's voice trembled now as she finally laid eyes on the brother she'd traveled across the ocean to find.

"Sure enough, little *dinué*. You not be thinking I'd leave you here with just these *grelún* for company, eh?"

Tears filled Raina's eyes as she practically barreled into her big brother, clinging to him as if to the edge of the world.

Akamu only patted her shaking back, smiling quietly into her hair.

Keira smiled at the sight but quickly turned back toward Neval's knowing smirk as confusion and suspicion hit her once more. "You—but you betrayed us."

Neval only shrugged, examining the back of one hand as if it might hold the answers she sought. "I had my own investigations to conduct, Keira dear." His smile faltered slightly as he added with a nod to Raina, "Didn't help that I had a young'un trailin' me, though, did it? Nearly unraveled everythin'."

Keira snorted, eyes narrowing in a glare. "So I suppose you had no choice but to take her prisoner, then, did you?"

Neval took a step forward, and she felt Cyrus tense beside her. She refused to give Neval the satisfaction of her fear, though, and so held her ground, chin up at an angle Raina would have been proud of.

"I'm flattered that you think I have such say-so around these parts, Keira dear, but I'm afraid I must tell you you're mistaken. It was all I could do to gather enough information about their plans to warn the City Guard ahead of time."

"You could have prevented that massacre in the first place," Keira snarled.

Neval's eyes narrowed, and he took another step forward so there were only a few inches between them. "And have 'em know for sure they'd been betrayed? I rather like my back to remain knifeless, I'll have you know. Besides, you'd never have caught them all. Their network is too deep and has been around far longer than I've been in the capital." Neval shook his head. "No, they'd know it was me, and then where would we be? Where would *she* be?" he added, nodding in Raina's direction.

Keira hesitated, lips pursing, and Neval grinned broadly at her indecision, emanating that cocky self-assurance that set her teeth on edge. But his words settled in her stomach with the weight of truth. It really had all been for nothing.

"Fine," she finally spit out. "Say you actually *are* on our side in all this—you can start by helping get us the hell out of here. We saw guards heading back in the direction we came from."

Neval nodded grimly. "Follow me, then. The drugs'll be wearin' off soon."

"Y-You did this, then?" Marti asked, gesturing at the thirty-odd slumped figures around them. Neval smirked in response.

"Not bad for an upland peasant boy, eh? Amazin' what the lure of good ale can yield."

Keira rolled her eyes but conceded to follow him, gesturing for the others to follow suit. Still, she kept a healthy distance. She told herself it was because she didn't trust him. She *didn't* trust him. But the faint twist of relief that had echoed in her stomach with every word of his professed innocence warned her that the true reason might be far more complicated.

TWENTY-SEVEN

876 Common Era (C.E.)

Danny barged into the kitchens, sending the door flying into the back wall. The cooks and servers all glanced up in alarm, the regular chatter of daily servant life coming to an abrupt halt.

"I-I'm looking for someone," Danny said, shifting his weight as he felt all eyes fall on him. "Moira. Moira Foléan."

A low murmur echoed around the room as the uplander servants eyed his sword and Bellatori cloak distrustfully. Danny shifted awkwardly, searching faces that refused to meet his gaze. He was just about to demand that someone had better start talking, when a rustle of movement from the back of the room caught his eye as Moira strode toward him.

She perched her hands on her hips as she reached him, brows raised to demand, "What in Séiro's name has gotten into you, eh?"

"He's dead," Danny spat, balling his hands into fists to keep them from shaking.

Moira's brow furrowed. "Who's dead?"

"Imperator Titus Longus. This morning." Moira's face paled as she seemed to fully take in his shaking, dirty appearance.

"Let's . . . go outside," she said finally, glancing around before steering him toward the kitchen door and the back alley beyond. Danny let her guide him, too weary to resist as the adrenaline that had laced his veins since the initial attack began to wear off. When they had reached the alley and the door was firmly locked behind them, Moira turned to face him, arms crossed and eyes guarded. "All right, then, say what you've come to say."

Her tone alone was enough to reignite the dying flames of Danny's fury. He rounded on her, voice trembling with rage as he threw his words like daggers. "He died in my arms, Moira! In his own piss and shit. He couldn't even scream at the end!"

Moira crossed her arms. "I'm sorry to 'ear that, truly."

Danny scoffed, running a hand through his hair.

Moira's eyes narrowed further. "I *am* sorry."

"Is that right? Well, you'll be more sorry to hear who killed him."

Moira's lips parted, and her throat bobbed. "Who?"

"Your friend, Arlan," Danny spat, trying and failing to keep his voice steady, even as he searched her eyes for any hint of surprise. He found none. "Don't worry, he's dead."

She blinked. "No doubt thanks to your Bellator friends," she said, voice icy.

Danny gritted his teeth to keep from shouting but could feel his nostrils flare. "No, we didn't get the chance. He was shot through the eyes before we could interrogate him. You can thank your own friends for that, I think."

Moira went absolutely still as she stared at him. "*My*

friends? You think I had something to do with this." She said the words stiffly, and there was no question in her tone.

"I sure as hell do. Arlan was *your* friend, and I was the one who told you what time Titus and I would review the troops, precisely where we'd be."

She didn't move, still regarding him coolly. "That means nothin'. It's not exactly a secret where the red cloaks train, and besides, I'm friends with lots of—"

Danny couldn't take the lies one second longer, and he lunged forward, grabbing her wrist. He yanked up her sleeve to see the image he'd glimpsed time and again in the hours they'd spent combing Cato's books and scrolls. Inked in bloodred, just above her inner wrist, was a willow tree, its curling fronds twisting around her arm in a branded bracelet of guilt.

Moira yanked her arm away, hand wrapping around her wrist to hide the evidence. But it was too late.

"*Long live the tree from which liberty springs,*" Danny whispered, voice shaking. "That's what he said before they killed him."

There had been a part of him that had hoped, desperately, to be wrong. But seeing the proof there, in ink and flesh, made the truth settle like a boulder in his gut. Then the weight of what he'd done washed over him.

"I-I gave you troop movements, camp locations," he said, searching her eyes for any sign of guilt or apology, any indication that the girl he'd thought was his friend still existed. "I'm a *traitor.* You *made* me a traitor."

Moira's eyes hardened then, and she met his gaze with steely-eyed determination. "You're no traitor, Danny O'Leary. You're just a soldier. You didn't ask for this, but you are good and brave and loyal." She said the words with a ferocity that made Danny wonder vaguely who she was trying to convince. "It's these *people*, who tried to turn you into somethin' else. You've seen who they are, what they've done. You know it's wrong. You *understand* what we're up against."

He shook his head, staring at her with eyes wide. "Sabotage, targeted assassinations, political stunts . . . you're terrorists."

Moira stiffened, straightening to her full height as her hands fisted at her side. "We're only fightin' for what's *ours*, what we're *owed*. We don't go after innocents, only the Bellatori and government targets. That isn't terrorism, Danny. It's war. It's a different kind of war than I'd wager you're familiar with, but it's still a war."

Danny hesitated, hearing the pull of her words settle around his own conflicted soul. She wasn't wrong, not entirely. And whether he liked their methods, he couldn't deny that their cause was just. "I have friends in the Bellatorio, Moira. People I care about in the Legion who are allied with them. I can't. I won't betray them, not again."

Moira pressed her lips into a thin line and jutted out her chin. "So what? Will you turn me in, then? Watch 'em execute me? That is, after they've tortured me for names I'll never give 'em. Is that what you want?"

Danny stared at her—this girl who'd reminded him of home, this girl he'd started to truly care for. *Not started*, a small voice reminded him, *a girl I did care about.*

"No," he said finally, the weight of guilt and defeat finally settling on his shoulders. "I won't tell anyone. But this—*us*, we're done. I'm done."

He caught a glimpse of Moira's parted lips, eyes wide with surprise, before he turned and left the alley. He felt her eyes on his back the entire way, but she didn't come after him.

～

THOUGH IT WAS HELD in a training field rather than a great hall, the coronation had all the pomp and circumstance that was expected of a Marian prince. Nothing short of a natural disaster could have postponed this event. Certainly not the assassination of the ranking Imperator, commander of the entire Eastern Imperium. Finely dressed courtiers lined the center walkway as the prince made his way at the head of the procession toward the dais, ornately draped in the red-and-gold colors of the Marian dynasty.

But Danny barely registered any of it, content to be carried along amid the Bellatori lines on the waves of ceremonial procession.

Tammy is gone. Titus is dead. Moira betrayed me. I'm a traitor.

Round and round his thoughts flew, his guilt and loneliness a thick smog that threatened to choke him. In that moment, all he could think about was her—Keira. Her laugh, her ferocity, her determination, and her protectiveness over those she cared about. He missed it all with an ache that sent shock waves through his body. It had been so long since he'd seen her, he'd thought that pain was fading. But he knew then he'd only buried it beneath layers of work, distraction, and good intention. But when all else was stripped away, she was what was left. And he wasn't sure he could bear it.

Time passed in a daze, and by the time Danny glanced back up, the prince had been crowned and was raising his hands for silence from the waiting crowd. The cheers quickly fell to a hush as Magnus laid cold, dark eyes on his rows of subjects.

"I stand before you as the newest Regio of the Marian Empire, ruler of the realm of Loren. And though she be the youngest jewel in the Empire's crown, I swear to lead her to glory and a place of honor among her sister nations. In my first act, I hereby declare this place our sacred capital, filled with promise and opportunity for whoever should be so bold as to claim it! I name our capital city Crîd Eálas. May she always serve as a haven to all friends of the Empire who seek refuge beneath her mighty stone walls."

The crowd erupted again in cheers at his words, and Magnus had to raise a hand to quiet the cacophony. "With my coronation begins a new era in the realm of Loren—one filled with promise, prosperity, and opportunity. In honor of this, I officially declare today the first day of the Marian Era!"

The crowd again roared its approval as Danny blinked in surprise and after a quick glance at Cato saw the old man visibly wince—no doubt imagining the confusion and clerical errors this would introduce into the historical record. But that was no matter, and no one dared contradict Magnus. After all, what the Regio wanted, the Regio got.

In that moment, Danny felt nothing but disdain for the Empire and its ever-expanding ambition. Opportunity? Promise? What more could they want that they didn't already have? That they hadn't already claimed? He was tired, so tired, of the fighting and the never-ending power struggles. For the first time in a while, he thought of the farmhouse back in Abalás and the happy years he'd spent there—what he wouldn't give to go back, to reclaim just a tiny sliver of the happiness he'd once taken for granted.

But that place didn't even exist yet.

So where could he go? What could he do? He supposed he could return to the Legion, but were they any better than the Empire? After everything he'd learned about their activities over the centuries, and all the questions still left unanswered, he wasn't at all sure he could stomach it.

A commotion at the back of the training field caught Danny's attention, and he turned to find lines of terrified servants in rattling chains being herded onto the training field by stiff-faced Bellators.

Danny's eyes shot to Magnus but saw no trace of surprise on his face—only cool expectation.

"Subjects, as you all know, we suffered a cowardly attack this morning. Our beloved Imperator Titus Longus, who served his Empire loyally for over twenty years, was assassinated!"

There was a rumble among the crowd. Though they'd all no doubt heard the news, it was hardly something to be addressed at a coronation. Magnus eyed them with keen anticipation before beckoning a hand toward the far end of the field.

A kernel of dread twisted in Danny's stomach as he watched the Bellators herd the fettered servants down the procession line—their chains rattling in cruel mockery of the jeweled finery of those whose steps they followed in.

"Citizens of Loren, they must know that an attack on one of us is an attack against us all. Our beloved Imperator was poisoned, in a cowardly act of sedition." Magnus paused, letting his words sink in. "The perpetrator is dead, but no doubt his co-conspirators still live among us."

There was another rumble from the crowd of downlanders, who turned faces twisted by rage and fear toward the chained servants. Young he may be, but Magnus certainly knew how to play an audience. Shouted epithets and cries for vengeance echoed around the yard as Magnus eyed them all expectantly.

Barely breathing, Danny searched the servants' tear-streaked faces, but he saw no sign of the girl with hair the color of fire. He exhaled, relief quickly followed by guilt as he saw the uplanders clinging desperately to one another. He turned then to see Magnus's face twist into a smug smile of satisfaction.

"These uplanders worked side-by-side the assassin and no doubt knew of his allegiances. Let this be an example to all who dare to stand against the might of the Marian Empire. Insurrectionists will not be tolerated, nor will those who accept them in their midst."

Danny felt suddenly cold as the ring of unsheathing metal echoed around the crowd. *They wouldn't. They couldn't—*

Then two Bellators grabbed a man at the front of the line, ignoring his squirming and pleas for mercy as they hauled him to face the crowd, forcing him to his knees.

Danny wanted to move, to stop this, but his legs remained frozen in place, and he felt his face settle into a horrified mask. Cries of outrage echoed among the crowd, and Danny glanced up, hopeful that others might see this injustice for what it was. But their fingers pointed, not at Magnus but at the man who knelt, trembling in the dirt, at the monarch's feet.

They want him dead.

And with that realization, something broke within Danny. He watched as if through a tunnel as Magnus gave the signal and the Bellator raised his blade. The screams and shouts faded to a muffled sound in his ears as he watched blood trickle through the grass, feeling bile rise in the back of his throat.

And then there was only carnage.

HE KILLED THEM ALL. Danny watched it, saw it happen. And yet something within him refused to believe it. Even after the crowd dispersed, Danny still stood alone, staring at the blood that had settled into stagnant pools in the grass. Around him, Bellators slowly cleared the field of the bodies. Danny clenched and unclenched his fingers, to find them stiff and frozen, as if there was one more corpse among the living

A voice behind him ripped him from his thoughts, and

Danny slowly turned to find a face he'd hoped never to see again.

"Millus Rommel," he said flatly.

"It's actually Imperator now," Rommel said, teeth glinting. "The Regio made the appointment this morning." He eyed the training field with distaste. "Rotten stuff, isn't it?"

When Danny didn't respond, Rommel cleared his throat, continuing, "After what happened this morning, well, I can't say I'm pleased with the promotion. But duty calls, after all."

While Rommel had the decency to at least look mildly abashed, Danny wasn't fooled. This man had always had a particularly cutthroat brand of ambition. And even if he regretted Titus's assassination, Danny didn't doubt he'd leapt at the opportunity to replace him.

"I just wanted to inform you that we have another lead on the assassin and their ilk. Some resistance group, it seems, the same one we believe has been harrying our supply chains. Anyway, one of the servants talked and gave us their meeting location. We're planning a raid at dusk, and I think it's only right you should join us. I know you and the Imperator were— close."

Danny stared at him, wading through the mental quagmire of his current state to understand what Rommel was actually saying.

The Resistance. Raid. Tonight. Moira.

Part of him knew he should just let it happen, let history unfold as it no doubt had. The Empire won. The Resistance failed. There was no changing that outcome. But then Danny remembered the smiling girl with a mother and younger brother to support, the same smiling girl who'd dragged him free from the despair that had held him all those months fighting with the Bellatorio.

He realized then that maybe he could change this one thing. Amid all the death, he could save Moira.

Danny straightened, just managing to slap a composed look on his face before turning to Rommel. "Thank you, sir. You know there's nothing I'd love more than to see justice done. I'll meet you at dusk. But in the meantime, I've got a few things to take care of."

Then Danny turned, striding away from Rommel's surprised expression with as much poise as he could muster, at least until he turned the corner out of the training field.

Then he ran.

CHAPTER

TWENTY-EIGHT

242 Marian Era (M.E.)

Wariness was a palpable force as Keira led the others back to the Vindolum—her legs aching with every step they made across the uneven cobblestones of the South End. It had been a miracle they'd encountered no further resistance on their way out of the sewers. But true to his word, Neval had slipped them out from under the guards' very noses.

Keira had gladly retaken the lead as soon as they'd emerged in clear night air. She'd checked and rechecked their rear and each alley they passed, half expecting a trap to be sprung at any moment. For his part, Neval kept a veneer of bored amusement plastered on his face, but Keira didn't miss the occasional flash of annoyance when he caught her glancing sidelong at him. No matter what he said, Keira still didn't trust him and had no intention of allowing any more of her friends to be captured.

She didn't breathe easy until the tall stone towers of the Vindolum crept over the horizon.

Inside, servants bustled about, readying the extra room Keira had requested for Neval—quite above his objections.

"You'll need to lie low for a while," she insisted, crossing her arms as she squared off against his narrowed amber gaze. "Once they discover Raina's gone, they'll be looking for someone to blame. You don't want to be around when that happens."

"I can take care of m'self, Keira dear. Though your concern is quite touchin'." Neval shot her the smirk he surely knew drove her nuts before continuing, "But I daresay it might look *more* suspicious if I'm nowhere to be found when she's discovered missing."

Keira shrugged. "You went back to the tavern. At least stay here a few days, just until we know what they're up to."

A shadow flashed across his face at her words. And though it was gone in an instant, Keira made a mental note to follow up on *that* particular tidbit later. Regardless, he conceded to stalk up the stairs behind a servant, and Keira turned to the next urgent task at hand—getting something solid in her stomach, which was threatening outright revolt.

The others had drifted off to their respective bedchambers, so Keira took the stairs to the subterranean kitchens two at a time, mouth practically watering at the thought of the beef stew one of the maids had mentioned.

Her feet slowed as she neared the bottom and voices rose up to meet her. Through the loosely woven sackcloth that covered the doorway to the kitchen, Keira could just make out two figures standing close together at the large plank table. It seemed the servants had made themselves scarce. Keira finally came to a complete stop at the sound of her own name.

"... Keira's plan. It was foolish, Marti. She likely would have gotten herself killed and very nearly took the rest of us with her. If it hadn't been for that Neval bloke—"

"That's not fair, Porah. She didn't order us to go, didn't even ask us, actually. She was willing to take the risk herself."

"That's exactly my point!" Zipporah's voice rose an octave, and Keira felt her teeth clench involuntarily. "She's always doing that, always going off on her own, consequences be damned. If she'd just talk to us, explain her plans, we could actually help—*improve* the plans, even. But no, Keira Altman trusts no one but herself, and that is *dangerous*, Marti."

Marti sighed. "You're not wrong, but she needs us, Porah. She's got no one left. She's all on her own."

The pity in her voice was like a kick to Keira's gut, even if she couldn't fault her logic.

"There's a reason for that, you know," Zipporah grumbled. "There's also something odd going on with her and Albert. I don't trust him, and I don't trust whatever garbage he's pouring into her head."

"Hope is a powerful thing," Marti murmured, tracing her finger along the whorls of the plank table.

"It can also be a dangerous thing," Zipporah replied, "when you let it distract you from the here and now, from the responsibilities that tie you to this world."

Keira watched as Zipporah stepped closer to Marti, covering her hand with her own, even as she lifted a hand to cup her cheek. "I made you a promise," she murmured, "that when things were settled, we'd get out of all this, go somewhere quiet. Don't think I've forgotten that."

Marti leaned into Zipporah's hand as she looked up into her eyes with a softness Keira had never seen before.

And just like that, Keira felt the intruder, a spy on a moment she should not be privy to. Her feet itched to turn around, to go right back up those stairs.

But something held her back, an aching in her chest that threatened to double her over the longer she continued to stare at the two of them—so happy, so in love. And Keira felt everything she'd lost with a sudden crushing weight.

She reached a trembling hand to the stair banister and half stumbled back up those stairs, fighting the tears that threatened. There was pain, yes, the pain of a life forever lost, beyond her grasp—a life with Danny. But there was also shame.

Zipporah was right. She had been foolish, endangering those around her for weeks now in her selfish quest to save him —to save *them*. It was the secrets, she realized. She risked their lives with every secret she withheld—her real reason for being in the capital, her dealings with Albert, all of it. They deserved to know, and she would tell them. But first, there were other secrets that needed uncovering.

THE SOUND of Keira's fist pounding on the door echoed down the hallway, but she didn't really care. To her surprise, the door opened before the third knock.

Neval stood before her, shirtless and with one eyebrow cocked, but with no indication of being bleary-eyed or recently roused from sleep.

Regaining her composure, Keira pushed past him, careful to avoid looking too long at the wiry muscles that spread across his chest and abdomen.

"Please, come in," Neval said snidely, closing the door behind her before turning with arms crossed. "Tell me, how can I help the great Keira Altman?"

Keira glanced around the room, momentarily flummoxed, before she rounded on him, arms crossed in perfect imitation as they squared off across from one another. "To *start*, you can tell me everything you know about this radical faction, including what their plans are. *Don't* pretend you don't know," she added as he opened his mouth in protest. "I saw your expression earlier. You know something, and I want to know what."

Neval's face had settled back into its look of bored curiosity. "Is that so? And why, might I ask, should I spill all my secrets to you?"

Keira let out the whoosh of breath she'd been holding. "Because," she said slowly, "I'm trying this new thing called honesty. Truth for a truth. I'll answer all your questions if you'll answer mine."

Neval's eyebrows had steadily risen throughout her speech, and he now stared at her with abject surprise, but there was still a glint of suspicion in his eyes as he asked, "Why? Why now? And why this sudden need for total honesty? As I recall, Keira dear, you rather like keeping things *close to the vest*."

Keira sighed again, rubbing a hand roughly across her face. An image of Marti and Zipporah flashed in her mind—their closeness, that connection, the *trust*. "Because I'm tired. I'm so tired, Neval. I'm tired of running, tired of questioning, tired of doubting everyone I've ever known. Aren't you?"

Neval's lips parted slightly as a look of surprise crossed his face, chased by something akin to curiosity. Keira didn't look closer as she turned instead to the table and chairs, yanking one out as she said roughly, "You mind?"

She didn't wait for a response as she collapsed into it, relishing the feel of her limbs going loose and jellylike. When she looked up, Neval was still staring at her. But seeing her gesture, he roughly yanked on a shirt and settled into the chair opposite her. She said nothing, merely waited.

He tented his fingers on the table before leveling her with a wary look. "They're called Red Willow, and they didn't start with the People's Council. No, they've been around for a very, *very* long time. I first learned about them back in the Claustranum—prison," he added, seeing Keira's confused expression. Keira blinked but kept her face carefully blank as he continued, "The other prisoners spoke of them in almost worshipful tones, an ancient organization committed to overthrowing the Marians, formed back in the early days of the invasion as a resistance movement. When it became clear the Marians were here to stay, they morphed into something else, a secret organization undermining them at every turn—politically, economically, and now . . . militarily."

Keira barely dared to breathe as she stared at Neval's face, half shadowed by the fading firelight. "So your attack in Rabonéis, the riots in the capital—you've been working for Red Willow this whole time?"

Neval snorted. "You flatter me, Keira dear. No, those bumbling attempts at revolution were wholly my own. But I believe they brought me to their attention. They thought I had . . . potential. They began recruiting me soon after. I'd made a name for myself, gotten a position on the People's Council. I was foolish enough to think I was the only one." Neval shook his head, a rueful expression on his face as a muscle worked in his jaw. "It wasn't until the attack that I realized how far they'd infiltrated the Council's ranks." He paused, eyeing Keira carefully even as she tried to maintain a blank expression, fighting the panic and horror that threatened to bubble to the surface. "I really did try to stop it, you know. Landry . . ." Neval shook his head. "Landry and I may not agree on everything, but I'd never want him dead."

Neval went quiet then, waiting for her to say something.

"I believe you," she said finally, meeting his gaze with as much openness as she could muster. "But how did they know? How did they know about Raina? Who she was? What she— what she means to me?"

Neval shook his head, face going hard. "I have no idea. Lisander —one of the Red Willow lieutenants assigned to the capital—he seemed to know exactly who she was, where she came from. All he told me was that a *friend* had mentioned she might be stoppin' by."

A hot stone settled in Keira's stomach, and she felt suddenly cold as she met Neval's gaze, both coming to the same conclusion.

They had a spy.

Keira's mind raced—flitting over familiar faces, the many friends and servants alike who knew who Raina was, had seen them together. There was no telling who it might have been.

But now it was Neval's turn, his eyes narrowing as he cocked his head to the side, surveying her curiously.

"Why are you really here?" he asked finally.

It was not the question Keira expected. She blinked. "To help Landry," she said after a moment. "He sent word to the Legion requesting aid, warning us of the discovered assassination attempt."

Neval waved his hand, brushing off this explanation. "We'll get to the *Legion* in a moment. I'm asking why are *you* really here?"

Keira gritted her teeth. "It's not enough that my *friend* needed help? Why shouldn't I have come?"

Neval's lips pulled back from his teeth in that Cheshire grin she knew so well. "Because the Keira Altman I know always has another play in mind. Besides, you seemed quite content to wait out your days in the festering jungles of the Southern Shield, as I recall. You lost your grounder and decided the rest of the world could go to hell."

"That is *not* what happened," Keira snarled. "And you don't know anything about it."

Neval's head cocked to the side again as he surveyed her closely. "Then explain it to me."

All her anger deflated in a moment upon seeing his earnest look. There was no judgment there, no condemnation, only genuine curiosity. He really wanted to understand.

So, taking a deep breath, she started from the beginning—the *very* beginning. How she'd arrived in Loren; the actions of the Legion there; training with Danny, Elliott, and Nazor; their mission to retrieve Landry and the resulting entanglement with the budding revolution in the capital. She sped through Danny's death, not trusting herself to dwell too long on the details. She described her time in the Southern Shield, Cyrus's arrival, Raina's stowaway, and their journey to the Legion headquarters in Port Galaén. She tried to explain her work with Albert as best she could, and Neval nodded along, though clearly confused by the exact mechanics. And she explained about Danny and the strange bond she didn't even fully understand herself. And, voice shaking, she confessed what she'd done, the torture she'd put the Red Willow operative through, all to save Raina.

When she'd finished, they sat in silence for a long while, and she was content to merely breathe. Keira felt a lightness that she hadn't experienced in a very long time, the relief of confession, of unloading your burdens onto someone else and finally being able to ... breathe.

"So that's it, then," Neval said finally. "You're tryin' to save him. Danny, I mean. That's why you're here, why you've been workin' with this Albert fellow."

Keira rubbed her cheek warily before burying her face fully in her hands. "I'm trying to save all of them," she murmured. "Danny, Landry, Raina. But the closer I get to one, the farther away the others seem. I'm really losing it, Neval. The equinox is only two days away, and I'm no closer to knowing how to bring him back than I was a month ago. And Landry—I thought we were done. After he survived the attack, I thought we'd done it. But now you're telling me there's this ancient organization that has been looking for ways to destroy him and his family for literally *hundreds of years*. How do I fight that, Neval? Where do I even start?"

Keira looked up from her hands to find Neval staring at her with a mixture of sympathy and something else she couldn't quite place. He leaned forward, gripping her forearm firmly, but with a tenderness that surprised her.

"You can't save everyone, Keira," he said quietly. "You're only one person. One very impressive person, I'll grant you," he added with a chuckle. "But still just one person. You have to let people in. You have to let 'em *help* you."

Keira snorted. "You're one to talk."

A shadow fell across Neval's eyes, and she instantly regretted her words. But he merely nodded. "You're not wrong, Keira dear. I decided a long time ago that I wouldn't lose anyone else I cared about, that I couldn't bear that pain anymore. And I have suffered because of that choice. As have you."

Keira stared at him, and he looked unflinchingly back at her. For the first time in what seemed an age, Keira felt like someone could really *see* her, that maybe she wasn't as alone as she'd thought. His hand was a scalding brand on her bare skin, and with a jolt, Keira suddenly realized how close they were now sitting. She swallowed, wanting to pull away, and yet somehow *not*. Heat rose to her cheeks, and she blinked. That seemed to break the spell, and Neval inhaled sharply, as if realizing the same thing. He quickly let go of her arm and leaned back in his chair. His Adam's apple bobbed twice, but then a lazy grin spread across his face and he reached up a hand to tousle his own hair.

"Well, now that that's settled, why don't we discuss how, exactly, we're goin' to go about catchin' these bastards, not to mention saving your grounder fellow."

Keira blinked at him, a blush further coloring her cheeks. "You—you mean you still want to help me? Even after everything? Even after I lied to everyone?"

Neval's eyes softened as he said, "Total honesty, remember? I feel we've made great strides today, Miss Altman, don't you? Besides, I quite like our chances. Red Willow may seem a worthy opponent, but after all, that which is *made* can be *unmade*."

Keira's entire body suddenly went deathly cold. and she stared at Neval with eyes wide. "Wh-What did you just say?"

Neval's brow furrowed, but he repeated, "That which is made can be unmade. It's something Lisander, the Red Willow lieutenant, told me once. I figured it was just an expression. Do you know it?"

Keira blinked, staring at him as her mind raced, putting the pieces together even as reality slowly dawned on her. Her mouth suddenly went dry, and she leapt to her feet, startling Neval enough that he yanked a knife from his boot, spinning to face whatever enemy she must have spotted. But their enemy wasn't there, not anymore.

"It was him," was all Keira managed to say to Neval's questioning look. "It was him all along."

Then she was running, barreling out the door and through to the West Wing. She felt Neval close on her heels, shouting questions she didn't dare stop to answer.

That which is made can be unmade.

The thoughts raced in her head as she ran. How could she have been so stupid?

Reaching her destination, she pounded on the door but waited only a moment before barreling in. The bed was made, drawers stood empty, and only a small sheet of parchment remained on the bedside table. With trembling hands, Keira reached for it, unfolding it and scanning its contents before turning to meet Neval's worried amber eyes.

"He's gone," she said simply. "Albert's gone."

By this time, I suspect you've stumbled across some rather unpleasant truths, Keira. I confess that I wish I could stay to explain the situation to you more fully. But as I'm sure you can understand, there is much for me to do. I pray you do not let the current situation dissuade you from your training. You have such potential, if only you'd be willing to grasp it. This certainly isn't goodbye, as I have no doubt our paths will cross once more. Yet until then, I wish you all the best in your efforts.

Your most affectionate mentor,

Albert

Keira read the note half a dozen times before handing it mutely to Neval, who whistled low as he finished.

"That is some creepy shite right there, Keira. You're tellin' me you actually thought this bloke was upstandin'?"

Keira merely shook her head. How could she have been so stupid? Elliott had warned her, hadn't he? He'd *warned* her Albert wasn't to be trusted. But had she listened? Of course not. That would have required far too much foresight for Keira Altman, Epic Screwup.

"What have I done?" she murmured, staring blankly at the surrounding finery. "I brought them here, all of them. I just— just wanted to save him. I *had* to save him. After everything, I couldn't let him down too."

Keira turned pleading eyes to Neval, silently begging him to understand. His mouth softened, and a look of sympathy flickered in his eyes.

"I know what it is to lose someone you love, Keira," he said, so quietly she had to lean forward to hear him. "And to be willin' to do almost anythin' to save 'em—even the despicable." His words pricked her curiosity, but at the shuttered look in his eyes, she quickly suppressed it. There'd be time for more questions later.

"So what do we do now?" she asked, rubbing a hand across her face.

"We try to get a step ahead of them, for once," Neval replied. "What does he want? What does he value? We find that out, and we make sure he doesn't get it."

Keira snorted. "Profound."

Neval shrugged, flashing her a grin. "I am just a poor upland peasant, after all. There *are* limits to my schemin', you know, Keira dear."

Keira started to roll her eyes but froze as a thought occurred to her. "The conduit."

"The what?"

"The conduit, that's what he wants. That was his whole reason for coming to Crîd Eálas, I know it!"

Neval started to ask another question, but Keira was already moving for the door, heart pounding against her breastbone. Neval had no choice but to follow on her heels.

TWENTY-NINE

The conduit was still there.

Keira heaved a sigh of relief. In the adrenaline-filled minutes it had taken them to sprint to the South Tower, she'd half convinced herself that Albert had managed to carve it out of the marble room and carry it off with him.

She watched as Neval approached it, his face a mixture of curiosity and excitement. He slowly reached a hand out and stroked the smooth marble lip.

"So this is it, then?" he murmured quietly. "The source of power Albert wants."

Keira shook her head. "It isn't the source. Pneuma comes from all around us. It's the in-between, the distance between the atoms and molecules of our world, which when slightly nudged cascade into a waterfall of motion." She didn't know where the words came from even as they spilled from her—no doubt stolen from one of Elliott's oft-repeated lectures. An image of Elliott's face lighting up with delight as he launched into one of his long-winded treatises caused a bolt of pain to shoot through her.

He warned you, told you Albert couldn't be trusted.

She ignored the thought, focusing instead on the marble basin as she ran her own hand along its smooth-lipped surface. Beneath the sheer, water-like glass surface, the pearl lay untouched, its silence a heavy thrum against her senses. "It's a conduit," she breathed. "Just like us. Pneuma doesn't come from us, you know," she added, glancing up at Neval's wary expression. "We're merely the channel, directing it where we will. The conduit is like that, but so much more powerful."

"How do you use it?"

Keira swallowed, eyes fixed on the pearl twinkling just beneath the surface. "I don't know. Albert didn't even know. I was training with him to hone my senses and ability to heal. He said when the equinox came, I would just . . . know."

From the corner of her eye, Keira saw Neval clench his jaw, eyes darting between Keira and the pearl she couldn't seem to look away from.

"If you really wanted to stop him, I think you know the best way to do that."

Keira's head snapped up, and she blinked once, twice, at Neval. "What are you saying?"

A muscle worked in Neval's jaw as he said, "You should destroy it." Seeing her aghast expression, Neval quickly added, "You said yourself, this is what brought him to Crîd Eálas. Whatever it is he's plannin', it has to involve this thing."

Keira folded her arms tight across her chest, glaring over at Neval. "Who's to say he won't achieve his goals some other way? We can't just—*destroy* it."

In truth, the thought of destroying the conduit made Keira feel physically ill, as if the world around her had turned sideways.

"You can destroy it."

The edges of Keira's vision seemed to darken as she watched the knuckles of her fingers gripping the basin turn white. Her heart hammered in her ears, and Neval's words seemed muffled.

"I-I can't. I can't do it, Neval." She turned to him then, vision blurred from the tears that suddenly filled her eyes. "This is my only chance. The *conduit* is my only chance to save him. I-I can't lose it, not as long as there's any chance of bringing him back."

Neval stared back at her for a long moment, lips pressed into a thin line as he searched her eyes, looking for . . . something. Finally, he nodded. "Just know, Keira, the time may come when you have to make a choice. When that time comes . . . I'll be here."

Keira swallowed and merely nodded, not trusting her own voice to speak.

"Well, I suggest we track down the rest of your motley crew," Neval said, that old glint coming back to his eye as he winked at her. "Seems we have some work to do, and I, for one, would like to know what we're up against."

Keira nodded, a sudden wave of gratitude flooding her for Neval's understanding, for his not pushing the question, at least not yet. "I'll talk to Akamu, see if there's somewhere he can take Raina, far away from all this." She gestured vaguely at her surroundings.

Neval pursed his lips, giving her a long, considering look.

"What?" she demanded when she could take his heavy silence no longer.

"You mentioned she had abilities," Neval said slowly.

"Yes, untrained and untried, but . . . yes."

Neval merely raised his brows pointedly, his meaning clear.

Keira ground her teeth together before snarling, "Absolutely not."

"Keira, if there's anything this week has shown you, it's that no one is safe. At least give her a fightin' chance. Teach her, train her."

"Neval, I'm not a mentor. I'm not even a full Legionnaire myself! I don't know the first thing about training someone. And Raina's gifts . . ." Keira trailed off, remembering the mysterious way in which Raina had manipulated the light around her. "I'm not even sure if what she does is pneumonancy. Albert seemed to think so, but I just don't know. I've never heard of anyone wielding pneuma in their first life."

Neval shrugged. "I know nothin' about that. But what I do know is that you can't just send the winnie out into the world without a means to defend herself."

He was right, and she knew it. Keira could only sigh and nod in agreement. "I'll do what I can, but as soon as things get crazy, she's gone," she warned.

Neval nodded solemnly before turning to the doorway. She followed him out of the room but couldn't help glancing back at the lone marble statue, its promise both ice and flame to her blood. She closed the door behind her.

THEY GATHERED in Landry's study, and though her friends had been roused unceremoniously from their beds mere hours after taking to them, each looked focused and alert, ready to get to work planning their next move.

"We have an opportunity here," Keira began. After a quick explanation of Albert's disappearance, her friends had seemed to grasp the stakes at play. "Albert thinks we're already three steps behind him."

"He's not wrong," Zipporah muttered, eyes narrowed as she scowled back at her. Keira gritted her teeth. No doubt the words *I told you so* would be close at hand. Keira pushed the thought away. There'd be time enough to suffer Zipporah's sanctimonious scoffing.

"He's involved somehow with these Red Willow people. From what Neval tells me, he's feeding them information about Landry and his movements, knowing it could get him killed. I still don't know why, but I intend to find out. He thinks he's got us on the ropes, but he doesn't know that Neval's with us, or that we know about Red Willow and what they're trying to do."

"A shame we don't actually know what they're planning," Zipporah added, eyeing Neval with undisguised suspicion. Neval merely smiled serenely back at her as he leaned against the bookshelf.

"Neval has to lie low for a while, but he'll be putting out feelers to his people to find out what he can," Keira explained, drawing Zipporah's baleful expression.

Zipporah opened her mouth, no doubt to retort something sarcastic, when a quiet voice from the corner put in, "We might have another option."

All eyes turned in surprise to Cyrus, who braced himself against the mantel as he gazed into the fireplace.

"What do you suggest, Cyrus?" Keira asked.

"I may know someone who can get us the information we need, about Red Willow, I mean." Cyrus hesitated, glancing toward them and then back to the fire.

"Well?" Zipporah asked sharply. "For Pneumos's sake, skip the dramatics."

Keira shot her a look before turning back to Cyrus.

"Her name is Aelianna," he said finally. "She runs a large . . . business out of the East End. If there's anyone who's heard rumors of Red Willow's plans, it's her. Her *employees* happen to be some of the best spies in this city."

Marti's brows bunched as she cocked her head at Cyrus. "She owns a business?"

"She's a madam," Zipporah said, smirking at Cyrus. "A prostitute," she added for Raina's benefit. "It seems our demure diplomat here has been keeping quiet about his *extracurricular* activities."

"O—Oh!" Raina said, eyes widening slightly as she glanced from Zipporah to Cyrus.

Cyrus had a crimson blush spreading from his cheeks to the tips of his ears, and Keira could see the whites of his knuckles gripping the mantle.

"It doesn't matter," Keira said quickly, waving off Cyrus's grateful smile. "If you think she can help us, we'll pay her a visit tomorrow."

"Better wait until afternoon," Zipporah put in, eyes glinting in the firelight. "No need to wake the poor lady after a hard night's work."

Cyrus clenched his jaw, cold fury shining in his gray eyes, but merely nodded in agreement.

"Very well," Keira said. "And I'll write to the Legion tonight, see what I can find out about whatever Albert's planning. Marti, if you have any contacts among the other amalgamors, we could use any insight into the conduit and what exactly it's capable of."

Marti nodded, and though Zipporah looked about to add something, Keira pointedly ignored her.

"In the meantime," Landry put in, "I've notified the City Guard to be on the lookout for anyone matching Albert's description. The moment he shows his face, we'll know about it."

"Fine, but tell them to be careful. He's powerful and won't take kindly to being cornered, which makes him dangerous. I wouldn't want any of your Bellators to be hurt."

Landry nodded and pulled Cyrus off to the side before Keira had a chance to talk to him, to apologize. With the meeting clearly at an end, Keira watched as her friends began to slowly set their plan in motion, each in their own way, and she briefly wondered when they'd next all be together like this, if ever. Neval caught her eye from across the room, his look pointed.

Keira sighed. He was worse than Nazor when he had a point to make.

"Raina," Keira called after her young friend, who was already heading back to her bedchambers. Meanwhile, Neval pulled Akamu aside, no doubt with some convenient question about the knowledge and allegiances of the Southern Shield delegation.

Raina spun around to face Keira, eyes at once surprised and instantly suspicious.

"I can help, Keira," she muttered stubbornly. "You know I can."

Keira rolled her eyes, crossing her own arms in perfect imitation. "Not untrained, you can't."

Keira kept her face in a mask of perfect stillness as she watched a flicker of understanding cross Raina's face, her lips slowly spreading into an earsplitting grin. "You mean—?"

Keira arched one eyebrow. "Well, you've shown an uncanny knack for getting yourself captured, so it seems only practical —"

With a whoop, Raina flung her arms around Keira's neck, and she staggered back in surprise. Slowly, fighting some deep emotion she couldn't quite name, Keira wrapped her arms around Raina and squeezed her tightly. A sensation of warmth flooded through her, followed quickly by a clench of fear in the pit of her stomach. She swallowed and gently pulled away.

"You'd better get some sleep. We start bright and early tomorrow morning," Keira warned, leveling Raina with the sternest impression of Nazor she could muster. Raina merely squealed in delight, scampering off to her rooms.

Well, so much for that.

Keira turned to Neval in exasperation, to find his hand covering his mouth and shoulders shaking in a gesture suspiciously reminiscent of laughter. She shot him a rude gesture and he laughed aloud, startling the others, who glanced between them curiously. Keira ignored them and headed for her own bedchambers and the few hours of sleep that awaited her, praying to Pneumos herself for the patience to withstand a training session with Raina.

THIRTY

1 Marian Era (M.E.)

Danny ran, shoving aside startled Bellators as he headed for the only place he could think of to find Moira, hoping she'd still be there—praying he wasn't too late.

Danny stumbled into the mess hall kitchens to find them . . . empty. The startling silence was enough to catch him off guard, and he stumbled to a halt, searching the kitchens for any sign of life. She had to be here. They hadn't brought her to the field, but what if they'd taken her to some other prison? Danny shook his head, banishing the thought. She *had* to be here.

"Here to finish up what your mates started?" The icy voice came from behind him, and Danny spun around to find Moira staring at him, eyes red and swollen and hands shaking even as she balled them into fists.

"Moira, I—"

"I don't want to 'ear it, O'Leary. You made your feelin's quite clear this mornin'."

"Moira, *listen* to me."

Moira did pause then, lips pursed as she raised her brows expectantly.

Danny took a deep breath. "I came to warn you! One of the servants, they talked. And now Rommel is planning a raid of wherever it is the resistance meets, tonight."

Moira's freckled face paled, her eyes going wide before narrowing into a wary examination. "That right? And I suppose you'd love for me to show you exactly where that is, would ya?"

Danny gaped at her. Really? After everything, *she* didn't trust *him*. He gritted his teeth, glaring. "Show me or not, but you'd better warn them somehow, unless you want that field painted an even deeper shade of red." His voice caught, and he swallowed, almost choking on the bile that rose to his throat at the memory of the slaughter.

Moira's eyes softened. Whatever she saw on his face was apparently enough to take the edge off her suspicion. "Were you there?" Her voice was barely above a whisper, as if to speak louder would lend further truth to the horror.

Danny nodded, but seeing his own pain reflected in her face opened up something inside him that he didn't know how to close. "I just stood there," he choked out. "I did *nothing*, just let them die."

Tears filling her own eyes, Moira reached for him. They sagged onto a nearby bench, and Danny let her pull his head to her shoulder as the tears finally flowed. He let everything pour out—every loss, every pain, every dream inevitably crushed under the cruel reality of the world. She made soothing sounds as she ran a hand over his hair.

"You did the right thing, Danny. If you'd stepped in, tried to stop 'em . . . well, then you'd just be dead alongside those poor souls."

Her words only made the twist of guilt's knife dig deeper, and Danny felt like his insides might actually come apart.

"But—" And here she paused, as if feeling out the words to come. "If it's guilt that haunts you, Danny, there is one way you can atone."

Danny blinked up at her, eyes questioning.

"Join us, Danny," Moira said, eyes fixed on his with blazing intensity. "Honor their memory and join us. You've seen the truth now. Lend us aid with your eyes wide open."

He stared at her, drawn to the fire in her eyes. But there remained that tug of duty, a thread so old he'd never questioned it—not once. That thread was dangerously frayed now, in danger of outright rupture. And what then? Who was he without the sense of honor and loyalty that had all but defined his life?

"You couldn't save 'em," Moira pressed, eyes boring into his. "But you could save others, so many others, Danny."

Could he live with himself if he truly turned traitor? Could he live with himself if he didn't?

What do I do, Keira? he thought desperately. *What would you do?*

Of course, there was no reply, only Moira's determined gaze shooting right through him. And he knew. He knew exactly what he had to do. And with a slow nod, he felt that last frayed tether to his old self snap, blowing away into the wind like so much dust.

Moira's lips spread into the truest smile he'd ever seen from her. And whether it was the emotion flooding over him, her closeness, or just a need to be with someone else, Danny felt himself leaning in closer. She bit the bottom of her lip as she moved to meet his lips with hers. The smell of her was intoxicating, and Danny felt himself press closer, wrapping one hand around her waist to the small of her back. Her hands reached up to twine themselves in his hair as her lips spread beneath his and the tip of her tongue brushed along his bottom lip.

And then he was somewhere else, another time, in another room, with a different girl—Keira. He remembered the feel of her curls running through his fingers, her sapphire-blue eyes gazing up at him with longing, the feel of her in his arms.

Danny jerked away, breathing heavily as he caught Moira's startled expression. He pressed his hands into his thighs as he let his pulse slow.

"I-I'm sorry, Moira. I can't. I just—" He trailed off, turning to search her face for some sign of understanding. She swallowed, color flooding her cheeks. But she nodded.

"It's fine, better this way, even," she said, flattening her skirts around her as she straightened to her full height. "Fewer . . . distractions."

He nodded and watched as she turned to gather her things from the nearby table.

"We'd best be goin', anyway," she continued. "Tonight was supposed to be an epic strategy meeting. If we want to warn the others, we've got a lot of ground to cover."

Danny got to his feet, still searching her face for any sign of anger. But he found only determined practicality. Meanwhile, his own insides churned with a new kind of guilt as he felt yet another part of himself crumble into ash amid this second betrayal.

What have you done? a voice so like Keira's asked.

He wished he had an answer.

THAT NIGHT, Danny dreamed of Keira.

They were back at the little farmhouse in Abalás, running through drill in the training yards, the same way they had countless times before.

"Press the attack when you have it," Danny prompted, swiftly parrying Keira's side slice and letting her drive him back a step. He then brought their blades curving above their heads, using his superior height and weight to press down on her. But she didn't buckle, instead angling her blade so she could spin off to the side.

The warm tone of her laughter echoed around the clearing, and on impulse, Danny grabbed for her waist, dropping his own blade to grapple with her wrist as he pressed her against his side. She laughed again, squirming slightly against his grip before dropping her own blade and sinking into him. Her free hand reached up to cup the back of his neck as she pulled him closer.

His breath caught as she paused, lips mere inches from his.

"What does it feel like?" she whispered. Her warm breath against his skin made every muscle in his body tense.

"What?" Danny inhaled the scent of her.

"Grounding."

Danny chuckled, running his fingers lightly up the back of her arm. He felt Keira shiver and press closer to him.

"I don't know. I suppose it feels like steadiness, protection. Sometimes it seems like the entire world is swirling around me and I'm untouchable, unshakable."

Danny watched Keira's brows crease as she gazed up at him from beneath heavy lids. "What does canting feel like?"

She pressed her lips together. "I'd say . . . it feels like the ocean, waves and waves rolling over you, threatening to swallow you whole."

She swallowed, and the desperation in her voice was heartbreaking. Danny placed one finger under her chin, drawing her eyes up to meet his.

"I will never let that happen." His voice was firm, belying the inner turmoil he felt as he took in her glassy blue eyes. Then he kissed her. It was a kiss born as much from desperation as love, and the ferocity with which she returned it told him she felt the same. He crushed her to him, twining a hand in her hair and another around her waist as he felt her take his face in both hands. His mouth moved from her lips down her neck, feeling the soft flicker of her pulse through her skin before dragging himself back up to her cheeks. He inhaled the scent of her, floral and salty all at once, as if he could breathe her in and never exhale. But when she pulled away, the taste of her tears was still on his lips, and he felt her shaking breath against his cheeks.

"I miss you, Danny."

"I'm right here."

There was utter sorrow in her eyes as she searched his face —as if trying to memorize every curve and line. Her fingers traced the contour of his jaw, and he shuddered.

"No, you're not."

CHAPTER

THIRTY-ONE

242 Marian Era (M.E.)

Keira awoke with a start. Her heart hammered as she stared up at the canopied ceiling, and she glanced down to find her sheets in a tangled, sweaty mess around her. The dream had felt so real. *Danny* had felt so real. She swallowed, fighting back the tears that burned in her eyes. She hadn't heard Danny's voice since the attack on the People's Council, but that dream . . .

That had been no ordinary dream, she knew. And even through the pain of its end, she knew one thing—that the tether was still in place. She still had a chance. She could still bring him back. *I'm coming, Danny*, she thought, slipping back into fitful sleep. *Just hold on.*

KEIRA WOKE early but waited a few hours to rouse Raina from her bed, deciding that her young friend was tough enough to deal

336

with after a full night's rest, let alone the couple of hours she'd managed to get before their meeting. Besides, after all she'd been through, the kid deserved a bit of rest.

Meanwhile, Keira could barely shut her eyes, her mind flying over the plan they'd discussed, and she woke up earlier than she'd planned to work on the letters.

She addressed the first one to the High Council of the Legion of Pneumos in Loren, and it briefly outlined what they knew of Albert's treachery—the information he'd been feeding to Red Willow about Landry, his disappearance, and that mysterious note.

The second letter was to Elliott, and it was at that far-too-blank page that Keira stared for an hour or more, searching for the words, any words, that might adequately convey what she had to say—what she owed him. In short, an apology, but also so much more than that. She needed his forgiveness, but also his understanding and advice. How had he done it? she wondered. Taken two surly teenagers and turned them into Legionnaires—well, almost. Although her failings on that front fell solidly at her own door, not Elliott's. He'd taught her and given her so much, and she'd thrown it all back in his face. For what? A lie? A secret about research he clearly still wrestled with the implications of. She'd been a fool to leave with Albert, a fool to trust him. The memory of Elliott's broken face floated across her memories, and she balled up the piece of parchment that she'd only managed to make splotchy with drops of ink fallen from a hesitating pen. She needed to move, needed to get out of this room. The letter to the council would just have to be sufficient. She'd figure out how to talk to Elliott when this was all over, if they even made it that far.

She was still wrapped up in her own thoughts when she

rapped on Raina's door and moved to lift the latch, convinced she must still be buried deep in her covers.

Instead, the door flew forward, and Keira blinked in surprise at Raina, her usually unruly hair looped into a side braid, dressed in loose-fitting attire. The look on her face was a mixture of excitement, nervousness, and—annoyance.

"Took you long enough," Raina said, crossing her arms as her eyes danced with excitement. "I thought you be saying how warriors be rising early, eh?"

All right, then.

Keira arched one eyebrow at her. "We're eager today, I see. Well, we'll see how eager you are after you've been puking your guts up in the courtyard."

Keira was rewarded with a flash of nervousness that flew across Raina's face as she turned to head down to the courtyard. Maybe this would be fun after all.

~

It wasn't fun.

Raina once again crashed to her knees, retching for what felt like the tenth time, only bile coming up at this point.

"You have to ground yourself first," Keira explained once again. She rubbed her face wearily as Raina slurped down ladles full of fresh water. Keira racked her brain, trying to remember how exactly Elliott had gone about getting her to *focus*.

"Your energy has to be focused down to a single point, the ball of energy that lies just behind your stomach. Once you feel it move, you have to immediately control it, send it shooting out through your feet, grounding you to the spot."

"I be trying!"

Keira bit back the angry retort that flew to her lips and

merely stood in terse silence as Raina climbed back up to her feet, limbs shaking with the effort.

"When I reach inside, I don't be finding any ball. Instead, it just be—chaos."

Keira felt the hair rise on the back of her neck at the words but kept her face carefully blank. "What do you mean?"

"It be like, the pneuma being an ocean, not a ball, and when I be trying to shape it, I feel it slip out through my fingers."

Like an ocean.

Keira shot a glance at the sea shell necklace Raina never removed from around her neck.

"When I saw you disappear during the attack, you gripped that necklace," Keira murmured. "Where did you get it?"

Raina's eyes hardened as her fingers curved protectively around the smooth chitin exterior, thumb roving almost absently over its perfectly curving spiral.

"Marné told me it be from my mother. Sometimes . . ." Raina trailed off, and her cheeks reddened.

"Sometimes what?" Keira prompted, taking a step or two closer as she reached for her own pneuma. If she could just look inside it—

"Sometimes I be hearing her speak through it." Raina's voice was barely above a whisper, but it sent an icy chill racing down Keira's spine. She froze, feeling the space where Danny had long since fallen silent shift slightly. When had she last heard his voice?

"You—hear her?"

Raina nodded. "The necklace grows warm, and I be hearing her voice in my head, telling me to run or hide, or—or fight. I know it be silly, but—"

"It's not silly." Keira's voice was rough even to her own ears as she continued, "Bring all of your attention to the necklace,

Raina. Try to channel your pneuma through it. Let it *hone* your pneuma for you."

Raina looked doubtfully down at the necklace that sat still in her palm, then back at Keira.

"You think my mother be actually . . . *speaking* to me through this?"

Keira lifted a shoulder in a noncommittal shrug. "I've stopped putting limits on exactly what pneuma can do in this world. Just try it."

Raina closed her eyes, palming the necklace flat against her chest as she placed her other hand on her stomach, just as Keira had shown her. She stood that way for a long moment, breathing in through her nose and out through pursed lips. Then it began, just as before.

The surrounding air became charged, and Keira felt her hair stand on end. Raina began shaking, but she pursed her lips and emitted a high whistle, far too high for normal ears to hear. Keira felt her excitement grow as the sound shaped the surrounding particles, dragging them in toward Raina, who was controlling them.

That's it, Raina. That's it.

Then Raina's knees gave out.

Keira staggered forward to catch her, but moving through the charged air was like wading through molasses. Too caught up in the channeling of her pneuma, Raina didn't move quickly enough to catch herself, and Keira's stomach lurched as Raina's shoulder crashed into the hard stone. She cried out, and Keira pushed through the soupy energy in order to reach her side, helping the trembling girl into a sitting position.

"Are you all right?" she asked tensely.

Raina nodded, but winced as she tried to rotate her shoulder.

"Here," Keira said, mouth pressing into a thin line as she pulled a strip of fabric from her bag and looped it into a sling. "Better?"

Raina turned to the side and dry-heaved onto the stone floor.

Keira sat back on her heels, holding Raina's braid out of the way as she dragged a wary hand across her face.

"I be trying *so* hard," Raina said when she'd finished heaving, turning back to Keira, eyes brimming with tears.

"I know." Keira sighed. "I think that's enough, though. We've been at this for hours, and you're clearly exhausted."

A bolt of pain shot across Raina's face, and her lip began trembling. "I can keep going."

"No, that's enough for today."

The tears finally overflowed, and Raina wiped them roughly away with her unhurt arm. "Fine. I'll just be going."

Keira's brow furrowed. "We can try again, Raina, later, once you've had time to rest."

"No need. We tried. It didn't work."

"Raina, I didn't mean—"

"Forget it, *grelún*. I be going to clean up now anyhow."

The words stung, and Keira blinked in surprise as Raina staggered out of the courtyard. Burying her face in her hands, she groaned aloud.

How did you do this, Elliott?

"Don't worry about it," a voice replied from behind her.

Keira spun around, only to find Neval leaning casually against the pillar.

She rolled her eyes at him. "I swear that girl is the most stubborn person I've ever met."

Neval snorted. "I believe the sayin' is, *takes one to know one?*"

"Ha. Ha," Keira replied dryly, glancing up at the sky. Nearly midday.

"The others will be here soon," Neval said, reading her thoughts. "And if I'm not mistaken, Master Flavius will have some unfortunate news for us."

"What news?"

Neval's eyes narrowed at her, and he pushed his hands into his pockets. "Nothin' good."

IT WAS JUST past midday when they all gathered in the central courtyard of the Vindolum, its clear reflecting pool mirroring the cloudless sky. Oddly, Cyrus was the last to arrive. But when he stormed into the room, face tight with fury, Keira felt her stomach flip on its edge. Neval had been right.

"What's happened?" she asked as he approached.

"The Council of Benadur, in their holy *wisdom*, have seen fit to call for the dissolution of the People's Council, considering their newest *radicalization*."

Landry glowered. "That is unacceptable. I won't allow it."

"Good," Neval said, grim-faced, as he stepped forward. "Because neither will the people. You promised them a council, representation. You can't take it away now. We've come too far." Neval's face held a ferocity that made Keira shiver.

Cyrus eyed him warily before turning back to Landry. "It will cost you, though, to overrule them. Everyone's running scared, and you don't exactly have many allies right now."

"What do you suggest, then?" Landry replied, terse but not unkind.

"Use the festival to your advantage."

Landry nodded, and even Neval gave Cyrus a considering look.

Keira's eyes danced between them. She was clearly missing something. "What festival?"

The three of them turned to her in surprise.

"The equinox festival," Landry explained. "It begins tonight and will continue until midnight tomorrow. If I can appeal to the people directly by . . ."

Landry's words continued, but Keira stopped hearing him over the roaring in her ears.

The equinox. Tomorrow. Danny.

A stone dropped in Keira's stomach, and she had to remind herself to keep breathing. She'd known it was close, but a deep panic gripped her as she realized she still had no idea what to do. And now, with Albert turned against them and a radical extremist group trying to kill Landry and send the city careening back into chaos, she had even less of a chance.

Keira rubbed her temple against the throbbing headache that had just begun. She was only one person, and this was all —too much.

"That settles it, then," Landry pronounced, snapping Keira out of her mental spiral. "Neval and Akamu will appeal to their people directly, and I'll stay here to make preparations for this evening. The rest of you will meet with Cyrus's contact, find out what you can about Red Willow and Albert's plans. I doubt the timing of all this is a coincidence, so we have to assume that Albert has influenced the Council of Benadur in some way. Perhaps he, too, plans to make his move at the equinox festival."

Keira could only nod along with the others as the groups went their separate ways. Raina had caught up with them as they'd spoken and would come with them to meet Cyrus's contact. Keira tried to catch her eye, tried to convey—what? An apology? Reassurance? She had nothing to offer her, not when the world was crashing down around them. All she could manage was to put one foot in front of the other. There had to be a way out of this. There just had to be.

CHAPTER
THIRTY-TWO

Strolling the prospering streets of the East End seemed a world away from the squalid lodgings of the dockyards. Here lived prosperous merchants, its streets graced by well-dressed patrons basking in the first truly sunny day of spring. All around them, bustling preparations were being made for the equinox festivities—from fabric banners strung across rooftops to the street musicians tuning their instruments before the coming celebration.

"This is—impressive," Keira said absently to Cyrus, who nodded, eyeing the thick crowd around them with undisguised suspicion.

"Here in the capital, the solstice celebrations pale compared to that of the equinox. While the uplands might revere the solstices for their agricultural implications, here it's much more about the magical and religious power that is said to be imbued in the equinox—dating all the way back to the Ancient Lorenans. The equinox holds power both for its symbolic meaning and its religious connotations."

Keira nodded, remembering the winter solstice celebrations back in Abalás. She didn't remember the equinox ever holding such sway, even as Elliott and Nazor always took time to honor the day when darkness and light, order and chaos, were held in perfect balance. Elliott would always read solemnly from a dreary Legion tome on the subject, but it was Nazor's epic recounting of some ancient battle or other such Legion legend that always kept Keira and Danny on the edge of their seats. Keira swallowed, banishing the remembered sound of their laughter and cheers from her mind as she focused on the here and now.

"It's just ahead," Cyrus said, rubbing the back of his neck as he weaved around a juggling street performer. Keira glanced at him, noting the beads of sweat across his brow and the reddish hue to the tips of his ears. He was nervous, poor guy. Cyrus had always been on the quieter side, a sensitive type better suited to the privacy of an artist's loft than the scheming courts of his diplomatic post. But he seemed particularly bothered by their current task. Perhaps Zipporah was right, and he knew this prostitute in a much more *personal* capacity.

Keira was about to quietly ask, when they rounded the corner and found themselves staring at a massive white stucco building. It was similar to its surroundings but notable for the greenery that arched around it, perfectly manicured gardens overflowing from the balconies and rooftops of the multileveled structure. Cyrus didn't hesitate outside, though, pushing forward until he could rap twice on the solid oak door.

The door creaked open a few inches, and a beautiful young woman appeared. She wore loose-fitting clothes better suited to a training ring, and her honey-colored hair was artfully braided over one shoulder as she smiled serenely up at Cyrus.

"I'm sorry, but we aren't open yet. Please come back at four for our thrilling equinox pageant."

She moved to close the door, but he stuck out a foot to block it. In an instant, the woman's face hardened, and Keira noted with alarm the glint of a blade at her hip. But Cyrus quickly explained, "I'm here to see Aelianna. Tell her—tell her Cyrus is here."

The woman's brows shot up, and she eyed Cyrus from head to toe with renewed interest. "Of course," she said demurely, that serene smile fixed firmly back in place. "Please come in."

Cyrus followed her in, and Keira caught a raised-brow look from Zipporah, merely shrugging before she, too, followed the woman inside. They emerged into a tavern hall unlike any Keira had seen before in Loren. Tall windows set high into the stone walls allowed long beams of light to fill the hall with the warm hues of midday. The tables had all been pushed to the side, and young women filled the space beneath the spilling golden rays. All were dressed in similarly loose-fitting attire as they moved perfectly in sync through a complicated choreography of painfully slow, flowing movements. Keira's own legs practically ached watching them hold deep squats as they flowed through a sequence that all seemed to know by heart.

"Wait here," the honey-haired woman instructed them, flowing up a staircase to their left. The five of them were left in awkward silence—Marti and Raina staring in frank curiosity at the crowd of women moving in perfect sync, while Cyrus stared at the ground, hands dug deep into his pockets. Zipporah, being Zipporah, scowled at anyone who glanced her way, looking for all the world like she'd been dragged here against her will.

Keira stepped to Cyrus's side, bumping him gently with her elbow as she nodded toward the women. "What's that all about?"

Cyrus eyed them with wariness but said nothing, and Keira was about to leave it when he suddenly replied, "It's an ancient practice, dating back to one of the earliest sects that worshipped Pneumos. They believe—well, they *think* that the power of Pneumos can be channeled through this practice. They enter a sort of trancelike state."

That caught Keira's attention, as she remembered Albert's offhand comments on the ride to Crîd Eálas. *The Legion would like to claim it has a monopoly on the practice of pneumonancy in this world, Keira. They don't.*

She turned back to the women, focusing her pneuma into a gentle probe. It felt almost like—Danny. Or rather, it felt like the grounding presence Danny had always conveyed. No wonder she felt so drawn to them.

"We don't think—we *know*."

The five of them turned to see a regal woman descending the stairs like a queen to her court. This could only be Aelianna. Her silk dress seemed to be a single sheet of fabric that fell in layers to the floor before wrapping several times around her waist and looping up to fall in two sheets across her shoulders and down her back. Though her once raven-dark hair was shot through with silver and wrinkles crinkled at her eyes, she was still one of the most beautiful women Keira had ever seen.

"I tried to teach you when you were a boy, Cyrus. You never had the patience for it, always running off with your paints or in search of some insect to collect." Aelianna smiled warmly.

"It wasn't *this* aspect of your practice that bothered me," Cyrus replied, eyeing Aelianna pointedly.

She brushed off his comment with a flick of her hand as she turned to the rest of her gathered audience. "Now, who are your friends?"

Cyrus subtly stiffened but continued formally, "We are a

delegation from His Majesty Landrianus Marian, Regio of all Loren, and we have some questions for you."

Aelianna arched one eyebrow as her lips twisted into a smirk. "Do you now? Well, good for you. I heard you'd finally escaped that dreadful Bellatorio."

Cyrus's hands curled into fists. "The Bellatorio is a noble institution. I was honored to—"

"Yes, yes, I remember," Aelianna said, waving a hand breezily. "It was all for the *honor* of the post, certainly *nothing* to do with how proud it made your father, oh he of frequent absence."

"Don't talk about him like that." There was an edge to Cyrus's voice that Keira had rarely heard before, and she shifted awkwardly, glancing from Aelianna to Cyrus and then back to her other friends, all of whom looked equally confused. They'd clearly walked into something here that none of them fully understood.

Aelianna's eyes narrowed, and she took a step closer to Cyrus, regardless of the fact he was a solid three inches taller. "I'll speak about him however I wish. Don't think you were the only person he hurt, Cyrus, the only one who would have given anything to see him return, just once more."

"That was a long time ago, Mother."

Keira gaped, looking from Cyrus to Aelianna, noting their shared dark olive skin tone and the long oval of their faces. How had she not seen it before?

Zipporah's mouth hung open, her cheeks coloring slightly as she no doubt regretted the relentless teasing she'd subjected Cyrus to the night before.

Aelianna merely inclined her head and gestured to the stairs. "Why don't we take this discussion *elsewhere*."

They all followed her up the stairs to an elegant sitting room off the top landing, the tension between them palpable.

Raina, for her part, was oblivious, merely asking, "What they be doing downstairs?"

Keira shot her a look and quickly came to sit down, nudging her pointedly. Raina shot her a look of surprise, but Aelianna only chuckled.

"It's quite all right." Turning to Raina, she added, "Fundati is an ancient practice designed to quiet the mind and ground the body, practiced by many of the earliest followers of Pneumos. Its daily practice is one of our many rituals."

Cyrus snorted, and Aelianna's eyes narrowed.

"Do you have something to add, Son?"

Cyrus's face was bitter as he said, "Only that you shouldn't dance around the nature of your other *rituals*. Go on, tell them."

"I wasn't dancing around anything," Aelianna said, turning back to the rest of them as she explained, "What my son is so rudely implying is that many of our rituals fall under a far more *carnal* nature. It's a similar practice, grounding the mind and body, funneling our energy into the creation of order out of chaos, fusing two parts into a whole, life from nothing."

"They're a sex cult," Cyrus said flatly.

Keira blinked, mouth opening and closing again, totally at a loss for what to say to that.

"We're a collective," Aelianna emphasized, scowling at her son. "Something I never hid from you. It wasn't until you went to that close-minded Academy Bellatori that you let it bother you."

"I was teased mercilessly, humiliated day after day." Cyrus's jaw clenched, and Keira saw the shadow of past hurts flicker in his eyes.

"You always cared far too much about what those friends of yours thought."

"I was a child!"

Cyrus and Aelianna fell silent then, merely staring at each other as they remained squared off a few feet apart.

As neither seemed inclined to break the silence, Keira intervened. "We need your help," she said to Aelianna. "With some . . . information."

Aelianna's eyes narrowed, but she inclined her head, gesturing for them to follow her up the stairs, leading them toward a private study. Upon arriving, Aelianna floated toward a well-cushioned bench, draping herself across the rolled arm and stretching her legs out in an effortless recline. Taking that as invitation, Raina promptly plopped herself onto a bench opposite her, feet dangling. Keira moved to perch beside the girl. Meanwhile, Cyrus leaned cross-armed against the wall, adamantly refusing to take the offered seat.

Keira sighed. Apparently, *she'd* be doing the talking. "We're looking for information on an organization called Red Willow. We think they're behind the attack on the People's Council and fear they may be plotting another assassination attempt on the Regio."

Aelianna's eyes narrowed, but she asked airily, "And why would you think I'd know anything about such an organization?"

"Because half the men of this city have graced your doorstep over the last few decades, and no shortage of women either," Cyrus answered coldly. "If there's anyone who's heard of this Red Willow, then it would be you."

Aelianna's lips pursed, but she didn't deny it. "Red Willow has been here since the birth of this city, longer, even. They've built themselves into its very fabric, entrenching themselves deep within the sewers and catacombs. They've had centuries to solidify their hold. You want to dig them out?" Aelianna eyed each of them in turn. "Be prepared to have this entire city come crumbling down around you."

They were all silent for a moment, letting Aelianna's words sink in. Finally, Cyrus pushed off from the wall. "That's ridiculous. Anyone can be killed. Give us names, Mother, and we'll make it happen."

Aelianna narrowed her eyes at him. "No doubt you'd love for me to destroy my business that way, Cyrus, but I'm afraid I must disappoint. You'll get no such names from me."

Finally, Keira said quietly, "This city is already crumbling, Aelianna. Red Willow has recruited a powerful pneumonancer to their side, a Legionnaire with his own agenda, intent on channeling chaos for his own ends. If we don't stop him, you'll have no business left to come back to."

Aelianna stared at her, and Keira thought she saw a flash of hesitancy, but it was quickly replaced by steely determination. Keira braced herself for an outright refusal, but instead Aelianna said, "If you are trying to determine their next move, I'd look no further than tonight's festivities. The Regio is making a public appearance, I presume? He will speak at the opening of the festivities to celebrate the cosmic balance of the equinox, as is tradition. If they're going to strike, they'll do it tonight."

Keira nodded, turning the words over in her mind. But before she could reply, Zipporah piped up from the corner.

"Tell us who we're looking for," she demanded.

Aelianna's eyes narrowed. "Red Willow or not, a client is still a client."

"Your *clients* are murderers," Zipporah snarled. Seeing Aelianna's only reply was an elegant elevation of her chin,

Zipporah turned instead to Keira. "Do a bind, then. Find out that way."

Keira hesitated, glancing from Zipporah to Aelianna, the memory of the prisoner Finn's screams still pulsing in her ears. Aelianna looked perfectly serene. If she knew what they were discussing, she gave no indication. Keira swallowed, feeling the others' eyes on her before slowly shaking her head. She couldn't do it. Not again.

Zipporah grunted in disgust before turning instead to Marti. "Well?"

Slowly, Marti rose to her feet and moved to stand before Aelianna, whose glittering eyes betrayed mild interest.

"I should warn you, I charge extra for binding," Aelianna crooned at Marti, whose cheeks colored slightly.

Keira heard the whistle, high and light, just before seeing Aelianna suddenly stiffen. The sensation of pneuma was palpable in the air, a buzzing as molecules moved and shifted, forging a path directly toward Aelianna. Every muscle in the older woman went rigid. Keira glanced toward Marti, seeing her brow furrow and beads of sweat appear on her forehead. Zipporah saw it too, and her fingers tightened around Marti's, no doubt infusing her with that grounding energy. Marti's breath came faster, until her eyes snapped open with a quick gasp.

"What is it?" Keira asked, glancing between Marti and Aelianna, who sat now with feet flat on the floor, breathing slowly and steadily through pursed lips.

"I-I couldn't get through," Marti gasped. "It felt like grounder energy, but more—impenetrable."

Frowning, Keira turned back to Aelianna and let out her own light whistle, feeling the tightly coiled ball of energy in the pit of her stomach respond instantly, grounding her first to her seat before springing toward the perfectly still Aelianna. Keira felt it immediately as her pneuma made impact, a jolt through her entire body as her pneuma encircled the invisible wall around Aelianna's mind. The buzzing of the air revealed every shifting molecule her pneuma touched. But behind that wall, Keira could feel only . . . stillness. Frustrated, she poked and prodded it, feeling for any weak point. It was Aelianna's mind alone that stood protected, grounded in place by rivets of impenetrable will. The tendons and sinews of her body were exposed, and Keira suspected a muscle bind or the torturous undoing that Albert had taught her would still take effect. Shivering, Keira withdrew, gasping as she settled back into her own body.

"How are you doing that?" she breathed.

Aelianna's eyes fluttered open, and though her breath came fast and shallow, her lips twisted into a wide smile of triumph. "As I told you, our practice is ancient and powerful. It's taken me many years to master the mind walls."

Keira stared at her. Mind walls? She'd never heard of such a thing. Elliott had never mentioned this type of pneumonancy, using pneuma to form walls around your own mind. Could it work against other types of binds? And then she remembered another of Albert's offhand comments.

It's even said that one can become so grounded that they actually cancel out the pneuma of others, like lightning rods funneling energy into the earth.

Keira's thoughts raced, filled with questions that yielded no simple answers. Like a tired old record, her mind kept coming back to one tantalizing possibility.

"Can you—could you extend this wall onto someone else?" Keira asked quietly.

Aelianna blinked, cocking her head slightly. "I've never tried. Why do you ask?"

Keira met Cyrus's wary gaze before turning back to Aelianna.

"We heard you were planning a pageant? How would your girls feel about a more *public* performance?"

THIRTY-THREE

The streets of Crîd Eálas were filled to bursting with the excited murmur of people bustling about in preparation for the start of the equinox. As the sun steadily approached the horizon, the flurry reached a fever pitch—children and adults alike eagerly readying their lanterns and bundling into cloaks as they made their way toward the grand plaza before the Vindolum. They waved twisting ribbons of black and white and carried candles of every shape and color, all unlit, as was custom, as they waited for the ancient ceremony to begin.

From the overhang of the Vindolum's central balcony, Keira scanned the faces of the crowd with furrowed intent, searching for recognizable features. But anyone could be Red Willow. That was their strength; their power lay in their universality. There was a rustle of movement beside her, and Landry appeared. He moved to join her, both carefully hidden by the lengthening shadows of dusk.

"Still no chance I can talk you out of this?" Keira murmured tensely.

Landry's brow furrowed, but he offered her a half smile.

"You said yourself the best way to lure Red Willow out into the open is to carry on as usual, make them think we've stopped looking for them."

Keira clenched her teeth as she eyed the masses of people gathered in the plaza below. "Haven't you figured out by now that I'm not exactly known for my great ideas?"

Landry laughed aloud and nudged her gently. "It'll be fine. I've a whole City Guard's worth of Bellators to protect me, not to mention Loren's fiercest Legionnaire."

Keira rolled her eyes at him, but quickly sobered as she said seriously, "Don't underestimate him, Landry. Albert is cunning as a snake and has had hundreds of years to hone his pneumonancy."

"Good thing you've found us some new allies."

Keira had opened her mouth to protest when the sounds of footsteps approaching made them both turn. Keira tensed on instinct but relaxed as she saw Cyrus emerge from the shadows.

"Ah, speaking of which," Landry said, "how are our new recruits faring, Cyrus?"

Keira saw Cyrus grimace at the word *recruits*, but he merely nodded.

"My mother and her ladies are setting up now. They'll perform throughout the ceremony. Hopefully it will be enough to discourage any binding attacks from Albert."

Landry shook his head. "It's hard to imagine why he'd attack now of all times. He stayed in the Vindolum for days. If he wanted me dead, surely he would have made his move then."

"Whatever his plans are, they require the power generated by mass chaos. He's experimented with it before," Keira added, bitterly remembering their discussion in the tower only a few days ago. Why hadn't she *seen*? She shook her head. "But killing you in front of the entire city might be just what he had in mind."

Landry inclined his head in acceptance of her explanation before chuckling. "Truthfully, I never thought I'd see the day when I'd have only a dozen escorts weaving ancient Lorenan sex spells standing between me and a murderous spirit-binder. To see the look on my father's face, if he only knew . . ."

Landry barked a laugh that Keira and Cyrus didn't share, and he clapped them both on the back.

"Cheer up, you two. We've got an equinox to celebrate." And with that, Landry steered them both around and toward the stairs that led to the waiting crowd. Keira stole a glance at Cyrus and found that he looked as grim as she felt. Landry could keep his airy demeanor, but they both knew full well the danger he was putting himself in, and Keira didn't like it one bit.

THE CROWD ROARED in excitement as Landry exited the great double doors of the Vindolum, flanked on either side by Keira, Cyrus, and half a dozen Bellators. He waved to the crowd, beaming as he descended the steps to the middle landing, where the twelve councilmen of Benadur were already arrayed. Six to a side, they stood regally in robes of deep ochre while an ornate brazier crackled with leaping flames, the only light to be found as the sun continued its steep descent beyond the western mountains.

On the steps leading down to the gathered crowd, Aelianna and her ladies were adorned in skirts of black and white that swished with their slow, gentle movements as they flowed through the motions of their practice. Even from here, Keira could feel the force of the wall being constructed by their movements, felt it wash over them all. Curious, she nudged at the ball of pneuma that lay just behind her stomach, testing it. It reacted sluggishly, unfurling with the speed of molasses. Keira withdrew, satisfied. It might not stop Albert completely, but it was certainly enough to slow him down.

Landry raised his hands then, and the crowd fell silent, waiting with hushed tones.

"Good people of Loren, I come before you as your Regio on this most holy of days to celebrate the joining of light and dark and the balance of order and chaos. As we emerge from the darkness of a long winter, rebuilding much that we have lost, let us enter a new spring of possibility. Light will soon conquer dark as we enter this new age."

Landry paused and the crowd cheered, children waving their lanterns and twirling ribbons above their heads. Then Landry's smile faded, and his voice turned somber. "But also, let us not forget the darkness we have come from and the chaos that yet swirls around us. There are many among us who suffer still, those who have lost much. And there are yet more who would seek to manipulate that pain, twisting it to their own ends. As we work every day to manifest the reality for which we hope, I pray we lean on each other, knowing success lies in our ability to heal our differences and make room at the table for all to venture near. Happy equinox, citizens of Loren!"

His words were met with a roar of applause that only grew as he lit the proffered torch from the massive brazier. As if on cue, each councilman stepped forward, kneeling and murmuring words of fealty to the Regio and Loren before lighting their own torches from Landry's. As the twelfth councilman lit his torch, Landry stepped forward and was met by a long line of men and women who emerged from the gathered crowd. They wore robes of every shade, symbolizing the various regions of Loren from which they hailed.

"The People's Council," Cyrus murmured beside her. "Landry insisted they be included in this year's ceremony, much to the Council of Benadur's chagrin."

Keira glanced toward the twelve and suppressed a smile at the looks of disgust on their faces. *Serves them right,* she thought. She watched as each member of the People's Council took their lit torch and began moving out among the people, lighting candles and paper lanterns as they went, twisting paths of light that curled through the gathered crowd. Yet another symbol of the value and impact of the People's Council, bringing light to the people.

Just then, Keira saw the dark green robes of the Southern Shield delegation, ornately decorated sashes of bark cloth draped across their shoulders. Raina walked beside her brother, her long, dark hair loose and woven throughout with bright blue flowers, her beautiful eyes shining out from the rich warmth of her brown skin. Keira exhaled and grinned broadly. She looked absolutely stunning. Raina caught her eye and waved, completely ignoring the formal solemnity of the rest of her delegation.

Keira turned slightly, about to point out the group to Cyrus, when a flash of movement caught her eye. She turned back and saw the flash of a familiar face in the crowd, just behind Raina's delegation.

Keira froze.

This wasn't happening. She couldn't possibly have seen what she thought she'd seen.

Mom?

When she looked again, the face was gone, and she heaved a sigh of relief. But another flicker of movement drew her eyes to the edge of the crowd on the far side of the plaza as long, dark curls flicked out of sight.

Before she'd consciously decided, Keira felt her feet moving, and a second later, she was down the stairs and plunging headlong into the throng.

The crowd was a swirling mass of color as Keira pushed her way through. Startled eyes met hers, and those who didn't jump out of her way were quickly elbowed past. Keira couldn't think, couldn't process what was happening beyond an all-encompassing desire to find her. She couldn't be real, couldn't possibly. And yet *she was*.

Finally, Keira reached the edge of the crowd and found—*nothing*. She spun around, searching every face for a glimpse of that familiar smile, those eyes she knew so well, better even than her own. Passersby eyed her with suspicion, and mothers clutched their children closer as she darted from person to person with the frenetic pace of a spooked horse. But there was no one. She was gone.

A hand on her arm made her spin around, a surge of excitement quickly fading as she met Cyrus's steely gray eyes.

"Keira," he murmured urgently, ignoring her attempts to peer around him, searching in vain for any sign of her mother. *She'd been right there.*

"Keira, it's Albert. He's been captured."

That caught her up short, and she stared at him, wide-eyed. "What are you talking about?"

"They caught him trying to sneak back into the Vindolum while everyone was distracted by the festivities."

Keira felt her lips press into a thin line as she murmured, "If he's allowed himself to be captured, it's because he's now exactly where he wants to be." She cursed, and Cyrus's eyes widened.

"What do we do?"

Keira hesitated, glancing to where Landry stood, still greeting each of the People's Council members in turn. Akamu and Raina, along with the rest of the Southern Shield delegation, stood nearby, patiently explaining their ornate accoutrements to the bolder city dwellers who curiously approached to ask.

Keira swallowed. Red Willow could still be here, could still be planning an attack. But if Albert had truly weaseled his way into the Vindolum, then he was surely up to something. She had to find out what. And there was something else, a niggling thought in the back of her mind that had only grown as the festivities had begun. The equinox was here, and this was her chance, maybe her only chance, to save Danny. Albert could very well be the only person with the answers she needed.

"I'm going to see him," she murmured quietly as she pushed past Cyrus, heading for the servants' entrance to the Vindolum.

He gaped and spun, catching her arm firmly. "Whatever it is you're planning, Keira, don't. *Please* don't." There was a desperate look in his eye as he continued, "We need you, Keira. We need you here. We're a team, you can't just—"

Keira shook him off. "You'll be fine. You have Aelianna and her ladies. And there's no sign of Red Willow anywhere. Albert is the bigger threat here. He's the one I need to deal with."

Keira turned then and pushed through the crowd, ignoring the pang of guilt in her stomach as she felt Cyrus's eyes on her. *They'll be fine*, she reminded herself. But even she couldn't fight the wiggling thread of doubt that coursed its way through the back of her mind.

THE DANK WALLS of the steep staircase closed in around her as she once again descended into the depths of the Vindolum's dungeon. Her shoulder brushed the freezing damp of the stone walls, and a shiver arced up her spine. With every step, the uncertainty bubbled up in her mind, and her thoughts flitted back to the friends she'd left behind and the gnawing sensation that this was likely a terrible idea. But still her feet carried her forward, drawn by something she couldn't quite explain but felt compelled to understand. It was that same sense that guided her toward his cell, a part of her knowing exactly which one she'd find him in.

Albert sat in a cell all his own, legs crossed and arms folded neatly in his lap. He sat serenely, a faint smile on his lips as he reclined with eyes closed. They fluttered open as she approached, and he leveled her with a knowing gaze. Even from the safety of the hallway beyond the cell, Keira felt her stomach drop, flames of fear flickering in her veins.

"I knew you'd come, my dear."

Keira said nothing, only stared at him as she worked to control her own breathing.

"Nothing to say?" Albert's voice was like liquid honey, curling around her with a sticky sweetness that made her stomach turn. But she squared her shoulders, refusing to give him the satisfaction of seeing her squirm.

"Why are you here, Albert?"

Albert's eyes shone with innocence as he crooned, "Why, Keira, I'm afraid it was *your* Bellators who captured *me*. You'll have to ask them."

Keira scoffed. "You and I both know you're only here

because you want to be. So just get on with it. Tell me what it is you're looking for."

Albert's smile widened into a hungry, angled snarl. "You know what I want, Keira."

"The conduit," she said flatly, daring him to contradict. He didn't. "But what do you want *with* it? And don't give me any of that crap about my *learning*."

Albert's eyes narrowed slightly, though his smile remained curious—teasing even. "I want the same thing you do, Keira. I want to get out from under the thumb of the Legion, away from the artificial limits they've placed on our power."

Keira was already shaking her head before he'd finished. *Lying snake.* She was about to tell him so to his face, when she saw his throat bob and Albert murmured, "Do you think you're the only one who's lost people?"

Keira froze, eyes narrowing. "Who? Who did you lose, Albert?"

Something like pain flashed across his face, and his voice croaked as he murmured, "I loved her, you know. No matter what he may have told you."

"Who?"

Albert let out a long breath before saying in a voice so low she had to lean forward to hear it, "Nazor."

Keira blinked, remembering the conversation they'd had in Port Galaén, what seemed like a lifetime ago. *Two men in love with the same woman*, he'd said. Could he really have done all of this just for a chance of seeing her again? *That's what you're doing, isn't it?* a small voice reminded her. Keira shoved it aside, shaking her head as she did so.

"Well, that's just tough. I still have no clue how to save either of them, so I'm afraid you're out of luck."

"No, not alone, you can't."

Keira scoffed. "Oh, and I'm sure you're the one to help me? What makes you think I could ever trust you again?"

Albert shrugged. "I honestly don't expect you to."

Exasperated, Keira replied, "Fine, I guess we're done here, then."

She was turning to leave when his voice came from behind her. "Very well, if you're content never to see him again." Keira paused as he continued. "You'll never manage it on your own, no matter how strong your tether. You simply don't have enough power."

Rage curdled in her stomach as she spun around to face him. "Don't you dare talk about him," she snarled. "He would despise you and everything you stand for. I refuse to dishonor his memory any further by listening to another word of your poison." Satisfied, she turned to walk away.

"Why do you think I did it, Keira? All of it?"

Yet again, she paused, her breath becoming shallow as the words spilled from him—uncrushed, unbothered, merely matter-of-fact, as if recounting the week's weather.

"Why do you think I told Red Willow how to get close to Landry? Who do you think planned the initial assassination attempt? Why else would I persuade the Council of Benadur to disband the People's Council? Hmm?"

Keira didn't answer, but she couldn't tear her eyes away from his.

"Power," Albert said, sounding almost regretful. "So unoriginal, I know, but the surge in power we need really could only come from one place."

Keira's breath caught and she felt her eyes widen. She shook her head. "No. If you wanted Landry dead, you could have just done it yourself."

"Ah, but you're still missing the point, Keira." His voice was patient, pedantic even. Explaining a lesson to a small child. "Chaos, Keira. That's what I'm after. Chaos on a massive scale. I realized it last summer, when you saved this city from the brink of disaster. I could feel it. And I knew then that that brand of chaos was the only thing capable of powering the pneumonancy I needed, the only thing that could bring them back."

Keira scoffed, though the sound came out strained, even to her own ears. "You actually expect me to believe that you've orchestrated all of this just to bring back a woman who already rejected you once?"

Albert's eyes tightened in anger.

Come on, Keira thought. *Get angry. Tell me what you're really after.*

Then a slow, serene smile spread across Albert's face, and he cocked his head at her. "Not just Nazor, Keira. But any number of long-departed Legionnaires. We've been under the Legion's thumb for far too long, you see. When I have the backing of my own army, they'll suddenly find that they're not the only ones capable of pulling the strings of power in Loren."

Keira felt like she couldn't breathe, and she searched blindly behind her for a handhold in the darkness. "And on the road?" she finally managed. "I guess those Worshippers of Séiro were your cronies too? Anything to stir up more chaos, I suppose."

Albert's grin widened as he shrugged. "No, that was for you, Keira. You needed some . . . prompting. Encouragement, if you will, to see the full potential of your gifts. Raina's kidnapping also served its purpose, motivating you to play the role I needed you to." Albert shrugged. "And it wasn't just that. It's the same reason I persuaded Red Willow that a seemingly useless girl from the Southern Shield might be just the leverage they needed, and it's the very same reason I trained that pathetic operative of theirs in the basics of resisting a mental bind."

Albert's smile grew wider, and Keira shuddered. "You needed a push, Keira. And I was the only one who could give it to you."

Keira felt her stomach roil as a wave of nausea brought bile to the back of her throat. "No," she whispered, the memory of Raina's terrified cries quickly morphing into the screams of the Red Willow prisoner. "That's—it can't—"

"Oh, but it can, Keira dear. The redoing is a tricky business, and you needed all the practice you could get—not to mention the motivation," he added, winking.

Keira shuddered.

She could only shake her head. Everything she'd done, everything she'd accomplished, had only served to further Albert's own plan.

"So, what do you say, Keira? Let's finish what we started."

Danny's soft green eyes flashed in her memory, and the ache in her chest was palpable, painful even. Then she heard it, the whisper of his voice in her ear. *Don't do it, Keira. It's ok, really. You can let me go.*

Keira blinked the tears out of her eyes as she practically sobbed, "No. No, Albert, I won't help you. You can rot down here, for all I care. They wouldn't have wanted this—neither of them."

Albert held her gaze for another moment, searching her eyes for something she couldn't quite make out. Finally, he sighed, nodding. "Fine, have it your way, Keira. I suppose I'll just have to do it on my own."

"Yeah, ok. Good luck with that, Albert."

His smile widened, and her gut clenched reflexively. "Don't you see, Keira? I've already done it. In the time you've spent with me, your friends are no doubt dead, the chaos I wanted already set in motion. If you listen carefully, I'm sure you can even hear the screaming. It's already begun."

Keira did listen, casting out her pneuma as far as she dared, searching, the terror of what she'd find rising with every moment. And there they were, screams, crying, flames . . . and death. Keira reeled back into her own body, staggering backward into the wall of the hallway.

"They're all gone, Keira."

"No," she gasped. "No, they can't be."

She blinked the tears away before looking up into Albert's cool amber eyes, no longer locked behind the cold steel bars that now stood open.

She gasped. "How did you—"

The sound cut off as his fingers closed around her throat, and all she remembered as the blackness curled in around her vision were his words.

"I'm sorry, Keira. Truly, I'm sorry it had to end this way."

THIRTY-FOUR

1 Marian Era (M.E.)

Danny's induction into the resistance movement was swift and seamless. In fact, his day-to-day changed little, even as the consequences of his actions multiplied. He met few of the other resistance members, sending the information he gathered through Moira to preserve anonymity. He'd insisted early on that he'd only pass on information about the Bellatorio's counterinsurgency actions, heading off the Bellatorio's efforts to weed out the resistance movement itself —he drew the line at targeting individuals. Moira didn't press the issue, though he could tell from her pursed-lipped expression that she found his scruples nonsensical. But they made him feel better, more in control, like he wasn't being tossed about on the eddies of events far beyond his understanding. He knew it was a lie.

Moira remained tight-lipped on the details of the resistance movement itself—deftly diverting Danny's increasingly frequent questions about the group's founding, its organization, and its ultimate goals, saying it was better if he didn't know the details.

That is, until one evening, several weeks after he'd first started working with the resistance, when Moira abruptly suggested they go to dinner at a local tavern. Though surprised, Danny had agreed, wondering just what it was she had up her sleeve.

He now followed Moira wordlessly through the winding roads of Crîd Eálas, their feet kicking up dirt where cobblestone had not yet been laid. And though it would be over two hundred years before the capital he remembered would rise into being, the salt in the air and the call of fishermen on the breeze echoed through the soul of the South End—a reverberation across time, binding what was to what would one day be.

Moira led him to a small tavern close to the docks, and they slipped silently into the bustle and warmth of its interior. They let the noise and life of the place wrap around them, absorbing them into its fibers as surely as any cloak of invisibility as they settled into a corner booth at the back.

Danny steepled his fingers as he stretched his legs out beneath the table, relishing the pull of sinew on bone as he turned to face Moira, brows raised in expectation.

"Well?"

She eyed the retreating form of the barmaid before meeting his gaze without evidence of discomfort or embarrassment. "I joined up just under a year ago, now."

"The resistance?" Danny pressed, leaning forward with interest.

"Shh," Moira hissed, glancing around. But no one paid them any mind. "Yes. When the siege of Ulgáris began, a lot of us realized right quick the Empire was here to stay. There was little choice at that point. It was submit or resist." Her eyes narrowed, and she eyed him shrewdly. "I chose resist."

Danny rolled his eyes. "Yeah, I got that, thanks."

Moira ignored his pointed tone and pressed on. "Red Willow shared my anger, they—"

"Red Willow?"

Moira grinned, rolling up her sleeve to again show him the inked tattoo of the tree on her arm, its fronds twisting and curling around her wrist to form a bracelet of ink.

"That's what we've taken to calling ourselves—*the tree from which liberty springs*. Anyway, it offered a lifeline, a way out of the mess we'd found ourselves in. I didn't have to think twice."

"Because of your father?"

Moira blinked, before murmuring, "Yes, yes, that's right."

Danny nodded. "Have you heard anything? From the letters you sent."

Moira twisted a napkin in her lap before saying coolly, "Nothin' yet, but there were a good lot of 'em, so . . ."

She trailed off, and Danny nodded. "Just a matter of time, I'm sure."

Moira took a deep breath before saying, "Anyway, the real reason I'm tellin' you this is that our *leadership* has taken a bit of an interest in you, Danny. They'd like to meet the Legionnaire who's joined our cause."

Danny swallowed, something like eagerness mixed with dread churning in his stomach. But a hesitancy held him back, and he asked, "Why? What is it they want, exactly?"

Moira's eyes fixed on him, and she leaned close. "You're special, Danny. Just look at those texts we've been translatin' about the Legion. You know as well as I do they hold power in this world. To have one of them, to have *you* on our side, it opens doors, Danny, you see?"

Danny did see, and her words sent a chill through him. But her expression was so earnest, so . . . proud. He didn't want to let her down. So he nodded. She grinned broadly and squeezed his hand, sending electricity coursing through his veins. He didn't pull away, though guilt prickled at him. "But we have to be careful, Moira. Look what happened to Arlan. This Red Willow may be revolutionaries, but they're also ruthless."

Moira shrugged, smiling darkly. "Better dead than in a Bellatori prison, I say."

Danny nodded, unable to fault her logic, but the weight of his choice settled heavily around him. And it left him wondering if he'd just traded one noose for another.

THEY SET the meeting with Red Willow leadership for the following night. Danny got ready, feeling a bit queasy after a dinner he'd barely been able to stomach. He strapped a dagger to his hip, beneath the folds of his tunic, and another in his boot. He may technically be on the same side as Red Willow, but that didn't mean he trusted them.

Danny was just contemplating exactly how early it was acceptable to be to this meeting when a knock at the door caught his attention and he glanced up, brow furrowed. He'd agreed to meet Moira at the tavern they'd been to the night before. She shouldn't be coming here. At the thought, hair rose on the back of his neck, and he fingered the hilt of his dagger, slowly moving to unhitch the latch.

Throwing it open, Danny blinked in surprise to see Tammy Altman standing in the pouring rain outside his door.

"Hey there, O'Leary. Miss me much?" Tammy tried to smile,

but it faltered, her lip trembling as her eyes slowly filled with tears. "Mind if I come in?"

The question shocked Danny out of his mute astonishment, and he yanked the door open farther. "Of course, come in. It's just—geez, Tammy, you look like hell."

Tammy tried and failed to smile at that but ended up just scrubbing her cheeks roughly. Danny dragged a chair over to the fire for her and quickly put a kettle on.

"Sorry, I don't have tea or anything," he muttered, rubbing the back of his neck as he took in Tammy's red-eyed, sniveling appearance. "But seriously, are you ok?" He pulled up his own chair and put a hand gently on her arm. "What happened in Port Galaén? Why are you back? You can tell me, Tammy."

Tammy's hands twisted in her lap, and then she looked up, pinning Danny with a grim expression.

"I-I'm pregnant."

Danny stared at her blankly. It took him a split second to register that his mouth was hanging open, and he snapped it shut. "That's, uh—congratulations."

Tammy snorted. "Yeah, thanks so much."

Danny ran a hand through his hair, searching for something, anything, he could say.

"How did . . . ? I mean—" Danny could feel the blush creep up over his cheeks, and Tammy rolled her eyes.

"The usual way, O'Leary. It was Fitz. He's the father, I mean."

Danny swallowed. It made sense, but still, Tammy—*pregnant*? Then his thoughts flashed to Keira. Well, at least he hadn't muddled things up too badly. She'd still exist, anyway.

"I mean, it's not the worst thing, is it?" he asked, trying to avoid looking at Tammy's stomach. The whole thing was just too weird.

Tammy's eyes narrowed. "You see any pregnant Legionnaires walking around, O'Leary? Any of them have kids they've been squirreling away somewhere?"

Danny blinked. He'd honestly never thought about it. But now that she mentioned it, he'd never heard of a Legionnaire having children.

"I just assumed they . . . couldn't."

"Yeah, that's what I thought too. Until a friend of mine found herself in a bad way. She went to her mentor, looking for help, and the next thing I knew, she was gone, just like that." Tammy's face had gone dark, and she rubbed her arms as if suddenly chilled. "I think it's gotta be pretty rare . . . even so, no one *talks* about it." Her eyes searched his, pleading for understanding. "You can't tell anyone, Danny. The Legion's got no room for rule-breakers, and a Legionnaire with a baby? You can forget about it. They'll discharge me, cut me off, and send me right back where I came from."

Danny blinked. "How is that even possible?" His thoughts raced. They wouldn't actually *kill* her, would they?

Tammy shot him an annoyed glare. "Hell if I know, O'Leary! And does it really matter? They've done it before, and they'll do it again. And I told you, I'm not going back there." Her voice took on a panicked edge, her eyes wide. "I'd rather die for real."

Danny felt torn and stood to pace around the room. On the one hand, Tammy was his friend, and he'd do anything to help her, keep any secret. But if she really was pregnant with Keira . . . she *had* to go back. Or did she? Danny shut that thought down quickly, not wanting to think about what would happen if Keira were born in this timeline, in this world. Would she ever become a Legionnaire? Ever live the life she'd had prior to coming here?

These were the sorts of questions that made his head hurt,

and he quickly pushed them from his mind. But how long could Tammy keep this secret, really?

"They'll find out eventually, Tammy. There's only *so long* you can hide it."

She shook her head. "Don't worry about that."

Danny shot her a dubious look.

"I have a plan," she insisted, brow furrowed as she gazed up at him. "Just, promise me you won't say anything, Danny—to anyone."

Danny swallowed, silencing once more the questions that stirred in his mind. They didn't matter. All that mattered was his friend, and she needed help. "Of course, Tammy. I won't say anything."

The relief that flooded her face was heartbreaking, and Danny felt something twist in his stomach as her shoulders sagged.

"Can I stay here tonight, please?"

Danny hesitated, glancing toward the door and thinking of Moira waiting for him in the darkness beyond. He was supposed to meet with Red Willow leadership tonight. But Tammy was here, shivering in her wet clothes, though she sat next to the roaring flames. There was a pleading look in her eye, a weakness there that he'd never seen—that she'd never let him see. And that decided it.

"Of course," he said, coming to sit beside her. He gently laid an arm across her shoulders and squeezed. "Whatever you need."

She leaned her head against his, and they sat that way for a while, until her shivering slowed and her shallow breathing told him she'd nodded off. But Danny didn't sleep, merely waiting as the hours passed and the life he'd known seemed to slip ever further from his grasp.

CHAPTER

THIRTY-FIVE

242 Marian Era (M.E.)

The equinox festival was probably the most exciting thing Raina had ever seen. Her neck ached from jerking her head from sight to sight, trying and failing to take in the full splendor of the capital bathed in light. The air was filled with music she couldn't help but dance to as torchlight flickered across the cobblestones, like waves lapping at the shores back on Tibolé.

Yet as Raina watched, the shadows seemed to grow longer, and her eyes drifted to the sky, pulled by an urge she couldn't name, a dread she couldn't explain. The very shadows atop the terra-cotta roofs seemed to shift as Raina watched, growing taller and multiplying.

"Akamu," she murmured.

"Hmm?" he asked absently, smiling indulgently at a downlander who lavishly praised the intricate paintings of his barkcloth sash.

"I think there be something wrong," Raina said, eyes

darting from rooftop to rooftop, trying to discern shape and movement from the shifting shadows but unable to shake the feeling of icy fingers running down her spine. "Do you see—"

An earsplitting roar sounded, and the ground around them vibrated. Raina glanced across the plaza just in time to see the westernmost tower of the Temple of Pneumos explode in a rain of stone, showering rubble onto the crowd of people below.

There was a moment of stunned silence as the cheers and laughter faded, only to be replaced by screams of fear and pain.

Then a second explosion sounded from behind her, and Raina spun to see the arched dome of the newly christened People's Council Chambers buckle skyward before sending stone and terra-cotta tiles raining down on top of them.

"It's an attack!" Akamu roared, grabbing Raina's arm as he dragged her forward, toward the massive stone archway of the Vindolum. "Take cover!"

Raina followed him, too stunned to resist the tight grip of his fingers. They had made it up the first flight of marble steps toward the door when the fireballs came. At first Raina thought them only stars flickering in the night sky, but as they arced and began their slow descent to the earth, she could see the truth. Akamu seemed to see it at the same time as her, and his face blanched. It was that look of fear on her brother's face that shook Raina to her core, far more terrifying than anything she'd experienced herself.

"With us!" a female voice cried, and the two of them turned to see Aelianna gesturing with an outstretched hand as she simultaneously moved in unison with her black-and-white-robed ladies. Their dance took on a faster beat, and sweat rimmed their brows with the effort.

Raina did as she was told, and when she and Akamu

reached them, Aelianna gripped her arm. "I've seen your power, girl. Help us stop this dark magic."

"I-I can't. I don't know how," Raina murmured, watching as the rain of fireballs slowed but still made their arcing descent upon the crowd.

"Do as we do," Aelianna growled, voice thick with effort. "Ground yourself into the earth and let your power flow through it. We will wrap this entire city in a wall if we have to."

Raina gaped at her before sparing a glance at Akamu. He nodded, glancing back to the rest of the council members, the bravest of whom were desperately trying to herd people out of the killing field the plaza had become. She had to do something, help somehow.

So Raina stepped to Aelianna's side, watching from the corner of her eye to mimic their movements. She focused on her breathing, just like Keira had showed her. If only she'd known she'd need to implement the lesson so soon. Moving in sync with the others, Raina desperately searched inside herself for the ball of energy Keira had described. But Raina felt only a chaotic churning of power, without beginning or end. There was nothing to grab hold of, no anchor to steady herself. She was drowning in it and felt herself being sucked under even as her stomach rolled with nausea. Only a growing warmth in her chest held her steady, and she clung to the sensation, focusing all her attention on it, a single unmoving point in a sea of shifting energy. No, not *in* her chest—*on* her chest.

All at once, she realized where the source of the energy was coming from—the sea shell necklace, her mother's necklace. She focused all her attention on it, siphoning everything else through that single point. The massive swirl of energy inside her became threadlike as she drew it through the tiny chambers of the shell's spiraling contours until it emerged, tightly woven and controllable. Remembering Aelianna's instructions, Raina sent it spiraling down through her feet to the earth below her, letting it tether her in place. She felt steady, untouchable.

"Now form a net." Aelianna's voice was strained, and Raina swallowed, trying to quiet the hammering of her own heart long enough to move through the motions as the older woman instructed. It was slow going, the movements like molasses, and her muscles burned with holding the positions, but gradually, she felt the thread of her pneuma slide up to join the others, forming an unseen but vibrating net that covered the entire plaza.

A gasp at her side made Raina's eyes flutter open. Aelianna was staring at something above them.

Keeping tight hold of that thread, Raina glanced up and nearly cried aloud at the sight of a thousand flaming balls hovering unmoving in the air, only feet above the heads of the panicking crowd. Raina barely dared to breathe, terrified of disrupting the spell they'd somehow woven.

But at that moment, the shifting shadows of the rooftops morphed into human figures as one stepped toward the edge. His furious expression was illuminated by the flame below as he looked down at the gathered crowd. But it was the spiraling black tattoo that cut a steep diagonal across his face that caught Raina's eye, and she had to bite back the wave of panic that threatened to choke her. Suddenly she was back in a clearing, tied beneath a tree as a half dozen tattooed faces leered down at her.

The sting of her nails cutting into her palm brought her back to the present, and she watched in horror as the hooded man raised one hand, pointing a single spindly finger toward the fountain at the center of the plaza, its sculpted figures celebrating some long-forgotten victory. Raina followed his gesture with her eyes just in time to see a gleam of metal turn its massive, cylindrical snout toward the fountain.

Raina's breath caught. Akamu.

He was there, beneath the flailing hooves of a stone horse, forever frozen mid-rear. She could hear his shouts from where she stood as he tried to guide the fleeing crowd.

"Akamu, run!" Raina screamed.

Aelianna barked a word of warning that Raina paid no mind to as she launched into motion, sprinting toward her brother. She summoned every ounce of strength she had, throwing that mysterious thread toward him, desperate to create something, anything, that might protect him.

But she was too late.

The blast hit her with a force like a breaking tidal wave, and she felt herself thrown wide of the explosion.

Raina blinked up at the sky, forcing air into her lungs as the stars swirled in her vision. No, not stars—flames. The spell seemed to break, and she watched in mute horror as the flames rained down upon them. She didn't know how long she lay there—maybe seconds or perhaps hours, staring in blank shock. She continued to blink up at the swirling night sky until a face appeared before her, mouthing words she couldn't hear as rough hands shook her.

Neval, her brain replied groggily to her unasked question.

Then the sounds came rushing back—screams, pounding feet, sobs, and the roar of flames.

"Can you walk?" Neval demanded, helping her into a sitting position. Raina nodded, then groaned as the motion sent icy shards piercing her head.

Twisting her fingers into his cloak, Raina scrambled to her feet, searching around them as claws of terror raked at her insides.

"Where is he?" she rasped, coughing out the smoke she'd inhaled. "Akamu," she said, seeing Neval's eyes tighten. Something about his expression made her pull away.

"Where is he?" she demanded again. Her eyes searched the running crowd, willing her brother's face to appear. But there was no one.

Raina turned and started pushing her way through the crowd, back toward where she remembered standing with Aelianna. She felt Neval following close behind, but he didn't try to stop her.

Raina emerged into a clearing of the crowd. She blinked, trying to understand exactly what she was seeing. Then she felt bile rise in her throat.

Bodies.

The clearing was strewn with bodies, loosely dressed in robes of black and white, except for a single figure in the center, the glittering blue sashes that had trimmed her body now bloody and torn. Dark curls shot through with silver fell loosely across her face, no doubt obscuring the worst of the damage. Raina heaved a sob.

Aelianna and her incredible ladies—all gone.

A howl erupted from across the clearing in the crowd, and Cyrus stumbled into the circle of bodies, falling to his knees beside Aelianna. Sobbing, he heaved her onto his lap, gently brushing the curls from her face with a trembling hand. Tears coursed down his dirt-stained cheeks as he rocked her back and forth. Even from across the bloody clearing, Raina could hear his sobs as he buried his face in her hair. "I'm sorry, Mama, I'm so sorry."

This was her fault, Raina realized. She'd broken the chain, failed them when they needed her most. Tears filled her eyes, but she blinked them away. Not now. She couldn't stop yet.

"Akamu!" she cried, spinning toward where the fountain had stood. Only rubble remained, and she took a few hesitant steps toward it before breaking into a run. The sound of her footsteps hammered into her brain as a barrage of frantic thoughts clawed at her.

Please be ok. He has to be ok. Where is he? I'll find him. I can't be losing him. I can't be losing anyone else.

Her eyes searched the ground for any sign of him, for that shaggy mane of curls their mother used to complain about, the tattoos curling up his arms that he'd been so proud of—*"a sign of manhood,"* he'd told her. *"More like stupidity,"* she'd replied.

Please be ok, she begged.

Finally, she spied dark brown skin beneath shaggy curls in the crowd ahead of her, and she wanted to sob with relief.

Two steps more, and she'd reached him, dragging on his arm to pull him around to face her.

It wasn't him.

Nusa, her brother's best friend, stared down at her. She could barely recognize him through the soot that covered his face and the jagged cut that still bled freely from his temple.

"W-Where's Akamu?" she asked. "Where's my brother?"

Nusa's face broke, twisting into a grimace as tears filled his eyes. "I'm sorry, little *dinué*. I'm so sorry."

"D-Don't call me that!" she screamed at him, voice raw. "Where's my brother?" she demanded. Nusa's face blurred before her as tears pooled and overflowed her own eyes, the cuts and scrapes on her face stinging with the contact.

Nusa reached a hand toward her that she slapped away, pushing past him, toward the fountain. *I saw him. Just over—*

Raina froze.

She couldn't breathe, air catching around the vise that

suddenly gripped her chest as she stared down at the crumpled body of the only family she'd had left.

"NO," she moaned, dropping to her knees beside him. "No, no, please, no!" Then she exploded. She felt a wail rip out of her chest as she collapsed onto him, twining her fingers in his shirt. She could feel the rough bark cloth of the sash he wore, that dumb sash he'd been so proud of. "Why?" she asked nobody in particular. "Why him?"

Nobody was there to answer.

She wasn't sure how long she lay there, broken and sobbing, sprawled across her brother's body. But it was long enough for blood to cake beneath her nails and for her sobs to run dry, having spilled every ounce of liquid she'd had left in her body.

Fingers wrapped around her arm, gentle but insistent.

"I'm sorry, little Raina, but we *gotta* go. I promised Keira I'd get you out if anyfin'—"

"Don't you say her name!" Raina screamed, eyes unseeing through the curtain of tears. She could barely breathe through the ripping sensation in her chest. "I HATE her! She promised, she *promised* me—" Raina's words dissolved into racking sobs that convulsed her entire body. *They're gone*, her brain kept repeating. *They're all gone. I'm all alone.*

She crumpled onto Akamu's body, fists balling into his shirt as she lay there—unable to move, unwilling to face a world without him standing over her shoulder, protecting her always.

Raina didn't know if Neval stayed, was unaware of anything beyond the feel of her brother's chest beneath her cheek. She could feel him growing cold, her big brother who seemed to radiate heat and light wherever he went, and she choked out another sob, willing her own body to melt into his, her own heat to fill him. But there was nothing left of him, of Akamu. He was like the empty shell the tiny *anomura* left behind as it moved on to its new home on a far-off shore. This was just the empty shell of who Akamu had been. She knew in her soul there was nothing left.

She let that settle into her gut before she raised herself up on trembling arms to look down into Akamu's face—smooth and far too still, without the smile he wore even while sleeping, and she leaned forward to kiss his cheek.

"Goodbye, Akamu," Raina murmured, racking her brain for the words of her ancestors. "Slip beneath shimmering waves, and rest in the arms of Mother Cála."

And with that, she glanced up to see Neval still there, standing guard over the both of them, dagger gripped tightly in his fist. She met his eyes and nodded. His brows furrowed, eyes softening as he held out a hand. She took it.

THIRTY-SIX

The first thing Keira knew was pain, and the second was an overwhelming sense of guilt. She heard herself groan as she blinked up at strange rafters that crossed a beamed ceiling far above. Then she sat bolt upright, heart hammering as she remembered in a panic what had happened.

She was out of bed and halfway to the door when a voice from across the room stopped her dead in her tracks.

"Easy does it. That's a sure way to find yourself unconscious halfway down the stairs."

Keira froze and slowly turned around, heart hammering for a completely different reason.

Elliott sat in a chair beside the window, an open book perched in one hand. He was apparently halfway through thumbing over a page, looking up at her from beneath comically large spectacles.

She would have laughed if it hadn't been for the overwhelming sense of guilt and shame that suddenly washed over her. Not to mention her knees were about to buckle. Determining they must be in no immediate danger, Keira consented to plop down in a chair opposite him and relished the sensation of solidity as the spinning room slowed to merely a slight tilting sensation.

"Where are we? A-And how are you here?" was the first thing she thought to ask.

Elliott shrugged in that noncommittal way he had, before saying, "We're in a tavern, not far from the plaza. As for how I got here, that's a discussion for another day. But the short answer is that I got word that you needed help and came as soon as I could."

Keira's brow furrowed at this cryptic response, and she was about to press the issue when a sudden memory had her leaping to her feet. "Albert!"

Elliott blinked, surprised, as his lips pressed into a thin line. "Indeed, it seems my old friend is up to his usual tricks. He and his cronies managed to wrest control of the Vindolum, I'm afraid. We've regrouped here for now."

A wave of guilt flooded Keira, and her mouth fell open as she stared at Elliott. She closed it, swallowing, before squeezing out the words, "I'm sorry, Elliott. I should have listened. It was a mistake to trust him, to think he might actually want to help me."

Elliott stood then, coming around the side of the bed to lean against one post. He squeezed her shoulder gently, eyes kind. "I'm sorry too. I'm sorry I didn't tell you the whole truth —about my past with Albert, about Nazor, and about Danny. I knew what you wanted, Keira. Pneumos knows I've wanted him back, too, him and Nazor both. And that scared me, scared me so much I rejected it out of hand. Because it *is* dangerous, Keira. If your interactions with Albert have taught you anything, it's the danger that such power brings. And how our own desires and vulnerabilities may make us blind to the risks."

"So, are you saying—" Keira's breath caught in her chest, and she swallowed, remembering the words Marné had spoken what felt like a lifetime ago.

"When rains do fade and waves be calm, then sun and moon be borne alike. Le'ena walk among the stromb, death be gone when Cála strike."

She glanced toward the open window, where day was just breaking over the horizon. It was well and truly the equinox now. If there was any chance of her saving Danny, it had to be today.

"If there's any way to save him, Elliott, I have to try. I owe him that."

Elliott's smile was drawn, and Keira flinched away reflexively from the pity she saw there.

"There may be a way to save him yet, Keira. But—" His eyes searched hers, and she let them, holding his gaze as she steeled herself against the bud of hope she felt fluttering in her chest. "—but you need to prepare yourself for what may come, the sacrifice that Pneumos may ask of you, if the chaos Albert's unleashed can't be stopped."

"How can we possibly stop it? He's too powerful, has too many allies."

Keira saw a spark gleam in Elliott's eyes as he said slowly, "Not *we*, Keira, *you*. You've managed to unravel the secrets of healing pneumonancy. Albert wanted to use your abilities to channel the chaos for his own ends. And if there's anyone capable of stopping him, it's you. But I'm not sure you can do it alone. You've made friends here, allies, even. Let them help you."

The dread once more built in her chest as she remembered Albert's words from the night before. "What happened? Is everyone—" Keira's voice again cut off. Raina? Cyrus? Neval?

What had happened to her friends while she'd foolishly run off to face Albert alone, walking right into the trap he'd set?

Elliott's lips pressed together, but he didn't avoid her gaze, instead staring her down as he mumbled, "They took losses, Keira. Too many."

KEIRA FIDDLED with the ties of her scabbard as she and Elliott descended the stairs to where her friends waited in the open air of the tavern's courtyard. They were all battered and bruised, nursing wounds of varying severity. Marti lay curled up against Zipporah, head cradled in her grounder's lap, as Zipporah stroked her flaming hair with a tenderness Keira had rarely seen. In the corner, Cyrus sat with head in his hands, and Keira glimpsed red, swollen eyes. Landry braced him across the shoulders, letting him lean into him. For his part, Landry looked in absolute shock, brow furrowed in disbelief as he stared at the ground, his security detail tensed on either side of him. Keira continued to scan the room, looking for the one person she was most terrified to find.

Raina sat on a bench at the far edge of the courtyard, hands hanging limp in her lap. Keira watched as Neval offered her a loaf of bread, a worried look in his eye as he tried to cajole the young girl back to life. Raina merely stared at the ground, eyes dry despite the tear-streaks on her soot-covered face. From the looks of it, she alone among them had refused to clean up after the attack. She likely hadn't slept either.

Keira's heart pounded in her chest, and she swallowed against the shame that stung her cheeks as she approached them. She cleared her throat, waiting for the reproachful looks she knew would greet her. But as weary eyes raised to hers, she saw no anger or blame. Instead, she found something far more terrifying—defeat.

"We've suffered a loss," Keira began, voice sounding strained even to her own ears in the silence. Keira's eyes drifted to Raina, who still hadn't looked up, then snapped away. "Albert once again outsmarted us, allying with both Red Willow and the Worshippers of Séiro in a combined attack." None of them looked surprised. She was telling them what they already knew. Keira took a steadying breath against her own fear. She felt like an imposter. Who was she to lead them? She'd failed them too many times to count. In the silence that followed, Keira's eyes met Neval's, and he gave a small nod of encouragement, even as Elliott shifted his weight against her, steadying and urging her forward. Keira cleared her throat and squared her shoulders.

"I need your help," she said simply, looking at each of them in turn. "I know you're tired. I know you've all given so much already. And Pneumos knows I've made mistakes, gone off on my own when I should have waited for backup. I left you all when you needed me most. And that is something I'll always regret." Her gaze strayed to Cyrus, who was staring up at her, eyes bloodshot. She swallowed. She knew what he was feeling, knew what it was to lose a mother. But she couldn't dwell on that now. She turned back to the others and pressed on. "But I can't do this on my own. I need you. Loren needs you. Albert may think he's beaten us, that we've given up. But he's wrong."

Then she fell silent, waiting for their reaction. There was a long pause, and then another, as her friends surveyed her, taking her measure. Keira shifted uneasily under their gaze but stood firm. This was their right—their choice. She'd failed them before. Let them choose to join her—or not. But let them choose.

Neval was the first to stand, striding toward her with a determination that belied his usually practiced indifference. He gripped her shoulder, and she returned the gesture. "My people, whoever I have left, are yours to command."

Keira nodded, feeling a rush of gratitude wash over her as she met his eyes. In his eyes she saw trust, support, and something else she couldn't quite name—an intensity that made her stomach clench. She glanced away before whatever it was could fully surface, and she waited for the others' answers.

Surprisingly, Zipporah was next. She stood, approaching Keira with quick strides that favored one leg, a bandage wrapped tightly around the other. "You say you have regrets, but talk is cheap. What will you do going forward?"

Keira met her gaze, making her eyes clear and open. "I've lost people," she said simply, honestly. "Too many people. It's made me cautious of letting those I care about take risks and put themselves in danger. But I see now that I can't protect them just by doing everything on my own. In fact, it's only put you in further danger. I have to trust you, all of you. And that's what I plan to do. From now on, we're a team. We plan together and execute together. And the losses we suffer, we do so together."

Zipporah's eyes narrowed as she searched Keira's gaze. But whatever she saw there must have been enough, because she nodded and clapped a hand to Keira's shoulder. "Then I'm with you."

"Me too," Marti piped up from the corner, rising unsteadily to her feet. Exhaustion painted her face in shadow, but her expression was determined.

Keira nodded her thanks.

Cyrus was next, and the look on his face brought a chill to

Keira's spine. "We'll make him pay," Cyrus growled. "For everything."

As Landry approached, Keira could see the strain that bent his shoulders forward, the weight of all that had happened bearing down on him.

"I've always been with you, Keira. And you've never let me down."

His words brought stinging tears to Keira's eyes, and she blinked them back as she gripped his forearm in thanks.

Finally, only Raina remained, unmoved from the ledge of the reflective pool as she stared at the ground ahead of her.

Keira's mouth felt suddenly dry as she stared at the young girl who'd become like a sister to her. The girl she'd met only a few weeks before but knew in her heart she'd do absolutely anything for, anything to protect her. But she hadn't. She hadn't been able to protect her, to save her from the pain and loss of the person who meant everything to her.

Raina dropped to her feet and came toward her, not meeting Keira's eyes until she stood directly before her. When Raina raised her red, hollowed-out eyes to meet hers, Keira felt something twist deep in the pit of her stomach. "Raina—"

"Don't," Raina said flatly. Her voice was like sandpaper, and Keira winced at the venom that laced through it. "You promised us, *grelún*," Raina hissed. "You promised us we'd be safe here, you and that one." Raina jutted her chin toward Cyrus, who looked abashed. "You promised us more, a better life. And now my brother—," Raina's voice caught, and tears filled her eyes. "And now he be dead."

Keira's mouth fell open, and she felt a stinging in her eyes. "Raina, I'm so—"

"I don't be wanting your apology. I be wanting my brother back." Raina's voice hitched on the words, a sob bubbling up in her throat that cut straight through Keira. She reached for her, but Raina jerked back, eyes narrowing. The look she gave Keira was one of pure hatred and sent a scorching dagger through her heart. "I will fight with you, to avenge Akamu. But I will never trust you again, *grelún*."

And with that, she turned on her heel and headed for the staircase. Keira lurched forward, a sound—half sob and half plea—on her lips, but a warm hand caught her arm, and she looked up through tears to meet Neval's face.

"Let her go," he said simply. "She has to do this on her own."

Keira swallowed, fighting back the whimper that would shred the last piece of dignity she had left. She nodded, but in her heart, she followed after Raina, begging her for the forgiveness she knew she'd never deserve.

"He can't possibly think he can win this thing," Cyrus growled, pacing up and down the courtyard. Temporarily freed from his grief by the purpose set before him, he'd thrown himself wholeheartedly into planning their next move. "Even holed up in the Vindolum with that damned Red Willow, he's no match for the Bellatorio. He *has* to know that."

"Don't forget the Worshippers of Séiro," Zipporah added, crossing her arms as she faced him. "From the looks of it, he has at least a couple dozen. They certainly won't go down without a fight. Not to mention, Albert himself won't be easily dealt with."

Keira stared at the ground throughout this exchange, Raina's words replaying in her head. *"I will never trust you again, grelún."*

A nudge from Elliott broke her reverie, and she glanced up at the others.

"He doesn't expect to win," she said quietly, feeling all their eyes turn to her, expectant. She cleared her throat. "Albert's goal in all of this has always been to generate chaos. He gains power from it and will twist it to his own ends if we try to attack him head on. We'd be playing right into his hands, practically handing him the power to do whatever it is he plans with the conduit."

Seeing the others' confused expressions, she quickly explained about the marble basin located in the South Tower of the Vindolum and its legendary placement there by the Legion. She explained Albert's claims that it could channel the redoing and bring back long-dead Legionnaires to Loren using the power of the equinox.

"I-I think he wants to build an army," she said at last. "He wants to challenge the Legion directly, and this is his best chance at doing that."

When she'd finished, the others merely gaped at her.

"Does that mean—" Landry finally began, swallowing, "you could bring back Danny?"

Keira took a long, steadying breath, feeling all of their eyes on her.

"That's what first brought me back," she admitted, meeting Landry's look with her own pleading gaze, begging him to understand. "Of course I wanted to help when we heard about the assassination attempt. But Albert promised me he'd help me tap into my own abilities. He said there was an object. I-I don't know what I was thinking, trusting him, I mean—"

She let her voice trail off and looked back to Landry, expecting ridicule, condemnation, even hurt. Instead, she saw only understanding. He missed him too.

"Do you think you could still do it?"

Keira opened her mouth but had no words to reply. She glanced to Elliott, but his face was carefully expressionless.

"I don't know," she said finally, ignoring the tightness in her chest. "But right now, my priority is stopping Albert. The rest—well, we can figure out the rest later."

The others nodded, apparently satisfied.

"Well, how exactly do you plan on beating Albert without generating more chaos?" Zipporah demanded. "Last I checked, assaulting a fortress required a bit of bloodshed."

"We need to find a back way in," she said, turning to Landry. "Is there any way in besides the front and servants' entrances?"

He considered that, rubbing a hand across his mouth. "There used to be," he said finally. "An old escape stair down the cliffside, to be used in case of attack. Similar to the one we used in Ulgáris. Junia and I used to play on it as children, daring each other to see who could make it down the farthest. But that was years ago. I don't know if they've sealed it since then."

Keira nodded, thinking. "We'll scout it out beforehand, make sure it's still an option. We'll need a distraction, though," she said, glancing between Cyrus and Landry. "Albert has to believe that we intend to launch an assault from the front."

Cyrus nodded. "I'll speak to the city garrison, gather a show of force to stage in the plaza."

"Be sure to clear civilians from the area," Marti added. "If we want to avoid the chaos of a mass panic, then we need to minimize the fallout."

"I'll go with you," Landry said, turning to Cyrus. "Albert will expect me to reclaim my home. He'll grow suspicious if I'm not there."

Keira bit her lip, looking between the two of them. "Be careful," she pleaded. "Both of you, but especially Landry. If you're killed, there'll be no stopping the chaos that will follow."

Landry grimaced, nodding, but Cyrus clapped a hand over his shoulder. "I'll look after him," he assured her. "No unnecessary risks."

"I'll take the rest of you with me around to the back entrance," Keira said. "Between the five of us, we should be able to handle whatever these Worshippers of Séiro have to throw at us."

"And Albert?" Zipporah asked.

"Leave him to me," Elliott said, eyes tight. "We have some *unfinished* business."

"It'll take all of us," Keira said, glancing around at her friends and ignoring the clenched sensation around her heart. "But if anyone can do this, it's us." She hoped she sounded more confident than she felt.

THIRTY-SEVEN

1 Marian Era (M.E.)

Over the months that passed, Danny kept time by the slowly rising walls of the Vindolum. Even as frigid winds battered the newly minted capital, workers continued lugging heavy stones up to the site of the Regio's future palace. The great hall was newly finished, and as the towers of the Vindolum rose above the city, Red Willow wound its tendrils beneath. Danny's meeting with the organization's leadership had been postponed after the announcement that construction would begin on the city's sewer system —supposedly because of Magnus's personal aversion to the smell. For Red Willow, this meant the perfect opportunity to solidify its hold—by embedding within the city itself.

It was for this reason that Danny found himself in the Wailing Mudder, waiting for his dinner companions, Tammy and Imperator Rommel, who happened to have been charged with overseeing the construction project. Officially, they were meeting to go over the arrangements for a cohort of Legionnaires who'd soon be arriving to pay respect to the new Regio and for his upcoming nuptials, but Danny had also been tasked with weaseling as much information out of Rommel about the new sewer system as possible.

He'd seen little of Tammy since she'd come to him in desperation that night, and when she waved to him from across the room, he couldn't help but notice she seemed a fair bit . . . rounder.

He swallowed, watching as she strode toward him, seeing every swish of her tunic press against the curves of her new form. She couldn't keep this hidden, not for much longer. It was in light of this and his continued work with Red Willow that the idea of a group of Legionnaires showing up to poke their heads around was far from reassuring.

They'd agreed to meet early to catch up before Rommel arrived and the business of the evening began. Danny waited until they'd ordered their drinks and caught up on the daily happenings of their lives. Then he cleared his throat, shifting slightly in his seat as he turned to meet Tammy's curious gaze.

"What's the plan, then, Tammy? Eventually it"—he nodded at her stomach—"is going to become obvious. You won't be able to hide it forever, let alone when the baby actually gets here . . ."

"I have a plan."

"Really? I'd love to hear it." His words sounded snide even to him, but he couldn't help it. He was worried and couldn't help but feel like everything was spiraling out of control.

"It's better you don't know," Tammy murmured.

That sent a shiver down Danny's spine, and he hesitated, weighing his words carefully.

"It's just that I might know . . . people—who could help. If you were looking to have the baby adopted or something—"

He trailed off, watching as Tammy's eyes narrowed, her piercing gaze missing nothing. "What people?"

Danny swallowed. "People who could get her—or him," he added quickly, "out of the city and away from the Legion. People who work *off the grid*."

Tammy cocked her head, surveying him with fresh interest. Then her voice dropped to a whisper as she said, "If I didn't know any better, Danny O'Leary, I'd say you were talking about the *resistance*." This last word came out in a hiss, and Danny felt his fingers go numb.

"And I'd say," he started, eyeing the people at nearby tables in the loud, bustling tavern, "that questions like *that* are less than helpful given the current situation." He met her gaze directly and saw her eyes widen.

"You're working with the resistance?" she hissed.

"Shhhh!" Danny's eyes darted around them, making sure they weren't overheard.

"Danny O'Leary, you better tell me exactly what's going on, right now." Tammy's voice dropped back to a whisper but lost none of its furrowed intensity.

Danny sighed, rubbing the back of his neck and kicking himself for even broaching the subject. He eyed her, mentally calculating the likelihood she'd spill her guts to the first Bellator they saw. But Tammy had secrets of her own, and she couldn't turn on him without endangering herself. Besides, it was *Tammy*. She was the first friend he'd made in this time. If there was anyone he could trust, it would be her.

So he started from the beginning—Moira's request for information about her father, Titus's assassination, her confession, the killing of the mess hall servants, and the raid that had forced his hand, made him pick a side.

When he was done, Tammy just stared wide-eyed at him. After a long moment, she asked slowly, "So let me get this straight. The steadfast Danny O'Leary has turned spy and is now feeding information on his Bellatori friends to a clandestine resistance group?"

At his curt nod, she whistled. "Dang, O'Leary. I didn't think you had it in you."

He scowled at her. "It's not funny."

"I beg to differ," she crowed. Then she sobered, seeing his expression. "I guess I mean it's more, just, *ironic*. You're literally the last person I thought could betray anyone."

Danny's jaw clenched, and he inhaled through the nose. *You and me both.*

"If you'd seen what I saw, Tammy, you wouldn't be so surprised."

Tammy nodded, brow furrowed. "I'm sure. It sounds so awful. But do you really think—" She shot him a glance, hesitating. "Do you really think you're better off with all the cloak and dagger stuff? All of this started out because you were looking for answers—about the Legion, the Empire, and why you were brought here in the first place. From the sound of it, you're as much in the dark now as you were at the outset."

Danny bristled. "I *do* know what's going on, Tammy. That's why I'm helping them. I finally understand what I was meant to do here—help my friends fight for a cause that—"

"Your *friends*?" Tammy snorted. "*Ok.* Yeah, why don't you ask little Miss Freedom Fighter how that search for her father is going."

Danny blinked, confused. "What are you talking about?"

Tammy threw her arms up in exasperation. "I'm talking about the fact that this girl has completely manipulated you, O'Leary. You fell hook, line, and sinker for the tears and the sob story, and now you're risking your life on something that isn't even *you*."

"What do you mean, it's not me?" Danny demanded, folding his arms over his chest.

Tammy sighed, gesturing around herself. "All this spy crap, Danny. You are the most honest, kind-hearted guy I know. This has to be eating you up inside."

Danny's jaw clenched, and he leveled her with a glare. "Look, Tammy, I get that you think you know me and all, but you left. And what happened here—" He swallowed. "I never want to see that again, ever."

Tammy looked at him for a long moment before shaking her head. Her voice was bitter as she replied, "Do what you want, O'Leary. I'll keep your secret, but I want no part of any so-called *resistance*."

Danny bit his lip, his eyes darting again to her stomach, swelling beneath her tunic. "Look, if you won't let the resistance help you, then maybe it's time to explain what happened . . . to the Legion, I mean."

Tammy went rigid, her eyes shooting to his and narrowing into slits. "I told you, O'Leary, I have a plan."

"Tammy, this isn't a secret you can keep. You're already starting to—"

"Shut. Your. Mouth," Tammy snarled, eyes darting around the room. "If I wanted your opinion, O'Leary, I would have asked for it. And if you say a word to anyone, including your uplander girlfriend—" Danny flinched at the term. "I will turn you and your resistance friends in so fast your head will spin."

Danny gaped at her, at the ferocity etched across her face as her nostrils flared and shoulders heaved. "Tammy, I-I would never—" He let his voice trail off, watching as her breathing slowed and her features softened.

"Good. Because I'm not going back there, Danny. I swear I won't."

At that moment, her eyes flicked up, and her face suddenly morphed into one of serene boredom. She lifted a hand and called, "Imperator, good to see you!"

Danny's stomach flipped, and he forced his own features into some semblance of normalcy. But inside, his pulse still hammered, and he knew the smile he offered Imperator Rommel wouldn't quite reach his eyes.

Because he believed her. Even if she was the best friend he had here, Tammy would turn him in in a heartbeat if she thought he'd double-crossed her. And that was a terrifying thought indeed.

"So . . . how's your search coming? For your father, I mean."

Danny said the words casually, even though his heart pounded in his chest. He really was hopeless at this clandestine stuff.

Moira paused, glancing up from the papers she'd been inspecting. "As well as can be expected. No word yet, but we're hopeful."

"We?"

Moira blinked, and something flashed in her eyes, a hesitancy, and something else, something almost like *guilt*. "Yes, *we*. All of Red Willow is eagerly awaitin' his return."

"He—he was in Red Willow, then?" Danny swallowed. This was a new twist on the story. *So much for the fisherman drafted against his will to Loren's defense,* he thought wryly.

"He was, and is still, well-respected. It was a blow to all of us when they caught him, to the entire organization, really."

"And your mother, too, I'm sure."

Moira glanced at him and then away. "I never met my mother, so I can't really say."

"I thought you said—"

"I know what I said," she snapped, hands splayed in her lap. He gaped, and she glanced at him and then away. "What do you want to 'ear, O'Leary? That I'm an orphan? That Red Willow and this fight are all I've got in the world? That I'd give anything to free Lisander? Pay any price? Tell any lie I needed to? Cuz I would, and you should know that."

Her eyes were fierce as they bored into his. Danny swallowed the rising frustration, not just at Moira, but at himself as well. Why hadn't he asked more *questions*?

"So this *Lisander*, he's not actually your father, then?"

"He's as much my father as any man ever was," Moira snarled. "Lisander took me in when I 'ad nobody. I would 'ave starved if not for 'im. And what's with all the questions, anyway? You think we're keepin' things from you, O'Leary?"

"No, not at all. It's just that Tammy and I were talking, and she just pointed out that—"

"You told TAMMY?" Moira demanded, eyes going wide. "What, *exactly*, did you tell 'er?"

Danny glanced up, startled, and instantly realized his mistake. "Not much," he muttered. "Just the basics."

"The basics?"

Danny shifted his weight, weighing his words. "Just Red Willow's goals in all this, why I'm doing what I'm doing— nothing specific, I swear."

Moira opened and closed her mouth, clearly at a loss for words.

Danny cleared his throat. "She won't say anything."

"That's so *comfortin'* to hear."

Danny's eyes narrowed. "Look, she has her own secrets, ok? She won't say anything."

At least, she did for the next few months.

Moira's brows raised. "What secrets?"

Danny's lips pressed into a thin line, but he said nothing.

Moira rolled her eyes, muttering, "Oh, *this* secret he'll keep."

"She's not a threat."

Moira's eyes narrowed. "You'd better 'ope not, Danny. I put my neck on the line, and my word, vouchin' for you. Don't make me regret it."

Danny nodded, and they both turned back to the work in front of him. But something nudged at the back of his mind. It was the fact that Moira had somehow steered the conversation well away from this mysterious Lisander—the absent father who wasn't actually her father at all.

CHAPTER
THIRTY-EIGHT

242 Marian Era (M.E.)

As Keira stared up at the winding staircase, narrowly cut directly into the cliff ledge, she couldn't help the flutter of panic that raced over her body, just beneath the skin. She hated heights—always had. She caught Neval's eye, and he winked in that way that always put her teeth on edge, as if he saw through all of her bravado to the terrified little girl beneath.

"All right there, Keira dear? Never fear, I won't let you fall."

"The only thing I'm afraid of, *Neval*," she said, smirking, "is that you'll get in my way."

The words were bold, fearless even, and speaking them aloud seemed to buoy her courage as she started up the first steps. She could have hugged him for it.

Neval merely laughed aloud as he and the others followed behind.

The wind caught at her hair, pulling it from its ties and whipping it around her face. She braced herself against the cliff wall but kept moving, glancing back only to check on Raina. She'd tried to insist the younger girl stay behind, but Raina was having none of it, swearing that if Keira left her behind, she'd only find a way to sneak out on her own. Given her track record, Keira didn't doubt she'd make good on that promise. So she'd come along, a brooding shadow at the rear of their group and a constant worry in the back of Keira's mind.

It was a long climb, and Keira's legs were soon burning with the effort. But she pushed on, determined not to waste the one and only chance they were likely to have. But that didn't stop the relief that rushed through her as they finally neared the upper ledge and the tunnel Landry had promised would take them straight to the Vindolum's kitchens.

She was so excited that she almost missed the sound of low voices that floated down to them from the ledge above.

Keira froze.

She reached out a hand to stop the others, barely breathing as she strained to make out the words. Beside her, Neval tensed, fingers reaching for the dagger at his hip.

Slowly, the voices floated down to them, coalescing into words as Keira tried to quiet the hammering of her heart in her ears.

"... don't see why we've got to wait out here in the cold."

"You 'eard him. Got to make sure nobody tries to sneak up 'ere."

"Who even knows about these stairs? It's a sheer drop to the waves below."

Neval's eyes met hers as Keira held a finger to her lips, slowly unsheathing her blade as she nodded toward the last few steps up to the ledge. He held up three fingers, then a fourth, as another voice floated down to them. Below, Marti was already crouched, fingertips lightly pressed into the stone stairs as Zipporah stood before her, sword unsheathed and grounding hand braced against her shoulder.

Keira counted them down. Three . . . She took a steadying breath. Two . . . Neval's fingers tightened on his dagger. One. . .

"D'you hear that?" a voice above asked.

Keira froze, putting a hand up toward the others to stop them racing forward.

"Hear what?"

Keira was barely breathing, even as her heart hammered in her chest.

"It's coming from the plaza, I think."

Keira let out the breath she'd been holding before straining to hear what had caught their attention. Sure enough, the sound of shouts and the march of footsteps floated down the cliffside. Keira smiled in satisfaction. Cyrus and Landry were taking their position. Her eyes met Neval's, and they both nodded in unison. The time was now.

They sprang up together, and Keira took the last few steps in two giant leaps, coming face-to-face with a shocked Red Willow guard, his pink face blanching at the sight of them.

He didn't even have time to react before her sword arced up and around, cutting deep into his side before she ran it straight through his middle. He sagged against her, and she rolled him off before turning to face his companion—already lifting his own blade in response.

Her sword met his with a clang that reverberated in her bones, and she staggered back, letting the metal slide off with a high-pitched shear.

Out of the corner of her eye, she caught the flash of Neval's dagger against one assailant as the fourth staggered back, making rigid, cogwheel-like movements, no doubt fighting off Marti's bind.

But Keira's attention was drawn back to the man before her, who was again on the attack. She dodged to the left as his sword came down, and she lunged for his exposed side.

He easily parried, forcing her to spin out of the way of his counterattack. Keira paused, dragging stinging air into her lungs as she took in her opponent. He was well-trained, much better than the usual Red Willow dregs. A former Bellator maybe?

Keira didn't have time to fixate on this thought, because he was again after her, and she stumbled back. She felt her mistake before her brain fully recognized it as her ankle rolled over an uneven rock and she was suddenly crashing to the ground.

She caught herself on one knee, wincing as pain raced up into her hip. But the guard was still advancing, and she threw herself to the side, rolling as his blade arced down into the space she'd only just vacated.

Keira kept rolling, hands scrambling at the rocky ground, catching herself perilously close to the cliff edge. She lifted her head, glancing down as she felt her stomach rebel at the sight of the dizzying drop. Motion to her left had her scrambling up, hands riffling desperately for the hilt of her blade as the guard descended on her.

Nothing.

Keira looked up into the man's eyes, seeing only his murderous intent. He was going to kill her, she realized. She reached inside herself, to Danny's reassuring presence in the back of her mind, but felt only a faint stirring. She wouldn't even be able to say goodbye.

Then a cry from the man made her glance up, and she saw his face contort with pain as he collapsed onto both knees. Behind his bulky frame, Raina's fierce green eyes met Keira's. She held a bloody dagger in one hand.

Keira lunged forward, grabbing the guard even as he grappled for his fallen blade. She gripped him by the straps of his leather armor and heaved him around, letting him roll off the cliff ledge.

His howls echoed off the rock walls as he fell, and Keira winced at the distant splash in the waves below.

She glanced at Raina, whose eyes were round as saucers as they looked between Keira and the bloody dagger in her hand. Raina dropped it with a clang onto the stone, and Keira reached for her, pulling her into a tight hug that Raina slowly returned.

"Well done," Keira said simply, looking over Raina's head to see the others slowly disentangling themselves from the other fallen guards.

Gradually, Raina's trembling ceased, and Keira held her out at arm's length, scanning her up and down in search of any injuries.

"Are you all right?" she asked. Raina's eyes met hers, and in their glassy appearance, Keira saw—not forgiveness, but perhaps something like acceptance. "Are *we* all right?" Keira asked instead.

Raina nodded before suddenly throwing her arms around Keira, burying her face in her shoulder as she gently rubbed her back.

"It's all right," Keira said quietly. Her eyes met Neval's as he bent to pocket the fallen dagger. He nodded, a small smile of encouragement pulling at his lips. "It's going to be all right."

～

1 Marian Era (M.E.)

THE LEGIONNAIRES' arrival was marked by all the pomp and circumstance the backwater capital could muster, and Magnus arrayed himself on the dais at the far end of the newly completed great hall like the imperial ruler he was—seemingly oblivious to the sounds of construction that echoed throughout as work continued on the East and West Wings.

Five legionnaires in total had come, and Danny easily spied Fitz leading the bunch, his startling blue eyes a mirror of Keira's. How had he never noticed that before?

"I told him," Tammy murmured, startling him from his thoughts. She nodded toward Fitz.

Danny shot her a glance. "About the baby?"

Tammy nodded. "He said we'd figure it out, find a way to make it work."

"So you're going to raise it yourself?" Danny couldn't help the flurry of hope that rose in his chest. Keira had grown up with her mother, so if Tammy was planning on raising her, then maybe things weren't as screwed up as he'd thought.

"We both are."

That caught him up short. Keira had insisted she'd never known her father. Danny glanced across the hall at Fitz, noting his affable demeanor and the relaxed tone of his arch British accent as he regaled the Marian courtiers with tales of his journey through the wilds of the uplands. Danny cringed at their tittering laughter. No, he didn't trust Fitz, not one bit.

But one glance at Tammy's awestruck face told him his thoughts would not be welcomed. So he kept those to himself.

"We're leaving the Legion, Danny. He promised me. We're catching the first ship out of here and heading to the Cross-Sea Lands. Apparently, the Legion has less of a presence there. They'll never know."

Danny swallowed, torn between happiness for his friend

and worry over exactly what this meant for Keira and the time-line they'd shared. He was saved from formulating a response by the sudden quieting of the crowd as Magnus raised his arms.

"Welcome, Legionnaires, to Crîd Eálas, the newly christened capital of Loren."

The cohort knelt upon reaching the stairs to the dais, but at some unseen signal, Fitz got to his feet.

"We thank you, Your Highness, for your hospitality. As a sign of the deep friendship between the Marian Empire and the Legion of Pneumos, and to honor your upcoming nuptials, we'd like to offer you this gift. May it grace your halls for a thousand years, as will our friendship."

Turning, Fitz gestured toward a wheeled cart that was, as they spoke, approaching the dais. With a theatrical gesture, he whipped away the large canvas that covered it, revealing an alabaster white marble basin. The marble was covered in intricate carvings that danced and wove in swirling spirals that seemed to burrow into the surface itself. And there was something else, a popping, crackling energy that caught Danny's attention, drawing him forward with one step and then another before he even realized what he was doing. He glanced at Tammy, who met his gaze with confusion of her own. She felt it too.

"What . . . is it?" Magnus asked, eyeing the marble basin with cautious interest. Clearly, he'd been expecting something more bejeweled, or at least with gold plating.

"It is an object of immense reverence and symbolism to our order—a gift only bestowed to the worthiest rulers of this world. It is a sign of our great respect for you and the Marian Empire. As long as it stands, it will serve as protection to you and Loren, a ward against the looming chaos and a preserver of the cosmic balance."

Magnus still looked dubious, but the flattery had clearly had its intended effect, as he inclined his head graciously. He gestured then, bringing forth servants to squirrel the marble basin away, no doubt to some remote cellar or tower where the rest of his more homely gifts were kept. Danny suspected it would simply gather dust and soon be forgotten, the Legion's favor along with it.

"There is one more thing," a cool, nasally voice said. Another legionnaire climbed to his feet. He was tall, with wide, intelligent eyes and a hooked nose over too-thin lips. Danny didn't know him, but something about the way the man took in the room with a single glance put him immediately on edge.

"Yes, yes, what is it? And who are you, exactly?" Magnus was clearly bored by the proceedings and eyed the tall Legionnaire with a look of annoyance.

"I'm called the Inspector," the man replied, seemingly oblivious to both Magnus's annoyance and Fitz's suddenly nervous shifting. "And the Legion has tasked me with seeking out one of our own—a Miss Tammy Altman?"

Danny froze, and Tammy inhaled sharply at his elbow.

Magnus raised one eyebrow before snapping his fingers impatiently. Rommel immediately stepped forward and, after a few whispered words to the Regio, turned to look directly at Danny and Tammy.

"Run," Danny said on impulse, turning to find Tammy staring at him with horror.

"How could you?" she whispered.

Danny gaped at her. "I didn't—"

But she was already running, shoving courtiers out of the way as she barreled toward the door and the free air beyond.

"Tammy—" He tried to run after her, but Rommel was too fast.

"Seize her!" Rommel cried, and Danny watched in cold disbelief as Bellators suddenly emerged from the shadows on either side of the hall. They lunged for Tammy, gripping her firmly under each arm. From behind him, Danny could hear the Inspector soothing a clearly ruffled Regio.

"Nothing to concern yourself with, Your Highness. Her presence is merely requested back at our headquarters."

Tammy writhed in their grip, kicking and twisting. But she was unarmed, as was custom in the presence of the Regio, and no match for two Bellators twice her size.

Danny didn't know what to do. He shot a glance at Fitz, who was staring resolutely at the floor, not even looking up as the mother of his child was hauled before the wide-eyed court.

Bastard.

Tammy's tear-filled eyes met Danny's before narrowing into slits of wrath.

"You," she snarled. "You swore! You promised me, O'Leary, damn you! First the Legion, then me! You and your resistance friends can go straight to hell!"

Danny's mouth fell open in horror as all eyes suddenly turned to him. He felt frozen, unsure whether to speak up or just run.

But one thing was for sure. He was finished being silent.

"Leave her alone," he cried, lunging forward even as firm hands gripped him on either side.

"What's this?" the Inspector asked, now staring at him with interest. "Are you saying he's turned traitor?"

"Tammy, *please*—" Danny pleaded, struggling against the arms that held him.

Tammy's eyes were cold as she gazed into his. There was no

mercy in their depths—only unadulterated pain. "I sure as hell am. You can search his tent. I'm sure you'll find all sorts of stolen documents. Troop movements, construction plans, all snatched from Rommel's own desk. He's been at it for months."

Danny felt the air squeeze from him in a rush, even as the hands that gripped his arms tightened.

"Oh dear," the Inspector said, tsking away like some disappointed schoolteacher. "Well, it seems we now have two cases to investigate. It is a good thing indeed you thought to bring me along, Fitz. Optimum efficiency, that's what I say."

The Inspector's jovial tone belied the nervous shifting of the spectators, and Rommel was having none of it. "If what she says is true, then we'd see justice done," he snarled, his face having turned the color of eggplant as he gazed furiously at Danny.

"Of course," the Inspector purred. "Just give us some time to get to the bottom of this. Justice will be done, I assure you."

Though they were discussing his own fate, Danny didn't spare a glance for the Inspector, Rommel, or even that scumbag, Fitz. He only had eyes for Tammy, and despite everything she'd just done and said, it broke his heart to see tears fill her eyes as she stared wide-eyed at Fitz. *He'd* been the one to bring the Inspector. She'd told him about the baby, and he'd brought the Inspector to have it dealt with.

With a snap of the Inspector's fingers, they were hauled from the great hall and into the Legion's own custody, and whatever punishment they had in store.

CHAPTER

THIRTY-NINE

242 Marian Era (M.E.)

The echoes of their footsteps resounded through the stone walls as Keira and the others crept through the tunnel that led toward the Vindolum's kitchen.

"Almost there," she muttered to no one in particular, willing the words to be true. She could have laughed with happiness at the sudden appearance of stairs as they rounded a corner. They hurried up, and Keira pressed an ear to the door before pushing through.

They were inside a storage room that Keira guessed to be just off the main kitchens. Sure enough, as they neared the door across the room, Keira spotted light spilling beneath its frame, and the smell of cooked meat permeated the room. And then she heard the voices.

". . . not what I signed up for," one voice hissed.

"Well, what exactly do you suggest?" another shot back. "It's too late now. The Bellatorio's already formed up outside. It's fight or die."

A low rumble of other voices joined in, and Keira blanched. It sounded like an entire room full of Red Willow guards, far too many to take on at once. She glanced at Neval and saw a look of equal consternation cross his face.

Slowly, she unsheathed her blade, but his hand on her arm made her pause. She shot him an annoyed look, but hesitated as she met his intent eyes.

"I know these men, Keira. They have no interest in making some suicide stand, especially if the Bellatorio really has gathered outside. If I tell 'em about the servants' entrance out of the Vindolum, they'll follow me."

Keira snorted, but her stomach clenched. "That or put a knife in your back," she hissed. "I don't think so."

Neval didn't laugh and his eyes caught hers, holding them fast. "There are too many of 'em, Keira, even with pneumonancy. I have to try, give us a fightin' chance."

Keira's mind churned with thoughts of how she could get them out of this. The Red Willow soldiers were blocking the only way out of the tunnels, the only means of getting to the South Tower—and Albert. They had to get around them.

"Trust me, Keira," Neval murmured quietly. "It's the only chance we've got."

Keira's breath caught as she searched his eyes, no sign of fear or doubt evident, only clear determination. And though every inch of her wanted to deny it, she knew he was right.

She nodded.

Neval's eyes sparkled with excitement mixed with no small amount of surprise. He hadn't expected her to trust him, she realized. Not really. Even as she thought the words, he suddenly leaned in, planting a quick peck on her cheek.

"Don't miss me too much, Keira dear," he said, winking. Then he ruffled Raina's hair, pulling the extra dagger from his back pocket and handing it to her. "Try not to stab anything you don't intend to, rabbit."

And then he was gone.

Keira gaped after him, feeling the others' stares on her back. She cleared her throat, as if that might clear the sudden fog that swept over her brain. She shook her head and pressed her ear to the door, straining to hear whatever might occur on the other side.

Neval's footsteps padded away as he emerged more fully into the kitchen, sporting the usual amount of jaunt to his step.

"Hello, boys. Looks like it's heatin' up out there."

There was a murmur of surprise at his sudden appearance, and Keira tensed, gripping the hilt of her sword as she prepared to rush out at the first sign of violence.

"I don't know about you all," Neval continued, "but I, for one, have no interest in waitin' for some damned Red Cloaks to come barging through that door. We've made our point. Perhaps it's time to save our strength for another day?"

There was a murmur of agreement and not a few relieved sighs.

"What do you lot say we make ourselves scarce? I happen to know a servants' entrance that the Red Cloaks are far too stupid to have caught on to yet."

There was a rumble of laughter and brief, muffled discussion. Keira held her breath, on edge as she waited for any sign of a decision.

Without warning, there came the sudden screech of stools on stone and the sound of voices and footsteps retreating into the distance. Keira breathed out a sigh of relief but couldn't squelch a pang of worry as she realized Neval would be forced to go with them, crawling back into whatever sewer hole they'd come from.

Keira and the others waited for several long minutes until all sounds from the kitchen had faded.

Raina's small voice at her arm caught her attention.

"Will he be all right, then?"

Keira glanced down into her worried expression as she turned the small dagger over in her palm and forced a smile onto her own face.

"Don't worry about Neval, Raina. It'll take more than a few angry revolutionaries to catch him. He'll be fine."

Raina nodded, the relief on her face a palpable pang as Keira shook off the guilt of her less than honest answer. But she didn't have time to worry about Neval. They still had to find Albert, and if the Bellatorio had already gathered, there wasn't much time left.

~

1 Marian Era (M.E.)

Danny and Tammy were hauled to the Legionnaires' quarters, a wood building not far from the Vindolum. He eyed their surroundings carefully, looking for any escape or means to fight their way out. But the room was the barest of guest lodgings, fit for purpose until the Vindolum could be completed. They were deposited unceremoniously in the center of the room, and Tammy's gag was the first to be removed.

"Who are you?" she demanded, eyeing the Inspector with unabashed suspicion.

For his part, the Inspector merely shrugged, settling himself in a chair across from them, hands folded neatly in his lap. "I told you, I'm the Inspector." Seeing their continued blank expressions, he sighed, looking thoroughly disappointed. "Honestly, we need to look at the expectations we're setting for our mentors. In my day, history and civic policy were a vital part of the trainee curriculum. But no matter. As the Inspector, I have the privilege of enforcing the Legion's rules and regulations. That said, since our rules haven't been updated in half a millennium, it means there are a fair number of *incidents* that slip through the cracks of strict fiat. I'm the unofficial arbiter of all such cases that arise within the Legion's jurisdiction."

Danny didn't have a clue what to make of this speech, and a quick glance at Tammy told him she was equally flummoxed.

The Inspector sighed again before addressing Tammy directly. "Let's make this simple, shall we? You're with child, yes?"

Tammy's lips pressed in a thin line, and she glared back at him. He'd get no confession from her.

"Well, you're not exactly hiding it, dear, if you'll excuse my saying so," he said with an apologetic nod at her abdomen. "Now, tell me, who's the father?"

She said nothing, and the Imperator made an exasperated noise before turning to the other Legionnaires, who now stood silently along the edges of the room. "Fitz?"

Tammy froze, eyes going wide as she stared at Fitz. He stepped forward, shifting awkwardly as he stood before the Inspector. "Sir?"

"Do you know who the father is?"

Fitz swallowed, and Danny saw Tammy's expression turn pleading as she stared at him, waiting for him to step forward, to claim her as his.

He didn't move. "I don't know, sir. She never said."

Tears filled Tammy's eyes, and she blinked them away, savagely biting her trembling lip until it stilled.

"Well, dear, have you nothing to say? No one else is to be implicated here?"

Tammy glared up at the Inspector, daring him with her eyes before giving two brief shakes of her head.

Danny felt her heartbreak then, the abandonment that weighed her down with every passing second. In a futile effort, he strained against the ties that bound his wrists. But they didn't budge.

The Inspector rubbed at his eyes, and Danny was surprised to see bags there. "Very well. You've left me with little choice, then."

"Is that it?" she demanded, gritting her jaw tightly enough that it almost disguised the tremble of her lower lip. "One screwup and I'm out? You're just going to, what—kill me now?"

The Inspector blinked before his face twisted into a look of incredulity. "Kill you? Whatever gave you that idea?"

Tammy blinked, betraying the surprise that crept over her features.

The Inspector chuckled. "My dear, you're not being punished. Quite the contrary. Do you know how rare it is for a child to be born to a pneumonancer? And if one were to be born to *two* pneumonancers? One in a million, my dear, and that's *not* exaggerating." He shook his head. And though his smile was warm, Danny couldn't help but tense at the fiendish excitement in his face as he gazed appreciatively at Tammy's abdomen. "Pneumos, my dear, has blessed you. *Now* will you tell me who the father is?"

Tammy hesitated, and from the corner of his eye, Danny saw Fitz stiffen.

Good.

But then she shook her head. "He can come forward if he cares to. I'm done giving out secrets." At that, she glanced apologetically at Danny, and he strained against his gag, his eyes trying to convey what his words could not.

It's ok. I forgive you.

"Well, if you're not going to kill me, then what's with the rigamarole?" Her hands perched on her hips, and she glared up at him.

The Inspector smiled kindly. "You're going home, my dear."

Tammy staggered back a step, paling. "N-No, I can't. I won't!"

"Don't worry, it won't hurt a bit. I'm not quite sure *how* it's done, but the High Council assures me—"

"I'm not going back," she said again, this time with a snarl.

The Inspector blinked in surprise before his expression turned hard.

"I'm afraid, my dear, that you don't have much of a choice. A child of the Legion cannot, *would* not, survive in any place beyond the home world. That first life *is* crucial, you know. Improper development can have disastrous effects—"

The words had barely escaped his lips when Tammy was up and sprinting for the door. It was Fitz who caught her there and, grim-faced, dragged her kicking and screaming back toward the Inspector.

The Inspector sighed. "Honestly, such theatrics. Very well, it seems we won't be having any *reasonable* conversation with you in this state. Go on, then, take her to the wagon. We'll just have to depart a bit earlier than planned—yet again, why I always insist on being ahead of schedule!"

Fitz handed Tammy off to the other Legionnaires, who dragged her outside. Danny squirmed in his seat, fighting the bonds as he tried and failed to catch her eye. But he could hear her shouts and pleading well enough.

The Inspector moved as if to follow, when a voice from

behind Danny asked, "Um, sir? What do we do with this one, then?"

"Oh my, so sorry. I'd completely forgotten!" The Inspector motioned toward the other Legionnaire, and Danny felt the gag pulled from his mouth.

He glared at the Inspector, snarling, "Is this really all we can expect? After loyal years of service to the Legion?"

The Inspector eyed him with remote interest, an inconvenience that needed to be dealt with, and quickly. "Loyal service? Is that what you call it, Mr. O'Leary? I thought you'd turned traitor."

Danny's nostrils flared, but he didn't argue.

"I'm afraid the Legion has little use for those we cannot trust. But ultimately, that decision is not mine to make. I'm sure the Bellatorio has already ransacked your quarters for any evidence that might be hidden there and is, as we speak, calling for your head. No, I'm afraid you'll have to be turned over to the Bellatorio. Let them deal with your betrayal as *they* see fit. They'd demand nothing less."

Danny felt suddenly cold, the image of the bloody coronation field flashing in his memory. But he sat still, refusing to give the Inspector the pleasure of seeing him squirm.

"Yes, I think that would be most fitting. And as for your future service, well, we'll let Pneumos deal with you in the between-worlds. Let her decide if you're truly worthy to call yourself a Legionnaire."

The Inspector snapped his fingers, and the door opened. Danny was barely aware of the approaching footsteps before rough hands seized hold of him and he felt himself dragged up and out of his seat. The heels of his boots scrabbled against the floor as he was hauled backward, trying and failing to get a grip on the dusty wood planks as his bound hands twisted uselessly before him. On either side, red-cloaked Bellators flanked him, their faces cut from stone.

When he glanced back, he saw the Inspector had already turned away, but one set of sapphire-blue eyes still gazed after him. Fitz watched as Danny was dragged out, his face betraying keen interest and a question burning deep in his eyes.

~

242 Marian Era (M.E.)

THE FIVE OF them moved through the Vindolum, slipping in and out of unused halls and diving through closed doors at the sound of approaching feet. Most had merely been servants bustling about their business, radiating fear as they tried to avoid the Vindolum's new occupants. Still, Keira knew they had to keep their progress a secret if they hoped to make it to Albert in time. From outside, the sounds of the Bellators' marching feet had been replaced by shouted taunts. Keira hoped Cyrus and Landry were keeping them in check—luring Red Willow and the Worshippers of Séiro out, distracting them without actually engaging. Even so, everything depended on them making it to the South Tower.

Keira was just debating the merits of simply making a run for it, curious servants be damned, when a ball of fire suddenly erupted from the doorway ahead of them.

Pneumonancers.

Keira's hand found Raina's, and they froze, eyes darting across the hallway for any sign of escape. But there was nothing. It was either go forward or fall back and find a different path.

A raucous chorus of laughter echoed from the open doorway. There were too many of them, Keira realized. They couldn't risk it. She raised a hand toward the others, gesturing back the way they'd come, and was met with nods of agreement.

"*Please!* Please, I have work to do. Just let me—"

Another jet of flame erupted from the doorway ahead, and laughter drowned out the panicked screech from the servant inside.

Every muscle in Keira's body tensed, and she met Zipporah's eyes, alight with fury. The sound of begging and sobs echoed down the hall, and she saw Zipporah's face harden into a look of grim determination.

"Zipporah—" Keira warned. But it was too late. Zipporah was already moving toward the open door. Keira lunged for her arm, but Zipporah easily shook her off.

"I'm not leaving them," she snarled. "I won't."

Keira glanced to Marti, expression pleading, but Marti's face was strained as she looked only at Zipporah, eyes communicating something Keira couldn't comprehend. Then she nodded.

Keira threw up her hands. "I know you want to save them," she hissed, turning back to Zipporah, "but there's no *time*. And if we don't stop Albert, it won't matter. They'll be here for good."

Zipporah crossed her arms over her chest, face like stone. Keira was just about to try another tack when a sneering voice echoed off the walls behind them.

"Now, who do we have here?"

Keira spun around, hand reaching for her sword as she came face-to-face with three leering men in black cloaks, their tattooed faces glinting in the flickering torchlight.

"Take Raina and go!" Zipporah snarled, lunging toward them. "Let us hold them off."

"N-No, that wasn't the plan," Keira sputtered, eyes darting around the hallway as more and more cloaked figures appeared. It was only a matter of seconds before the pneumonancers in the room heard the commotion and came to investigate. She turned to Elliott. "*You* were supposed to face Albert. I-I can't. I already failed—"

She couldn't leave them, couldn't abandon her friends to a fight they'd never win.

"It's the only way," Elliott snapped, holding her gaze as her eyes pleaded with his. "There are too many of them. Zipporah and Marti can't hold them off alone. We'd never make it to the tower. Only you can do this—now."

"What are you talking about?" Keira demanded, not bothering to hide the panic rising in her voice. "I don't even have a grounder. I can't stop him."

Elliott's eyes bored into hers, and she saw something like amusement there. "You don't need a grounder, Keira. You never did. Everything tethering you to this world, this life, is right in here." He gripped her shoulder then, thumb digging into the place just below her collarbone. "You know what needs to be done—the only way to stop him."

Keira's eyes widened as she stared at him. "N-No, I can't. *Please*, Elliott."

But he only shook his head. "I can't do this for you, Keira. Now go. You're almost out of time."

He glanced pointedly at Raina, whose trembling lip betrayed the terror beneath her brave expression as her knuckles turned white around the hilt of Neval's dagger.

Keira nodded. She didn't trust herself to look back at her friends, didn't trust the emotion that was rapidly filling her chest as she gripped Raina's arm and they turned to sprint past the open doorway.

They had to find Albert. It was the only way to stop this.

~

1 Marian Era (M.E.)

DANNY SPENT a week in the Vindolum's newly constructed dungeons, awaiting the start of his trial. Cold, hungry, and increasingly desperate, he spent his days tightly bound and gagged, according to the strict instructions of the Inspector. He suspected that this fact alone had kept him from the torture room—his captors were too afraid of exactly what his pneumonancy might do if he were ungagged long enough to give names. Still, he spent his days lying on cold stone as he listened to the screams of those far less lucky than him. And slowly the despair sank in. Once in a while, his thoughts would flit to Keira, to her soft curls or teasing smile, but he'd quickly banish the thought—determined not to let the desperation of that place sully what precious memories he still had.

Finally, the day of the trial arrived, and Danny was hauled from his cell, blinking at the shock of sunlight and the world above. The trial, if that's what you wanted to call it, was over in minutes. Imperator Rommel read the list of Danny's crimes and presented the evidence gathered from his quarters. Magnus passed the sentence.

"Guilty."

Danny blinked. That was it. It was all over. His eyes searched the gathered crowd, and he thought he saw a flash of red hair. But when he looked again, it had disappeared into the mass of jeering spectators. It was just as well. There was nothing Moira or Red Willow could do for him now.

"The sentence for such treason is, of course, death. However," Magnus paused, letting the words hang in the air as the crowd fell silent, "I'm willing to show mercy and commute your sentence to life imprisonment, on one condition."

Danny waited, staring bleary-eyed up at the Regio. Weariness weighed on every inch of him, and he wanted nothing more than to fall into the deepest sleep of his life.

"Give us names. Tell us who all you worked with."

Danny blinked slowly at him before clearing his throat pointedly. Magnus snapped his fingers, and the gag was removed. Danny swallowed, relishing the feeling even as a Bellator stood with a knife pressed to the hollow of his throat, lest he get any ideas.

"Well?" Magnus asked, impatient now to have things over and done with.

Danny stared at him, remembering the coronation field painted red with the blood of innocent servants. His eye traced the hard, unyielding angles of the Regio's face before drifting down the soft lines of his body—evidence enough of his privilege and power. This man was nothing. A king, yes. A Regio, yes. He had armies at his disposal, soldiers to command. But in the end, he was just a scared bully. And Danny knew well enough how to deal with bullies.

"Long live the tree from which liberty springs." He said each word like a chant, building in power and volume as he went. "Red Willow rises!"

There was a gasp from the crowd as the gag was shoved roughly back into his mouth. They forced him to his knees, bones cracking with the impact, but not before he saw Magnus pale, his eyes going wide and darting around the gathered assembly. And in his heart, Danny knew that, powerful as he was, Magnus would sleep with one eye open from now on, never knowing who to trust and who to fear, the paranoia slowly eating away at him. Danny hoped he choked on it.

They placed a wooden block before him, and Danny swallowed the tang of fear that coated his mouth. This was it. His number was finally up.

"Centus Flavius, if you please."

Danny glanced up in surprise. But of course, it wasn't the grizzled Gaius Flavius who stalked toward him, though they shared the same steel-gray eyes. Perhaps a great-great-grandfather, he thought remotely. There was some irony in that, he decided.

The Centus approached with sword drawn and gleaming in the noonday sun, and rough hands pressed Danny's head against the block with enough force to leave bruises. *Not that I'll have time to bruise*, he thought remotely. And something about that seemed almost funny. He really was losing his mind.

Danny glimpsed light reflecting off metal as the blade was raised above him, and his eyes drifted to the sky and the lazy dance of two swallows through the clouds. And he let himself think about her, just this once. For the last time, he imagined Keira turning toward him, face lit up in surprise, her smile broad as she beckoned him toward her.

Then everything went black.

242 Marian Era (M.E.)

They made it to the tower with only a few unexpected encounters, all of which were easily dispatched. Raina proved surprisingly adept in the use of Neval's little dagger, and Keira made a mental note to make sure she got some proper training once this was all over. If they made it that far, that is.

When they finally reached the winding stairs of the South Tower, Keira heaved a sigh of relief tinged with trepidation. How, *exactly*, was she going to do this?

She turned to Raina. "Wait here. I'll deal with Albert."

Raina snorted. "I don't think so, *grelún*. I be coming with you, thank you very much."

Keira rubbed a hand roughly across her face. She didn't have time for this. "Look, Raina, I need someone to guard the stairs. I don't know what Albert will do, and I don't need anyone getting hurt."

"And what if you be getting hurt?" Raina demanded,

crossing her arms in a perfect imitation of Zipporah. One eyebrow arched imperiously.

"I'll be fine," Keira said, infusing confidence she didn't really feel into every syllable.

Raina said nothing, but her mouth was fixed in a straight line, and her chin jutted up at an angle that Keira knew all too well. She felt the seconds ticking by with the force of a dirge as she stared Raina down.

Keira groaned. "Fine," she snapped. "But stay back, and if I tell you to run, then I don't want one word of argument." Her eyes narrowed as they bored into Raina's, widened in innocence but unable to hide the excitement that gleamed there.

Raina nodded vigorously, and Keira reluctantly turned to climb the stairs.

BY THE TIME they emerged into the airy room, Keira's nerves were wound taut, and her eyes darted around the tower's interior. She spotted the marble basin first, standing alone in the same alcove as before—only now Keira could feel the power pulsing from the conduit within it, intensified by the power of the equinox and drawing her toward its inscrutable depths. She'd already taken two steps forward without consciously deciding to do so when a voice from behind caught her up short.

"So lovely of you to join me," Albert crooned.

Keira slowly turned, to find him leaning casually against the far wall, not even bothering to face them as he gazed instead out on the city below. Keira surreptitiously moved to put herself between him and Raina.

"I didn't know we were invited," she said acerbically,

quickly scanning the length of him. No sign of weapons. Albert didn't reply, only continued staring out at the city below, as if their drawn blades were of no concern to him.

"It's intoxicating, isn't it?" he asked instead. "The chaos. It's really more than I ever expected, and it's all thanks to you." Finally, he turned toward her, his smile widening into a pointed grin.

Only then did Keira hear what had clearly caught his attention. The Bellatori taunts that had crept through the Vindolum's open windows during their ascent to the tower had turned into shouted orders, screams, and the clash of steel. The shaky standoff had finally collapsed. Keira felt the blood drain from her face.

Landry . . . Cyrus . . . Neval.

The Bellatori show of force had been intended as a distraction, drawing the attention of Red Willow and the Worshippers of Séiro so they could make it to the tower. They weren't supposed to fight. And yet there it was, the thrum of chaos building around them. It echoed off the stone walls of the Vindolum, and she could feel the pulse of it emanating from the marble basin behind her, the conduit's power practically throbbing within.

Keira pressed her palm flat against her thigh to keep it from shaking. And she swallowed the swell of panic in her throat. She had to focus. As if reading her thoughts, Albert's smile grew wider.

"Yes, you brought chaos directly to my doorstep, Keira. And now here you are. Are you ready to help build my army?" He pushed off from the wall, coming to stand before her.

"Like hell I am," Keira spat, twisting the hilt of her sword in her hand, imagining what it would feel like to plunge it through his heart. It was because of him that Akamu and Aelianna were dead. He'd killed them as surely as if he'd run them through himself.

"We're here to stop you, Albert."

Albert arched one eyebrow at her. "*We?*"

Keira's eyes darted to her side, but Raina was nowhere to be seen. She spun around, but the room was empty but for the two of them. Slowly, with dawning horror, Keira turned back toward Albert's smug condescension. And there she was, dark hair fanning out and green eyes glinting with fury at Albert's unsuspecting back, Neval's dagger clutched in one hand.

Keira's eyes widened, but she didn't dare call out as Albert's eyes narrowed further in suspicion.

Then Raina lunged, the knife digging deep into Albert's side as she stabbed once, twice.

Albert howled, grabbing for her as she leapt out of the way, falling backward. Keira dove forward, gripping hold of one arm just as a blast of energy sent them both flying back.

Keira landed hard, the wind knocked out of her as she rolled over, scrambling for the sword that had flown from her hand. Her fingers found it as she spotted Albert stalking toward Raina's sprawled form, eyes murderous. Keira heaved herself to her feet, staggering toward him as another blast of energy hit her.

But instead of throwing her back, this one latched onto her. Keira squirmed as she felt talons of Albert's pneuma pierce her, sinking deep as she tried desperately to writhe out of his grasp.

But the more she pulled away, the tighter his grip became, and Keira felt a rising swell of panic as she felt control of her own body wrested from her and she was forced down to her knees, barely noticing the sharp pain as they made impact with the cold stone floor.

Remember . . . lessons.

Danny's voice was far away, as if shouted from across a field, but Keira seized onto it in her panic.

Can't pull away . . . dig in.

And then Keira was back at the farmhouse near Abalás, facing off against one of the Séiro Worshippers. Keira remembered the icy feel of the woman's pneuma after she'd lured Keira into attempting a bind, the talons that seized hold, threatening to suck her into her own stream of consciousness.

Keira stopped fighting.

Albert's pneuma surged forward, and she thought she caught a whiff of his surprise in his pneuma's swift advance.

She waited until his muscle bind was almost complete, feeling his pneuma inch a centimeter too close to her own subconscious.

And then she lunged.

She dug her own talons in this time, suppressing a shudder as she let her pneuma wind in and through Albert's. She felt the surprise that gripped him and smiled in satisfaction as it swiftly shifted to panic. He tried to withdraw, tried to pull back from her viselike grip. But she only dragged him deeper, pulling him toward her own stream of consciousness, to the murky depths that would leave him *undone*.

He would pay. She would make him pay.

A cry broke the trance.

Keira's eyes flew open to find Raina held tight in Albert's grip, a blade pressed to her throat. Without thinking, Keira released her pneuma's hold on him, letting his talons slither away to the safety of his own body.

Albert was breathing heavily, eyes still glassy from his canting. How had he moved?

Albert chuckled breathlessly, no doubt seeing her confusion.

"There's still much you don't understand about the art of pneumonancy, Keira. I could teach you, would love to teach you. You'd be the most powerful Legionnaire of your generation. But first, I need something from you."

"You can go to hell, Albert," Keira spat.

Raina whimpered as Albert's blade pressed harder to her throat, and Keira's breath hitched.

"Now, now," Albert tsked. "There's no reason to be rude. No, go on, Keira. The conduit is ready, practically *humming* with power, actually. You should be able to make quick work of the job. You can even start with your grounder—Danny, was it? I know how long you've been waiting to see him again."

Keira's thoughts raced, eyes roving from Albert to Keira and then to the dais. The temptation was there, stronger than she'd like.

"Why me?" she asked instead, buying time. "Why not do it yourself? You're clearly powerful enough."

Albert laughed aloud at her blatant pandering but inclined his head, considering the question. "The conduit can't be wielded by just anyone, Keira. But *you*, you're special—your gifts with healing pneumonancy second to none. I likely could develop the technique, but it would take a while, and I find myself—*impatient*. And with your tether to your grounder, Danny, I think he'll be the perfect test case. Once you've grown more confident in your skills, we'll turn your gifts to more *practical* purposes."

"And you'll what? Hold Danny hostage to make me do it?" The bitter taste of fury coated her mouth, and she felt an echoing twinge vibrate along her tether to Danny.

Albert's grin widened and he shrugged. "I play the long game, you see, Keira. It will take more than one equinox bloodbath to see my plans fulfilled. But this is a fine start."

Danny would hate her, hate himself, if she left him to that. But the desire to see him, to *hold* him, was a palpable ache in her soul. Keira swallowed the lump that had formed in her throat, blinking away the stinging in her eyes. Albert had left her with little choice.

"I'll do it," she said finally. Albert's smile was broad, victorious. "But first, let Raina go," she added. "She's just a kid, and you only get one hostage today."

Albert considered her words, taking her measure, before slowly releasing his hold on Raina. She staggered forward, and Keira reached out a hand to pull her close, squeezing her tightly.

Albert cleared his throat pointedly.

Keira intertwined her fingers with Raina's before turning toward the marble dais and the thrumming conduit within it.

Don't . . . Keira.

Danny's voice was pleading, but Keira ignored it, leading them across the room. Albert trailed them but kept his distance, arm clutched protectively around his bleeding side.

When they were several yards away, Keira murmured out of the corner of her mouth, "You remember Aelianna's practice?"

Raina's wide eyes raised to meet hers, and she gave a tiny, almost imperceptible nod.

"On my count."

With every step, the conduit drew closer, its beckoning energy pulsing in Keira's veins.

"One . . ." Keira's fingers tightened around Raina's hand. "Two . . ." Raina squeezed her fingers in silent encouragement. "Three!"

Keira dropped Raina's hand and spun around, dropping to a crouch as her fingers pressed to the ground. She whistled, and her pneuma sprang forward, hitting Albert like a javelin. He staggered back in surprise. She spread her pneuma out thin, seeping into every corner of him. The sense of being untethered was nearly overwhelming, but Keira suppressed the nauseous upheaval of her rebellious stomach, focusing instead on evading the talons of Albert's own pneuma. She just needed to hold him, distract him long enough for the pneuma-suppressing net of Raina's practice to settle in. *Come on, come on*, she thought, gritting her teeth against the force of Albert's bone-rattling attacks on her bind.

And then she felt it. Like an icy mist settling in overhead, Raina's net settled around them, and Keira felt her bind sputter and dissipate. She quickly withdrew it, staggering back into her body.

She turned to see Raina, a look of fierce concentration on her face as she moved through the movements Aelianna and her ladies had taught her, beads of sweat already lining her brow. Released from her own bind, Albert's hands balled into fists, and Keira felt his pneuma twisting and curling as it burrowed into the invisible wall that stood between them.

He's too powerful, Keira realized. Even from this distance, she could feel the strength of it. From outside came the clash of steel as the Bellators launched their assault on the Vindolum. And within the fortress itself echoed the faint explosions of fire and flame as her friends battled the Worshippers of Séiro. There were just too many of them.

"It's no use, Keira," Albert snarled through shallow breaths. "You can't save them all. You'll be lucky if you can save yourself. Give it up. *Join me*, and we'll bring back everyone we've ever lost."

The temptation was palpable, an ache in her chest begging her to just give in as Danny's olive-green eyes twinkled in her memory. What she'd give to see him again. She'd once thought she'd give everything—anything to hold him in her arms once more.

But that was before. Before she'd found a family, friends who were at that very moment risking their lives for her. And she knew then that as much as she might wish to save the person she'd loved and lost, it couldn't be at the cost of the family she'd only just found.

With a strangled cry from Albert, his pneuma pierced through Raina's wall, and he took two staggering steps toward them.

"Prepare yourself for what may come—the sacrifice that Pneumos may ask of you if the chaos Albert's unleashed can't be stopped."

And with a jolt, Keira suddenly knew exactly what she had to do.

"Hold him!" she screamed at Raina as she sprinted for the conduit. He was simply too powerful, the carnage he would have wrought too horrendous. She couldn't let him do it, couldn't let him destroy everything they'd tried to build here.

I'm sorry, Danny, she thought, feeling the tears slip down her cheeks as her fingers curved over the cool marble lip of the basin.

"NO!" Albert cried from behind her, and Keira heard Raina let out a squeak of pain as he blasted apart the last remnants of her wall.

Fury flared inside, and her grip tightened on the basin. How dare this man threaten her and the people she loved. He'd already taken so much. Well, she'd take something in return. She'd make him pay, even if it cost her everything.

And with that, Keira dug deep down inside herself, toward the pulsing ball of pneuma. And with a high-pitched whistle, she sent it coursing through the marble itself. Inside, Keira saw the pearl grow red-hot as the encasing glass rippled, its molecules shifting to an almost liquid-like consistency.

Keira poured yet more pneuma into the stone, ignoring the ripping sensation in her own body as the conduit's energy pulsed through her. It was like straining against an immovable boulder as Keira tried desperately to tease apart the ancient molecules that held it.

"Hurry, Keira!" Raina cried.

More, Keira thought. *I need more.*

She dug deep then, deeper than she ever had before, as she dredged up every last piece of pneuma she could. She poured it all in, every single piece of her scarred and weary soul. Keira gave it all away.

She knew the moment it happened, when she peaked the initial energy hump, catalyzing the conduit's own self-destruction.

For a split second, the roaring in her ears ceased, replaced by a ringing silence that threatened to shatter her very bones.

And then she was flying through the air.

Her last thought was of her mother's laugh, the spatter of rain against a windshield, and the flash of headlights coming directly toward her.

Then there was nothing.

CHAPTER

FORTY-ONE

She felt the light before her eyes even opened, its warmth spreading across her face. Her eyes flickered open to meet the dark burgundy of an overhead balcony. She registered it mere moments before the pain hit.

Every inch of her body felt like it had been run through a meat grinder, and she groaned aloud.

"Take it easy," a low voice murmured. "No need to rush things."

Keira glanced over to find Elliott perched on a seat beside a roaring fire. A savage bruise stretched across his cheek, and Keira could just make out the tip of a blistering burn peeking out above his collar.

It all came back in an instant, and Keira heaved herself upright, instantly regretting the motion as a piercing pain shot through her skull. She groaned again, blinking away the stars that suddenly blurred her vision and breathing through the nausea that swept over her.

"I told you to take it easy," Elliott chided. A cool, damp rag suddenly appeared in her vision, and Keira gratefully

438

accepted it, pressing it against her forehead with a relieved sigh.

"What happened? Where's Albert? Who—who made it out?"

"The Bellatorio took some heavy losses, but otherwise we fared quite well, thanks to you." Elliott's smile was kind, and pride shone from his eyes. "You did well, Keira. Better than I expected, even. The conduit is gone, destroyed. The strength of the blast took out half the South Tower, thus the source of your headache, I presume."

"Cyrus? Landry?"

"Both fine."

"Neval?"

"Broken arm, but sporting it bravely. Preening about, actually, like some sort of war hero." Keira registered his sarcasm but couldn't muster up the strength to laugh.

"That sounds like him," she said wearily. "Marti? Zipporah?"

"Scrapes and bruises, a few burns, courtesy of the pneumonancers, but recovering nicely."

A terrifying thought suddenly occurred to her, and Keira's eyes shot up to meet his. "Raina! Where's Raina? She was in the tower with me—"

"I'm fine."

Relief flooded through Keira as she looked over to see Raina hovering nervously at the foot of the bed. Had she been there the whole time? She hadn't even heard her come in.

"I told *you* to get some sleep," Elliott chided gently, one eye arching imperiously. "Seems someone's gotten better with their light bending."

Raina grinned broadly, eyes shining with pride at the compliment.

"And what about Albert?"

Elliott's eyes clouded at her question, and his lips pressed into a thin line. "There's been no sign of him. We don't know if he was killed in the explosion, or—"

"If he's off plotting something new," Keira finished. She sighed, feeling her headache spread down into the muscles of her neck.

"We'll sort that out later," Elliott said gently. "For now, let's just be grateful we all made it through this round."

Keira nodded, massaging the base of her skull.

"You're really ok, Keira?" Raina asked in a small voice, and Keira glanced up to see worry painting those bright green eyes in muted shadow.

Keira forced a smile onto her face and flicked Raina's nose gently. "I'll be fine, *dinué*. Nothing to worry about."

"Now that we're all reassured, I think it's time we got some sleep. There are still several hours before dawn."

Keira nodded and eased herself back onto the bed. Raina crawled up beside her, curling into a ball, eyes daring Elliott to say something about it. Keira could hear his chuckling recede into the hallway as she drifted off to sleep.

KEIRA SLEPT FITFULLY. Tossing and turning between dreams of a dank cell and shadowed faces passing judgment.

When her eyes flickered open, it was just after dawn, and Raina was still fast asleep beside her. Keira slipped gingerly from the bed, trying not to wake her as she pulled on clothes and boots and crept out of the room. Her feet carried her, almost of their own volition, down through the spiraling servants' staircase and out the side entrance of the Vindolum.

Outside, she gulped down the moist morning air gratefully, letting the light mist soothe her still-throbbing head.

"Up early, aren't we?"

Keira blinked and found Elliott perched on the garden wall, book in hand. "I could say the same of you."

Elliott shrugged, snapping his book closed and getting to his feet. "Care for a walk? It really is a lovely morning."

His eyes were kind, as if he understood her desperate need to escape, the tightness in her chest that demanded free air beyond the stone confines of the Vindolum. Perhaps he even shared it.

She nodded, and the two of them started down the path that led to the markets. All around them, the city bore the scars of the last two days. The streets were littered with rubble and refuse, while many shop fronts stood burnt out or with holes in their crumbling exteriors. The people around them moved quickly, scurrying about their tasks without making eye contact, as if to linger too long might draw unwanted attention.

Keira remained silent. In truth, she didn't have the energy to comment. It took everything she had just to put one foot in front of the other, following Elliott with little sense of where they were going.

Finally, they found themselves at a graveyard, of all places. Keira gaped. Unlike the rest of the city, the graveyard was filled with townspeople gathered in groups and murmuring quietly. Each bore brightly colored flowers, candles, and cloth decorations. And though their voices were muted, they acted not as mourners but as celebrants.

Keira glanced curiously at Elliott, who shrugged.

"It's a tradition," he explained. "The morning after the equinox, families gather to visit the graves of their ancestral dead. It's always a balance, you see. At equinox we celebrate spring and rebirth, but we never lose sight of all we've lost. We honor the harmony between order and chaos—bringing light into the darkness and honoring death even amid the joy of life."

Keira contemplated his words as she watched a woman sweep the ashes and fallen debris from a grave, gently laying her flowers before it even as she pressed a hand from her lips to the stone surface, gently tracing the letters as she went.

"Why did he do it?" Keira asked finally, staring at her. "I don't understand how anyone just gives up everything for power, for a chance at control."

Elliott considered her for a moment, lips pressed tight. "Albert always felt like a leaf on the wind, tossed from one path to the next and buoyed by the expectations of others. I think he felt that he never really had control of his own life, that things in this world or the last always happened *to* him rather than *by* him. And loss, Keira," Elliott added quietly. "Never underestimate the power of loss and grief. When we feel everything has been taken from us, we may very well stop at nothing to reclaim what we believe to be ours."

The silence that followed was pointed, and Keira kicked up the dust around her feet as her hands clenched and unclenched around the lip of the bench.

"I wanted to save him so badly," Keira said, voice raw as she choked back tears. "I would have done anything—I almost did."

"But you didn't," Elliott replied gently. "When the stakes were made clear, you chose your love for your friends. You gave up the thing you wanted most. That's what being a leader is, Keira."

"But I hurt so many people. I lied and manipulated and risked their lives. I'm a selfish piece of shit."

"You're human," Elliott said quietly, squeezing her arm

gently until she met his eyes. "We hurt people. Whether intended or not, it's what we do. What matters most is how you try to fix it."

Keira nodded, and they sat together in silence. She understood what he was saying, knew she had to find a way to forgive herself and move on. There were people counting on her now and a city to rebuild—again. Once more, she reached out to that space in her mind where Danny and his tether had lain for so long. Its absence felt like a gaping hole, a piece of herself that had gone missing in the equinox's aftermath, blown apart as surely as the exploding conduit.

"What do I do now?" she asked finally, feeling the emptiness pulse, threatening to expand and encompass all that she was.

Elliott considered her. "What do you want to do?"

What did she want? Part of her thought she'd want nothing ever again. But there was another part, a truer part, that knew the answer.

"I want to go home."

Elliott nodded, the sadness in his own eyes a perfect mirror of her own, and he put an arm around her shoulders, tugging her close. She leaned into him, relishing the solidness that seemed to keep the void in her heart at bay.

"Let's go home, then."

Keira nodded, standing to follow him from the graveyard. Then a flash of movement caught her eye and she turned, blinking against the sun toward a figure that stood half-shadowed in a nearby alleyway. Familiar hazel eyes gazed back at her.

Mom?

She blinked and her mother's face seemed to morph before her eyes, skin glowing an ethereal shade and curls rippling in a non-existent breeze. Keira squeezed her eyes shut, opening them to find the mirage disappeared. She let out a breath she didn't know she'd been holding. The concussion, it had to be the concussion making her see things.

This fight isn't over yet, Keira.

The voice was clear, echoing in her mind with the same solid surety as Danny's had. But it wasn't Danny's voice this time, and it certainly wasn't her mother's. Though it shared a similar timbre, this voice was richer and far more ancient than anything Keira had ever heard before.

Who are you?

The voice made no reply.

"Keira?" Elliott's voice was soft, but she started as if the words had been shouted. She turned to find his eyes creased with worry. "Is everything all right?"

She glanced back once more, reassuring herself of the alley-way's emptiness before nodding weakly. It hadn't been real. It *couldn't* be real. She squelched the nagging sensation that pulled at the edges of her mind and followed Elliott back to the Vindolum.

CHAPTER
FORTY-TWO

Two Months Later

Keira's face hit the dirt as she sprawled on the ground. She jerked to the side, staggering into a crouch as she squared off against the massive black panther before her. Its great purple eyes glinted with an otherworldly intelligence, and its lips flared into a snarl as it prowled around her. She was completely unarmed, equipped only with her bare hands and the pneuma that vibrated like a coiled snake in her gut.

This was the final trial—the last obstacle that lay between her and claiming her place as a full Legionnaire. The panther paced around her, and she moved with it, poised in a half crouch, arms up and at the ready—useless though they might be.

She waited, slowing her breathing to barely a whisper as every nerve in her body homed in on the opponent before her. She kept her eyes trained on the panther's chest, attuned to any shift in the rippling muscles beneath its skin.

A moment passed, and then another, before a flicker of movement to her left caught her attention.

"Keira, look out!" The voice was Raina's, and Keira's eyes shot to the spectator booths that rose high all around her before she spun on her heel to face a second panther that suddenly sprang from the shrubbery and joined the first in their spiraling death stalk. She tried to keep both in her line of vision, but they moved in perfect sync, diametrically opposed as they paced around her.

Any moment now, they'd strike. Keira's eyes darted around the clearing, searching desperately for something, anything, she could use as a weapon. Nothing. Even the spectators above her had fallen silent, all waiting for the strike they knew was coming.

A flicker of motion to her left was the only warning she had before the panther struck, leaping toward her with inch-long claws extended.

Keira dove, rolling under the panther's arcing leap and emerging in a crouch, fingers digging deep into the moist earth. She pumped everything she had into the ground, the coiled snake in her belly finally getting its chance. The panther hit the ground where she'd just been as the earth beneath it crumbled.

The panther screamed as it fell through the ground itself—a deep pit materializing in the void left by her pneuma's path—every atom of the soil shifted out of place, leaving an epic chasm.

Keira's eyes flashed to the second panther, the keen intelligence in its unnaturally violet eyes gleaming with fury. It sprinted for her, dodging the clefts her pneuma carved through the ground in its path.

The distance between them evaporated, and suddenly the

panther was on her—claws outstretched as it reached for her throat.

She hit it with everything she had, throwing her pneuma in a wide net that wrapped around it. The animal thrashed, shredding its confines as she desperately clung to it, burrowing her pneuma into every nook and cranny she could find.

And then she *was* the panther.

She stretched languidly, admiring the feel of rippling muscle down her back as her claws dug deep into the soft, moist earth. Opening her eyes, she saw the world no longer muted in darkness, but clear and detailed despite the low light. She saw herself kneeling with fingers wound deep into the soil.

Keira sifted through the creature's mind, soothing as she went, quieting the panther's thoughts until she felt it settle to the ground, curling in on itself as it collapsed into a deep, unnatural sleep.

Keira slowly began to untether herself, methodically unwinding every inch of pneuma from the creature's psyche as she reeled herself back into her body. The distance was short, manageable even without a grounder, but still she worked slowly, careful not to lose hold of that tiny thread of tether tying her pneuma to herself.

And then she was back.

Keira's eyes flickered open to see the panther melt away, dissolving into its constitutive molecules. She staggered to her feet, exhausted but triumphant. The crowd roared, and Keira turned in a circle, admiring the sheer number of Legionnaires who'd come to watch, to watch *her*.

"Congratulations," a young girl's voice announced, and Keira spun around to find the members of the High Council striding toward them. Each was bedecked in long, flowing robes, and they were led by a young girl who looked no more than eight or nine. Keira wasn't fooled, though, recognizing Zoya from her appearance before the council only a few months before.

Keira knelt on one knee, as was custom, and from the edge of her vision, she saw the council members stop before her. Zoya's braids were piled into a crown that steepled high above her head, adding several inches to her diminutive frame. Her dark skin gleamed in the torchlight that had flickered to life with the panther's dying breaths.

"Keira Altman, defender of Pneumos and enemy of Séiro," Zoya began, raising a hand to quiet the crowd even as her voice echoed around the spectator boxes, "you have fulfilled the ancient rites of the Legion of Pneumos. I hereby declare your Trials complete. Rise, Legionnaire!"

The crowd erupted in applause, and Keira rose to her feet, a sensation of buoyancy fluttering to life in her chest. She'd finally done it. After everything, she'd finally completed the Trials.

You'd be proud, Danny. I just wish you were here to see it.

She nudged the empty space where Danny's voice had been. It had been silent since the conduit was destroyed, and there had been no recurrence of the strange, ancient voice she'd heard in the cemetery—the one that seemed to speak from her mother's altered, ethereal countenance. She'd long ago chalked up *that* particular encounter to traumatic brain injury.

She was soon drawn from her musings by the sound of the audience dispersing. She shook hands with each council member, thanking them for the opportunity. They murmured their congratulations and best wishes for her service moving forward. When she'd finished, she took a deep breath, rubbing the back of her neck as the creeping sense of exhaustion teased at the edges of her waning adrenaline.

"That was amazing!"

Keira turned just in time to see Raina pounce. Keira caught her with a laugh tinged with a grunt of pain as the young girl collided with any number of partially healed bruises. It had been a long two weeks. The Trials were an ancient rite of passage for all Legionnaires, and the rules dictated only twenty-four hours of rest between each challenge. Stamina, after all, was essential to the well-trained Legionnaire.

These particular Trials had drawn more attention than usual. Upon returning to the Legion's headquarters in Port Galaén, Keira had found herself something of a celebrity, as word of the events in the capital had spread not only across Loren but throughout the Legion's extensive network.

Glancing up into the spectator boxes, Keira glimpsed the thick furs and pelts of Grumaérians and even the colored headscarves of Legionnaires visiting from the Cross-Sea Lands.

Keira frowned at the somber countenance of this last group. They'd arrived the night before, at the tail end of the annual Trials, and something about the furtive looks and whispered discussions between the delegation and the High Council made Keira suspect their true reason for visiting was far more serious.

"What you be frowning about?" Raina demanded. "You've done it! You be a full Legionnaire now!" Keira couldn't help but chuckle at the look of rapt awe that spread over Raina's face. Since they'd arrived back in Port Galaén, Raina had thrown herself into her training with a ferocity that was borderline worrisome. She was just a kid, after all. The thought of her training herself into a lethal warrior brought a twinge of sadness to Keira's chest.

But as she scanned Raina up and down, she couldn't help but admit that the transformation was impressive. Clad in the simple leather armor of a Legionnaire-in-training, Raina's gangly length had filled in with stringy muscle. Her brown skin had become less ashen, and the haunted look that had filled her eyes since Akamu's death had lessened, even if only slightly, in the excitement of the Trials.

And she'd made friends. Over the past few weeks, the Legion headquarters had filled to the brim with other eager Legion trainees, brought to Port Galaén by their mentors for the annual Trials. Raina had fallen in among their ranks with an ease that had frankly surprised Keira. After all, this was the same stubborn girl who'd been as likely to fight the other kids back in Tibolé as befriend them. But here she seemed focused, determined.

"You seem . . . happy," Keira said finally, wary of breaking whatever spell had caught hold of this girl who was as much a sister to her as a friend. The light in Raina's eyes flickered slightly, but her smile held.

"I am," she said simply. "I be missing him, but I'm glad we be coming here. I be learning a lot—about pneuma, and I think about my mother too. I think she was like you, Keira."

Keira blinked in surprise but nodded. Since hearing the story Raina had told her about her close call with drowning, she'd suspected the woman might have wielded her own vein of healing pneumonancy. "That's good," she said. "We all need to know where we come from."

"It will help," Raina said simply, "when it be time."

Keira frowned slightly. "Time for what?"

Raina's expression was unchanged, her eyes boring into Keira's. She said almost casually, "Time for me to be killing him."

The air around Keira felt suddenly frigid, and a seed of dread rooted itself deep in her stomach. She met Raina's frank, untroubled eyes and knew in her heart she meant every word.

"Albert?"

Raina nodded, eyes fierce. "Someday, somehow, he be paying for Akamu's death."

Keira tried to swallow but found her throat suddenly dry. Her heart ached for Raina, but she knew there were no words she could offer that would take away the pain. It would be an insult to even try. So instead, she only reached forward and squeezed Raina's shoulder.

"Together," she said simply. "We'll do it together."

Raina's eyes shone with a fierce light, and she nodded, returning the gesture. From the corner of her eye, Keira spotted Elliott striding toward them, a broad grin stretched across his face. Whatever was coming, Keira knew she wouldn't be alone.

Back in the training room where she'd lived for the last two weeks, Keira eased herself onto a bench, wiping at the dirt and blood smeared across her skin. A small knock on the door made her glance up.

"Come in," she called.

Zoya entered, the tiny girl looking out of place amid the heavy weaponry.

"This is a surprise," Keira murmured, eyeing the girl warily. Though Zoya had tolerated her presence just fine in the weeks leading up to the Trials, Keira still suspected that she didn't quite trust her.

"I'll get right to the point," Zoya said, coming to stand before Keira. "With Albert gone, there's a vacancy on the High Council." She spoke in her usual direct style, all formality with no hint of emotion. "Now that you've completed your rites, you're eligible to apply for it."

Keira snorted. "Me? On the High Council? Aren't I a little . . . young?"

Zoya's nostrils flared, and Keira blushed, remembering the woman's childlike appearance.

"Age is of little importance to the Council. We look for leadership ability, and after hearing Elliott's debrief of the events in the capital, I'd say you've proved yourself quite worthy." Seeing her dubious expression, Zoya's tone softened as she added, "He won't stay hidden for long, Keira. The next equinox is only four months away. If he's going to make a move, he'll do it then, when he can channel the power of the cosmic balance. And then, with the winter solstice soon after . . ." Zoya shook her head, brow creased with worry. "Pneumos help us."

Keira exhaled sharply. The High Council? Her? She didn't exactly relish spending her days deep within the bowels of the Legion's headquarters. But Albert was still out there, and Keira knew in her gut that Zoya was right. He wouldn't give up, not ever.

"But what can he do?" she asked. "Without the conduit, he has no way of building his army."

Zoya pursed her lips, a flicker of something like guilt in her eyes. "We don't—well, we don't *exactly* know how the conduit worked. Our amalgamors are hard at work unearthing every record we have on the subject, but much of the history from the early days of the Marian invasion was destroyed and none of the current High Council members were stationed in Loren during that time. In fact, most of us arrived in this world well after then. We believe that the Legion here constructed the conduit to channel pneuma, but there are some who believe its role might have been far more *protective* in nature. And we certainly don't know if it was the only one like it."

Keira's breath hitched as she thought about the significance of Zoya's words. If there were other conduits like the one in the Vindolum ... She swallowed, shaking her head.

"I need time to think about this," she said. "I promised Landry I'd return to the capital to help him, and with Raina still early in her training ..."

Zoya put up a hand to halt the flood of excuses, the many reasons Keira was not right for this task. "Take the time. Think it over. After all, we're the Legion. We've got nothing *but* time."

Keira blinked. Was that actually a joke? From the stern expression on Zoya's face, she couldn't be sure, so she merely nodded.

"What will you do now?" Zoya asked.

"I think I'll return to Crîd Eálas," she said finally. "Landry needs help to get things in order, and from the sound of it, Cyrus is about ready to strangle him. Besides, I've written to the Royal Hospital there, and they've agreed to take me on as an apprentice." At Zoya's raised brows, Keira added, "I feel like it's about time I learn more about my healing pneumonancy, the proper way this time, with people who've dedicated their lives to the care of others. No more shortcuts."

Zoya nodded, eyes sparkling with approval, and she reached out a tiny hand. Keira took it.

"Until next time, then, Keira Altman."

KEIRA SPENT the rest of the afternoon going through her belongings back in her old bedroom in the Legion's headquarters. It was a paltry lot, but she supposed she honestly didn't need much. She could get whatever else she needed back in the capital.

"Leaving so soon?"

Keira glanced up from her packing to find Zipporah leaning casually against the doorframe. She shrugged. "I was just finishing up packing. I'd have come to say goodbye," she added, feeling a twinge of guilt. She might not have sought out Zipporah specifically, and instead let Marti convey the message. Even Keira's masochistic tendencies had a limit.

Zipporah snorted, and from beneath her arm, two faces appeared—Marti and Raina. Keira's smile widened. "I'm glad you all came by, though. I have some things for you."

Keira reached into her bag and pulled out the wrapped packages, handing them out one by one. Marti and Raina lunged for them, squealing in delight. Zipporah's brows rose in surprise, but something like pleasure flickered in her eyes as she reached for hers.

Raina tore hers open first, eyes widening at the turquoise beads that made up the small necklace. The shell necklace her mother had given her had been lost in the conduit's explosion and Raina had been working hard to learn to channel her pneuma without it. Though Keira knew nothing could ever replace that loss, when she'd spotted the necklace in the stall of an Olphéis nomad at the market, she couldn't resist.

"Do you like it?" Keira asked nervously. Maybe it *was* too soon.

Raina threw her arms around Keira's neck in response, and Keira laughed, squeezing the girl tightly. By the time she'd set Raina back on her feet, Marti was already oohing and ahhing over the leather-bound field journal she'd unwrapped.

"That one's really from Elliott," Keira said. "I'd mentioned your interest in the botany of Loren, and he insisted you have this." Marti muttered her thanks absently, already absorbed in the journal's pages as she thumbed through them.

Finally, it was Zipporah's turn, and Keira shifted her weight nervously as she slowly untucked each fold of the gift-wrapping.

At the bottom of the wrapping was a leather scabbard, its worn surface shined to a deep mahogany hue, and on its golden crest, a roaring lioness reared back on hind legs.

"It's—beautiful," Zipporah murmured, glancing up at Keira with widened eyes.

"It was my old mentor's. Nazor would have wanted you to have it. I-I think she would have liked you, actually," Keira added, grinning nervously.

"Thank you," Zipporah said quietly. "I'll treasure it."

Keira shifted her weight, looking between these new and unexpected friends.

"I'll miss you. All of you," she said, meaning every word. "I couldn't have done any of this without you."

"We know," Zipporah said nonchalantly. "That's why we're coming with you."

Keira blinked, looking between them for confirmation.

"We can't split the team up, now, can we?" Marti added brightly, tucking the field journal into her satchel.

"But what about your work with the amalgam?" Keira asked. "I thought they needed all the help they could get?"

Marti shrugged. "They'll get on without me."

"You really want to come with me?" Keira asked again, this time to Zipporah.

Zipporah picked at some invisible piece of dust on her arm before Marti nudged her with an elbow. Zipporah shot her a glare before finally meeting Keira's questioning gaze.

She rolled her eyes and said with exasperation, "Yes, all right? We want to come."

Keira grinned broadly, earning a scowl from Zipporah, who muttered, "Well, there's no need to gush on about it. Someone's got to keep Keira Lone Warrior in check."

Marti snorted and shook her head before reaching down to finish tying up the last of Keira's bags.

Keira shook her head as she looked between them, eyes finally settling on Raina. "You have your training. You're getting so good. You can't give up now."

Raina shrugged, eyes twinkling. "Good thing I be having a brilliant teacher to work with."

Keira shook her head, suddenly having a hard time swallowing. She blinked against the burning sensation that filled her eyes. She looked at the women before her—one still a girl, and the others little more than that. Her family. Not the one she'd been born into, or even the one the Legion had assigned her, but the one that she'd chosen and who had chosen her back. And even though they were about to depart on yet another journey that promised danger and violence, Keira couldn't help feeling, for the first time since leaving Abalás, that she was well and truly home.

EPILOGUE

Danny gasped, his eyes flying open as he stared uncomprehendingly at the stone ceiling above him.

Where am I?

No sooner had the thought occurred than a wave of nausea flooded over him, and he rolled over to heave onto the straw pallet beneath him. But nothing came up, his stomach bone-dry and completely empty.

"Oya, easy does it, Danny-boy. You don't want to make a mess after you've only just arrived."

Danny felt his entire body go rigid as he slowly raised his gaze. He blinked, unable to believe what he saw.

"Nazor?" he asked in disbelief. "Is it really you?"

His old mentor stood solidly before him, hands braced on her hips and eyeing him with that same twinkle in her eye as when a training session had left him flat on his butt. She was dressed in her old leather armor, a familiar longsword strapped to her back. Her dark eyes stared down at him, and her long braids swished against her back.

"It is, indeed, Danny, and I'm quite happy to see you as well."

"B-But how? Where am I?"

"An ancient fortress on the coast, not far from Port Mârfa. More like a ruin, really," she said, eyeing the beads of condensation that gathered on the stone walls around them. Seeing his confused expression, she added quietly, "You're back in Loren, Danny—the Loren you first knew, that is."

Her words crashed over him, and he sat back on his cot, eyes going wide. He wanted to ask *how, why.* A whole host of questions swirled in his mind, but only one thought emerged from their murky depths. *He was back.*

"Ah, I'm glad to see our guest is getting settled."

The arch British voice unfurled from the darkness as a tall figure slowly emerged into the light. His brown hair was cropped short, and he now sported a curling mustache. But Danny would have known those piercing blue eyes anywhere.

"Fitz," Danny snarled. "What the hell are you doing here?"

"Calm down, Danny," Nazor chided, shooting him a stern look. "Albert's a friend."

Fitz—or Albert, whatever his name was—only smiled serenely down at Danny as he moved to stand beside Nazor, laying an arm casually across her shoulders. Danny glared at the two of them.

"What the hell is this, Nazor? Don't you know who he is?"

"Of course I do," Nazor said simply. "Albert Fitz and I have been friends for a very long time. I know this must all be unnerving, Danny, but we do have work to do. And only you can help us do it."

Danny shook his head, rubbing his temples as a throbbing sensation began just behind his eyes. "How am I even here?"

Fitz chuckled. "That's the age-old question, isn't it? Well, the short answer is, you have your friend Keira to thank for that. She swore she'd bring you back, and by Pneumos, she did," Fitz replied.

"Y-You've met Keira?" Danny asked, startled.

"Yes, yes, and before you ask, I'm well aware of who she is. Why do you think I invested so much time in training her?" Fitz sighed, expression turning nostalgic. "I knew it the first time I laid eyes on her. She's the spitting image of her mother, you know. But I suppose I don't need to tell you that."

Danny stiffened at the mention of Tammy.

"I wondered if it might be you Keira kept going on about, the strange Legionnaire I'd met so long ago, supposedly newly arrived from a future time." He chuckled. "It seems I was right."

Danny leveled Fitz with a glare. "You betrayed her," he hissed. "Tammy loved you, and you turned her over to the wolves."

Fitz sighed. "A necessary evil, I'm afraid. I've been searching for a way to channel the arrivals for years, you see—centuries, even. And there was always one thing in my way." He paused theatrically, eyeing Danny with an almost childlike excitement. "The conduits, Mr. O'Leary—dozens of them, spread all over this world. At first, I thought they were the answer, the conduits through which the arrivals were formed. Then I discovered a long-buried secret." His voice grew in both excitement and volume as he pressed on. "The conduits don't just strengthen our power but protect the balance of order and chaos in the area under their purview. I'd never have been able to harness enough chaos to channel the arrivals while its power still held firm. And I knew that there was only one person with the power to destroy it. *My* daughter, the child of two Legionnaires. Only someone with the power of rebuilding could have channeled its destruction. When Keira destroyed the conduit, it finally gave me the opening I'd been waiting for all these years."

Danny's eyes danced around the room, looking for some way, any way, out. *Just keep talking*, he thought.

"And here you are, the first of my army. You wouldn't have been my choice, honestly, but Nazor here insisted you'll be *useful*. I do hope you don't let her down."

Danny swallowed, shifting in his seat as Fitz's Cheshire-like grin grew wider by the minute. "The first?"

"Why, of course. And you're not the only one," Fitz said, smiling as he gestured toward an open window.

"Your old friend Junia says hello," Fitz crooned. "And this time, she's brought some friends."

Danny felt something hard settle in his gut, and he glanced from Nazor to Fitz.

"It was the only way, Danny," Nazor said quietly. "The only way to preserve order in this world."

Danny stood, moving stiffly toward the open window, even as his feet dragged with the weight of molasses. The sunlight reflecting off the water was blinding, and he had to blink to clear it from his eyes. But there they were, the smooth outline of hundreds of ships dotted across the horizon. Their colorful sails marked them as hailing from the Cross-Sea Lands, an old score finally ready to be settled. At that moment, the kernel of dread that had seeded itself deep in Danny's gut blossomed into outright horror.

This was the end of everything.

SEE WHERE THE JOURNEY BEGAN...

FREE for Newsletter Subscribers!

www.hbreneau.com/thecantor

One life at an end, another just beginning.
Chaos looming in the distance.

See where the journey began in this prequel to *Chaos Looming*,
Book 1 in The Legion of Pneumos series.

EXPLORE MORE OF THE LEGION OF PNEUMOS WORLD

With death on the line, could you choose between duty and honor?

Loren 218 M.E. - See where Gaius's and Aelianna's story began in this much-awaited prequel novella to the Legion of Pneumos series.

Read on for a sneak peek . . .

THE CENTUS

CHAPTER ONE

218 Marian Era (M.E)

In his nearly six years in the Bellatorio, Gaius Flavius had served under many incompetent commanders. But Millus Szerio had to be the worst. Most days Gaius could handle that. Most days he could consider the realities of bureaucratic incompetence with something akin to muted tolerance. Today was not one of those days.

Gaius heeled his horse on as he raced into the Bellatori camp, the frigid mountain wind cutting at his cheeks and sending his blood-red cloak flying behind him. Pulling up abruptly outside the Millus's tent, he swiftly dismounted, plucking off his plumed helm and bracing it under one arm as he stalked toward the tent flap. The two foot soldiers outside snapped to attention, thumping their chests in salute. Gaius returned the gesture, trying and failing to regulate his tone as he spat out a greeting.

"Centus Flavius, here to see Millus Szerio."

"Of course, Centus! The Millus is regrettably occupied at present. May we—"

"It is urgent," Gaius said, gray eyes narrowing to hooded slits. "I'll see him *now*."

Not waiting for them to open the flap, Gaius pushed past, throwing it open as he stalked inside. The tent room was warm, in stark contrast to the frigid temperatures outside. Gaius stopped short at the food-laden table, overflowing with the most scrumptious of delicacies. The soft tittering of laughter filled the warm interior. Millus Szerio had guests.

As his eyes adjusted to the shadowed interior, they flew from face to face, finally falling on the portly Millus Szerio. He reclined lazily on his side, gesturing with the thick turkey drumstick he held in one hand.

Gaius gritted his teeth, somehow managing to restrain the sneer he felt bubbling beneath the surface. He instead snapped to attention, loudly thumping the metal gauntlet of his forearm against his embossed leather cuirass with a clang that brought the entire dinner party up short, staring at him in surprise.

Szerio was the last to respond, only glancing up when he noticed his conversation partner to have been distracted from the no doubt enthralling tale he'd been sharing.

"Yes, Centus? Can't you see I'm otherwise occupied?"

"Sir!" Gaius responded, voice echoing. "I'm here with an urgent message from the front. My Bellators are poorly rationed, without the food or equipment we were promised. If we are to hold our position to the west—"

"Yes, yes, Centus, I received your communiques. The issue is being looked into."

Gaius felt his teeth ache as they ground together. He resisted the urge to stare pointedly at the lavishly decorated table overflowing with sweetmeats and pastries.

"Sir, the men and women who serve under me *need* to be properly rationed if we are to fulfill our mission. We cannot leave the western front—"

"Centus!" A note of annoyance crept into Szerio's voice as he leaned forward, drumming his fingers rhythmically against the chair arm. "I *told* you that the matter is being *looked into*. Now, please, you're disturbing my guests."

There was a soft tittering of laughter from the aforementioned dinner companions. A vein in Gaius's temple throbbed, and his hands curled into fists of their own accord. His rising rage was truly making it difficult to see straight. This man was not fit to wipe the scum from the boots of even the lowest foot soldier in the Bellatorio, who served admirably and with honor. Whereas this man, no doubt descended from ancient Marian nobility, had barely even seen a battlefield before being commissioned as a Millus and charged with the war's execution. Didn't he understand what was at *stake*? How could he sit here in his warm quarters, eating delicacies, while men and women starved on the battlefield? It was unconscionable.

"You are *dismissed*, Centus."

Gaius thought briefly about skewering Szerio then and there, taking his overpuffed ego down a few notches. Gaius's fingers twitched toward his sword's pommel, relishing the thought of unsheathing it and showing this man what a true Bellator looked like. Then he thought of his Bellators, huddling around barely concealed campfires, trying to keep warm and desperate for rations that only he could bring them. He realized with frustration that he'd have some difficulty doing that from inside a prison cell, which is undoubtedly where he'd end up if he treated this Millus as he deserved.

So instead, Gaius gave Szerio a curt nod before saluting and spinning on his heel as he stalked out of the room. He was met outside by Decius Braína. Her straw-colored hair was plaited in the Bellatori fashion, her icy blue eyes scanning the garrison. She raised one delicate eyebrow at him, and he realized with sudden embarrassment that he'd likely outpaced her some ways back. In the meantime, she'd caught up and wisely watered the horses after he'd dismounted in a rage.

"Any luck?" she asked, but seemed unsurprised when he shook his head, the success of his mission written on his face.

"Well, it was worth a try," she said. "We could try the quartermaster directly, see what the garrison itself can spare."

"It's no use," Gaius said, rubbing a hand across his face. "None of them will dare act without Szerio's direct say-so. Reallocating rations is an offense worthy of court martial."

She nodded. Decius Erin Braína had served under him for two years now. An uplander by birth, she'd grown up in a tiny fishing village near the Western Plains. Gaius didn't much care for uplanders, typically. He found them uneducated, provincial in their outlook, and hostile toward outsiders. But Braína was different, curious about the world and smart as a whip. She'd done well in the Bellatorio and was respected by both commanders and subordinates. She'd quickly risen through the ranks, one of the few female Bellators to have received a commission. Even two hundred years after women had been allowed to enlist, it was still an uncommon profession for them to pursue.

"Well, what is it you're plannin'?" she asked, offering him his horse's reins. At his shrug, she raised an eyebrow. "You know as well as I do that this isn't the end of it."

Gaius was about to reply when a young messenger boy appeared, standing awkwardly in the periphery. Gaius turned to eye the boy pointedly.

"A-are you Centus Flavius?" the boy sputtered. "I-I have a message for you, sir."

Gaius put his hand out for the message, intentionally ignoring Braína's knowing look. He certainly wasn't done fighting, but he refused to give her the satisfaction of having her suspicions confirmed. He flicked a coin to the boy in thanks, noting with satisfaction how the boy's face lit up. The messenger thanked him profusely before scampering away.

Unfurling the scroll, Gaius scanned its contents, brow furrowing further by the line.

"What is it?" Braína asked.

"It's a summons," he said, voice disbelieving even to his own ears. "A summons from Imperator Lanus. He wishes to see me."

Braína's eyebrows had shot up at the first mention of Imperator Lanus, chief commander of the entire Western Imperium.

"That's incredible," she said finally. "When?"

"Tomorrow. Apparently, he's making a brief stopover in camp tonight before continuing on his tour of the western front."

"Well, this is perfect. Ask him about the rations."

"Millus Szerio won't take kindly to that."

"Screw the old fatbag."

Gaius's head cocked toward her, eyebrows raised.

Her eyes narrowed. "He doesn't give a fig about any of us. You tried appealing to him directly. You brought your concerns, and he's done nothing. You are fully within your rights, no, your *responsibilities* as a commander, to take your request up the chain of command."

Gaius nodded, considering. The thought made him uneasy. He disliked complaining to a commander's boss about his behavior, preferring instead to settle his disputes in person. But Braína was right. He'd tried everything, and he wasn't about to return to his Bellators empty-handed. If Szerio wouldn't help him, then Gaius would have to go over his head.

The story continues . . .

About the Author

H.B. Reneau is an author of fantasy and contemporary fiction. Author, medical student, and proud dog mom, she is known for her character-driven, genre-crossing fiction that draws on her experiences in both medicine and the military. She has a particular love for strong female characters who face up to adversity and manage to subvert some expectations along the way.

To learn more, head over to her website at www.hbre neau.com. There you'll find her books, blog, and fun extras. Or reach out directly! Follow on social media and sign up for the monthly newsletter to receive receive free gifts, awesome discounts, and updates on all her latest projects.

If you enjoyed this book, please consider leaving a review at your favorite online storefront!

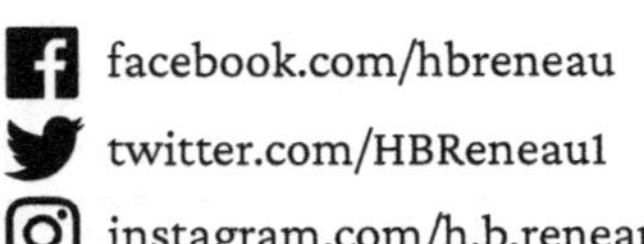

facebook.com/hbreneau
twitter.com/HBReneau1
instagram.com/h.b.reneau

ALSO BY H.B. RENEAU

<u>The Legion of Pneumos</u>

Chaos Looming

Haven Enduring

<u>The Legion of Pneumos: Novella Collection</u>

The Cantor

The Centus

The Rebel

The Remnant